AN EGGNOG
to
DIE FOR

A Cape Cod Foodie Mystery

AMY PERSHING

BERKLEY PRIME CRIME
New York

BERKLEY PRIME CRIME
Published by Berkley
An imprint of Penguin Random House LLC
penguinrandomhouse.com

Copyright © 2021 by Amy Pershing
Penguin Random House supports copyright. Copyright fuels creativity, encourages
diverse voices, promotes free speech, and creates a vibrant culture. Thank you for buying
an authorized edition of this book and for complying with copyright laws by not
reproducing, scanning, or distributing any part of it in any form without permission.
You are supporting writers and allowing Penguin Random House to continue to
publish books for every reader.

BERKLEY and the BERKLEY & B colophon are registered trademarks and
BERKLEY PRIME CRIME is a trademark of Penguin Random House LLC.

ISBN: 9780593199169

First Edition: November 2021

Printed in the United States of America
1   3   5   7   9   10   8   6   4   2

Book design by George Towne

For Bill, for always

"Can I refill your eggnog for you? Get you something to eat? Drive you out to the middle of nowhere and leave you for dead?"

—Chevy Chase as Clark Griswold in *National Lampoon's Christmas Vacation*

ONE

~~~~~

"THEY WANT TO call it Santa's Seashore Selebration," Jenny said, spearing a succulent morsel of lamb tagine from my plate and plopping it into her mouth. "Mmmm, yummy," she said, reaching over again.

I smacked her hand away. "Keep your mitts off my tagine," I said. "You've already eaten your own entire"—I glanced at the menu again—"Marhaba Meat Extravaganza."

This was true. Jenny had polished off a generous sampling of the barbequed kufta meatballs, a lamb and beef gyro, and three grilled baby lamb chops. Which hadn't surprised me. Jenny Snow Singleton, whom I'd known since we were Minnows together in swimming lessons, is a confirmed meat eater. She was loving the Marhaba, a tiny Middle Eastern restaurant with a menu designed to please everyone from the dedicated omnivore to the most devoted vegetarian.

"That's not fair, Sam," Jenny protested loudly. "You had some of *everything* on my plate."

"I'm *supposed* to have some of everything on your

plate," I said, lowering my voice to just above a whisper. "*I'm* the restaurant reviewer."

For the past six months or so, I'd been critiquing restaurants for the Cape Cod *Clarion*. Not that I did much actual critiquing. If I tried a place and it was truly not very good, I simply didn't review it. I wanted no part of trashing someone else's dream. But if a place had promise, was doing its business honestly and with passion, I was happy to tell the world (or at least our little corner of Cape Cod) about it.

Truth be told, I wasn't sure how much longer I'd be able to get away with this gig. A large part of reviewing restaurants depends on the anonymity essential to an honest review. Anonymity, however, has never been my strong suit. First of all, I stand well over six feet tall, so I'm kind of hard to miss. Second, I have an awkward history of going viral online.

Through no fault of my own, I might add. Was it my fault that someone posted online a very unfortunate video they'd taken with their cell phone of me, Samantha Barnes, up-and-coming New York chef, mixing it up with my rather volatile chef husband in a kind of chefs' fencing match? (Which I won, I might add. My knife skills were always better than his. Which is why he is now missing the tip of his pinky finger.) Once that video hit YouTube, I almost instantaneously became Samantha Barnes, ex-chef.

So when I found I'd inherited my Aunt Ida's house on the Cape, I reluctantly retreated home to Fair Harbor, where my old friend and now publisher of the *Clarion*, Krista Baker, gave me a job writing restaurant reviews. And, much against my better judgment, I had allowed Krista to talk me into a series of video food features for the *Clarion*'s online edition, starring yours truly as "the Cape Cod Foodie." The good news is that they've been something of a hit. The bad news is that they've been something of a hit.

So, though I still wasn't sure what I wanted to be when I grew up, I was making ends meet as the Cape Cod Foodie and the *Clarion*'s restaurant reviewer.

And now Jenny was blowing whatever cover I had left by arguing with me. Loudly.

I looked in mute appeal to my other fellow diners, Helene Greenberg and Miles Tanner, willing them to distract Jenny from my falling-off-the-bone, meltingly delicious lamb and to *keep her voice down*. Miles, an old high school buddy and dedicated organic farmer, was too busy spooning the sinfully rich yogurt labneh over his falafel to notice, but Helene, my sixtysomething next door neighbor and the town librarian, jumped in, bless her heart.

"So tell me about this Santa seashore celebration," Helene said, as she dipped a piece of pita into her eggplant baba ghanoush with one beringed hand.

Jenny grinned at her. "'Celebration' with an *s*," she said.

Helene shuddered. Librarians as a rule don't like cute misspellings. "I'm assuming that the celebrating"—she pronounced it "ssssselebrating"—"is mainly about buying stuff?"

Helene has no illusions about people's motivations. That's what happens after twenty-five years as a legal psychologist with the Manhattan DA's office.

"Well, sure," Jenny said. "I mean, according to the select board, the whole point this year is to bring in some extra tourist dollars during the off-season. You know how usually we just have Santa come through town on a fire truck and throw candy canes to the kids? Well, this year, there's going to be a Santa Trolley to take people around to all the stores, and everybody gets a wish list to fill out and give to their significant others. And the kids, of course, get to tell Santa what they want."

Miles dabbed some rogue yogurt off his beard. "But there's other fun stuff, too," he said defensively. Miles is the optimist yin to Helene's pessimist yang. "I'm personally looking forward to the pancake breakfast hosted by Mrs. Claus . . ."

"Archaic and sexist," Helene muttered to herself.

"And the 5K Santa Stroll, where all you have to do to qualify is wear a Santa hat. You don't even have to run, just walk. *And* the best Santa lookalike wins."

Miles stroked his bushy beard and beamed at his considerable paunch. "I'm gonna win," he said with all the complacent pride of the five-year-old he still was deep inside. "I have the whole outfit. I've been playing Santa for my sister's kids like forever."

This, I knew, was no exaggeration. Miles's sister had been popping out kids at a rate of one every two years for the past ten years and showed no sign of slowing down.

"So why aren't *you* playing the town's Santa?" I asked.

"Apparently the role had been filled," Miles responded with great dignity, "by Caleb Mayo, the latest member of the Fair Harbor select board."

"Santa is always played by someone from the select board," Jenny explained. "They rotate. Last year it was Monique Holden. She was terrific. Very jolly. That's going to be a tough act for Caleb Mayo to follow. On the other hand, he'll be the first Santa to arrive at Town Cove by boat."

"I like that," I said, imagining a red-suited Father Christmas chugging in at the helm of a fishing boat to the delighted cheers of the Fair Harbor citizenry.

"Ah, I'm not sure you will, actually," Jenny said, her blue eyes dancing with mischief. I groaned. Jenny in a mischievous mood is not someone I trust.

"The boat is going to be the Harbor Patrol's Grady-White," she continued. The Grady-White is the Harbor Patrol's main powerboat. I know this because my gentleman friend, as my Aunt Ida would have called him, is Jason Captiva, the town's harbormaster.

"Why wouldn't I like that?"

"Well, the Grady-White is going to be piloted by Jason," Jenny said, and left a significant pause.

I stepped right into her trap. "That's fine. How is that a problem?"

"It will be piloted by Jason wearing an elf costume," Jenny said gleefully. "An elf costume with red-striped stockings and curly-toed shoes!"

Jason in an elf costume. That would *not* be fine. That would be something I could never unsee. Jason was hot to death, but even he could not pull off red-striped stockings and curly-toed shoes.

I was so stunned, I didn't even notice Jenny snatching another huge forkful of tagine off my plate.

S AM, SAM, SWEETHEART, is that you?"
    What I sort of wanted to say was, *Who did you think was going to answer* my *phone that* you *called?* Because I'm snarky that way. But I love my mother, most of the time anyway, so I didn't.

Instead, I said, "Hi, Mom. Yeah, it's me."

"Hi, sweetheart. Hold on a minute while I put you on speaker. Your dad is here, too." I'm not sure if my mother knows that she can actually put her phone on speaker *before* she calls, thus minimizing the chance that she will press the wrong button and cut the call off completely. This happens often. But not this time, miraculously.

My father's voice came booming in my ear. "Sam! How are you? Is everything okay?" This greeting is also par for the course. As is the shouting.

"I'm fine, Dad. Everything's okay. No need to shout, I can hear you fine."

"Excellent," he shouted. *Sigh.*

"So, what's new?" I asked. Actually, it had only been a

few weeks since I'd been down to Florida to visit them over Thanksgiving, so I doubted anything much was new. There's almost never anything new going on in Cedar Grove, Florida.

"Much the same," my father said glumly.

"Same old, same old," my mother said gloomily.

What was this I was hearing? Boredom, perhaps? Had they grown tired of endless sunshine, health food, yoga, and aerobics at the senior citizens center? I hoped so. I really did. My parents, Robert and Veronica Barnes, were not to my mind senior citizens. It had been only two years since my father had had a mild heart attack and they'd taken early retirement from the *Clarion*, where they'd been the editor in chief and senior journalist, respectively. These were people who were used to an environment that challenged them both physically and mentally.

"Anyway," my father continued, "we were talking and we decided that we really didn't enjoy spending Christmas down here last year, so we thought maybe we'd come up to the Cape over the holidays."

This was more like it! The Florida honeymoon was wearing off. This was a good first step.

"That's a great idea!" I said. "You can make your standing rib roast for Christmas dinner! And you and I can go shopping, Mom."

I knew the roast beef plan would seal the deal with my dad. After his heart attack, my mother had gone on a total health kick, tossing out his favorite meal of meat loaf and mashed potatoes in favor of a diet of mostly fruits and vegetables. So far, the menu still included chicken and fish but was beginning to veer perilously close, in my dad's opinion, to vegetarian.

I couldn't really blame him for his dismay. Plant-based cooking can be out of this world, but you've got to have the knack and the right ingredients—good olive oil, the best produce, tons of lentils and chickpeas, lots of freshly ground spices, great handfuls of fresh herbs. (Tip: Avoid generic vegetarian cookbooks and look instead for solid introductory Italian, Middle Eastern, and Chinese cookbooks like Marcella Hazan's *The Classic Italian Cookbook*, Yotam Ottolenghi's *Ottolenghi Simple*, and Fuchsia Dunlop's *Every Grain of Rice*.)

That is not what my mother did. What my mother did was present my father and me with a prepackaged tofu turkey for Thanksgiving. This was not good. In fact, I was pretty sure it was the threat of two tofu turkeys in the space of a month that had inspired my father's sudden urge to come up to the Cape for Christmas. Because my father has exactly one meal that he cooks every year and that meal is a juicy prime rib roast for Christmas dinner.

"Well, I'm not sure about the roast beef," my mother said. *We'll see about that, Mom.* "But the shopping sounds like fun. And we can be there for your birthday, too."

My birthday. *Uh-oh.* My birthday falls on the worst possible day of the year—January 1. All my adult life I have woken up on my birthday with a hangover. And it was only as an adult that I realized that for all of my childhood my parents had probably also woken up on my birthday with a hangover. Oh well. It looked like this year we'd be hungover together. *Doesn't that sound like fun, Sam?*

"Where are you going to stay?" I asked. "You know, Tina Eldredge has turned their family's big house into a bed and breakfast."

Over the past twenty years or so, a number of retired couples had turned their family's rambling summer houses (known as big houses) into B and Bs. After the necessary renovations, they were as charming as they were expensive.

"That sounds a little pricey," my father said doubtfully.

This was another downside to my parents' retirement—my smart, intellectually curious father had turned his brain power toward clipping coupons and saying things like "Take care of the pence and the pounds will take care of themselves," instead of "I think I'll write an editorial about overbuilding near the marshes."

"We thought we'd stay with you," my mother said.

"With *me*?" I squeaked.

"Sure," my dad said. "In Aunt Ida's house."

There were two reasons why I didn't think this was a good idea. The first was Aunt Ida's house itself. When I'd moved in last spring, it had been barely habitable except for a small studio ell that Aunt Ida had added when it became clear that maintaining the rest of the rambling old place was too much for her. Little by little, Miles had helped me spackle and paint, but despite our best efforts it was not exactly ready for prime time.

The second reason for my hesitation was the certainty that a couple of weeks with the 'rents as roomies would put the final kibosh on my very confusing relationship with Jason (which would already be at significant risk from the elf costume).

So what I wanted to say was, *Don't come.* Don't come because I have mice in the wainscoting and am uneasy about sharing my space with you while I try to understand the man in my life.

But what I said was, "Sounds great." And then I added the fateful words: "What could go wrong?"

You'd think you'd learn, Sam.

I N AN ATTEMPT to distract myself from the challenges of putting my parents up in a house where hot water for your shower is pretty much a roll of the dice, I turned for consolation, as I always do, to food. More specifically, to making food for the people I love. Before my career and marriage went south, I'd spent eight years in New York City creating very imaginative, very delicious concoctions for very discerning patrons to some very nice reviews. But never once did I feel the satisfaction that I felt when I watched my friends dig into my chicken potpie and clamor for more.

So I decided that what would cheer me up was to go all-in on a Christmas Eve Friends and Family Feast of the Five Fishes. Okay, so traditionally it's seven fishes or even twelve. But times have changed. The holidays are stressful enough. Christmas Eve should be *fun*.

You would think my friends and family would get that, but no. Nobody was exactly cooperating. My mother began sending me recipes for soy "fish." Jenny said she'd only eat real fish and then only if it didn't "smell fishy" (which it doesn't if it's fresh, but try convincing her of that). Her kids, known collectively as the Three Things, essentially only ate sugar, and Miles only organic. Helene, being Jewish, wanted the traditional Chinese takeout. My friend/boss Krista said she didn't care what she ate as long as she didn't have to cook it. (Krista's lack of sentiment is sometimes a good thing.) I'd also invited a newish friend, Jillian Munsell, the manager of Shawme Manor, Fair Harbor's combined nursing home and assisted living facility, who'd announced that she would bring dessert. She wouldn't tell me what it would be, though, insisting that it should be a surprise. (*Not* a good thing. When I plan a meal, I don't like surprises. I like control.)

The only thing anyone could agree on was that there had to be eggnog.

But, it turned out, my guests had strong feelings there, too. My e-mail was dinging regularly with "best eggnog ever" recipes—rum eggnog, bourbon eggnog, vanilla bean eggnog, you name it. I didn't have a dog in this fight, but I was going to have to declare a winner. This could not end well.

* * *

A FEW WEEKS BEFORE Santa's Seashore Selebration, I'd managed to talk Jason, who had been a bit elusive recently, into checking out the Ginger Jar, Fair Harbor's first-ever small plates and craft cocktails restaurant. The restaurant had opened in the summer and had been a big hit with Fair Harbor's younger crowd, who totally fell for the menu's New England sensibility with an Asian twist. But the town's old guard still had misgivings. Who would want to eat a *small* plate of anything? (Answer: me. I've always found that appetizers are the best part of almost any restaurant meal, so why not just get a bunch of those for the table and have at them?) And what's wrong with a good old-fashioned Manhattan? (Answer: nothing. A good old-fashioned Manhattan is a fine thing indeed. But so is a cold-smoked Manhattan.)

Dinner at the Ginger Jar was terrific, so I'd suggested to Krista that I cover the restaurant for the *Clarion*. Usually when I make a recommendation to Krista, she tells me to take Jenny, Miles, and Helene so I can get a reasonable selection of dishes to taste and discuss. Krista has about zero interest in food unless it sells newspapers. But in this case, her eyes lit up and she insisted that she and I go together, rather than me and my usual posse. Her business rationale was "You've already gone once with Jason, so you don't need to spend the paper's money on dinner for another three people." Her personal rationale was "I hear the Ginger Jar's bartender is H-O-T." *Uh-oh.*

W E CHOSE A Tuesday for our visit on the grounds that Tuesdays tend to be a quiet night for restaurants. But not for the Ginger Jar apparently. As we pushed through the front door from Main Street, almost every table was taken.

"I like the vibe," Krista said, as we followed the greeter to a corner table. "Cool, but still relaxed."

She had it right. The space was at once spare and yet warm, with industrial chic elements marrying seamlessly with wood accents. An enormous painting of a blue-and-white-flowered Chinese ginger jar almost filled one whitewashed wall, though the rest were bare. The simple rattan chairs and bamboo-trimmed tables were well spaced, and tin pendant lamps over each provided a golden pool of light. The long mahogany bar, where the cocktail magic happened, was trimmed in the same bamboo as the tables, though the metal shop stools lined up in front of it did indeed give it a kind of cool edge.

Our server, a twentysomething neatly dressed in black jeans, a crisp white cotton shirt, and a short, pocketed waist apron, offered us a couple of thick cardboard menus, one simply labeled DRINKS, the other FOOD. For purely professional purposes, we each started with one of the Ginger Jar's seasonal cocktail specials. I went with the Caribbean Christmas eggnog, Krista for something called a Santa Clausmopolitan made with vodka-infused cranberries. As our server headed over to the bar to put in our order, Krista caught her first glimpse of the bartender. Who was indeed H-O-T with his shoulder-length blond hair and a bicep-hugging black T-shirt.

"Ladies," she murmured almost to herself, "start your engines."

Which, of course, made me all flustery.

"It's sexist comments like that one that feed the rumor mill about the Brunis," I objected primly.

I could almost see Krista's ears prick up. "What rumor mill? And who are the Brunis?"

"The brother-sister team that owns this place." I nodded

over to the sexy bartender, who was now leaning over the servers' end of the bar, listening earnestly to a young woman with a mane of curly red hair wearing cowboy boots and a dress that clearly came from some high-end vintage store. I placed them both in their early to mid-thirties.

"That's Julie and Martin Bruni," I said. "He's the brains behind the craft cocktails. She's the brains behind the kitchen and the business by all accounts. I hear from Jenny that some of Fair Harbor's old guard aren't exactly fans of this restaurant."

She knew instinctively what I meant by the old guard. Like every small town, Fair Harbor has its unoffical roster of prominent citizens (including, once upon a time, my mother and father)—school board officials, local business owners, members of the town's board, people like that. Good people, in the main, who love their community and want to serve it. But even good people can be suspicious of change.

"I can see how the hipster look might not endear them to everyone," Krista admitted. "But aside from that, what does the old guard have against them?"

"Well, not all of the old guard," I clarified. "But Jenny says there are a few who just don't trust them, probably because of the hipster look but also because Julie and Martin are from off Cape. Just Boston, but still . . ."

"But how does Jenny *know* these people don't trust the Brunis?" *Krista, ever the journalist.*

"Jenny says you can always tell when a Cape Codder doesn't like or trust someone," I said, grinning. "They call them 'that,' as in 'that boyfriend of yours.'"

Krista laughed. "Oh yeah, I know what you mean. The New England equivalent of the southern 'bless her heart.' But it's still not much to go on."

"I know," I said. "And normally I wouldn't think much of

it, but Jenny also says that there's a move to revoke the Ginger Jar's liquor license on the grounds that the Brunis aren't of"—and here I made air quotes with my fingers—"'good moral character.'"

"Seriously?" Krista said. "That's a thing?"

As someone who had worked in the food and drink biz for more than a decade, I knew this was a *serious* thing.

"Oh, yeah," I said. "In states like Massachusetts that have the good-moral-character clause, anyone who holds a financial stake in an establishment that serves liquor has to be of sound character."

"And who, exactly, gets to make that determination?" Krista asked.

"Well, in Massachusetts, it's the selectwomen and selectmen on the town's select board."

"This may be something we need to look into," Krista said thoughtfully. "It sounds to me like someone has a personal ax to grind."

At that point, we got distracted by the arrival of our drinks. Which were fantastic. And strong. But even better, I took one sip of my eggnog and realized it was the answer to my eggnog dilemma.

"This is the best eggnog ever," I said ingratiatingly to the server. "Do you think if I asked nicely, I'd be able to get the recipe?"

"I doubt it," the young woman said flatly. "Martin is pretty serious about keeping his concoctions proprietary."

Oh well, it was worth a try.

Krista, who could walk home to her apartment over the Shear Beauty hair salon just down the street, downed her Santa Clausmopolitan with gusto, but since I'd be driving home after dinner, I drank only half of my cocktail.

"Waste not, want not," Krista said, reaching over to take my glass from me. I watched it go with a sigh. Life is so unfair.

Further discussion of the Brunis and the Ginger Jar was postponed while we ordered a series of delicious small plates, including a cup of oyster stew that almost made me swoon and a Maine peekytoe crab dip with wonton chips so yummy that we got into a fight over who got to finish it. Krista won, I'm sorry to report.

But I was willing to give her that one, because I wanted her to say yes to something else.

Usually I have to be coaxed into doing a Cape Cod Foodie video. They have not always brought me the kind of notoriety one would wish for. But this time it was my big idea.

"What do you say Jenny and I do a Cape Cod Foodie video featuring Martin Bruni doing his holiday thing behind the bar?" Jenny, aside from being my oldest friend, is also a very talented videographer and the director and editor of the Cape Cod Foodie videos.

My secret plan was that if we did a nice piece on the Ginger Jar, Martin might agree to give me his amazing eggnog recipe and I could avoid taking sides in the great eggnog debate.

"Great thinking!" Krista responded enthusiastically. "Merry Margaritas, a possible scandal, and that bartender's biceps? That's a perfect storm of clickbait." *Whatever.* I just wanted that eggnog recipe.

"I'll talk to the Brunis," Krista said. "Maybe we can film the piece on the Saturday of the Santa Selebration. You and Jenny could film with Martin around twelve, which would give you an hour before the place opens for business. Then Jenny can get a few shots of holiday makers coming in." And then, in an uncharacteristic awareness of others outside of herself, she added, "Do you think that timing will work for Jenny?"

"I think Jenny will be delighted with that timing," I said. "It means that Roland will have the boys, who will have been transformed into the Three Things from Hell by the combination of Santa, shopping, and sugar."

"Great," Krista said. "Then it's a win-win for everybody."

Well, in retrospect, not everybody. Not Santa, as it turned out.

TWO

A T FIRST, ALL seemed to be going well at Santa's
Seashore Selebration. It was the Saturday a week before Christmas, and although a cold northern front had
moved over the Cape overnight, the sun was shining. On
the Cape in winter, that is reason enough for high spirits.

Precisely at ten o'clock, I pulled my ancient and very
cranky pickup truck, Grumpy, into the municipal lot at the
Town Cove, which shone blue and silver in its cradle of
winter-bleached marshes. A crowd was already forming
down by the pier, with what seemed like hundreds of
screaming kids working themselves up to a fever pitch of
excitement. This made me nervous. Am I the only one who
thinks children en masse are kind of scary? Also, it seemed
that everyone was sporting a Santa hat except me. This
made me feel like Scrooge, but I wasn't willing to add another four inches to my already considerable height.

Earlier that morning, Miles had stopped by to see if I
wanted to go with him to Mrs. Claus's Pancake Breakfast
at the Lions Club. Mrs. Claus was actually Nellie Tompkins
of Nellie's Kitchen, home of the best buttermilk pancakes

this side of the Cape Cod Canal. (Tip: Let the batter sit for at least ten minutes—thirty is better—before cooking. Even if your kid—or Miles—is getting cranky.)

Much as I hated to miss this exercise in pancake gluttony, I'd had to say no to his invitation in favor of making myself presentable for my upcoming work assignment. In my Cape Cod Foodie persona, I try to spiff myself up a bit, switching out my usual jeans and a sweatshirt for a funky dress and a pair of dangly earrings. In honor of the season, I dressed up a bit more, donning a red knit dress, black boots, and sparkly silver beads swinging from my ears. I've always claimed that I'm not exactly beautiful, but Krista says the camera loves me (or at least my cheekbones). She says my height gives me presence. And it's true that there are moments during filming when I feel completely poised and at ease in a way that I seldom do in real life.

I got out of the truck and scanned the crowd for Jenny and her boys, Thing One, Thing Two, and Thing Three. For the record, their names are Ethan, Eli, and Evan, and they are ten, eight, and six years old, respectively. I finally managed to spot Roland, who, despite the crowd's preference for holiday headgear, was wearing his usual hideous yellow-and-black-checked wool cap with the earflaps tied securely under his chin. Not for Roland Singleton to choose fun over comfort. And yet Jenny loved him.

I pushed through the crowd and enjoyed a series of high fives with the Three Things. Suddenly, the crowd began to cheer, and I turned back toward the water. Coming around the curve from the narrow, reed-rimmed estuary that leads into Town Cove from Crystal Bay was the Harbor Patrol's Grady-White with Santa Claus standing in the bow, resplendent in his plush red suit and an enormous white polyester beard. As the boat nosed its way up to the dock, he waved one white-gloved hand and the kids in the crowd went wild. All except Evan Singleton.

I like this kid a lot. He is serious and thoughtful and

seems much wiser than his six years. Also, he has no filter. He says whatever he is thinking. While his brothers rushed forward to catch one of the candy canes that Santa was now tossing to his adoring fans, Evan stepped back, surveying the scene solemnly. There was a temporary hush when Santa raised his hand for silence, presumably so the crowd could hear him ask the obligatory "Have you been good boys and girls?" But before he could say his line, Evan took the opportunity to pipe up, high and clear, "Santa Claus has a nose like a potato." *Awkward*.

Santa Claus did indeed have a nose like a potato, large and bulbous and kind of mashed in on one side, but I didn't have much time to absorb that fact before my eyes were drawn to something even more disturbing: Jason at the wheel of the Grady-White. Not the tall, dark, and handsome Jason I knew and (usually) hoped to know even better. No. This was Jason in an elf costume. With red-and-white-striped stockings and green shoes that turned up at the toes. I had been right about the buzzkill effect of this getup. The sight would be forever burned into my retinas unless I did something fast.

I turned to Jenny. "Get me out of here," I commanded. "I need a cocktail."

Yes, it was ten o'clock in the morning. And, yes, though I like a cosmo as much as the next girl, I usually try to wait until the sun is, as we sailors like to say, over the yardarm (whatever that means—even we sailors don't know). But today was different. And not simply because I'd just seen the world hottest harbormaster reduced to being Santa's little helper. Today, Jenny and I had a job to do.

"We aren't supposed to start filming until noon," Jenny pointed out, "so that gives us a chance to do some Christmas shopping with the boys."

Well, it was better than Jason the Christmas Elf. But not by much.

* * *

IT WAS WITH great rejoicing that Jenny and I finally handed the Three Things off to Roland and drove off to the Ginger Jar. The restaurant fronted on Main Street, but Julie Bruni had suggested that Jenny and I park in the gravel deliveries lot behind the building that they shared with the Lucky Strike Lanes, the local bowling alley.

Jenny pulled into a spot near the restaurant's back door next to a battered pickup full of buckets, mops, and cleaning supplies. Parked on the other side of the truck was what even I, a vehicle illiterate, could identify as one of those sleek all-electric Teslas. Across the lot, nearer the back door of the Lanes, stood a nondescript beige sedan in unlikely partnership with a shiny red muscle car.

"Okay!" Jenny said gleefully. "Time to play Match the Car to the Owner!"

Match the Car to the Owner is one of Jenny's favorite games. Jenny was convinced that cars say a lot about the people who drive them. I drive a pickup named Grumpy. I didn't want to think what that said about me.

"The truck belongs to Liz the Cleaning Lady, of course," Jenny announced.

I could have guessed that. First of all because "Liz the Cleaning Lady" was neatly lettered on the truck's door. Second, because everybody in Fair Harbor knew Liz the Cleaning Lady's truck. Liz the Cleaning Lady was a sturdy middle-aged woman with short salt-and-pepper hair that she clearly cut herself and who never met a mess she couldn't wrestle into submission. I'd scraped up a little extra cash to hire her to clean out the decades of empty paint cans, three-legged tables, and other assorted detritus from Aunt Ida's cellar because I simply couldn't face the legions of daddy longlegs (*eeuuw*) that would be fighting for their home. She'd attacked the junk and the spiders with impressive vengeance. Then she'd insisted on scrubbing and whitewashing the old stone and plaster walls. When I tried to be politically correct and said she was a great cleaner, she had snapped at me, "I'm a cleaning lady, not a cleaner. Cleaners are guys in coveralls who don't give a rat's ass what kind of job they do." So Liz the Cleaning Lady she remained.

"And the trying-too-hard Camaro has to be Wally Lipman's," Jenny said. "He manages the Lanes now."

I remembered Wally Lipman. In high school Wally had been the ringleader of a group of morons who thought it was the height of wit to plague me with questions like "How's the weather up there?" Wally was short. Maybe as some sort of compensation, he'd also been into bodybuilding in a big way. I comforted myself at the time with the thought that probably the only thing worse than being a very tall, very visible teenage girl would be to be a very short, very invisible teenage boy. So now I wasn't surprised that the fire-engine red, trying-too-hard car might be Wally's. That was not an automobile you could be invisible in.

"Wally Lipman manages the bowling alley?" I asked. It was hard to imagine Wally in a position of responsibility. He had never been the brightest bulb in the box.

"Well, in a manner of speaking," Jenny acknowledged. "You remember his mother, Mrs. Lipman?"

"Sure," I said. "Mrs. Lipman was about my favorite teacher ever."

Jenny nodded in agreement. Dorothy Lipman had been our physics teacher when we were sophomores in high school. She had high standards—any cheating or causing a ruckus and you were *out*, no excuses. But never had science so come alive. Mrs. Lipman believed in hands-on learning.

"You remember the fireproof balloon?" Jenny asked, laughing.

"I liked the Popsicle-stick catapults the best."

"Yeah, that was sheer chaos," Jenny agreed. "Well, anyway, when she retired last summer she bought the Lucky Strike, mostly I think for Wally to manage. So now she spends a lot of time here trying to manage him. Can't be easy, but at least for the first time in his adult life he actually has to stick to a job."

I wasn't that interested in Wally's adult life. But the news about Mrs. Lipman surprised me. I had been away a long time. I was still catching up with everything that had changed in Fair Harbor over the past decade.

"Mrs. Lipman retired?" I asked. "But she wasn't that old."

"Yeah, she's probably only in her mid-fifties," Jenny agreed. "My second cousin Jaye, who manages the high school cafeteria, told me she heard that Mrs. Lipman had applied for the principal's job when it came open two years ago. When she didn't get it—they gave it to that young guy, Inglesby, from Barnstable High—she stayed on one more year to get her pension, then took it in a lump sum and bought the Lanes with it. That sensible ten-year-old Honda has to be hers."

"So that leaves the super-cool Tesla to the super-cool Brunis?"

"I would think so," Jenny said. "Sustainable *and* hip. Perfect for the Brunis."

We climbed out of Jenny's gas-guzzling SUV ("I need a big car. I want those smelly boys as far away from me as possible") and headed to the back door of the Ginger Jar, which was propped open with a bucket full of dirty water. The door opened into a storeroom crowded with bottles of organic tomato juice and vodkas with unpronounceable names. In the dim light from the room's one small window, I just managed to avoid tripping over a wooden box full of coconuts and Jenny almost collapsed a pyramid of canned apricots. Disaster averted, we shouldered past a clothesline pinned with damp compression knee-highs and nylon cleaning smocks, and came out into a hallway.

Across from us and to the left were the men's room, then the ladies' room, and finally a door marked "Private," probably to the office, with a small wooden chair next to it. Directly to our right a pair of swinging doors, each with a glass porthole window, marked the entrance to the kitchen. Across from the kitchen another hallway led out into the restaurant proper, where the roar of a professional-strength vacuum cleaner announced that Liz the Cleaning Lady was already beating any rogue speck of dust or dirt into submission.

From inside the kitchen a thumping R & B beat competed with the racket from the invisible vacuum. Jenny and I walked over to the swinging doors and peered through the portholes into the kitchen. Martin and Julie, wearing tightly wrapped red bandanas around their hair, were prepping for the afternoon rush of Santa Selebrators. In a nice switch of typical kitchen gender roles, Martin was deftly carving impossibly long and delicate garnish twists from what looked like real key limes while Julie effortlessly hauled great tubs of pre-prepped vegetables out of the walk-in refrigerator.

Jenny stuck her head into the kitchen to say hello, and Julie came out to greet us in the hall, pulling off her headscarf. A great fall of red curls tumbled free around a small triangular face and brilliant green eyes. Julie was slight, almost waiflike, and was wearing a long peasant dress with bright red cowboy boots, but, as when Krista and I had introduced ourselves the night we'd eaten at the Ginger Jar, I'd sensed real professionalism and steely resolve behind that boho facade.

I introduced Jenny to Julie. "Jenny's the videographer and brains behind the operation," I said. "I just do what I'm told."

"Thanks for coming," Julie said, briskly shaking Jenny's hand.

Martin came out behind his sister, carrying a Lucite garnish holder piled with lemon and lime twists, thin shards of crystalized ginger, a small hill of pomegranate seeds, and vodka-infused cranberries. In his other hand he held a pitcher filled with something frothy and creamy and which I hoped desperately was the secret ingredient for his signature eggnog.

With my usual subtlety, I asked, "Is that your secret ingredient for your eggnog?"

It's a funny thing, but I've noticed that people tend to feel they have to respond to questions from the press or law enforcement. They don't have to, of course. It is everyone's right not to. But they do. It never ceases to amaze me.

"It is," Martin said, holding the pitcher out to me. "Take a sniff."

I sniffed. This was something I was good at. The heady aroma of coconut wafted up like a soft kiss. "Coconut cream," I said.

Martin smiled at me the way Alex Trebek used to when a contestant aced a particularly tricky question.

"You got it," he said. "We have a supply of coconuts in the back room. We grate and toast the coconut meat ourselves then cook it in the water from the coconut and lots of heavy cream. Once it's cooled, we strain out the coconut and voilà!"

Voilà indeed! My quest was fulfilled! Not that I was probably going to make it from scratch, but I knew a lot of grocery stores stocked canned coconut cream.

Jenny made a little ahem noise, and I came back to earth.

I made the introductions, and Martin smiled shyly at Jenny but said nothing. This didn't surprise me. Behind the bar, Martin was a showman and a charmer, but offstage, so to speak, he had a vulnerable, nerdish quality, only coming alive when explaining the science behind his mixology.

Martin was wearing a breathtakingly tight black T-shirt with long sleeves that he'd pushed up on his forearms, revealing full-sleeve tattoos in a kind of jungle motif with a few semi-naked ladies peering through the foliage. I'm not a huge tats fan, but even I had to admit these were pretty spectacular.

The three of us followed Julie out into the restaurant proper.

As I'd suspected, Liz the Cleaning Lady, resplendent in opaque flesh-colored knee-highs and navy blue cleaning smock, was slamming a vacuum cleaner under the tables. She barely gave us a glance as we stood there.

"Liz, you wanna give that a break?" Julie shouted.

Liz kicked the machine's off switch.

"Happy to," she said, her voice almost as loud as the vacuum had been. "I hate this SOB." So saying, she dragged the monster off behind her toward the storeroom.

"And keep it quiet back there, okay, Liz?" Julie called after her. "Especially if the kitchen crew comes in."

"No problem," Liz said over her shoulder. "I'll set 'em to cleaning out the freezer. They hate that."

"How do you want to do this?" Julie asked Jenny as Martin began arranging the tools of his trade behind the bar. "We have about a half hour before the rest of the kitchen and waitstaff get here. But they know to come in the back, so they won't disturb us."

"Well, first of all, a little costume change," Jenny said, pulling a Santa hat out of her capacious shoulder bag and holding it out to Martin. He grinned and pulled off his bandana. You'd think he'd look ridiculous, but when he plunked the Santa hat on and grinned at us, it all worked charmingly.

"That's great," Jenny said, just a little flushed. "And if you could pull down your sleeves?" She eyed the artwork on his forearms. "We need to keep this PG."

Martin grinned again and slid the sleeves down obediently. The only tattoo still visible was what looked like some kind of constellation wrapped around his left wrist.

"Is that Orion's Belt or something?" I asked.

Before Martin could answer, Julie jumped in. I got the feeling she talked a lot for her brother. "It's kind of a private joke," she said. "It's the molecular formula for serotonin, you know, the happy hormone?"

I laughed and said, "I'll take your word for it. What I don't know about chemistry is a lot."

I slid out of my down parka and dropped it on a chair.

"I'll just go see if I have anything between my teeth before we get started," I said, and made my way back to the hallway and down to the ladies' room.

I checked myself in the mirror, vaguely hoping that I had turned beautiful since I'd left the house that morning. Nope, no such luck. Though I was blessed at birth with my Italian American mother's clear olive skin and my Yankee father's high cheekbones, my brown hair and eyes have always been unmemorable. And they were still unmemorable. No matter what Jason said. I slicked on a little mascara and some tinted lip gloss and grimaced at myself in the mirror.

"Showtime!" I said, and headed back to the bar.

I slid onto a bar stool facing Martin on a diagonal and waited for my instructions from Jenny.

When I first got roped into this Cape Cod Foodie gig, Jenny had filmed the video clips with her iPad just for fun. But since then, she'd gone pro, opening her own videography studio in downtown Fair Harbor and using a fancy-schmancy Canon PowerShot for filming. She pulled the camera out of its case and placed it on the bar.

"It's very simple," she said to Martin. "Just start making a few of your favorite holiday cocktails, and while you work Sam's going to ask you some questions about your technique and your ingredients."

Martin looked a little apprehensive and Jenny hastened to reassure him. "It's just a conversation, just say what comes naturally. We already know you love what you do. That will come through."

"So you don't want to do a whaddayacallit, a rehearsal?" Martin asked.

"Nope," Jenny said firmly. "Rehearsals are deadly."

In retrospect, perhaps not the best choice of words.

O VER THE COURSE of the next half hour or so, Martin concocted and I sampled a few holiday-themed cocktails, including a dynamite Mistletoe Margarita and a highly potent Peppermintini, all the while also devouring plate of walnut-crusted salmon bites with apricot-ginger dipping sauce. As Jenny had predicted, the conversation was easy, with Martin's natural enthusiasm for his craft overcoming his initial reticence.

"There's a lot of science that goes into cocktails like this," Martin explained, as he prepared the bar's signature drink, the Ginger Man, as his finale.

"First," he said, "I grate some fresh ginger." So saying, he took a knob of ginger from a wire basket and grated it with a microplane—which I knew from experience was fine enough and sharp enough take the tip of your finger right off if you're not careful—into a cocktail shaker. "Then, we add liquid nitrogen. . . ." So saying, Martin took up what looked like a sleek black thermos with a spout on it and, pressing a lever, shot a white cloud of liquid nitrogen into the shaker with a whoosh that almost made me fall off my bar stool.

"Jeez," I said, regaining my composure. "You could've warned me."

Martin just laughed and began what he called nitromuddling the ginger, then, lightning fast, added acidless grapefruit juice ("that process alone takes an entire day"), aquavit, saline solution (I am not making this up), and crystalized simple syrup.

I took a sip and pronounced it ambrosia. Because it was. Jenny pronounced us done.

"This is great stuff, Martin," she said. "I'll just take a few shots of the Santa Selebrators coming in and we'll be done. I can't even imagine how I'm going to boil it down into a five-minute segment."

I knew she was being modest. Through inspired editing magic she could and would create five minutes of sheer foodie (drinkie?) infotainment. And somehow I would come across as much more knowledgeable and attractive than I knew I really was. That was Jenny's real talent, in my book. (Helene, on the other hand, says that I *am* knowledgeable and attractive and that the camera is showing me my *real* self as others see me. She says I need to stop seeing myself through the lens of my internal locus of evaluation, whatever that means.)

Jenny and I had arranged to meet Krista, Miles, and Jason at the bar for a quick lunch before moving on to enjoy the rest of the Selebration. As Julie unlocked the front door for the first revelers of the day, the bell over the door chimed and, right on cue, our friends piled in.

Jason (thank you, God) had ditched the elf suit in favor of black jeans, a red sweater, and brown leather hiking boots. With his unruly black hair tumbling over his forehead, he looked super manly and good enough to eat with a spoon.

Krista, of course, had donned a *very* sexy elf outfit complete with short skirt and fishnet stockings, which somehow worked with her sleek black bob and expertly applied makeup.

Miles was in his usual red flannel shirt and saggy blue jeans. Apparently, he'd decided against the full Santa regalia. But he had poured what looked like at least a pound of white flour on his bushy beard and perched an enormous Santa hat on his head. He looked like Saint Nick if Saint

Nick had been a lumberjack. Apparently the judges had
been lenient in their definition of what made a Santa lookalike, because he proudly waved a Santa bobblehead doll at
me. "You see? I won the contest! I told you I would win!"

"Miles," I said, "I couldn't be prouder." Miles stuck out
his tongue at me.

I wished Helene could have joined us, but she was holding the fort at the library, reading "The Night Before
Christmas" and *Hanukkah Bear* to little kids (or more
likely their exhausted parents) who needed a little down-
time before venturing back into the excitement of Santa's
Seashore Selebration.

Julie welcomed the gang and excused herself to go over-
see the kitchen crew. Martin wandered over and gave each
of the newcomers a friendly fist bump hello when I introduced them. I noticed Jason eyeing the ink bracelet on
the bartender's wrist, but I didn't think anything of it.
Everybody stares at unusual tattoos. That's kind of their
point. Martin handed Krista the drinks and food menus.
How everybody always knows that Krista is the boss is ever
a mystery to me. He pointed to a long table along the far
wall, saying, "Why don't you all grab that six-top in the
corner. Your server will come by in a second to take your
order."

As we settled ourselves, three young women in Santa
hats, very short skirts, and very high heels clattered in.
Jenny took a final quick take of Martin greeting his customers and then put away her camera. Inspired by Jenny's
example (or maybe Martin's biceps), one of the mixologist's
admirers started filming him with her cell phone as he
mixed a Santa Clausmopolitan.

Our server came over and introduced herself as Erica,
and my friends began the lengthy process of ordering. I decided to pass and, while Krista was carefully dictating her
order ("Belvedere vodka, straight up, super cold, two lime
twists and an order of those sugarcane sticks wrapped with

bacon, broiled crisp"), I slipped away for a much-needed bathroom break.

But when I got to the ladies' room, there was one of those yellow "Restroom Being Cleaned" signs in front of it and I could hear Liz the Cleaning Lady at work inside, clanking and clanging. No matter, I knew the restrooms were singles. I'd just use the men's room. I was pretty sure it was the door to my left, the one with the chair next to it. And, as I was by this time in a bit of a rush, I completely missed the "Private" sign on the door when I pushed it open.

So I was just a little confused when I found myself in what was clearly an office, if the sturdy metal desk across from me and matching file cabinet to its left could be trusted. *Oh, right.* The men's room was on the *other* side of the ladies' room. I started to back out, but was arrested by the sight of the open top drawer of the file cabinet. A fan of manila folders was sticking up raggedly from the drawer and a confusion of forms and correspondence had spilled onto the linoleum floor. And that wasn't all.

It was only then that I realized that my heart was hammering and why. Next to the papers on the floor, just peeking out from behind the desk, was what looked very much like a boot. A big, shiny, black boot.

None of this was making any sense to my shocked brain. I moved forward to peer at the floor behind the corner of the desk. Sprawled on the worn linoleum, one hand still clutching a manila file folder, lay the Santa with a nose like a potato, his head neatly caved in at the temple.

Oh god, oh god, oh god.

There was little blood, but that the man was dead was unmistakable. Sightless eyes stared at the wall and the cheeks above the false beard were waxy and pallid. Nonetheless, I crouched down and felt for a nonexistent pulse in a wrist that was already cooling.

Aghast, I stood and stumbled back to the front room,

where the Martin groupie was still filming. I gripped the edge of the bar to keep my legs from folding underneath me like a rickety lawn chair.

"It's Santa Claus," I stammered with my usual eloquence. "Santa Claus is dead."

Thus engendering yet another viral YouTube video starring the infamous Samantha Barnes.

THREE

~~~~~~~~~

As I stood there, the room, which only seconds before had been happily buzzing with holiday cheer, went abruptly silent.

And then all hell broke loose. Questions flew at me, none of them penetrating my stunned brain. Martin stared at me and almost unconsciously dropped three cranberries into the drink he was holding. I noted that they did not cause it to overflow its banks. (This reaction, Helene was to reassure me later, is a classic symptom of shock, in which the brain attempts to maintain its hold on reality by focusing on one very small thing. Like not flooding a Clausmopolitan.)

"Okay, everyone, let's please give her a chance to talk."

Jason. Jason politely ordering people around. Jason, his arm solid around my shoulders, leading me over to the table and sitting me down. Miles and Jenny each silently taking one of my hands, and Krista placing her barely touched drink in front of me. The last thing I wanted or needed was vodka, but I appreciated the gesture. At least it wasn't brandy. I pushed away the drink and began to gather my wits. My friends were there for me. Jason was there for me. I wasn't alone in this.

Jason crouched down next to me, his dark eyes at a level with my own, holding me steady, willing me out of my shock.

"You said somebody was dead," he said firmly. "Who? Where? Tell me, Sam."

I didn't want to talk about it. The words would make it too real. I took hold of myself. *Get a grip, Sam. You once cut a crazy man's finger off with a knife. You can do this.*

"The guy playing Santa Claus, the one you brought to the pier," I said. "He's in the office. Next to the desk. Somebody hit him on the head. He's dead."

To his credit, Jason did not tell me I was crazy. This was a good thing, as I was beginning to wonder about that. Instead, he stood up to his full six feet three and began politely ordering people around again.

"I'd like you all to please stay where you are while I check things out."

The three young women at the bar, who had been gathering their things to leave, sat back down and, as one, pulled out their cell phones.

"And until we understand what's happened here, phones away, please," Jason said.

There is something about the quiet voice of authority. As one, the revelers tucked their phones back in their purses.

"Erica," Jason said to our server, "could you lock the door?"

She nodded, went over to the front door, flipped the deadbolt, and even had the presence of mind to turn the "Open" sign in the window to "Closed."

"Martin, where's the office?"

"Third door on the right," Martin said, his voice panicky. "But I need to go tell Julie. She's in the kitchen."

"That's okay," Jason said, his voice calm but firm, "I'll

take care of that. You just stay here, okay, keep an eye on things."

With a shock, I realized that Jason, despite his calming tones, didn't want Martin going anywhere, telling Julie anything.

Jason turned back to me. "You okay now?"

I just looked at him, then shook my head. *Who knew that finding dead bodies didn't get any easier?*

"You'll be fine," he said, almost as if he believed it.

From where I was sitting, I could see Jason walk down the short hallway toward the kitchen, then turn right into the hallway toward the office. I imagined him opening the office door, taking in the open file cabinet, the waterfall of papers, the black-booted foot. Walking around to the side of the desk. He would know what to do next. As harbormaster, Jason's brief is the waters that give Fair Harbor its name: Town Cove, Crystal Bay, and the many smaller salt ponds that lead off the bay. But a harbormaster is also an officer of the law and can detain and arrest suspects and lead an investigation, though only within the tidal range of the waters he is responsible for. But in this particular case, he was the first law enforcement officer on the scene, and he would follow protocol. He would do his best not to disturb the scene while viewing the body and determining that the victim was in fact beyond any medical help. He would then call the appropriate authorities and detain any witnesses until the police arrived.

After a few minutes, I saw him crossing back toward the kitchen, his face grim. In the hushed bar, I could hear his voice but couldn't distinguish the words as he informed Julie and the kitchen staff what had happened. After a minute or so, he reemerged with Julie behind him, her face white and drawn. They came out into the bar, and Julie immediately went to Martin and began talking to him in low, reassuring tones.

Jason turned to the rest of us. "Sam was right," he said. "It's Caleb Mayo, and it looks like murder."

The word "murder" is not one that most people (*except yours truly*) experience in real life. It is not a good word. It is an ugly word. I looked closely as the others in the room absorbed what Jason had said. One of the threesome at the bar began to cry quietly. The others tried to soothe her but looked ready to crack themselves. Martin, his face a picture of confusion, turned to Julie, as if she could somehow make what he'd heard comprehensible. Julie, on the other hand, had immediately understood the implications of Jason's words and looked deeply worried.

My friends, though shocked, were not new to this scenario. They'd helped me through something similar when I'd first arrived home last spring, and I could see Miles and Jenny sharing a look that said "What? *Again?*" And Krista, of course, looked understandably electrified. How often is a newspaper editor on the spot when a murder is discovered? As unobtrusively as possible, she slid a small notebook and a pen out of her shoulder bag and began to jot down notes.

"We need you all to stay here until the police arrive," Jason continued, quelling some rebellious murmurs from the young women at the bar with a look that brooked no argument.

He took out his cell and moved back into the hallway where he could keep an eye on both the bar and the kitchen but could talk in relative privacy.

I knew who he was calling. Everybody knew who he was calling. He was calling my least favorite officer of the law, Police Chief George McCauley. While Jason spoke in rapid, low tones to McCauley, I tried to make sense of what I'd stumbled across. All I knew about Caleb Mayo was that he was—that is, had been—the town selectman whom Jason had ferried to the town pier just a few hours earlier. And that he had had an unfortunate nose. But Jenny could help me there. Jenny has deep roots in Fair Harbor, going back to her great-great-great-grandparents Patience and Ephraim Snow, who rest in the shady cemetery next to the Presbyterian church. Jenny had a vast network of siblings, aunts, uncles, and first, second, and third cousins. Their annual family reunion required the entire Odd Fellows' Hall to hold them all. Jenny knows everything about everybody in this town.

"Caleb Mayo?" I asked, turning to her. I kept my voice low, but nobody was paying attention to me anymore. Everybody was trying to hear what Jason was saying to the police chief. "Any connection to Mayo of Mayo's Clam Shack?"

Usually when I ask about somebody in town, Jenny regales me with a long and rambling mix of fact and rumor, but this time, in deference to the circumstances, she kept it short.

"A second cousin, I think," she said. "Owned Cape Concrete but semiretired. An upright man. Big into public service, elected to the town's select board a couple of months ago, been serving for forever on the school board. Married to Wilma Mayo, very nice lady, one son who moved off Cape, Miami now, I think."

Listening to her, I began to get a very bad feeling.

"Was Mr. Mayo the one who thought the Brunis were shady?"

Jenny knew exactly what I was asking. "Yeah," she said quietly. "By all accounts, that was Caleb Mayo."

I looked over at Martin and Julie, still huddled together behind the bar. Martin simply looked stunned, but it seemed to me that Julie was more than shocked: she was frightened. Before I could speculate further, I was distracted by Liz the Cleaning Lady stomping past Jason and into the bar, annoyance clear on her face.

Jason, still talking to McCauley, looked up in alarm as she elbowed her way past him. He raised his eyebrows at me quizzically, and I realized he had no idea who this woman was or where she'd come from. I myself had forgotten all about her. Everybody had. The cleaning lady had missed everything, including my dramatic announcement, while she'd been busy scrubbing the ladies' room. I stood up and moved to head her off, to tell her what had happened, but, as it turned out, Liz the Cleaning Lady already knew.

"Well," she snapped, pulling off her smock and stuffing it into a capacious tote bag, "looks like somebody else wasn't a big Caleb Mayo fan."

She'd been in the office? Alarmed, I put a hand on one skinny arm.

"You went in there?" I asked.

She cocked her head back at Jason. "I saw that guy come out. Thought I better check what he was up to."

"You didn't touch anything, did you?"

She shook my hand off her arm and looked at me like I was a complete idiot. "I'm not the one taking other people's stuff," she said.

That wasn't what I'd meant, but never mind. Jason was off the phone now, and I wanted to hear what he had to say.

He walked over to Julie and Martin behind the bar and talked to them in low tones before turning to the rest of us.

"I'm going to have to ask you all to sit tight until the police get here," he said.

Jason came over to where I was standing with Liz. I explained the situation to him. I could tell he was not happy about her little visit to the office, but he simply asked her politely to stay around and make a statement when the police arrived.

He turned to Julie. "In the meantime, maybe some coffee for everybody?"

Julie hurried back to the kitchen, grateful, I thought, to be doing something reassuringly normal in such abnormal circumstances.

In no time at all, we were all gratefully sipping some truly fine Sumatra and taking full advantage of a plate of mini sweet potato pancakes topped with avocado sour cream. The comfort food was disappearing fast by the time McCauley was banging on the front door and Jason unlocked it to let him in.

George McCauley is of average height but above-average girth, and it seemed to me that since our last unfortunate encounter, he had substantially increased his belt size. He was accompanied by a thirtysomething woman dressed in a blazer, slim jeans, and some really cool ankle boots. She had dark hair pulled back at the nape of her neck in a casual bun and smooth, clear skin the color of weak tea. Something about her was familiar, but I couldn't place her. A young patrolman who looked barely out of his teens followed them, locking the door again behind him. Obviously nobody was going anywhere for a while.

Through the plate glass window, I could see Santa Selebration revelers passing, though nobody seemed particularly interested in the patrol car parked on the street in front of the building or in coming into the cocktail bar. At first I wondered at this and then with a shock, I realized it was only two in the afternoon. It felt like I'd been trapped in this nightmare for days.

Jason led the police chief and his minions back through the bar toward the rear of the building, McCauley giving me the side-eye as they passed. The last time we'd talked, I'd needed a lawyer at my side. Police Chief McCauley and I were never going to be buds. He had literally no emotional IQ. But even I had to admit that the man knew his job.

Once he'd reviewed the crime scene and had barked some incomprehensible orders into his phone and shooed three rather frightened-looking kitchen staff into the bar proper, McCauley swaggered up to the front of the room.

"Okay, people, for those of you who don't know me, I'm Police Chief George McCauley, and this here," he said, nodding his head (dismissively, I thought) to the woman in the cool boots standing next to him, "is Detective Vivian Peters."

Vivian Peters. *Of course. Vivvie Peters.* I hadn't seen Vivvie Peters since high school. She'd been a few years ahead of me, but it would be hard to forget her. Vivvie was one of the few kids in our school descended from the Cape's original Wampanoag people and as such was considered wicked cool by the rest of us. Way too cool for the likes of me certainly.

McCauley gave another nod of his head, this time in the direction of the young cop now sitting at a table, typing at blistering speed into his tablet. "That's Officer Sandy Snow over there."

Officer Sandy Snow glanced up and (rather charmingly, I thought) gave us all a little finger wave. I noticed Jenny giving him a little finger wave back. This guy had to be another one of her bazillions of Snow cousins.

"It's gonna take the forensics guys"—*like there were no women on the team?*—"at least a half hour to get here from Bourne," McCauley continued. "I want the kitchen staff, the waitress"—*server, please*—"and the girls at the bar"—*young women, please*—"to give Officer Snow your names and contact details and then you can clear out. We'll follow up with you in the next day or so." The "girls at the bar" gave a little cheer, maybe at the thought of leaving or maybe because Officer Snow was so cute. McCauley ignored them.

"Once you're done, Snow," McCauley continued, "I want you to go wait by the back entrance for forensics and the ambulance. There'll probably be some big shot from the Bourne BCI, too."

I looked at Jason quizzically and he mouthed "Bureau of Criminal Investigation."

"And tell them to try and keep it on the down low, okay? The last thing we need is a bunch of little kids watching Santa getting wheeled outta here."

Snow winced a little at his boss's gallows humor but nodded gamely.

"Detective Peters and I are gonna need statements from the rest of you," McCauley said, looking balefully at our little group.

At me, actually.

FOUR

I GET IT, I really do. I was the one who'd found the body. But I didn't like the look in McCauley's eye. McCauley took his considerable paunch over to a separate table and, ever the gentleman, gestured at me with his chin to join him. Jason made a move as if to come with me, but I shook my head slightly and he settled back in his chair. Jason had to work with McCauley professionally. I wasn't going to put him in the middle. And besides, I was a big girl. I could handle McCauley.

But the man really needed to improve his bedside manner. As his questions for me got more and more aggressive, I got snarkier and snarkier. At least in my head. Aloud, I tried to crush him with my dignity. As if.

"What was your relationship with the deceased?"

What I wanted to say was, *Um, I found his body.*

What I actually said was, "I had no relationship with Mr. Mayo. I don't think I'd ever even heard of him until a few weeks ago. I'd certainly never met him."

"Why were you here before the place was open?"

Because I just couldn't wait to find a dead body? "We

were working on a video we're doing for the *Clarion* on holiday cocktails."

At this, McCauley swiveled and glared at Krista, who'd been unapologetically listening in on our conversation and scribbling into her little notebook. I could tell the lack of privacy annoyed him. But really the only other room where he could have talked to witnesses in private was the office and that was, shall we say, occupied.

"What are you doing?" he snapped at Krista.

"Just making sure I keep my facts straight, Chief," Krista said neutrally, somehow managing to give the impression of the total professional in spite of her flamboyant costume. Krista's always been able to handle McCauley. She's a little scary that way.

McCauley turned back to easier pickings. "Why did you go into the office?" he barked at me.

"Because I got confused looking for the ladies' room," I said.

"Why didn't you call the police right away?"

Because there was already a law enforcement officer in the building, and I like him a whole lot better than I like you?

"The harbormaster was here," I pointed out. "I told him immediately." *Okay, I told the whole bar immediately, but still.* "I thought it would be more appropriate for him to inform you."

McCauley finally dismissed me, sending me over to Detective Peters at the next table, who had just finished up with Jenny and Miles. Then he did that same chin thing to the Bruni siblings, who trotted over to him double time. I have to say I felt sorry for them. Martin still looked stunned and Julie was clearly apprehensive, maybe more than a little bad publicity from finding a dead man in your back room might warrant, I thought.

"Word is Caleb Mayo wasn't your biggest fan," I heard

McCauley start out in his typically diplomatic manner. Martin just nodded, but Julie went whiter if that was possible.

Detective Peters coughed politely, bringing my attention back to her. I smiled and sat down. I didn't mention remembering her from high school. Somehow it didn't seem like the right time to pull out the old yearbook, so to speak.

"What I'd like to do here," she said, tapping a slick little computer tablet on the table in front of her, "is create a timeline from when you arrived to when you found the body."

"Mr. Mayo," I corrected her quietly. "I found Mr. Mayo."

I didn't know the man, but until I knew differently, I felt he deserved the dignity of his name.

Detective Peters nodded. "Yes, of course," she said, conceding the point. "Mr. Mayo. Up until you found Mr. Mayo."

She then proceeded to take me through my day, almost minute by minute. Her fingers were a blur on the tablet's keyboard and yet somehow she managed to maintain eye contact with me at the same time. It was impressive. Everything about her was impressive.

The whole thing probably took ten minutes. When we finished, I went back to join my friends at our table while Detective Peters called Liz the Cleaning Lady over and began the same process with her.

"This is like speed dating," Miles said, "except they want to know the worst stuff about you instead of the best."

"You've done speed dating?" Jenny asked, incredulous. "You never told me that."

I sighed. Sometimes it is very hard to keep Miles and Jenny on topic.

"Hush," I said. "I want to hear what Liz the Cleaning Lady has to say."

Truthfully, I would have preferred to listen in to Mc-

Cauley's little chat with the Brunis, but they were speaking too quietly. In contrast, Liz's voice, like her vacuum cleaner, kind of commanded the airwaves.

According to her, she'd got to the Ginger Jar around a little before ten that morning. She'd unlocked and propped open the back door like Julie had told her to because some people were coming to do some movie or something. She'd immediately gone into the kitchen, cracked the window for ventilation, and started in on the kitchen cleanup, even though it had been wiped up the night before by the kitchen crew, because, as she put it, "those guys can barely wipe their bums, let alone a kitchen counter." She hadn't particularly noticed if the office door was open or shut when she arrived, but she assumed it was shut. No, she didn't go into the office. "I don't clean in there," she explained patiently, "on account of 'cause it says *private* on the door."

She turned to give me an accusatory look. Oh yeah, like I'd been sneaking around *looking* for dead bodies in defiance of all social norms.

She'd heard nothing out of the ordinary, she continued, while she'd been working in the kitchen. "Besides," she added, "I had the radio turned on loud to WKLB." WKLB is Boston's kickass country and western station. Quiet it is not. Through the open kitchen window, which looks out to the deliveries lot, she'd seen Martin and Julie pull up in their car an hour or so later. They'd come directly into the kitchen, where she was just finishing up the floor. ("Walked all over it, thanks for nothing.")

Riveting as Liz's story was, my attention kept wandering over to where McCauley was questioning the Brunis. Or trying to question the Brunis. Most of their conversation had been drowned out by Liz's recitation, but if body language was any clue, McCauley was not, shall we say, happy.

Finally, he shoved his chair back from the table and stood, hands on hips, saying loudly enough to be heard in the next county, "You're sure? You're sure you don't want to do this friendly?"

He did not sound friendly. He sounded mean. The rest of the room went very quiet.

You could have knocked me over with a feather when Julie Bruni responded firmly, "I've already told you. Apart from helping you logistically so you can get on with your investigation, we're only going to take further questions in the presence of our lawyer." *Wow. Why hadn't I thought of that?*

With a snort of disgust, McCauley sent them over to Detective Peters, and they joined Liz in confirming the timeline. Or Julie confirmed the timeline. Martin mostly confirmed Julie. They'd left the house around eleven, but Santa Selebration traffic had held them up so it took them maybe fifteen minutes to get to the restaurant. They'd parked in back and gone directly to the kitchen. Julie was fairly sure the office door had been shut when they passed it. ("I usually close it when I leave, so there'd be no reason for it to be open.") In the kitchen, they'd talked briefly to Liz, and Julie had started prepping bar food while Martin made a fresh supply of coconut cream and drink garnishes. Liz had moved to the front of the house to start vacuuming. Both Brunis said that from that point until Jenny and I had arrived at quarter to twelve, as arranged, the sound of the vacuum cleaner being pushed back and forth in the bar area never stopped. Neither of the Brunis left the kitchen or, indeed, went into the office during that time. Neither the cleaning lady nor the restaurant's owners had heard anything out of the ordinary, though it would have been difficult given the noise from the vacuum cleaner.

They were just wrapping up when Officer Snow came back into the bar area accompanied by a rather rabbity-looking man in an enormous down parka. I thought the rabbity persona might be misleading. The eyes that swept us held a quick intelligence, and I thought I saw a spark of recognition when he came to Jason, though he said nothing.

"Chief, this is Lieutenant Hammond," Officer Snow said, "from the BCI. He's got the forensics team waiting out back."

McCauley sucked in his gut a little and shook the lieutenant's hand in a manly fashion. "Thanks for coming, Hammond. I think we got it under control, though. I was tight with Caleb Mayo. I'm gonna make sure we get the guy who did this."

The lieutenant just nodded. Apparently he wasn't as impressed as he was supposed to be.

McCauley turned to the rest of us and said grandly, "This place is a crime scene. I want you all out of here. I'll be in touch."

It seemed to me that he was looking directly at the Brunis. It also seemed to me that in the course of fifteen minutes, he had decided who his primary suspects were. Which of course put me solidly on their side. Not that I had any business taking sides. But I'm only human.

For the first time Lieutenant Hammond spoke. He turned toward Jason.

"Captiva, you want to stick around?" It wasn't really a question.

Jason just nodded and turned to me. "Are you going to be okay?" he murmured. "Do you still want me to come over tonight?"

My parents were arriving the next day, so Jason and I had planned for a last evening alone before the invasion.

"Sure. Come over. I'm fine," I lied. For one thing, I have my pride. For another, I wanted to pump him for info. I couldn't help it. See "only human," above.

* * *

JENNY AND I left through the front door and said
goodbye to Miles and Krista on the sidewalk. Krista set
off down Main Street toward the *Clarion*, shouting over her
shoulder, "I've got to get this story posted online. Call me
if anything else breaks, okay?" She meant if I weaseled
anything more out of Jason. Krista knows me so well.

"You're sure you're okay?" Miles asked. "I can come
home with you, if you want some company."

I appreciated Miles's offer, but I knew he had plans to
meet his boyfriend, Sebastian Wilkes, at the Crying Tiger
for dinner that night. Sebastian was a pediatric oncologist
at Hyannis Hospital and rarely had a free night or weekend.
This was a source of tension between the two men. Far be
it for me to get in the way of their date night.

"I'm fine," I said firmly. Oddly enough, the more I said
it, the more I thought it might be true. "Helene should be
back home soon. I might wander over there for some free
counseling."

I grinned to show I was kidding. But only sort of. For
more than two decades, Helene had worked with the Manhattan DA's office evaluating people facing criminal
charges, talking with witnesses, and consulting on murder
investigations. I'm not huge on introspection, but Helene's
professional expertise as a psychologist as well as her personal good sense had helped me through tough times before. I knew I could count on her if I was having trouble
coping.

Miles grinned back at me. "By which you mean wander
over there for some free wine."

"That, too," I said, laughing. It felt good to laugh. Good,
but wrong. *Was I getting used to finding dead bodies?*

Miles, his bobblehead Santa clutched in his hand, hurried off. Jenny and I walked along the sidewalk in front of
the restaurant over to the driveway leading back to the de-

liveries lot, swimming upstream against a current of holiday makers heading for the menorah and tree lighting at Town Square. We turned into the driveway and walked back to the lot where the police from Bourne, despite the presence of one marked and one unmarked car, an enormous police van, and an ambulance, were doing their best to keep things low-key. They were helped by the fact that their work was mostly blocked from view by the bulk of the Ginger Jar itself in front and the bowling alley behind. The EMTs waited in the ambulance for their melancholy cargo while the forensics team moved briskly back and forth from the bar's back entrance to the open rear doors of the police van. One white-suited woman was carrying a Santa hat in a plastic evidence bag.

"Found this just outside the kitchen window," she said, handing it to one of the Bourne cops. "Might be the victim's. There was no hat in the room where he was killed."

Jenny and I hesitated, unsure if we should be trying to make our way to Jenny's car, but Officer Snow recognized us and waved us through. He was talking with Wally Lipman and his mother, who'd clearly come out to see what all the excitement was about. Despite the chilly day, Wally was wearing only a tight beige T-shirt bearing the logo of Fitness World, a local gym favored by bodybuilders, and tan cargo pants. If he felt the cold, it didn't seem to bother him. He'd lost a lot of hair since I'd last seen him but, maybe in compensation, had somehow managed to put new muscles on top of the old ones. He was now almost square. Mrs. Lipman, on the other hand, seemed to have shrunk. I remembered her as a commanding presence, tall and angular, who could freeze any class clown with what everyone called The Look. Huddled there now in a threadbare camel hair coat, shivering against the chill wind, she was almost reduced to insignificance. I looked away, as if I'd seen something private, and Jenny and I shared a glance.

"I swear that boy just sucks his momma dry," Jenny murmured as we headed toward her SUV.

"He's no boy," I said, also keeping my voice down. "He's our age, a grown man."

"One, he still lives at home. Two, until she bought him one, he could never hold a job. And three, he spends most of his time at the gym, playing he-man, or on the couch at home, playing World of Witchcraft—"

"World of Warcraft," I corrected her.

"Whatever. In my book, all that makes him a boy."

I couldn't argue with her on that one. Nor did I ask how she knew all this. Not with her network of informants.

"I just feel bad for Mrs. Lipman," she added. "It couldn't have been easy being a widow trying to raise a boy alone. Especially one who's thick as a brick."

While we were disparaging our old high school classmate, McCauley had come out to talk to Officer Snow. Wally grabbed the chief by the elbow.

"What's going on?" Wally demanded. "This guy won't tell us anything."

McCauley shook Wally's hand off his arm. "Nothing for you to get excited about, Wal. Some trouble in that new place." The way he said "that new place" made the Ginger Jar sound like a house of ill repute.

The police chief turned to Mrs. Lipman, probably sensing in her a more reliable source of information than her son. "Did you happen to see anybody or anything suspicious here in the back lot over the past couple of hours?"

"No," Mrs. Lipman said firmly. "I got here around ten. I saw the cleaning lady's truck parked where it always is and a few revelers, including our esteemed high school principal, on the sidewalk." She paused for a moment, then continued. "Walter gets in shortly before me. Did you see anything, Walter?"

Wally shook his head. "Like she said, I got here when I usually do, a little before ten, after my morning workout. I didn't see anything." He looked distinctly dissatisfied that he couldn't play star witness.

"And we've both been inside ever since, me doing paperwork in the office and Walter up front stocking the bar," Mrs. Lipman concluded. "I'm sorry we can't be more helpful."

"Yeah, well, don't worry about it," McCauley said. "Probably an inside job anyway." *There's the Chief Mc-Cauley we all know and love, master of snap judgments.* "You all can go on back to your work. I'll send somebody by to get your statement later."

Wally, clearly jazzed by all the excitement, didn't look like he wanted to go back to his work. But at a quelling glance from his mother, he followed her back to the Lanes, if sulkily. At least Mrs. Lipman still had The Look.

HERE'S THE THING about dogs. Nobody loves you better. People try, but dogs win hands down. Dogs jump all over you and lick your face *every time they see you*, even if you've only been gone half a day. Then dogs demand that you stop feeling sorry for yourself by taking you out for a good brisk walk. Then they cuddle up next to you on the couch and put their head on your lap so that your leg falls asleep and when you stand up you fall back down again, thus increasing the amount of cuddle time. At least that's how Diogi did it when I finally stumbled home to Aunt Ida's house. Okay, *my* house. I'm working on that.

Diogi (pronounced dee-OH-gee, as in D-O-G, get it?) is your typical Cape Cod mutt, part yellow Lab, part whatever. He loves the water, is great with kids, is loyal and well-meaning, but he is not particularly intellectual. Miles has a dog named Fay Wray, an exceptionally intelligent, beautifully trained Australian shepherd. Miles claims she knows at least fifty commands, including "Go get daddy a beer from the cooler." The only commands Diogi responds to are "shut up" (on occasion), "sit" (on occasion), "stay" (almost never), and "go find Helene" (always). And, oh yeah, "sic 'em." *Don't ask*.

Diogi is the best dog in the world, of course, but others could be forgiven for thinking he was in no way remarkable except for his size. At eight months old, he was about the size of a Shetland pony. I was beginning to think his "whatever" gene might be Great Dane.

But where the pup really shines is his emotional intelligence. By the time he'd covered all his therapy-dog bases, I was feeling much better. Nonetheless, once I got sensation back in my leg, I pushed him away again. It is not easy to shove the dead weight of a ginormous Cape Cod yellow dog off your lap, but I did it. I needed a bath and a glass of wine. Ideally at the same time. Self-care. I am a believer.

Lying there in my Aunt Ida's big old claw-foot tub, occasionally tweaking the hot water with one foot to keep my body temperature at almost boiling, I began to take stock of my psychological temperature as well. I didn't try to minimize what I'd seen. It had been shocking, terrible. But at least this time I hadn't known the victim, and aside from checking for a pulse, I hadn't really had contact with the body. And most of all, this time I wasn't compelled to prove that the death was a murder. That somebody had done away with Caleb Mayo was obvious. The investigation was in good hands, assuming Lieutenant Hammond and Detective Peters were smarter than Chief McCauley. Which wouldn't be hard. The bar was low. And this time, I wasn't personally involved. I had a natural curiosity about the case (or at least I told myself it was natural), but I had no horse in this race. As far as I could see, there was no way I was mixed up in this. I had nothing to worry about.

Which was good, because I had other stuff to worry about.

Partly it was that my parents were arriving the next day and *I wasn't ready.*

But mostly it was Jason.

FIVE

~~~~

I WAS BORN AND raised in Fair Harbor, Massachusetts, a small town on Cape Cod, that fishhook-shaped peninsula jutting out into the Atlantic Ocean just southeast of Boston. When I was seventeen, Jason Captiva, at twenty-one, had been the unwilling object of my first, disastrous teenage crush. So, with romance off the table, we had instead become friends. Until I had turned my back on him when he needed me most.

So, Jason and I had been, by mutual unspoken agreement, taking things slowly since we found each other again in the spring. There were good reasons for that. Sure, Jason was everything a woman could want—kind, intelligent, funny, dedicated to his work, and apparently to me. Also, let's be frank, Jason Captiva was one long, lean hunk of man and undoubtedly the world's best kisser. And yet, at least initially, I'd held back. Was I ready for a committed relationship with Jason? Wouldn't I always wonder if I was just trying to make up for hurting him so long ago? And what if I hurt him again? How could I trust myself?

And I knew that Jason was being equally careful with me. As a girl, I'd shared my hopes and dreams with him. I would become a professional chef. I would open my own restaurant. Unbeknownst to me, Jason had decided then and there that he would never be the one to hold me back from achieving those dreams. And still, it seemed to me, he worried that he might be standing in my way, that I might even now be longing for the bright lights, the excitement of my life and career in the city.

I say *seemed to me*, because, aside from one very good conversation five months ago when I'd tried to convince him that I was now exactly *where* I was supposed to be *when* I was supposed to be there, we'd never broached the topic again. Actually talk about our issues? Heaven forfend. I knew that he cared for me. Or I was pretty sure anyway. But both being born and raised Cape Codders, we didn't talk about it. Instead, we took it slow. Very, very slow.

Which wasn't hard, since summer on the Cape is no vacation for a harbormaster. It means long days and weekends keeping people safe from Mother Nature and Mother Nature safe from people.

Which isn't to say that Jason and I hadn't had some wonderful times together. Whenever he could spare the time, we'd rent a sailboat from Alden Pond boatyard and head out to my favorite place on earth, Crystal Bay. Once or twice we'd managed to snag a Baybird, which made me really miss my family's Baybird, the *Nellie Bly*, named in honor of the first woman investigative journalist, sold when my parents had left the Cape.

In my opinion there is no truth greater than what Ratty famously says to Mole in *The Wind in the Willows*: "There is nothing—*absolutely* nothing—half so much worth doing as simply messing about in boats." As a child and later a teenager, I had loved every minute of messing around in the *Nellie Bly*, from the moment I pulled up the sails and set off onto the clear blue waters of the bay to tacking back to the mooring hours later, lowering the sails, and making everything shipshape. It was all a joy. Especially, of course, the time on those clear blue waters, the salt breeze winging me across the bay, the sky like an azure bowl overhead. So to have the chance to sail in one of the two Baybirds at Alden boatyard was a delicious treat to me, and Jason knew it. I had a suspicion that on occasion a few extra dollars might have changed hands to jump the line.

But now, in the off-season, with its promise of a little more free time for Jason, we seemed to be seeing less of each other, not more. That the chemistry was there was never in question. There was enough chemistry between us to blow up a meth lab. And though we still had that easy camaraderie that we'd always had, I did wonder if Jason wasn't beginning to question, as I was, whether we were, in fact, a good fit.

I am impulsive and energetic to a fault, a little snarky when my dander is up, but basically cheerful and outgoing. Jason, on the other hand, is thoughtful and deliberate. When Jason is provoked, he gets very, very still and very, very quiet. I enjoy and seek out the company of others. I collect friends the way other people collect PEZ dispensers or vinyl records. I delight in new pals like Helene and Jillian and in old friends like Miles and Jenny and (on occasion) Krista. And though Jason likes being with people, and can in fact be the life of the party, he is perfectly happy on his own, reading up on the history of Byzantium (whatever that is) or tinkering with the Harbor Patrol's Grady-White.

But the biggest disconnect now seemed to be how much time we wanted to spend together. Despite my earlier reservations, I increasingly wanted to be in Jason's company, reveling in his dry sense of humor, his bed-head hair, his bedroom eyes. Jason, on the other hand, seemed to me to be even busier in the off-season than he'd been in the summer. Things had gotten to the point where I was beginning to wonder if his excuse for not spending more time with me—"I've got a boat that needs a lot of attention"—wasn't just that, an excuse.

Okay, enough of that, Sam. It wasn't like me to sit in my bath and mope. I climbed out of the tub and I told myself it was because of what had happened that day, the shock of finding Caleb Mayo. Nonetheless, it was a relief when my cell buzzed and I saw Helene's text.

Heard you had a tough day. Want to come over to talk?

I texted back a thumbs-up emoji, toweled off, and pulled on clean jeans and my favorite red sweater. Grabbing the bottle of wine that I'd opened for my bath libation, I said, "C'mon, Diogi, let's go find Helene."

Diogi had been dozing happily on the couch, but at the sound of Helene's name, he exploded off it and ran to the door of the ell. Diogi *wuvs* Helene. Diogi *respects* Helene. Diogi wuvs me, but he doesn't respect me. Which is why Helene is the only human being able to teach him commands. Granted the commands are a little idiosyncratic, along the lines of "shut up" instead of "quiet," but at least he's learned them.

It was five in the afternoon and darkness had fallen, but the path through the overgrown yew hedge that separated Aunt Ida's house from Helene's was so familiar I could do it with my eyes closed. I was almost at the front door when it popped open and Helene appeared like a genie out of a magic lamp. She always knows when I'm about to knock on the door. Don't ask me how. She looked pointedly at the bottle of wine clutched in my hand.

"Well, if you must self-medicate, by all means do it with a Willamette Valley pinot noir."

Helene is a tiny sixtysomething woman with electric blue eyes; a halo of long, curly silver hair; and a penchant for overloading the jewelry and wearing whatever she damn well pleased. Tonight she was sporting black leggings, black UGG boots, and an oversized orange sweatshirt that reached to her knees and was emblazoned with the words "Hey, don't judge my journey." I would never judge Helene's journey. I wanted to *be* Helene when I grew up. If I grew up.

She took the wine from me and ushered me into the house. Unlike my rickety old antique Cape with its many small rooms, Helene's home had been built in the mid-1950s and was essentially one large kitchen, dining, and living space with a roof that soared to almost double height at the wall of windows at the other end of the light, open space.

She poured a little of the wine into two stemless Museum of Modern Art tumblers (no boring old wineglasses for Helene) and settled me into one of the two sleek mid-century modern lounge chairs facing her sleek Swedish woodstove. Then she sat quietly in the other chair, letting the flames behind the window in the stove's door work their calming magic.

Little by little, I told her the story of my day. Mostly she just nodded, occasionally adding an "uh-huh," which was enough to keep me going and not enough to stop the flow. The woman hadn't forgotten her craft. When I'd gotten it all out, I felt better. Though not as much better as I'd hoped.

With that witch's sixth sense of hers, Helene asked, "What else is bothering you, Sam?" Then she poured a little more Willamette Valley truth serum in my glass.

And so it all came pouring out. Jason. Me. Jason and me. Was Jason tired of me? Avoiding me? Did he think we weren't a good fit?

"Nonsense," Helene said briskly. "Of course he's not tired of you. The man's besotted with you."

Besotted? You could have fooled me.

"Then why doesn't he want to spend time with me?" I said. Okay, I whined.

Helene was having none of my self-pity. "He *does* want to spend time with you. Just not *all* his time."

"But I want him to *want* to spend all his time with me," I said. Okay, I whined.

"Have you never heard of extroverts and introverts?" Helene asked. "It's basic Psych 101."

"I never took Psych 101," I muttered sulkily. "I went to cooking school, remember? Not college. But, yes, of course I've heard of extroverts and introverts. Extroverts are social and outgoing. Introverts are shy and retiring."

"Not exactly," Helene said. "It's not as simple as falling into one camp or the other. Those are really the two ends of a spectrum, with most of us falling somewhere in the middle and some of us closer to one end or the other. More important, it's not so much about how outgoing or shy we are. Introversion and extroversion actually relate to where we get our energy from."

"I don't get it," I said. I get my energy from grilled cheese sandwiches. Simple. "Why are people so complicated?" I whined again.

"Think of your brain like a rechargeable battery," Helene explained patiently and took another sip of her wine. "Introverts enjoy being social but only to a point. They are drained of energy from being around people for long periods of time, particularly large crowds. And even when the time spent is with people they care about, there is always a point when they need to retreat, to recharge by being alone."

I nodded. "Okay, that explains Jason," I said. "But what about me?"

"You, my dear, are a classic extrovert," Helene responded. "Extroverts *get* energy from other people. Extroverts actually find their energy is low when they spend too much time alone. They recharge by being social. And there's nobody they want to be with more than the people they are closest to."

So. Jason needed more alone time. And I needed more Jason time. I didn't see how this was going to work.

"So we're doomed," I intoned dramatically as I drained the last of the wine from my glass.

"Nonsense." "Nonsense" is often Helene's response to my, well, my nonsense. "It's like yin and yang. Introverts and extroverts can complement each other. But they have to *talk* to each other." *Well, that ain't gonna happen.*

I looked at my watch and struggled up from the low-slung chair.

"Thanks, Helene. That helps," I lied.

I didn't think for a moment that she believed me, but it was better than saying, *Thanks, Helene. That stinks.*

"And now, ironically, I have to go home and drain Jason's battery."

"Believe it or not, Sam, you are exactly what that man needs," Helene said. "You are the buffer between him and the world, the one who smooths the sharp edges of reality."

I had no idea what she was talking about, but I would take it.

A ND MAYBE HELENE was right. Certainly, Jason seemed *very* happy to see me. If this was a man with a drained battery, I'd eat my chef's toque. But then he, as usual, pulled away.

"You're sure you want to cook?" Jason asked. "You've had a rough day."

How could I ever be annoyed with this guy?

"Cooking is therapy for me," I reminded him, adding with a grin, "And anyway, I'm feeling ever so much better now."

He pulled me into another melting kiss, and then took my hand and led me into the kitchen. "Good," he said. "'Cause I'm starving." *Men.*

Aunt Ida's kitchen had been the first room in the house that I'd really worked on. In my opinion, there is no more important room in any house than the kitchen. But the first time I'd laid eyes on this one I'd despaired. The corner cupboard had held mostly cobwebs, the splatter-painted floor was caked with mud, and the greasy stove looked like it was just short of spontaneously combusting. The pine kitchen table hadn't seen polish in years. A grimy picture window ran the length of the wall behind the table, the window seat below it embellished with a faded cushion of a color very close to snot.

It still thrilled me to see the change a little elbow grease, a lot of paint, and some fresh fabric had wrought. The beeswaxed table now gleamed and the windows sparkled. With Miles's help I'd painted the walls and ceiling a fresh cream and the kitchen cabinets a deep blue-gray. And since the bank account didn't allow for new appliances, I'd disguised the avocado fridge and stove with white enamel spray paint. Jenny had run up new cushion covers for the window seat in a cheerful yellow toile print. The old corner cabinet proudly displayed Aunt Ida's collection of blue willow patterned china. The kitchen was still old-fashioned—no granite cooking island, no gleaming stainless steel fixtures—but it was warm and welcoming and I loved it.

I took the mushroom and béchamel lasagna I'd made the day before out of the fridge to come to room temperature while the stove preheated. (Tip: Unless you make your own lasagna noodles—and if you do, I salute you—try to find the thin, no-boil, oven-ready ones, not the fat, curly-edged ones that you boil first. The difference is amazing.) Jason pulled a Sam Adams beer out of the fridge, uncapped it, and settled into one of the two old but sturdy captain's chairs at each end of the table. He smiled at me, took a sip of his beer, and then set it on the table, his face suddenly serious. "I mean it though, Sam," he said. "Are you okay?"

"I'm fine," I said. Nervously, I started pulling salad stuff out of the fridge. "I talked it through with Helene, so that helped. And it wasn't as awful as the last time, you know? It was shocking, but I didn't know the man. And you saw . . . it. It wasn't, um, that messy or anything. He was just . . ." I found I couldn't say it.

"Dead," Jason supplied gently. "And dead is pretty awful."

He stood up, came over, and wrapped his arms around me. I leaned into his chest, his warm, solid chest, and for the first time that day, I cried.

I DON'T KNOW WHAT helped more, the weeping and wailing (okay, no wailing, but close) or the two large helpings of lasagna, but I was pretty much back to my normal self by the time Jason settled me on the couch in the ell and built up a small fire in the woodstove. I nestled into the deep down cushions with a sigh of contentment.

I loved Aunt Ida's ell. I loved the uncluttered feel of the space with its white walls and open ceiling. I loved the huge casement window that, now that I'd tamed the briar patch, had a view over Bower's Pond and offered lots of natural light. I loved my mahogany four-poster bed with its handmade blue and white quilt. But most of all I loved the sitting area with its floor-to-ceiling bookshelves on either side of a small Vermont Castings woodstove and its chintz-covered couch.

What I'd learned from my first winter on the Cape as a functioning adult (I'd been a barely functioning eighteen-year-old when I'd left for cooking school) was that winter on the Cape actually had its joys. On sunny days, gulls wheeled and cried overhead against crisp blue skies like so many glowing white pinwheels in the reflection of the low winter sun. Occasionally, a flock of wintering buffleheads would fly in from Canada, bobbing like little fat black-and-white bath toys on Bower's Pond. And, on the grey days, nothing, simply nothing, was as comforting as the gold and orange embers of a fire in a woodstove.

"Better now?" Jason asked, as he pushed Diogi off the couch and settled in next to me. This was fine with Diogi, who simply jumped back up and snuggled into Jason's other side. He was just as happy drooling on Jason's lap as mine.

Jason was the Man with the Boat. And Diogi *wuvs* riding in Jason's boat.

"Much better," I said. "I've almost gotten over that terrible sight." I shuddered. "All that green and those stripes . . ."

Jason looked at me blankly, and I snorted with laughter. "The elf costume," I said. "That hilariously bad elf costume."

I swear Jason blushed, though it's hard to tell with a man whose face is perpetually tanned from wind and sun.

"It wasn't so bad," he said weakly.

"If it wasn't so bad, why did you change out of it just as soon as you possibly could?"

"I felt my dignity had been compromised enough," he admitted.

"Well, I've always thought that only a real man can wear curly-toed slippers," I said in his defense. "You wouldn't see McCauley threatening his fragile male ego that way."

Jason didn't take the bait. He knew I didn't like the police chief and he knew why, but he wasn't going to badmouth a fellow law officer.

"McCauley handled himself pretty well today," he said mildly.

He clearly wasn't going to jump into shoptalk without a little nudge. I couldn't help myself. I nudged.

"I admit, he did everything by the book in difficult circumstances. But it was pretty clear that he had his prime suspect fingered within fifteen minutes of walking in the front door."

Jason didn't even ask who I meant. "Well, Martin Bruni *is* the obvious suspect."

This surprised me. I was used to McCauley going with the obvious choice, but not Jason. With Jason the jury was out until all the evidence was in.

"You mean because of the rumors that Mayo wanted to shut the Ginger Jar down?" I asked.

"That," he acknowledged, "but other factors as well. For one thing, it would take a pretty strong guy or someone who really knew what they were doing to take down a man like Mayo with one blow to the head."

"What was the weapon?" I asked. "Did they find it?"

He shook his head. "We'll know more after the postmortem, but it looks like it was something smooth and round, maybe a rock. And if it was a rock, all the killer would have had to do was wipe it and toss it. McCauley's got his team searching the lot behind the bar now."

Good luck with that. The deliveries lot was all gravel and rocks. "What about the timing?" I asked. "How long had he been . . . dead?" It was still hard to say it. "He wasn't . . . cold . . . when I tried to find his pulse. But he was . . . chilly."

"Again, we'll know more later, but the preliminary examination pointed to two, maybe three hours."

I did some rough calculations in my head. I'd found Mr. Mayo around one. "So probably between when the cleaning lady opened the back door around ten and when the Brunis got there at eleven fifteen."

"Maybe," Jason said, but he sounded doubtful. "Although it could have been done *after* they got there."

"But Martin and Julie never left the kitchen until we arrived," I said.

"That's what they say anyway."

"You don't believe them?"

"I don't believe them or not believe them," Jason said. "I'm just saying that we can't know."

"Okay," I conceded. "But don't forget that anyone could have come in through the back door before the Brunis got there."

"I haven't forgotten that," Jason said. "And I also haven't forgotten that the cleaner was alone in the building for more than an hour."

I snorted. "You don't honestly think Liz the Cleaning Lady is our killer?"

Jason grinned. "She's a tough cookie. But no, I don't think Liz the Cleaning Lady is our killer."

"And anyone could have come in through the back door while she was mopping the kitchen," I pointed out.

"True. But she says she didn't hear anything."

"I'm not sure she would have," I said. "She had the radio on."

"And maybe there wouldn't be that much to hear," Jason said. "The thud of the body falling, maybe the door being shut behind the killer. I don't think Mayo would have cried out. I doubt he even saw his killer. I think it all happened too fast."

"And he was too absorbed in going through the Brunis' files," I added dryly.

"Right," Jason agreed. "Which makes you wonder who would want to stop Mayo from going through the Brunis' files."

"Which is why you think Martin is a possibility?"

As for myself, I thought Julie was the more likely of the two to conk someone on the head for going through their business files. But Julie stood maybe five feet two in her cowboy boots and weighed maybe 110 pounds. She looked like she had the upper body strength of a ten-year-old. So not Julie.

"That," Jason said. "That and the ink on his wrist."

"Oh, that," I said dismissively. "That's just the chemical formula for the hormone that makes you happy," I said. "Julie told us. Seri something."

"Serotonin," Jason supplied.

"Yeah, that."

"And it's not."

"Seri-whatever's not the happy hormone?"

"Serotonin *is* the happy hormone. But the tattoo on Martin's wrist is not the chemical formula for serotonin," Jason said flatly. "It's the chemical formula for MDMA, the active ingredient in Ecstasy."

Now, Ecstasy I *did* know. I'd lived in New York City. I knew about E, the drug of choice at dance clubs and raves, though I, needless to say, had never tried it myself. For one thing, I worked nights. For another, I was too chicken. Drugs, even so-called recreational drugs, scared me. I didn't like the kind of people who made them or sold them. I stuck to wine. I *liked* the kind of people who made and sold wine.

"So Martin did Ecstasy," I said. "A lot of kids did Ecstasy. It doesn't make him a killer."

"Martin *sold* Ecstasy," Jason said. "A tattoo like that is an advertisement, a very effective way in a noisy club to let people know you're a dealer."

I sat in silence for a moment, absorbing the implications of this. If Martin had been a dealer, even of a party drug, he'd never be allowed to own a bar or restaurant.

"But a tattoo isn't *proof*," I said, almost to myself. "You'd have to have proof."

"And maybe Mayo was looking for or found that proof in the filing cabinet," Jason said.

I didn't have to say the next logical conclusion aloud: and maybe Martin killed him for it.

I sighed. I'd liked what little I'd seen of Martin and Julie. They were dedicated and enthusiastic and hardworking. But I knew from experience that even the nicest people could be deeply flawed. And yet I felt responsible for them, or at least for what had happened.

I leaned away from Jason. "It's my fault," I said.

Jason blinked. "What's your fault?"

"Everything," I said. "It's not a coincidence that I was the one who found Caleb Mayo. I was the one who *brought* him there."

"You," Jason said firmly, "are talking like a crazy person."

I pulled out my cell, clicked on the icon for the *Clarion*'s online edition, and scrolled through the site until I found it.

"Here," I said, passing the phone to Jason. "Look at this."

I leaned over and pointed to a banner at the top of the newspaper's Living section. *Coming soon from the Cape Cod Foodie: As part of Santa's Seaside Selebration, a sampling of holiday nibbles and cocktails at the Ginger Jar!*

Jason looked at me blankly. "And this makes you responsible how?"

"If the rumors are true, Mayo wanted the Ginger Jar shut down. What if he saw that banner? What if he wanted to head off this good publicity? What if he took a chance on finding something incriminating in the Brunis' files today, hoping it would stop the whole thing?"

"Sam," Jason said, taking both my hands in his, "look at me."

I looked at him. At his tumbled head of hair that no brush or comb could tame. At his deep brown eyes, fringed with thick, dark eyelashes that my grandmother would have called "wasted on a man." At his mouth. That mouth.

"No fair," I complained. "You're distracting me."

He smiled, eyes dancing, and then grew serious again. "It may not be a coincidence that you and Mayo were both at the Ginger Jar today. But that does not make you responsible for his death. The only person responsible for Caleb Mayo's death is Caleb Mayo's killer."

I nodded, half convinced. "But . . ." I said weakly.

"No buts. Sam, just repeat after me: Not my circus. Not my monkey."

I had to smile at that. "That sounds like something Helene would say."

Jason grinned. "It was on a T-shirt she was wearing last week at the library."

I had to admit, I felt a lot better. The day had been a terrible one, but now Jason was here—my old Jason, my funny Jason, my Jason with all the time in the world for me.

Not so fast, Sam.

Jason leaned forward and gave me a quick kiss on the forehead. There is nothing more dismissive than a quick kiss on the forehead. Then he pushed Diogi off his lap, stood, stretched, and said, "It's late and you're tired. And I've got a lot to do tomorrow."

And just like that, my Jason was out the door and gone.

SIX

I DID NOT SLEEP well that night. When I woke, I had a confused memory of a circus, of me as ringmaster, of Diogi dressed up like an organ grinder's monkey. But like all of my dreams, it faded fast. What didn't fade was the memory of Jason's abrupt departure the night before. That still stung. But a steaming cup of coffee while sitting on the window seat in the kitchen soon put me to rights. It was a brilliant, blue-sky Sunday and my natural optimism (or maybe just the caffeine) was kicking in.

"C'mon, Diogi," I said, putting down my mug, the one with my favorite Julia Child quote: "If you're afraid of butter, use cream." "We're going for a walk."

Diogi had been lying in a pool of sunlight on the floor doing his usual solar-powered dog routine, but at the word "walk," he sprang to attention. I went over to the kitchen door and snagged his leash hanging from its brass hook.

"Sit," I said. And Diogi sat. Attaching Diogi's leash to his collar preparatory to going for a walk is virtually the only time that I can count on Diogi to obey the command "sit." This is a dog who'd long ago mastered selective deafness. But he wanted to go for a walk as much as I did. In the warm sunlight streaming through the picture window, one could almost believe that it was just as balmy outside.

If one was an idiot.

It was freezing. Or at least unusually cold. Because the Cape juts out into the Atlantic Ocean, its weather tends to be more temperate than the rest of New England's. In the summer the Cape is cooled by ocean breezes and in the winter, warmed by them. Only by a few degrees, but enough to ensure that daytime temperatures rarely dip below freezing. Rarely, but not never. And not today. The stiff breeze was out of the northwest, which meant it was coming straight from Canada.

Diogi was, it appeared, less bothered by the cold than I was. While I shivered in my parka, he dragged me around the sandy roads of Bayberry Point, sniffing like a bloodhound on the trail of runaway convicts. But still, the walk was good for me. It blew away the cobwebs, as my grandfather would say, and with them, the shock of yesterday. I found I could think about what had happened, what I'd seen, without totally freaking out.

Which was a good thing, because in approximately one hour I would be picking up my parents in Hyannis. And if I knew my mother, a quick rundown of the day's events was not going to be enough. This was a woman who had the journalistic mantra "who, what, when, where, and why" baked into her DNA.

Once back at the house, I left Diogi happily chowing down on a bowl of kibble and some leftover lasagna (dog does not live on kibble alone) and snuck out before he could register my defection. Grumpy deigned to start on the third try, which was pretty good for a cold morning. The truck was a loan from Miles's mother and was about a hundred years old. Once again I wondered what this ancient and temperamental truck said about me. Probably that I am grumpy. Mostly when I am trying to get Grumpy to actually start.

The buttons on the radio had long since seized up except for the one for WKLB. Which was fine by me. I have no voice and no ear, but I sang along at top volume. Anyone can sing along to country and western music.

When I pulled into the parking lot of the Hyannis bus station, my parents were waiting for me. I could see them through the plate glass window, sitting on a bench talking nonstop to each other as if they hadn't just spent three hours talking nonstop to each other on a flight from Miami to Boston and then two hours talking nonstop to each other during the bus ride from Boston to Hyannis. In my entire life, I have never known my parents not to have something to talk about. Looking at them now, I felt a half-happy, half-sad tug at my heart. I loved them, and I missed them. They also drove me absolutely batty. Especially since this retirement thing. The whole reason I was picking them up at the bus station was because of my father's new retirement hobby, saving money. He'd done the math and decided it would be cheaper to take a bus to the Cape than to rent a car. Which would be fine except it also meant, given Grumpy's peculiarities, that yours truly would be their driver for the next two weeks.

But *whatever*. There they were, my wonderful parents. My father tall and thin and a little stooped, with his long, deceptively melancholy New England face. My mother tall, but not as tall as my father, olive skinned and dark haired with fine, flashing dark brown, almost black, eyes, the legacy of her Italian mother, my Nonna. They loved me more than anything in the world. Playing taxi driver was a small price to pay for that kind of love.

I beeped the horn and waved to catch their attention. They looked up, saw me, and hurried out, dragging their wheelie suitcases behind them. I got out and threw their bags in the back of the truck, then opened the passenger side door for them. My mother looked in doubtfully.

"We're all three sitting in the front seat?"

"It only *has* a front seat, Mom," I said. Which was true. Grumpy wasn't one of these newfangled trucks with a full back seat and surround-sound speakers. Grumpy was a classic truck. A crappy radio and one long bench seat with a small well behind it for your tools. "But it has three seat belts, so we'll be fine."

She lifted her eyebrows in an "if you say so" manner, but climbed in, followed by my father, tucking his long legs in like a stork.

"So this is your . . . vehicle," he said doubtfully, eyeing the cracked plastic of the dashboard and the three-on-the-column stick shift. I was glad I hadn't turned off the engine when I'd gotten out to help them with their bags. Now was not the time to display Grumpy's favorite trick.

"Well, it's not mine exactly," I said. "Miles's mom loaned it to me. I'm just borrowing it until I save up enough to buy something secondhand."

My father had enough sensitivity to not bring up the fact that six months is a long time to be borrowing somebody else's car.

"How are the Tanners?" he asked as we pulled out onto Route 6 toward Fair Harbor.

"They're great," I said. "Miles has the farmhouse now. His parents built themselves a nice, one-level cottage on the far side of the property when the stairs got to be a bit much for Mr. Tanner's arthritis."

My mother, who is quickly bored by discussions of older people's ailments, which she calls "the organ recital," broke in. "But what about you, Sam? What's happening with you?"

I knew that question was coming. And I knew they had to know. At least it was easier to tell them while I was driving, eyes on the road. *Just the facts, ma'am.*

It took the entire half-hour drive home to go through my unfortunate Santa Selebration. As I expected, my mother wanted to know everything. Honest to god, if she'd had her reporter's notebook with her, she would have been taking it all down in that incomprehensible shorthand of hers.

Fortunately, as we turned onto the Fair Harbor exit, my big news was dismissed as my parents went into paroxysms of nostalgia over the town that had been their home and their life's work for more than forty years until they'd packed it in for fresh grapefruit and bridge. (I have an unreasonable prejudice against playing bridge, which looks to me an awful lot like work. That being said, a fresh Indian River grapefruit that has never seen the inside of a refrigerator is a fine thing indeed.)

But when we finally parked at the end of Aunt Ida's pot-holed driveway, all conversation stopped. My parents simply stared at the house that I had finally, albeit reluctantly, learned to love and call home. I remembered how my heart had sunk when I'd first clapped eyes on my "inheritance."

In the fading light of that gray spring day six months ago, the house had definitely showed its age. The yellow paint of its clapboard facade had faded to a sickly, peeling beige. The rest of the house, sided with silvered cedar shingles, was streaked with long patches of damp where the original wooden gutters above had rotted away. Shutters hung at limp angles. Scrub oak, bayberry, and pitch pine encroached on all sides. The once-beautiful view of Bower's Pond from the screened-in porch was obscured by a great barricade of briars that only served to heighten the shabbiness of the house.

Back then, I couldn't see how all this was going to work. My usual unquenchable optimism had been all but extinguished by my imploding marriage, career, and self-respect. But I hadn't counted on Miles. Miles is the poster child for optimism. Under his tutelage, I'd learned to scrape, sand, prime, and paint. Pretty much anything is improved by scraping, sanding, priming, and painting. When I wasn't writing restaurant reviews or playing Cape Cod

Foodie, I'd worked on the house. The clapboard front was now back to its original cheerful yellow. Crisp white trim outlined the windows and the front door. Miles had replaced most of the gutters. The original wooden shutters he deemed "priceless," and I had spent countless hours stripping and painting each individual louver. But the effort was worth it. The shutters now gleamed black against the sunny facade, contrasting nicely with the glossy lipstick red I'd chosen for the front door.

As I sat there in the truck with my parents, looking at my humble abode with new eyes, I wondered what they'd make of it.

My mother finally broke the silence. "You've done an amazing job," she said.

I had to agree with her. It seemed to me that maybe I had done, if not an amazing job, at least a pretty good one. Well, Miles and I had done a pretty good one.

"I remember what this place looked like in the last years of Aunt Ida's life," she said. "Except for that ell, she wouldn't spend a penny on it."

"Now, Ronnie"—my father is the only person on earth who has ever dared call Veronica Barnes Ronnie—"that's not really fair. Aunt Ida was living on a fixed income. She didn't have a penny to spend."

"But we offered to help," my mother protested. "And she refused to take it."

My father just smiled his gentle smile. "She was a proud woman, my aunt. Cape Codders of her generation didn't take what they called charity."

My mother just snorted. As an off Caper, she'd never had much time for the myth of the self-sufficient Cape Codder. "She was pigheaded, that's for sure."

I broke into this fascinating discussion in favor of something really interesting. "Could we get back to the amazing job I've done with the place?"

"It looks great, sweetheart," my father said as he opened

the truck's door and gently eased his cramped legs out onto the crushed shell driveway. "And you can see the pond now!"

I hopped out of the truck and stood for a moment, looking over to where the land behind the house sloped down toward Bower's Pond. What had once been a wilderness of brambles was now not what anyone would call a yard—it would have to have grass for that—but was what I liked to think of as a meadow. In the summer, its sandy soil was graced with wild daisies and blue chicory. A path zigzagged from it down the hillside to the pond and Aunt Ida's rickety dock. I'd spent countless hours as a child sailing my tiny Sunfish on that pond.

"It was me against the brambles," I said as I lifted one of the suitcases out of the truck bed. "It was a close-fought battle, but I won in the end."

"Can't wait to see what you've done inside," my mother said as she wrested her bag from me, muttering something about not being dead yet.

I tried to manage expectations.

"Weeeell, Miles and I needed to get the outside ship-shape before turning our sights on the interior. We've really only just started. Just getting things neat and clean has been a challenge."

Sam Barnes, master of understatement. Getting things neat and clean had practically killed me.

I opened the red door and my parents and I crowded into Aunt Ida's minuscule front hallway. A set of crookedy, splatter-painted steps led directly up to the second story with its three tiny attic bedrooms. To our right a door opened into the small, formal parlor; to our left another gave access to the downstairs bedroom my parents would be camping out in.

"You're in here," I said, pushing the door open and standing back to let them through.

Silence.

"This is . . . charming," my mother finally said.

I knew what "charming" meant. "Charming" meant decrepit or, at best, shabby.

My father and I fell in behind her and surveyed the situation. I'd done my best with what had been Aunt Ida's bedroom before she'd moved into the ell. I'd scrubbed and waxed the wide pine floorboards and washed the windows until every tiny pane of antique, bubbled glass gleamed. I'd thrown out the old, yellowing curtains, and Jenny had run up simple white cotton ones with a trim of white bobbles at the bottom. I'd done my best to temporarily stick the worst of the peeling flowered wallpaper back up with Elmer's glue, but I could see one piece behind the bed's headboard already curling off again. Oh, well, the good news was you hardly noticed it once you clapped eyes on Aunt Ida's bed, a dark wood Victorian monstrosity, its headboard reaching almost to the ceiling.

The good news about the bed was that the mattress was fairly recent and had not become a mouse condominium (unlike the cushions on the couch in the living room). The best news was that the cedar hope chest against the wall opposite the bed was full of soft linen sheets, warm woolen blankets, and a number of pristine white and blue woven coverlets, one of which I'd used as a bedspread to very good effect. My mother now pounced on this with the practiced eye of a woman who had never met an antique store she didn't like.

"This," she said, fingering the fabric, "is the real thing. Wool and linen jacquard, probably woven by hand around 1830 or so."

She stood back and regarded her find.

"Reversible square and circle pattern," she said. "Color still a strong indigo. Primitive style. Excellent condition. No moth holes."

She turned to me. "What do you think this is worth?"

I stared at her. "What is this?" I asked. *"Antiques in the Attic?"* My mother's favorite TV show is *Antiques in the*

Attic, where people bring in their family heirlooms for appraisal by expert dealers. "How would I know what it's worth?" I hardly ever watch *Antiques in the Attic*. I pretty much only watch reruns of Julia Child in *The French Chef*.

My mother continued as if I hadn't spoken. "I'd estimate at auction this could bring something around five hundred dollars."

And then I said what all those stunned people on *Antiques in the Attic* always say. I said, "Wow. I had no idea."

"Do you have any more of these?" she asked.

I pointed to the cedar chest. She raised the lid, knelt, and began rifling through its contents. "One, two, three, four . . ." She stood up. "Ten. You've got about five thousand dollars' worth of hand-loomed coverlets in here."

I was dumbstruck. The Universe, or maybe Aunt Ida herself, had just handed me five thousand dollars. So far, my investment in Aunt Ida's house had been mostly sweat equity. But there were major expenses coming down the road, prime among them the replacement of the wonky furnace. And the bank account of the Cape Cod Foodie didn't have nearly enough in it to cover that. But Aunt Ida's cedar chest did. And I was very, very grateful.

And not for the first time, I sent Aunt Ida and the Universe a little mental thank-you note.

J ASON AND I had agreed that my parents would probably want alone time with their one and only child on their first night back. We'd save the fancy Meet the Parents dinner for Monday. So I kept our family meal that night to yummy but simple comfort food: a thick lentil stew; fresh baked, crusty sourdough bread (yes, I have my own starter and, yes, I fuss over it like a helicopter mom); and a romaine salad with buttermilk ranch dressing, topped with toasted chopped walnuts.

My mother gave my dad a warning look when he went

to the fridge for butter to slather on the warm bread, but otherwise the evening was without discord. Mostly we talked about their plans for the next week or so. Or, more worrisome, my parents' lack of plans. Robert and Veronica Barnes are like curious toddlers: if you don't keep them busy, they will get into stuff.

Like, in my father's case, my love life.

"Don't worry about us, sweetheart," my father said. "We'll just hang out with you. We're eager to get to know Jason Captiva."

Oh god, oh god, oh god.

Or like, in my mother's case, my unfortunate habit of finding dead bodies. "We need to put our heads together about this Mayo murder, Sam," she announced firmly.

Oh god, oh god, oh god.

SEVEN

～～～

MONDAY'S BREAKFAST WAS a blast from the past. After letting Diogi out to do his business, I wandered bleary-eyed into the kitchen, desperate for my first cup of coffee. There I found my father wearing his traditional Sunday Morning Dad costume—apron tied around his waist, spatula in one hand, coffee cup in the other.

He waved the spatula at me cheerfully. "What do you want for breakfast? I can do eggs or pancakes."

He didn't really have to tell me that. Aside from standing rib roast, the only thing my dad knew how to cook was eggs and pancakes. But every Sunday that I could remember, he'd asked the same question. And every Sunday I'd said the same thing.

"Both," I said.

I grabbed a mug from the corner cupboard and reached for the coffeepot.

"And by the way, today's Monday," I said. "Why are you doing Sunday breakfast on a Monday?"

"We were traveling yesterday," he said, briskly cracking eggs into a stoneware bowl, "so we missed Sunday breakfast. And since it's the only meal of the week that I'm allowed to eat what I want, I'm not losing that opportunity."

I laughed and settled into the window seat, my hands wrapped gratefully around the steaming mug. "Where's Mom?"

"She'll be back soon," my dad said. "She borrowed your down jacket for her power walk."

I shuddered. *Exercise. Ugh.* As far as I was concerned, the only good workout was the one that didn't happen.

With that, my mother blew into the kitchen, accompanied by Diogi, a blast of cold Canadian air, and unexpectedly, Helene.

"Look who we found on our walk," my mother announced. "Your next door neighbor!"

Helene's face was rosy with the cold, and her silver locks were doing their best to escape from a turquoise woolen turban that she'd obviously knitted herself. You can always tell a garment that Helene has knitted because it looks like no other garment you've ever seen before.

"I was just going out for a walk when Diogi spotted me," Helene said. *What is it with all these people exercising?*

"That dog *really* loves Helene," my mother added, like I'd never noticed.

"So we all took our walk together," Helene said.

"And now I know all about your life here," my mother said with deep satisfaction. *Oh, yeah? Like what?*

I narrowed my eyes at Helene, who just grinned back at me.

My father came over to Helene and offered her his hand. "Robert Barnes," he said. "And you must be Helene Greenberg. Sam's told us so much about you."

Now it was Helene's turn to look at me askance. I just grinned back at her.

"It's a pleasure to meet you both," she said, "but I'm afraid I've got to get to work."

"We'll see you on Saturday for the Feast, right?" my mother confirmed.

"Wouldn't miss it," Helene said gaily and disappeared through the door in a whirl of scarves and silver hair.

Diogi in the meantime had ignored me completely and was looking at the Man with the Food worshipfully. The dog has no loyalty. My father gave him a strip of cooked bacon that had somehow found its way onto the menu in defiance of my mother's dietary laws.

My mother leaned down and gave me a kiss on the cheek. "Good morning, lazy bones!"

I glanced at the kitchen clock. "It's seven in the morning," I pointed out.

"Your father and I have been up for hours," she announced cheerfully. "We've got a full day planned."

I groaned and gestured to my father with the mug. He winked and gave me a refill.

"A full day of what?" I asked.

"Well, your dad wants to get the Christmas tree . . ."

"We're getting a *Christmas tree*?"

Truthfully, I hadn't even considered getting a Christmas tree. I hadn't had a Christmas tree since, well, since I'd left home ten years ago. There is literally no room for a Christmas tree in a four-hundred-square-foot New York City apartment.

"Of course we're getting a Christmas tree," my father said, as shocked as if I'd questioned the existence of gravity or something. "Why wouldn't we get a Christmas tree?"

Well, for one thing, I thought, *I don't have any ornaments. Or a place for it*, unless you counted Aunt Ida's living room, which was in even worse shape than Aunt Ida's bedroom. But I knew there was no sense in arguing. If my father wanted a Christmas tree, we would get a Christmas tree.

"And what else is on the docket?" I asked.

If I'd hoped Veronica Barnes was somehow going to forget what she'd said the night before and just go holiday shopping like other girls' moms, those hopes were quickly dashed. My mom had never been like other girls' moms. But I loved her anyway.

"Well," she said briskly, tucking into an enormous pile of pancakes, "I want to talk to Krista about this murder. She's never covered something like this before."

Krista had been brought on board the *Clarion* as a recent college grad back in the days when my father was the editor in chief and my mother the senior journalist. Within weeks Krista was writing feature stories. In two months, she was moved to news. She was a dynamo. She was brilliant at the work. When my parents moved to Florida, I had assumed the chronically unprofitable *Clarion* would be shut down by the small New England media company that owned it. But Krista had convinced the big cheeses that the future of newspapers was local and online. She walked out of that meeting as the *Clarion*'s new editor in chief. Two years later, the *Clarion* was a print and online publication with a growing reputation and even a small profit. But as far as my mother was concerned, Krista was still a kid learning the ropes.

"I don't know," I said. "I read Krista's story in the *Clarion*'s online edition last night and I thought it was good. Just the facts, no sensationalism. Clear and concise."

"She learned from the best," my father said, leaning down to give my mother a kiss on the forehead.

"True," my mother said with her typical lack of modesty. "But now comes the tricky part, separating the facts from the rumors. I just want to make sure she's up to speed on next steps."

"The next step," my father said firmly, "is getting a Christmas tree."

I HAVE TO ADMIT, buying the Christmas tree was fun. We drove, as we always had, to the parking lot of Turner's Hardware, where Mr. King, a weathered and taciturn Christmas tree farmer from Maine, had been supplying Fair Harbor with Christmas trees for as long as anyone could remember. The only person more disinclined to gush than an old Cape Codder is an old Down-Easter, but I could tell Mr. King was delighted to see my parents again by the length of his handshake with my dad.

The wind was shifting to the southeast, bringing clouds but slightly warmer temperatures, so wandering around—arguing as we always did about blue spruce versus Fraser fir and skinny-and-tall versus short-and-fat—was not painful. We settled on a short-and-fat blue spruce, which Mr. King, who was eighty if he was a day, threw into the back of the truck as if it weighed no more than a feather.

Diogi greeted us happily when we got home—until he saw us taking the tree out of the truck. Diogi did not like the tree. A volley of barking greeted the tree. As far as Diogi was concerned, trees belonged in the ground. They were not supposed to move. They were certainly not supposed to move into *his* house. Which *he* was responsible for protecting. It wasn't until we'd wrestled the tree into a corner of the living room and set it up in a rusty old red and green metal holder that my father had found down in the basement that Diogi was satisfied. He still didn't like that tree, but at least it wasn't moving anymore.

My mother had called Krista earlier that morning and arranged an eleven o'clock meeting at the *Clarion*'s office, just saying she wanted to "catch up." I was almost looking forward to the look on Krista's face when she figured out that my mother was going to instruct her on how to cover Caleb Mayo's murder.

The *Clarion*'s offices occupy a long, low-slung building in a commercial zone just off 6A but still close enough to Main Street that Krista can walk there from her apartment over Shear Beauty. I use the term "apartment" loosely. It's probably more accurate to call it Krista's bedroom, because essentially the woman lives at the *Clarion*'s offices. By the time my mother and I walked in at eleven, I knew Krista had probably already put in a full five hours' work. And still she looked like she'd just been washed and polished. I, in contrast, looked like I'd just wrestled a Christmas tree into submission.

She came around from her desk to greet my mother, pristine in a slim black pencil skirt and white silk blouse. (*When was the last time you washed those jeans you're wearing, Sam?*) As she leaned forward to give my mom an air-kiss, her sleek black bob swung forward like a bell and then fell back into perfect place. (*And did you even comb your hair this morning?*)

Krista, as always, kept the preliminary chat short. As far as she was concerned, a quick "How's Florida?" and "How's Mr. Barnes?" for politeness' sake sufficed.

"So, Mrs. Barnes," Krista said, switching gears abruptly, "I assume you want to talk to me about the Mayo murder."

"You know me so well, Krista," my mother said.

They shared a conspiratorial smile, and Krista nodded, saying, "Two of a kind."

And then it was all business.

As my mother outlined the best approach to take with witnesses, the victim's family, and law enforcement, I realized that I'd been wrong about Krista's probable response to the interference. In fact, the look on Krista's face was less that of someone who wishes someone else would butt out than that of someone who had just been given a wonderful gift.

When my mother finally got through her little seminar, Krista smiled broadly. As a rule, I don't trust Krista when she smiles broadly.

"That's really helpful, Mrs. Barnes," she said. "You know, I'm down one reporter while Guy Flynn is visiting his folks in Vermont over the holidays." She turned to me. "Sam, I was thinking about asking you to take it on . . ."

I stared at her. I'd reported on a story once before for Krista and it had not worked out well. *Understatement.* But it had been, I don't know, exciting, fulfilling, intellectually stimulating? *And terrifying, Sam. You do remember the terrifying part, right?* But still . . .

Yes, I decided. I wanted this assignment.

But before I could say anything, Krista kept going. "But why don't you cover it, Mrs. Barnes?"

"You want *her* to cover the story?" I asked, dismayed.

"You want *me* to cover the story?" my mother asked at the same time. But she didn't sound dismayed. She sounded thrilled.

"Sure. You covered that case in Northam, that fisherman who killed that guy. And you'll be here for what, two weeks?"

"But she's here on *vacation*," I protested, telling myself I was looking out for my mother's interests, not my own.

My mother put a quieting hand on my arm. "It's okay, Sam. I'm happy to help out." Her eyes were bright, her mouth determined, her face alive in a way I hadn't seen in years.

"Sounds great," I lied, consoling myself that, since my mother would be relying on me to ferry her around town for her interviews, I'd be privy to everything she found out without actually having to do any of the work. *Win-win, Sam.*

"Good, then that's settled," Krista said. "Vivian Peters is in charge of the investigation. I'm talking to her this afternoon, and then I'll take care of today's follow-up for the online edition. Not that I expect much that's new from her. By all accounts the coroner's office isn't going to be able to tell us anything until after Christmas. But I'll let her know you'll be covering the story after today, Mrs. Barnes."

Krista stood up to indicate that our meeting was over. As we were gathering our things to leave, though, she turned to me, a slightly wicked smile on her Chanel Rouge lips.

"By the way, did you know you've gone viral again?"

I sat down hard.

"Don't tell me," I moaned.

Krista leaned over, punched a few keys on her computer,

and turned the monitor to face me: "The Cape Cod Foodie Finds Dead Santa." And there I was on YouTube once again, in all my glory. "Santa Claus is dead." *Had I really said that?*

"More than a hundred thousand hits already," Krista said with enormous satisfaction. For Krista, all publicity is good publicity. *Well, nice that somebody's happy.*

"And Jenny says she'll have her Ginger Jar video edited by this afternoon," Krista added.

I stared at her. "You're going to run it?"

She stared right back. "Of course we're going to run it. It would be a little insulting to the Brunis not to, don't you think? It would kind of look like Samantha Barnes, Girl Detective, had decided that the cute bartender is actually the killer."

She had me there.

"Well, have you checked with them?" I asked. "They're okay with you putting it up?"

"Totally cool with it," Krista said. "If anything, it will counteract the negative buzz of a dead body in the back room. And that Martin is a total hottie."

Uh-oh.

EIGHT

D URING THE DRIVE home I tried very hard to set some limits with my mother.

"Unless you can convince Dad to spring for a rental car, which isn't likely, you're going to need me to drive you around for any interviews you don't do by phone. That means working around my schedule, okay?"

"I can drive myself," my mother protested.

"Not gonna happen," I said. "First of all, Grumpy needs very special handling to be convinced to start, let alone stay running. Second of all, if I give you my truck, I'm stuck home while you go off gallivanting. I have a life, too, you know."

My mother laughed. "I swear that was exactly what I used to say to you every weekend when you first got your driver's license." *Oh jeez, I was turning into my mother.*

"But, okay," she continued. "I get it. I can do a lot of this by phone. And face-to-face appointments will be checked with you first, okay?"

"Okay," I said, though I still wasn't convinced this was going to work.

"So, I thought this afternoon we could go see Wilma Mayo," my mother said brightly.

I nearly drove off the road.

"You want to interview the *grieving widow* two days after her husband was murdered?"

"Not *interview* her," my mother said. "I *know* Wilma. We were both in the choir at church until she quit."

"Why'd she quit?" I asked idly.

"I don't know, now that you mention it," my mother said. "Something about it taking up too much of her time."

"It was a half-hour practice every Thursday evening," I pointed out.

"Well, anyway, I do know her," my mother said. "And I want to pay my respects."

I snorted again, and she added, "And maybe ask her a few questions."

I gave up. "Okay," I said, "but I've got some stuff to do first."

"Good," my mother said. "That gives me a chance to make her a tuna casserole."

I shuddered at the memory of my mother's tuna casserole, but I knew she was right. In Fair Harbor you never enter a house of mourning without a casserole in hand.

And I had to admit, I was curious about what my mother might learn from Caleb Mayo's widow.

AFTER DROPPING OFF my mom and picking up Diogi, my next port of call was Shawme Manor, the local nursing home and assisted living facility. I'd first visited the nursing home last spring, when I'd gone to talk to Suzanne Herrick, a sweet older woman in the early stages of Lewy body dementia. With Lewy's the issue is less memory loss than real-time confusion and hallucinations. In Suzanne's case, the delusions were fairly benign—

often seeing children or small animals. But she loved talking about the past, and I'd promised her after that first visit that I'd be back. I'd tried to keep that promise, visiting once a week if possible, usually with Diogi in tow. Suzanne adored Diogi. Mostly because he didn't chase her imaginary kitty.

Over the course of these visits, I'd also become friends with the manager, Jillian Munsell, a registered nurse specializing in geriatric care. On my visits to see Suzanne, Jillian often invited me into her cluttered office for a cup of tea and whatever wonderful treat she'd baked the night before and brought in for her residents. Jillian was a wonderful baker, which really impressed me because I am not. You have to be a combination wizard and chemist to be a baker, and both of those qualifications elude me.

When Diogi and I walked in, Jillian was behind the front desk doing paperwork. Jillian is in her fifties, though she looks at least ten years younger. Her dark mahogany skin has yet to show a single wrinkle or her close-cropped hair a single gray strand. She stood up with a smile to greet me. Jillian is almost as tall as I am, but more graceful with it. When Jillian stands, she gives the impression of royalty bestowing her presence on you. When I stand, I give the impression of a telescoping aluminum ladder that might topple over on you.

"Hey, Sam," she said with a warm smile. "I'm glad to see you brought the hound."

She dipped a hand into a glass jar of homemade dog treats that she keeps for the therapy dogs that come in three times a week. Diogi took a treat politely and then swallowed it in one gulp.

The three of us made our way down to the hall to Suzanne's room, a pleasant space filled with light from a south-facing window, holding two small armchairs and a tidy hospital bed. Suzanne was in the chair by the window, gazing contentedly at a pine tree decorated with twinkling colored lights. Jillian knocked politely at her open door.

"Suzanne," she said, "I've brought Samantha to visit you. And Diogi, of course."

Suzanne's face lit up. I wasn't sure who she was happier to see, me or the dog. "Come in, come in," she said. "Just mind the kitty."

I knew Suzanne's imaginary kitten well, and shooed it gently off the other chair. Diogi sat next to Suzanne and put his head, very softly, into her lap.

"Isn't the tree lovely?" Suzanne said, stroking Diogi with one hand and pointing out the window with the other. "I remember when I was a little girl, we made popcorn and cranberry garlands for our Christmas tree. And when we took the tree down, I would hang them on a little spruce tree in the back yard for the squirrels and birds."

Suzanne chattered happily about Christmases past while I listened with half an ear. I was kind of worrying about my own Christmas. After about fifteen minutes she tired, as she usually did, and Diogi and I took our leave, taking care not to let the kitty run out the door.

Jillian was still at work behind the front desk when we got back to the lobby.

"We're off," I said. "I'm not sure if I'll make it here next week. Things are complicated with the holidays and work."

"Let me get someone to watch the front desk," she said, "and we can go into my office for a chat." As if I needed any inducement, she added, "I made gingerbread cookies."

"I can't stay long," I said. "I promised my mom I'd take her and her tuna casserole over to Wilma Mayo's."

"Oh, that's nice," Jillian said. "I'm taking over a carrot cake when I get off work. Wilma used to be a volunteer here."

"Used to be?"

Jillian looked uncomfortable. "I think she decided it was taking up too much of her time."

Jillian managed to corral a passing aide into covering the desk and led me back into her office. She held out a plate of tiny brown star-shaped cookies, each piped with an intricate design in white icing. I took one. If it was possible, it tasted even better than it looked.

"You use real ginger," I said with my mouth full. *Chew ush weal ginguh.*

Jillian nodded and popped a cookie into her mouth. "Fresh *and* crystallized," she said. *Fwesh an cwishayized.* She swallowed. "And molasses. My momma always used molasses."

"Can I take one for my mother?" I asked.

"Sure, take two," Jillian said, holding the plate out to me again. "How was your visit with Suzanne?"

"Oh, she's such a love," I said. "Spent most of her time talking about decorating Christmas trees. Which just got me worrying about my own."

"How is it possible to worry about a Christmas tree?" Jillian asked. "I mean, you put it up, you put on the lights, you put on the ornaments, you forget about it."

"I don't have any lights," I admitted. "I don't have any ornaments. And Christmas is five days away."

"That is why the good Lord invented the Christmas Tree Shoppe."

I shuddered at the thought of the Christmas Tree Shoppe five days before Christmas, packed with harried moms dragging crying kids through the aisles. I also shuddered at the cost of buying lights and ornaments.

"I don't actually have any money either," I confessed to my friend. Even though Miles and I had done most of the work on Aunt Ida's house ourselves, the supplies had cost more than I'd expected.

"Okay, then," Jillian said firmly. "That makes it easy. We'll do it the old-fashioned way. An all-edible tree."

"What does that even mean?"

"Popcorn and cranberry strings," she said. "Candy canes, frosted holiday cookies with ribbons to hang them. I have plenty of cookie cutters and baking sheets and you probably already have the ingredients we need in your kitchen. I'm off Wednesday and Thursday, as usual." Jillian works weekends at the nursing home, as Saturdays and Sundays are the busiest visiting days and she likes to be available to talk to her residents' families and friends. "I'll come over on Thursday and we'll get this done. It'll be fun."

There is a reason why Jillian is so good at her job. She is a project manager. And my Christmas tree was now her project. I could have kissed her. Instead, I fist-bumped her.

"You are the best," I said.

"Go," she said, waving me and my thanks away. "I'll be over to your house Thursday morning, nine sharp, okay?"

I thanked her again, snagged two more gingerbread cookies for myself, and left, feeling about ten pounds lighter, metaphorically speaking. As I was climbing into Grumpy, a text from Jason popped up on my phone.

We still on for dinner tonight with your folks?

And just like that, my other worry was put to rest. I hadn't been concerned about how Jason and my parents would get along. I had just worried that he might find some excuse not to show. I was, once again, ashamed of my own insecurities.

U bet! 7 o'clock. I added an emoji of blowing a kiss.

Ok see u then. No emoji.

Well, a girl can't have everything. And anyway, my native optimism had already kicked back in. My mother would be doing all the work on the Mayo murder, but I'd get to satisfy my own curiosity. Jillian was going to help me decorate my Christmas tree. Jason was on for Meet the Parents night. Except for that little issue of the Santa Claus is Dead video (159,000 hits and counting), all my problems were solved.

As if.

NINE

$\sim\!\!\sim$

T HE GRIEVING WIDOW was not at all what I had expected. Or what my mother had expected. And my mother *knew* Wilma Mayo.

I'd had a few hours that afternoon to prep dinner but my mother had finally dragged me out of the house, impatient to pay her condolences, as she insisted on terming it. With no irony whatsoever, I might add. The woman has no shame.

"Wilma's a mousy little thing," she said as we drove around the curve of Crystal Bay toward the Mayos' house in south Fair Harbor. I have no idea why we have a south Fair Harbor, an east Fair Harbor, and a Fair Harbor proper but no west Fair Harbor. The answer, I'm sure, is shrouded in the mists of time.

"She's one of those women who spend a lot of time 'tidying' the house," she continued, "and whose opinions are always preceded by 'my husband says.'"

"What about her husband?" I asked. "Did you know him?"

She shifted the casserole on her lap. "I didn't know Caleb personally, but by all accounts he was a good boss. The men who worked at Cape Concrete knew they were lucky. During the recession, he managed to keep everyone working, even if their hours were reduced. But he didn't like workers with what he called attitude. Kind of a one-strike-and-you're-out kind of guy."

"It would be interesting to know if he'd fired anyone recently," I said.

"Aren't you the suspicious one," my mother said, surprise in her voice.

"Well, somebody killed the guy," I pointed out.

T HE MAYOS LIVED in a winding neighborhood of neatly kept two-story full Capes and the occasional slope-roofed saltbox, most pleasantly shaded by red maples and locust trees.

"There we are, eighty-seven McKinley Drive," my mother said, pointing to a saltbox notable primarily for its overall insistence on a beige palette—mushroom trim, tan shutters, taupe front door. A few cars were already parked along the road in front of the house, and I wondered how my mother was going to discreetly pump Wilma Mayo.

A rather subdued young man in his middle thirties, slight and with a hairline already beginning to recede, opened the door to our knock.

"Hi," he said, giving us a sad smile. "I'm Tim, the son. Come on in."

We introduced ourselves and murmured our sympathies. He noticed the casserole and directed us to the kitchen. "Just off the living room. My mom's in there."

"How is she doing?" my mother asked.

He gave us an odd look. "I don't know. You tell me."

Glancing sideways at each other, my mother and I made our way through the living room, where a handful of older men sat watching the Bruins game on a wall-mounted TV with the sound turned off. The kitchen, on the other hand, was lively with the sounds of women talking and even the occasional burst of laughter.

The laughter, it turned out, was Wilma Mayo's.

I needn't have worried about my mother getting information out of Wilma. Wilma was in no need of discreet questioning. For what was probably the first time in her life, Wilma Mayo was the star of the show and she was milking it for all it was worth. She was holding court at a heavily varnished kitchen table with four other women, all with Shear Beauty's signature haircut for women of a certain age, though each sported a dramatically different shade of hair color. They were sipping coffee and enjoying the show. For a show it was.

Wilma Mayo, as my mother had warned me, was the definition of mousy with her thin brown hair streaked with gray and her tan cardigan, white blouse, and slightly wrinkled tan corduroy skirt. But this was the mouse that roared. This woman was high as a kite.

"So what I want to know is did you all know about this Valiant stuff or whatever it's called?" Wilma waved one arm grandly and almost fell off her chair. She laughed gaily and righted herself.

"Valium," a woman with red hair of a shade never found in nature corrected her. "It's called Valium. And of course we knew about it."

There was a chorus of agreement from around the table.

"They gave it to me when I had shingles," said another, this one with what could only be called pink hair. "It almost made shingles worth it."

The woman to the left of her, with startling jet-black hair, nodded. "I took it when Herbert was out of work. I gave one to Herbert, and I never got the bottle back."

Everybody laughed.

At this point Wilma Mayo noticed my mother and me standing in the kitchen door. Her eyes widened and she smiled with delight.

"As I live and breathe, if it isn't my old choir buddy

Veronica Barnes! Come sit down, dear." She waved grandly at the single empty chair next to her.

My mother put the casserole on the kitchen's Formica countertop next to all the other casseroles and sat down as commanded. I stayed where I was, leaning against the doorway.

"I was so sorry to hear about Caleb, Wilma," my mother said. "How are you doing?" *Like it wasn't obvious.*

Wilma made an effort to respond appropriately. "Well, it was a shock, of course. But I'm doing as well as can be expected. The doctor gave me something to settle my nerves, and that's helped." She giggled a little. "We've missed you, Veronica dear. Where did you go? No, don't tell me, it will come to me. Florida?" She didn't wait for my mother to answer. "You know my boy, Timmy, and his wife, Cindy, live there, just outside Miami. It's real nice there. They just had a little girl, my first grandchild. Gosh, I would love to move to Florida, but that takes money." For the first time Wilma looked like she might cry.

"But, Wilma," the woman with the red hair interrupted, "I heard Caleb got a real generous offer for Cape Concrete from that big Rhode Island company, whaddayacallit, Hanson Construction."

At this, my mother sat up a little straighter in her chair. If she'd been a dog, you would say she pricked up her ears.

Wilma nodded and sighed. "He did get a nice offer, but he wouldn't take it. He said he wasn't going to sell to off Capers who would probably fire all of his people and bring in their own. Which didn't make any sense to me. Why would they do that? Their people live in Rhode Island, for goodness' sake." She shook her head sadly. "I thought it might be a good idea for Caleb to retire and we could move to Florida where it's warm and we could be close to our grandbaby. And Timmy, of course. I really miss my boy." A shadow of longing crossed her features. "I tried to convince Caleb, but he said it wouldn't be right. Caleb always does the right thing."

The ladies around the table shared a glance at the present tense, but said nothing.

"Caleb says, 'Here we live and here we stay.'" Wilma's faded blue eyes widened. "Caleb *said*, not says," she amended. "Caleb can't say anything anymore, can he?"

Which was the point where you would expect Caleb's widow's face to crumple as she burst into tears. But no, Caleb's widow's face, in fact, held a look of delighted wonder.

TEN

J ASON ARRIVED FOR the Meet the Parents dinner exactly on time. Which wasn't ideal. Why after six months, did he not understand that for me seven o'clock means *at least* 7:15? I was bent over, bottom sticking out attractively, sliding a buttermilk-brined chicken into the preheated oven, when I heard the kitchen door open and a cheerful "Knock, knock?"

Startled, I stood up too quickly and managed to bang my head on the corner of an upper cabinet door that I'd failed to close earlier *because I was busy rushing around.*

"Ow, ow, ow," I moaned, rubbing my head with one hand and very well aware of what a mess I must look, all nice and sweaty faced from the heat of the oven.

Jason, to give him credit, was suitably apologetic. "Oops, sorry. I didn't mean to startle you. Am I late?"

"Oh, no," I said sourly. "Right on time."

Only then did I notice the enormous bouquet of sunflowers he had in his hand. My favorites. Especially in bleak midwinter.

"Don't you look pretty," he said, as he presented the

flowers with a flourish. "All nice and rosy." (Note to self: Apparently men like sweaty girls. Probably best not to inquire too closely into why.)

"You look pretty pretty yourself," I said.

Which was, in my opinion, almost always the case. His teeth were white against the bronze of his face and his dark eyes under straight black brows were large and well spaced. A girl could drown in those eyes. Plus, though he was not a man who thinks much about clothes, he was blessed with one of those tall, lanky frames—all long legs and slim hips tapering up to nice square shoulders—that can make even a pair of faded jeans and a T-shirt (pretty much his standard uniform) look pretty darn good.

But that night he'd clearly made an effort for the occasion. He was wearing a pair of slim gray dress pants that I'd never seen before and a crisp white button-down shirt that still had creases in it from the dry cleaner's. His dark, almost black, hair, which usually looks like it's been styled by an eggbeater, was merely tousled, and I suspected some gel had been involved in the taming effort.

Jason glanced around the empty kitchen. "Where are your parents?"

"They're having drinks in the living room, such as it is," I said. "My father spent the whole day cleaning it. I haven't seen it yet. He said he wanted to surprise me."

"Then now's my chance," Jason said, tipping up my head with one finger and kissing me softly on the lips. Six months and I still got all melty when that man touched me.

I pulled away reluctantly. "Grab yourself a beer," I said taking up my own half-empty glass of pinot noir. In the words of the immortal Julia, I enjoy cooking with wine. Sometimes, I even put it in food. Jason poured a Sam Adams into a tall glass.

"I don't think I've ever seen you drink a beer out of a glass," I said.

"I want your parents to think I'm civilized," he said,

only half kidding. It occurred to me then that Jason was actually nervous about the evening.

"My father's already met you," I pointed out. "He knows you're civilized."

"He met me once years ago, and the conversation was an uncomfortable one," Jason said dryly.

"Uncomfortable" is one way of describing my father, generally the mildest of men, sternly advising the twenty-one-year-old Jason to stay away from his seventeen-year-old daughter. What my father didn't know then was that *I* was the one doing the chasing, not Jason.

"But he respects you," I pointed out. "He told me so. He was impressed by the way you handled yourself." The way Jason had handled himself was to stay away from me for *the next ten years.* Which my father had never intended. But never mind.

"And my mother's going to love you," I said. I knew this was true. Jason is a mother's dream—funny and smart and polite, and he treats me with great respect and tenderness. *When he's around*, a little voice whispered in my ear. *Which isn't much lately.*

Jason took a large gulp of his beer, grinned at me, and said, "Well, let's get this party started."

I plopped the sunflowers into a vase that I set on the kitchen table, and we made our way from the kitchen through an unused, empty dining room and into the living room. This was the heart of the original house, built in 1795 by Eliakim Higgins, first mate on the whaling ship *Bathsheba* out of Barnstable. Eliakim had gone for a full Cape, shingled except for its clapboard front with a rather imposing front door with sidelights. I've always thought that full Capes look like a child's drawing of a house—two windows on either side of a front door and a chimney poking up through the middle of a peaked roof. Over the years the house had been added on to in the typically haphazard Cape Cod way, with a full kitchen in the back, a dining room, a bathroom adjoining the downstairs bedroom, a large screened-in porch, and finally Aunt Ida's ell.

My father had worked wonders in the living room. He'd sponged down the whitewashed original shiplap walls and vacuumed and dusted every corner of the room. He'd polished the furniture, including the classic old rolltop desk in one corner, until every surface gleamed. He'd found a worn but still beautiful wool rug in faded blues and greens rolled up behind the couch and had unfurled it to great effect over the wide-plank pine floorboards. The old couch itself he'd brightened up by draping one of Aunt Ida's blue and white coverlets over the back. He'd also apparently raided the attic, coming up with two antique Chinese wooden armchairs, which he'd placed opposite the couch. An old flat-topped trunk served as a coffee table.

In the glow of the logs crackling in the fireplace, and with Diogi sprawled on the hearth like a big doggy rug, the room was homey and welcoming with a kind of austere beauty. But best of all was the heavenly scent of pine from the Christmas tree in the corner. I was beginning to like that tree.

My parents were sipping their drinks on the couch as Jason and I entered. I introduced Jason to my mother, and my father stood to shake his hand.

"It's good to see you, Jason," my father said warmly, completely ignoring the circumstances of their previous encounter in the way that only old-school New England WASPs can do.

My mother and I settled into the remarkably comfortable (once the mice had been evicted) couch, and Jason and my father took the wooden armchairs. I'm not a great believer in stuffing people with cheese and crackers before a good meal, but I offered a small dish of marcona almonds for those who wanted to nibble. Out of sheer nerves, I grabbed a handful for myself.

But my nerves were unwarranted. As I'd suspected she

would, my mother clearly thought Jason was the real deal, and my father was full of questions about his work as the town's harbormaster. After a few minutes, I left them happily chatting about the silting up of Namskaket Inlet (a source of endless interest to everyone in Fair Harbor and intensely tedious to anyone from away), while I pulled together our meal. I don't think they even noticed I was gone.

Once again, I had decided to go with delicious but simple because, quite frankly, I had enough going on without worrying about whether I was overcooking the veal or something.

I opened the fridge and pulled out the first course, an appetizer of braised leeks with parmesan cheese, which I'd made earlier in the day. I would let it come to room temperature and then just pop it in the oven to heat up for about ten minutes before we ate.

Then we'd go on to the star of the piece, the roast chicken, which had required literally nothing more than marinating it in buttermilk for twenty-four hours before roasting for an hour.

The chicken had been roasting at an initial high heat for about fifteen minutes, so I lowered the temperature a bit and slid a sheet pan of cubed butternut squash tossed with extra virgin olive oil, salt, fresh pepper, and a few sprigs of rosemary onto the rack below the chicken. In twenty minutes or so, I'd take it out again, toss the squash a bit with a spatula to get it browning all over, then scatter some thinly sliced garlic tossed in a little olive oil over the squash and return the pan to the oven. (Tip: Add the garlic to oven-roasted vegetables about halfway through the cooking time so it roasts rather than burns.) There is nothing as yummy as oven-roasted butternut squash. Unless it's buttermilk-brined roast chicken. Or braised leeks with parmesan.

And finally we'd finish up with what I like to call the Dummies' Guide to Chocolate Mousse, made, I kid you not, in a blender. Earlier that morning I'd cracked two eggs into said blender, added some chopped dark chocolate, then poured hot sugar syrup in with the motor running, thus cooking the eggs and melting the chocolate at the same time. Then I folded this cooled mixture into softly whipped cream, spooned it into individual bowls, and put them in the fridge. Voilà, done.

Aside from my mother firmly moving the bowl of additional whipped cream out of my father's reach, dinner was an unqualified success. The wine and the conversation flowed freely. My mother and I caught the men up on what we'd learned about Caleb Mayo's death, and they in turn talked to us about the Celtics chances for making the playoffs. We were all BFFs by the time we finally pushed ourselves away from the table. My parents insisted on cleaning up, with my mother shooing Jason and me away as we tried to help clear.

"You kids go on," she said, waving us toward my ell. "We'll finish up here and make sure that the fire is out in the living room before we hit the hay."

This sounded like a fine plan to me. I was jonesing for some more of Jason's kisses. But my hopes were once again dashed when he said, "Actually, I've got an early start tomorrow, so I'd better head home."

Then he shrugged on his parka, waved good night to my folks, and gave me a quick peck on the cheek before heading out into the cold night.

What had just happened?

ELEVEN

M Y MOTHER GREETED me the next morning with a handwritten list at the top of which was printed NEXT STEPS.

1. Set up meeting with Detective Peters
2. ~~Talk to Tony Scalifa~~
3. Buy Christmas presents

"Who's Tony Scalifa?" I asked.

My mother looked shifty. "Just an old source of mine from when I was looking into that drug bust in Barnstable."

Now I remembered Tony Scalifa. *Oh god, oh god, oh god.*

"Tony Scalifa is a *drug dealer*!" I said. Well, maybe shouted.

My mother was unfazed. "A *retired* drug dealer."

"And why did you talk to this *retired* drug dealer?"

"I had an idea that this murder might be connected to Providence organized crime. I thought Tony might know more."

Tony. Like they were best buds.

"Well, I'm glad you decided *against* talking to him," I said, taking comfort in the firm strike-through across Step 2.

"Actually, I didn't decide against talking to him," my mother said briskly. "I just crossed him off the list because I've *already* talked to him. Last night after dinner."

No wonder she'd shooed Jason and me away. And there I'd thought she was just being diplomatic.

"What on earth made you even *think* the mob was involved in this murder?"

"Wilma said Caleb got an offer from a Rhode Island construction company, right?"

I nodded.

"Construction in Rhode Island has been known to be connected to the mob," my mother explained. "I thought Tony could tell me a little bit about this Hanson outfit that offered to buy Cape Concrete."

"And could he?"

"Well, not them in particular," she said. "But he did tell me about this old capo who's just gotten out of jail after serving six years for conspiracy. He never turned on his pals, so now they owe him big-time. Tony says the word is they're looking for a nice, legitimate business for him to 'run' on the Cape. Apparently that's where he wants to retire. So they're asking around, seeing who can fit him in."

"C'mon, Mom," I said. "You don't even know if Hanson is mobbed up. And even if they are, which I doubt, you can't think that they, what, whacked Mayo in a fit of temper when he turned them down? Come on, you know organized crime is a business like any other. They make *plans*. They have a *strategy*. If they can't buy one company, they'll buy another. They don't wait around for a guy to go into a public place and then follow him in and knock him on the head on the off chance that nobody will see them."

My mother was not so easily dissuaded by my arguments. "Well, Tony's going to find somebody high up in the organization who'll talk to me about Hanson," she said. "So we'll see."

All my alarm bells were going off. My mother wanted to talk to *more mobsters*? She really had been away from work too long. And she had that look in her eye that I knew from old, the look that said "Outta my way."

This reminded me of something Jenny had once said to me about Eli, aka Thing Two. "He's one of those kids who, once they want to do something, there is simply no way to tell him no," she'd said. "The only thing to do is to redirect him, get him excited about something else."

So, I knew what I had to do. My mother wasn't going to stop going down this particular road unless I offered her another, more interesting road. I needed to cast around for other, more interesting suspects for her to sink her journalistic teeth into. I knew I could find them—I'd done it before. But I also knew from bitter experience that sometimes you *really, really* don't like what—or who—you find. . . .

B UT FIRST THINGS first. I needed to make sure there were some presents under the tree for my father and me from my mother. Because if Veronica Barnes was in work mode, you could never be sure that she'd remember her personal obligations, even if they were on her Next Steps list.

"Have you got a present for Dad yet?" I asked her.

"No, not yet," she replied, "but there's plenty of time."

"Not really, Mom," I pointed out. "Christmas is Sunday."

My mother frowned. "What day is it today?" *Is this what happens when people retire? They never know what day of the week it is?*

"It's Tuesday," I reminded her. "And I have to work tomorrow. And on Thursday, Jillian's coming over to help me with the tree."

"Well, we can go shopping on Friday then."

"C'mon, Mom," I said. "Let's get it over with. And besides, you'll love this new shop I want to take you to. It's all local art and handicrafts. Really beautiful stuff."

"But I've got work to do. . . ." *Yeah, trying to track down some mobster.*

And then inspiration struck. "And after shopping we can have lunch at the Windward," I said casually. The Windward was a venerable Fair Harbor bar, notable for its long list of craft beers and its amazing fried clam platter. But more to the point, the Windward's owner was Tom Wylie, who also happened to be a town selectman.

"I've been thinking," I said. "You and I both know the authorities aren't going to give you any more than they have to on this Mayo thing. But it seems to me that the first thing to look into is whether those rumors about Mayo trying to shut down the Ginger Jar were even true."

My mother nodded thoughtfully.

"So, what we need to do is to talk to someone on the select board," I continued. "Tom Wylie's usually keeping an eye on things at lunchtime at the Windward. You know him and he trusts you. He'd talk to you off the record. He'd tell you whether the rumors had any basis in fact."

My mother's eyes lit up. "Good idea!"

"What's a good idea?"

Neither my mother nor I had noticed my father coming into the kitchen, an empty coffee cup in his hand.

"Mom and I are going to the Gilded Lily to do some Christmas shopping, then to the Windward for lunch. You want to come along?" I asked.

"No thanks, kiddo," he said. "All my shopping is done." Of course it was. My father had long ago realized the efficacy of catalog shopping, particularly, in my mother's case, the Tiffany catalog and, in mine, Williams Sonoma's.

"How about lunch?" I said. "We can stop back to pick you up."

My dad looked uncomfortable. "Ah, actually I have other plans for lunch."

"How can you have other plans?" I asked. "You don't even have a car."

"I have friends here with cars, you know," he said defensively. "I made plans with a friend."

I waited for some further explication of who this friend might be, but nothing was forthcoming except a kind of stubborn set to my father's mouth. I felt as though I had become a parent to a difficult teenager. *Okay, be that way.*

T HERE IS SOMETHING magical about a small New England town like Fair Harbor over the holidays. Pine garlands loop along white wooden fences, candles shine in the windows of four-square captain's houses, wreaths with big red bows hang on the front doors of modest Capes, little wreaths with smaller bows on the dormer windows—it never changes, and it never fails to lift my heart.

Fair Harbor's downtown shopping area, too, was essentially unchanged since the days when I was getting my picture taken with Santa at Taylor's Department Store. The big white snowflakes made from some unidentifiable furry stuff still hung over Main Street. The store windows were still outlined with fairy lights, the huge blue spruce in Town Square still sported what seemed like hundreds of multicolored bulbs. The only thing new since my day was a very large Hanukkah menorah with blue-bulbed candles next to the Christmas tree. That also lifted my heart.

We turned right off Main Street onto Route 6A, the two-lane road also known as Old King's Highway that meanders through many of the Cape's prettiest towns, and pulled into the small parking lot in front of what had once been Fair Harbor's Army & Navy store. As a child, the Armynavy, as we kids called it, was my favorite store ever, an Aladdin's cave of World War II–era aluminum canteens, olive-green webbing belts, military patches, what have you. The treasures were endless.

But the Army & Navy had succumbed to modern tastes (or perhaps run out of surplus) and closed a few years ago. Various other emporiums had tried to take its place and failed, but I had high hopes for the latest, the Gilded Lily. The shop, run by a local mother and daughter team, focused on handcrafts, home decor, and jewelry made almost exclusively by Cape Cod artisans.

I'd been in just before Thanksgiving with Jason, ostensibly to look for something for Jenny's birthday. It was not an accident that I also spent much of my time on that trip exclaiming over a pair of dangly silver earrings cunningly etched to resemble the wavy lines left by the tide on sand flats. After all, Christmas was coming. Sometimes the dudes need a little nudging in the right direction.

On this trip, though, I wasn't shopping because 1) I didn't have the money, and 2) I had actually covered holiday presents already. For Jason I'd arranged for a *fantastic* (and practically free) gift to be delivered on Christmas morning. And each of my friends was getting a pound of my homemade chocolate fudge wrapped in wax paper and packed into vintage holiday cookie tins that I'd found in Aunt Ida's pantry. The tins, though they had to be fifty years old, were pristine and utterly charming, with scenes of carolers under old-fashioned streetlights and sleighs, carrying gentlemen in top hats and ladies with fur muffs, jingling down snowy lanes. For my father, I'd found a copy of the Heritage Press's 1968 illustrated reprint of Henry David Thoreau's 1865 classic *Cape Cod* complete with slip-case in a secondhand bookstore in Wellfleet. For my mother, I'd gone with the last collection of poetry from the late, great Mary Oliver, Cape Cod's unofficial poet laureate. For my parents, you can't go wrong with books. So no retail therapy at the Gilded Lily for me that day.

My mother, on the other hand, was spending money like water, picking up a handsome leather-bound notebook for my father, a brass beer bottle opener in the shape of a horseshoe crab for Jason, sandalwood-scented beard oil for Miles, a pair of earrings in the shape of tiny scallop shells for Jenny, a purple silk-screened scarf for Helene, and for Krista a tote bag emblazoned with the words "I'm not bossy, I have leadership skills." Which made me ashamed that I'd ever called Krista bossy.

"Why are you buying presents for my friends?" I protested. "We've always just done family." This was true. We'd had a small family, but we compensated for it with numerous stocking stuffers and presents from Santa.

"They *are* your family now," my mother said with very uncharacteristic sentimentality. "They love you and take care of you and tell you when you're being totally stupid." *Now, there's the mother I know and love.* "So, if they're your family, they're our family. Obviously."

I nodded and tried not to show how touched I was.

"You're not wrong there," I said, and my voice only wobbled a little bit.

"Now go away so I can shop for you," my mother said. "What do you want from Santa?"

What I wanted from Santa was for Jason to stop acting so weird. What I said was what I'd said every Christmas since I was nine.

"I want a pony."

But I knew I wouldn't get a pony. I never did.

L UNCH AT THE Windward was actually quite successful, both in terms of the food and in terms of information received. The Windward is maybe not where you'd go for a fancy dinner out but it is great for lunch. It has its own idiosyncratic charm—the walls are plastered with license plates from all fifty states going back decades, and the red-checked tablecloths give the place a warm feel that was very welcome on a chilly day. We'd missed the lunch rush and had our choice of tables, choosing a two-top in the corner where we could talk in relative privacy. We both went for the special, clam pie, which is, despite the way it sounds, actually super yummy—think fresh chopped sea clams in a lemony cream sauce and topped with crumbled Ritz crackers. (Tip: Ritz crackers are nothing to be snobby about; they are the real deal.)

As I'd hoped, Tom Wiley, a small, wiry man with faded blue eyes and grizzled hair, was perched on his usual stool at the far end of the bar, which he tended to use as his unofficial office. There he could look over the never-ending paperwork involved in running a bar/restaurant while still keeping an eye on his customers, bartenders, and waitstaff. By the time my mother and I were on to our homemade cinnamon apple crumb cake (because it is the law that lunch with your mother *must* include dessert), the other stools at the bar were empty and Wylie was beginning to pack up his paperwork. Now was the time for my mother to make her move.

"C'mon, kiddo," she said. "Let's go talk to the nice man." *Hallelujah.*

IT DIDN'T TAKE much for Tom Wylie to spill the beans. He welcomed my mother as an old friend and spoke to her as the same, even after she'd told him she was reporting on the Mayo story for the *Clarion.*

"You've always been a straight shooter, Veronica," he said, patting the bar stool next to him for her to take a seat. "If you say it's off the record, it's off the record. And, look, we all want this thing settled as soon as possible. The publicity isn't good for the town. If you think you can get to the bottom of it, have at it."

My mother hoisted herself onto the bar stool and I discreetly sat my butt two seats down and ordered another coffee. I wasn't going to miss this.

"Tell me about Caleb Mayo," my mother said. "I didn't know him other than through his wife."

Wylie looked conflicted. "Well, I want to be fair," he said. "Caleb had very high standards, you know? He was completely straight with his customers and with the guys who worked for him at Cape Concrete. And he was big into public service, as he called it. He's been on the school board for years, and nobody was surprised when he ran for town selectman after Sally Nordlinger finished her term in September. He'd wanted that job for a long time. And I gotta admit, he took it seriously."

Wylie paused, and appeared to be thinking about what to say next.

"I hear a 'but' in there," my mother prompted.

Wylie nodded. "But he had a real bee in his bonnet about bars and drinking, seeing as his dad pretty much drank himself to death. Caleb would look for any loophole to shut a bar down. Moral character, shady suppliers, health and food service violations, whatever. To tell you the truth, he could be a real pain in the behind. Even before he was a selectman he was always asking me who I had to shut off, who got his car keys taken away. He didn't even think it was right that the bowling alley had a full bar, even though they do food, too. Honestly, if he could have made this a dry town, I think he would have."

Then, looking like he wished he hadn't said that, Wylie added hastily, "But he was okay with the Windward. Maybe because, when my dad ran it, the Windward was the only place in town that wouldn't serve his dad. But we always gave him coffee, sobered him up a little. So I guess Mayo figured he owed me."

"But he didn't owe the Brunis?" my mother asked.

"Not no how, not no way," Mr. Wiley said, reminding me of my Grandpa Barnes. "Like I said to Detective Peters,

Caleb Mayo didn't like the idea of a restaurant making a big fuss over fancy cocktails. Said it made the place more about drinking than eating. The rest of us pointed out that the select board's responsibility is just what it says in the town bylaws."

"Which is?" my mother prompted.

"Which is"—and here the selectman seemed to be reciting from memory—"'to provide for a reasonable number and variety of well-run establishments for the sale and service of food and drink as will meet the public need and serve the common good.'"

"And what made him think the Ginger Jar wasn't serving the common good?"

"Well, I think he just didn't trust those off-Cape kids. He didn't like the tattoos and the hair and what he called their 'city ways.' We explained to him we'd done the required due diligence on the Brunis when they'd first applied for their liquor license last year, that they were clean."

"How did he like that?" my mother asked.

"Not much," Wylie admitted. "But there wasn't anything he could do about it."

"So how did the rumor get started that he was going to get the place shut down?"

Wylie looked uncomfortable again. "Well, probably when he stormed out of the board meeting into the town clerk's office shouting, 'Those Brunis are bad news. And I mean to see them shut down.'"

TWELVE

T HANKS FOR THE shopping and lunch," my mother
said as we carried her packages into the house. My
father was nowhere to be found, presumably still out with
that mysterious friend of his. I followed my mom back through
Aunt Ida's living room, redolent with pine, and into the
guest bedroom, where we dumped her purchases on the top
of the Victorian bureau in the corner.

She turned to me. "What Tom Wylie had to say about
Mayo's problem with the Ginger Jar was interesting," she
said thoughtfully. "It really doesn't look good for Martin
Bruni, does it?"

I agreed that it didn't. "For sure the Brunis had heard
about Mayo's threat," I said. "*Everybody* in town had heard
about it. But there's something even more damning."

"Do tell," my mother said with relish.

So I told her about Jason's suspicion that Martin at some
point dealt Ecstasy at clubs in Boston.

"Even if he's never actually been arrested or convicted,"
I concluded, "if some record of it could be found, there
might be enough guilt by association for the select board to
revoke the Brunis' license."

My mother picked up the thread. "So maybe Martin panicked at the rumor and killed Mayo to keep him from digging further. In which case," she added with a shrug, "he's the primary suspect and I'm not likely to find out anything more than the authorities, with all their resources, can. If anything, I'd just get in the way of their investigation. Just in case, I think I'll keep following up the organized crime angle."

Great. My big Tom Wylie idea totally hadn't worked. Instead of steering my mother away from the mob and toward other less potentially lethal suspects, all I'd done was point the needle right to Martin Bruni, the one suspect my mother wasn't interested in pursuing.

Think, Sam, think.

Something had rung a little bell. Something that Tom Wylie had said.

"You know, Tom Wylie said Mayo had it in for pretty much any bar, not just the Ginger Jar. The Brunis just topped the list because they were off Capers and Martin has a lot of tattoos."

"True," my mother mused. "Makes you wonder who else he might have had in his sights."

"Mr. Wylie actually mentioned the bowling alley," I reminded her. "He said Mayo didn't think it was right that the Lucky Strike Lanes has a full bar, even though it does food, too."

My mother snorted derisively. "You can't close down a bar because they have lousy food."

"Well, yes, you kind of can," I corrected her.

I'd worked in bars and restaurants all my adult life. I knew that in Massachusetts, as in New York State, a full liquor license allowing the sale of hard liquor in addition to wine and beer requires that the holder, even if just a bowling alley, also serves food, real food, made in a real kitchen or food prep area.

Since I'd been back in town, I'd been to the Lucky Strike Lanes once or twice with Jenny and the Three Things. I'd enjoyed myself and had admired the Lanes for their commitment to that uniquely New England sport of candlepin bowling. In candlepin, we use smaller balls with no finger holes to knock down skinny pins that look like, well, candles. There's a certain finesse to candlepin bowling that we like to think makes it superior to its less demanding ten-pin bowling cousin, with its finger-holed fat balls and fat pins. Not that I was prejudiced or anything.

However, I *was* prejudiced against the Lucky Strike's food offerings. If you could call microwaved burgers and Tater Tots food. Which I don't. And maybe Caleb Mayo hadn't, either.

I explained all this to my mother, adding, "So maybe Mayo also had his knives out for the bowling alley if they aren't doing real kitchen prep."

My mother's eyes lit up as she made a connection that had actually escaped me. "And the bowling alley shares a common deliveries lot with the Ginger Jar," she pointed out.

I took the opening. "And I bet Mr. Wylie didn't mention anything about Mayo's having it in for the Lanes to Detective Peters," I pointed out. "He only mentioned it in passing to us. She probably just asked him about the Ginger Jar rumor and left it there."

"You're right," my mother said cheerfully. "It might be worth my while to follow up on that lead."

Good. Let's keep her focused on anything other than her mob buddies.

A PPARENTLY TUESDAY WAS the 'rents "date night" and even time with their beloved daughter wasn't going to keep them from it.

"You've got to keep the spark alive," my mother said significantly. I pretended not to hear her. I didn't want to hear about my parents' "spark," thank you very much.

I dropped the lovebirds off at the Bayview Grill, easily the best restaurant in Fair Harbor. (Though it still holds some uncomfortable memories for me, which is what happens when you find a floating body ruining your bay view.)

"Tell Carol I sent you," I said as they were getting out of the truck. "And give her my best regards." Carol Bryant, the owner of the Bayview, had been very kind to me during the aforementioned floating body debacle.

"Will do," my mother promised.

"You're sure you don't want me to come pick you up after dinner?"

"No, thanks," my father said. "We'll call for a car. I have the app on my phone." My father had a ride-hailing app on his phone? My, how times had changed. "You go have fun with Jenny and the boys."

My parents have an unaccountable fondness for the Three Things. It may date from the time we were all at the Singletons for dinner and Jenny had tried to convince Eli that the greens he was refusing to eat were "superfood." To which Eli had said flatly, "Well, I say it's spinach, and I say the hell with it." Hard not to like that kid.

Jenny and the boys and I were going to have our own little bowling tourney that evening. I'd wanted to go to the Lanes to check out the food situation. Jenny wanted to go out of sheer desperation.

"All the boys can talk about is what they want for Christmas, which changes minute by minute," she'd said when I'd called. "I'll do anything to change the channel."

I sincerely doubted that bowling a few frames was going to be much help there, but held my tongue. Life is tough enough without friends pointing out the obvious.

THE LUCKY STRIKE Lanes, which occupied a long low white-stucco building just a block around the corner from Main Street on Route 6A, was the unintended beneficiary of the current nostalgia for all things retro. All it had had to do was not change a thing since the bowling alley opened in 1954. It still sported the same red and white letters spelling out B-O-W-L-I-N-G over the glass double front doors. The seating inside was still the same turquoise molded-fiberglass benches; the scoring tables were still topped by boomerang-patterned gray and white Formica; the tomato-red automatic scoring machines still looked like something out of the *Jetsons*.

The newer bar area to the left of the entrance included a number of tables, some of them six- or eight-tops for larger groups, as the Lanes enjoyed a thriving candlepin league culture. Just beyond the bar was a swinging door to what I assumed was the kitchen. Between the bar and the kitchen was a cut-through window with a sign over it reading "Order Here." Next to it hung a blackboard with the remarkably limited options I remembered from earlier visits.

As Jenny, the boys, and I made our way to the shoe rental counter, I saw Wally Lipman behind the bar mixing drinks. I found myself turning away instinctively to avoid catching his eye. *Good lord, Sam, are you still afraid Wally Lipman is going to call you Big Bird?*

Just renting the shoes was an ordeal, as each boy had strong feelings about what color he wanted. Evan, who at six had already established a firm no-negotiation policy, wanted red shoes to match his hair. Eli, at eight a devoted follower of the International Candlepin Bowling Association, wanted black shoes like the current Hall of Fame champion. And Ethan, at ten the oldest of the three and therefore the coolest by law, said he "didn't give a poop" as long as his shoes weren't the same as either of his brothers'. Thank god for the red and blue model.

As it turned out, we'd come on league night, and the place echoed with the din of balls scattering pins and bowlers shouting encouragement to their teammates and talking trash about the competition ("Split happens!") to gales of laughter. There seemed to be an intense rivalry between a team with the proud tagline "My drinking team has a bowling problem" on the back of their bowling shirts and another group with shirts proudly proclaiming them to be the Oddballs.

"The Oddballs?" I said to Jenny, raising my eyebrows.

"A bunch of teachers from the high school," she explained. "Well, except for the tall guy with the weak chin. Kevin Inglesby. The high school principal."

I remembered Mrs. Lipman saying something about "our esteemed high school principal" to McCauley. She hadn't sounded like she esteemed him one bit. I looked at Kevin Inglesby, youngish, maybe in his midthirties, who had just bowled a strike and was doing an awkward science nerd version of a victory dance. He seemed nice enough. Just a bit goofy.

"Am I wrong that Mrs. Lipman doesn't like him?"

"She didn't like him getting the principal's job over her," Jenny explained. "On account of 'cause he had almost no administrative experience and she'd been running the whole science department for years."

"Ah," I said, nodding my understanding. "But everybody knows that a principal has to be a man."

"Something like that," Jenny agreed. "Anyway, his contract comes up for renewal this year and since he is, or was, Caleb Mayo's golden boy, he's a shoo-in. I'm sure he's a perfectly nice fellow when he's not busting a move in a bowling alley."

We turned back to the boys, who, once they had accomplished the delicate process of choosing their footwear, had managed to snag the single open lane, which happened to be next to a group of women wearing bowling shirts proudly announcing the wearers as the Lucky Ladies.

"I used to be a Lucky Lady," Jenny said, waving over to the group. "Back in the good old days before kids."

"You're kidding!" I exclaimed, laughing. "Why didn't you ever tell me that?"

"Because you'd laugh is why," she said. "Like you just did."

"I'm sorry," I said, still grinning, though. "Did you have a Lucky Lady bowling shirt?"

"And my own candlepin balls in their very own sparkly pink carrier case," she said, grinning back at me.

"I never should have left town for ten years," I said. "I missed so much."

But Jenny had been distracted by a shout of laughter from one of the Lucky Ladies. "Tell me that's not Mrs. Mayo," she said, scandalized.

But sure enough, there was Wilma Mayo surrounded by the kitchen brigade from yesterday. She was again doing her best Merry Widow routine, though the mood enhancer of choice tonight seemed to be white wine.

Wilma raised her wineglass to her friends and giggled. "You know, I used to come home from league night and Caleb would absolutely grill me about who was there and if they were drinking too much or any other shenanigans. Once I told him about Mr. Inglesby's victory dance and he did not like it one bit!" She giggled again, but all I could think was what a prig her husband must have been.

"I told you so, Wilma," Pink Hair said. "Sometimes you just have to get out of the house, have a glass of wine, bowl a few frames, forget your troubles for a little bit."

Jenny looked at me, one eyebrow raised.

"Well, it's certainly working for Wilma," she said. "I just hope she doesn't drop a ball on her toe or something. Those suckers are heavy even if they are small. They can do real damage."

But fascinating as it might have been to watch the further antics of the Lucky Ladies, we were unfortunately sidetracked by the Three Things arguing over who would roll first.

"Oldest to youngest," Jenny ruled, which the boys accepted without question.

"And now," she proclaimed like an Olympics announcer, "let the Games begin!"

If Goofy Bowling were ever an Olympic sport, the Singleton boys would win it hands down. If a ball could be bounced down the lane, they bounced the ball down the lane. If they could throw the ball directly into the gutter, they threw the ball directly into the gutter. If they could slide and fall down on their butts in the run up, they did that, too. And all of this with great good cheer and incurable optimism.

"We're getting really good," Thing Three announced with enormous satisfaction after the final frame and scores so low they barely hit double digits.

"You really are," Jenny agreed. "Now go wash up and we'll order some burgers and Tater Tots."

Perfect. She was playing right into my hands.

While the boys trundled off to pretend to wash their hands, Jenny and I made our way over to the order window. I was relieved to see that Wally was busy filling drink orders for the Lucky Ladies, who, it appeared, had wiped the floor with their rivals, the Wicked Good Women, and were now gathered around a table for celebratory drinks. While Jenny went through the countdown of hamburgers (2), hot dogs (1), Tater Tots (3), and juice boxes (3), I peered through the window. As I'd suspected, the "kitchen" was essentially a fridge, a freezer, and microwave.

"You want anything?" Jenny asked me.

"Not on your life," I said.

"Good choice," she said.

The boys were less picky and settled into their dinner with gusto. For a few minutes, their chattering stopped, and the relative silence was filled in with occasional snippets from the Lucky Ladies' conversation at the table next to us.

"Did you hear that Ethel Cohen is divorcing Sanford?" Pink Hair asked.

"No! After, what, thirty-five years of marriage?" This from Black Hair.

"Well, you know what Sanford's like. Always putting her down."

"But still, he's always been like that. Why divorce him now?"

At this, Wilma finally spoke.

"It adds up," she said quietly.

* * *

WHILE I WAS still absorbing this comment, the boys began clamoring for ice cream sandwiches for dessert. I have to admit I was tempted to indulge. There is nothing quite as satisfying as an ice cream sandwich dripping down your chin. But at that moment I spotted Wilma heading toward the ladies' room and before I even knew what I was doing, I got up and followed her.

No, I did not follow her *into* the ladies' room. That would just be weird. But I did lie in wait in the hallway outside, pretending to look at a lighted display case filled with dusty league trophies going back decades.

When Wilma came out, walking just a tad unsteadily, I looked up and said, all innocent-like, "Mrs. Mayo! How nice to see you again!" Like we were old friends or something.

Wilma looked at me blankly, and I added quickly, "Samantha Barnes. My mother and I came by the house yesterday."

"Oh, of course," Wilma said. "That was really very good of you. Did you know Caleb?"

"Well," I said, feeling like a heel, "not really. But I was . . . there . . . in the Ginger Jar, I mean, when he was . . . found." I did not add "by me." There is such a thing as too much information.

"Oh, dear," Wilma said, her face creased with real concern. "I am sorry about that." Which made me feel even more like a heel. I reminded myself that my mother was probably talking to a mobster as we spoke. I had a responsibility to continue this conversation. And besides, I really, really wanted to know who killed Caleb Mayo.

"It's a terrible thing to have happened," I said. "I can only think that your husband must have come into the wrong building by mistake, maybe interrupted a burglary or something." As an opening gambit, this was about as lame as they come, but Wilma seemed to consider it seriously. Then she shook her head.

"Oh no, dear," she said. "Caleb had every intention of going into the Ginger Jar. I told that nice lady detective that. You see, after Caleb was brought to Town Cove by that nice harbormaster—I forget his name but you know who I mean, the handsome one, although I must say he could use a haircut and he really did look a little silly in that costume of his—"

I don't need to be reminded of Jason in the elf outfit, thank you very much. I brought Mrs. Mayo back to the subject at hand. "Yes," I interrupted, "after that?"

"Well, after that, I was driving Caleb over to the Christmas tree lighting—usually he insists on driving but he couldn't that day because of that silly hat and beard all in his face—and we were just turning up Main Street, where, if you look left you can see that parking lot kind of hidden behind the Ginger Jar, you know?"

I nodded. "The deliveries lot," I said.

"I guess so," she said. "Anyway, we were arguing about moving to Florida. That's all we do . . . did . . . these days. Argue. Which wasn't like us. I mean, not like me. I never really argued with Caleb before. But this was different. I just couldn't help myself. I wanted to move nearer our boy. You know?"

I did my best sympathetic nod, which seemed to pass muster.

"Anyway," Wilma continued, "I'm driving down Sterling Street real slow because there are a lot of people walking around and crossing the street not at the corners and that makes me nervous. I was just across from where you can see into the lot behind the Ginger Jar, I remember because I saw the cleaning lady's truck back there parked by that red car the Lipman boy drives and that reminded me that I'd been meaning to call her about cleaning out our basement. And then I got distracted again when I turned onto Main and saw Kevin riding his bike and I slowed down to wave to him. I remember we were just in front of the cut through to the Ginger Jar's back lot, and all of a sudden,

Caleb tells me to pull over and let him out. So I say, Caleb, you'll miss the tree lighting and he says he'll catch up with me. 'I need to talk to someone,' he says. 'It's the right thing to do.'"

She paused, remembering. "Caleb believed that it was the right thing to tell people bad news face-to-face. At Cape Concrete, he was the one who fired people, not Joe Cotton, the foreman. He said he wasn't going to hide behind Joe. But sometimes I thought he kind of enjoyed firing people. . . ."

She trailed off, and I tried to bring her back from her unhappy memories. "But that day, the day of the Selebration, who did he want to talk to?"

Wilma looked uncomfortable, then said firmly, "He didn't say."

"And you don't know what was on his mind?"

Wilma hesitated again, and I thought I knew why. She had to have known about her husband's animus against the Brunis. But she didn't want to point the finger of suspicion at anyone.

"Well, I knew whatever it was, it wasn't good. I didn't really want to know. I just asked him if whatever it was couldn't wait until after Christmas and he told me not to be a sentimental fool."

"So you don't know who he talked to?"

Wilma hesitated again, choosing her words carefully. "I left him there. I never . . . saw him . . . again."

Was I finally seeing some emotion? I wondered. What was it? Regret? Guilt? Grief?

But Mrs. Mayo had clearly decided enough was enough.

"Well, Samantha," she said, trying for bright. "It's been nice to chat with you, but I've got to get home."

"You're not driving are you?" I asked, not very subtly. "Because I'm happy to give you a ride."

"That's very sweet of you, dear, but I'm fine. I'll just call for a car. I've got the app." *Of course she had the app. They all had the app.*

She waved over at her peeps, who were packing up to leave. Most of the bowlers had their own balls and the true fanatics were using the lane's ball polisher before storing their babies away in personalized carrier cases. We said our goodbyes, and I walked over to Jenny.

"Well," Jenny said to the boys, "time for us to wrap things up, too. Why don't you guys go get your sneakers?"

This took a bit more time than I expected, as apparently Thing Three was only just learning to tie his shoes and refused to allow anyone else to help him. That is why I blame him for Wally Lipman hailing me before I could make my escape.

"Yo, Sam!" he shouted, barreling out from behind the bar, where he'd been tucking his personal bowling balls into a flashy black and gold carrier. "Yo, dude! Wait up!" *Dude?*

I turned and plastered what I hoped was a polite smile on my face. "Hi, Wally," I said.

Wally pushed his flushed face way too far into my personal space, looked up at me with bloodshot eyes, and said, slightly slurring his words, "When did you get so hot, Samantha Barnes?"

So Wally the Bully had turned into Wally the Lech. I wasn't sure this was an improvement. As there didn't seem to be any appropriate answer to his question, I didn't give him one. Not that he noticed.

"Come have a drink with me," he said. "It's on the house." In my considered opinion, the last thing Wally needed was another drink.

"No, thanks," I said coldly.

For a moment, anger flashed across my admirer's blunt features.

"We were just leaving," I added, pointing to Jenny and the boys coming up behind us. Apparently Thing Three had conquered the shoelace challenge. Thank god.

Wally squinted at Jenny. "You're hot, too," he announced. "You'd go good in my car."

"The Camaro, right?" Jenny asked.

"You bet," Wally said.

Jenny grinned at me, triumphant. "I win again," she said.

THIRTEEN

I WOKE UP ON Wednesday to a text from Jason.

> hi beautiful. hows it going with the folks

I smiled to myself. There's no woman in the world who doesn't like waking up to someone calling her beautiful.

> hi handsome. dad being mysterious and mom talking to drug lords so business as usual ha ha

> dinner tonight your choice my treat?

> you're on!

So my man had not forgotten me completely. Granted, by making plans for the evening he had also effectively told me I wasn't going to see him that day, which I knew he had off, but I wasn't going down that road. Instead, I would turn my mind to deciding where to eat and picking out just the right floaty dress and dangly earrings.

And finishing my work for Krista. Just incidentally.

I'd tried to talk her into letting me take the week before Christmas off so that I could have time to shop for and prepare the Feast of the Five Fishes. Somehow this had turned into another assignment for me. That's how negotiations tend to go with Krista. My big mistake was getting carried away, as I inevitably do when talking about food, in describing why this Christmas Eve ritual was so important to me.

"It's an Italian American tradition," I explained. "It goes back to when Christmas Eve was a fast day, so you couldn't eat meat. When I was a little girl, my Nonna spent days preparing it. Traditionally it was seven courses, but some families went up to twelve."

"I couldn't even *name* twelve fishes," Krista interrupted. This didn't surprise me. Krista probably couldn't name the five food groups.

I continued unabated. Don't interrupt me when I'm talking food. "It was usually homely fish, like salt cod for codfish balls in tomato sauce, stuffed mussels, fried calamari, spaghetti with clams, but finally culminating in some kind of whole baked fish or, more recently, stuffed lobster tails. But we always finished with Nonna's fish pie in puff pastry."

The stuffed lobster tails got her attention. "You know," she said, "now that you mention it, this five fish feast—"

"Feast of the Five Fishes," I corrected her.

"Whatever. It's a great feature story idea. Why don't you write a piece with the whole history, maybe talk about your Italian American roots, put in a couple recipes like the stuffed lobster tails?"

It wasn't really a question. It was more of an order. Another example of Krista's, um, leadership skills.

So I spent Wednesday morning researching and writing up the story while my parents took Diogi for a walk and then poked around in Aunt Ida's unheated attic for what my mother called "buried treasure." She'd been researching the woven coverlets online and been buoyed by the auction prices she'd found.

"Apparently there's some new thing called 'farmhouse chic' and Aunt Ida's coverlets are hot stuff right now," she informed me over our morning coffee. All I could think was I never imagined a world in which the words "chic" and "Aunt Ida" would be found in the same sentence.

"I want to see what else Ida squirreled away," my mother said with the kind of light in her eyes that you usually only see in those guys who walk along the beach with metal detector thingies.

"Have at it," I said. "I could use the money." Which was true. Visions of a new furnace danced in my head. "Also, I won't be home for dinner tonight so you'll have to fend for yourselves."

I don't know why I was reluctant to say I was going out with Jason. Maybe I didn't want to raise her expectations that there was more to our relationship than there apparently was.

"Don't worry about us," my mother said. "You just go have fun with your man." So much for not raising expectations. In her mind, I probably already had four kids and a dog. Well, she'd just have to be satisfied with the dog.

I WENT BACK TO the ell and tried to concentrate on my work, but questions about Mayo's death kept popping up in my mind like Whack-A-Moles. As I saw it, we had two possibilities for who Mayo wanted to talk to the day he was killed—Martin Bruni and Wally Lipman.

If Mayo had wanted to talk to Wally, what was the "bad news" he wanted to deliver in person? That he was looking into whether the Lanes was in violation of its liquor license because of its barely legal "food service"? If that was the case, I could easily imagine Wally losing it completely and happily conking Caleb Mayo on the head.

So Wally was a possibility, but that didn't mean Martin was in the clear. If Mayo got out of the car to talk to Martin Bruni, it could only have been to tell him in person what he already knew, what everyone in town already knew—that Mayo was determined to shut down the Ginger Jar. And if the Brunis already knew about that, then it didn't sound to me like Mayo was doing the "right thing" in telling them. To me it sounded like a chance to lord it over the off Capers with their city ways. And it sounded like a man who was pretty darn sure he had, or could get, some evidence to back up his claims. The more I found out about Caleb Mayo, the more I didn't understand him. Here's a guy who wants to rub salt in the wound on the same day he plays Santa for the town kiddies?

Despite these distractions, I managed to finish and send off the Feast of the Five Fishes piece to Krista by noon. I trundled into the kitchen, where I pulled a loaf of sourdough out of the freezer, wrapped it in tinfoil, and put it into a low oven to thaw. There was plenty of leftover lentil stew for lunch, as I'd made a huge pot in anticipation of my parents' visit and we'd barely made a dent in it.

It occurred to me that under the pretense of taking some of it over to Helene, I could pick her brains about what kind of man Caleb Mayo really was. In her work for the DA's office, Helene had evaluated countless people facing criminal charges. I'd come to rely on her deep, if cynical, understanding of human nature. My understanding of human nature is wobbly, to say the least.

Helene usually came home from the Fair Harbor library for lunch, leaving her assistant librarian in charge. "The best way to get your office phone to ring is to take one bite of a sandwich at your desk," she'd once told me.

I left a note for the 'rents about the bread and the stew and whistled up Diogi. "Come on," I said as I pulled on my down jacket, "let's go find Helene."

We trotted down the path through the yew hedge, me with a Tupperware container of lentils in hand and Diogi with his disgusting tennis ball in mouth. As always, I was struck by how much Helene's house, so different from Aunt

Ida's traditional Cape, pleased the eye. Designed by Luther Crowell, a local builder descended from a long line of early Cape Cod ship captains, it was one of the first of the mid-century modernist houses that later made his name. The roof is flat and slants up from the front of the house, facing the road, to the back, which looks out over Bower's Pond through what is essentially a wall of glass. The rest of the house was sheathed in the traditional, silvery cedar shingles, with crisp white trim outlining the windows and door, which Helene had seen fit to paint a brilliant and very untraditional neon yellow.

Helene opened the door to Diogi and me before we'd got halfway up the path to the front door. That day she was wearing a bright orange down vest over a knee-length purple sweatshirt and black leggings. Her mane of silver curls was held back from her face by a red headband that I was pretty sure she'd knitted herself. Helene is an enthusiastic if haphazard knitter.

"I brought you some lentil stew for your lunch," I said, thrusting the plastic tub into her hands.

"Lovely!" she exclaimed. "Come in and have a cup of tea with me. You, too, Diogi. But not that slimy ball. Spit it out."

And Diogi *spit it out*. It was amazing. I'd been trying to teach him "drop it" for weeks. Apparently, I wasn't using the right words.

Helene led us into the house's open living space, with its wooden ceiling soaring to almost double height at the wall of windows. Sliding glass doors led out onto her expansive deck complete with brightly painted Adirondack chairs looking out over Bower's Pond. I was jealous. Someday, I thought, I am going to have a deck like that. *Yeah, Sam. Someday when you win the lottery.*

But this chilly day was not the time for deck sitting, so we settled ourselves on stools at the kitchen island, our hands wrapped around Helene's hand-thrown mugs, sipping our Earl Grey.

"What's on your mind, Sam?" Helene asked with her usual directness.

"How do you know something's on my mind?" *Besides you being a witch and all.*

"Well, you've got that crease in your forehead that tells me you've been worrying about something."

I felt my forehead with a tentative finger. Sure enough, I could feel a crease like the Grand Canyon between my eyebrows. Great. On top of everything else, I was an early candidate for Botox. Which I also couldn't afford.

I poured it all out to Helene. The disconnect between Mayo the public man—the upright, highly respected business owner and public servant—and Mayo the private man, who'd apparently belittled his wife for years, enjoyed firing people, and was prepared to conduct smear campaigns against anyone who offended his sense of propriety. I felt guilty even drawing this picture. Somehow I must have misread Caleb Mayo.

"It's okay," Helene said when I'd talked myself out. "It's okay to say it. The man was a self-righteous bully."

I laughed. It felt good to laugh. "Is that the technical term?"

"Actually, bullying *is* a technical term," Helene said. "Both in children and adults, it's a distinctive pattern of harming or humiliating others, specifically those who are in some way smaller, weaker, younger, or in any way more vulnerable than the bully."

"But by all accounts, Mayo wasn't aggressive," I said. "He was more subtle than that, I think."

Helene nodded. "Bullying isn't typical aggression. It's a deliberate, repeated attempt to cause harm to others of lesser power. Your Mr. Mayo was one of those people who enjoy making their petty power very clear to those who have none."

"But then why all the public service?" I asked. "The school board, the select board, the willingness to play Santa to a bunch of screaming kids? Was that just to hide what kind of man he really was from the world?"

"More likely," Helene said dryly, "to hide from himself what kind of man he really was. In the words of the Bard, a 'proud man dressed in a little brief authority, most ignorant of what he's most assured.'"

Helene's voice held an unaccustomed bitterness. I looked at her closely.

"It seems to me that you have some pretty strong feelings about a man you've never met," I said.

Helene had the good grace to look uncomfortable.

"Well, we did meet once," she admitted. "Actually, it was the Thursday before he was killed."

Well, I hadn't expected *that*.

"Go on," I said as neutrally as I could.

"I didn't know who he was at the time. He was just some older guy who wanted help using the library's computers for some online research. I handed him over to Beth Voorhees, my high school intern."

I didn't actually know Beth, but Helene had told me a bit about her. A good student, a whiz with technology, the first in her family to aim for college. She'd been a summer intern at the library, and Helene, impressed by the girl's smarts and work ethic, had offered her a part-time job a few afternoons a week and the occasional Saturday during the school year.

"Turns out, Beth knew him slightly," Helene continued. "I think they lived in the same neighborhood or something. Anyway, she settled him into the computer lab and got him started, explaining how to do advanced searches on Google."

She paused.

"And?" I asked.

"About ten minutes later, I look up from the front desk and I see Mayo talking at Beth, almost lecturing her, it seems to me. Then she stands up and I can see that she's white as a sheet and her hands are shaking. I went to the door of the lab and called her into my office, where I could ask her in private what the problem was. All she would say was, 'That Mr. Mayo's not the nice guy he pretends to be.'"

Helene paused.

"What happened?" I asked impatiently. "What did he say to her? Did she tell you?"

"She did," Helene said, "but only after I promised to keep what she said confidential."

Well, that was disappointing, but I couldn't argue with it.

Helene got up from her stool at the kitchen island. "Anyway, it's all moot now," she said with uncharacteristic satisfaction. "The man is dead."

W HEN DIOGI AND I got back to Aunt Ida's house, my parents were sitting at the kitchen table spooning up their stew and talking nonstop. In their turtleneck sweaters, down vests, and jeans, they looked like teenagers planning some mischief. My mother's thick dark hair, with just the beginning of a silver streak at one temple, was pulled back by a scrunchie, though a few stray locks had escaped to frame her face, and my father's usually meticulously shaved chin was sporting a day's worth of stubble. Both of them were happily sopping up the last drops of their stew with crusty slices of sourdough. Suddenly, I was ravenous.

"I think I'll join you," I said as I ladled the steaming stew into a blue willow bowl, tore off a few chunks of bread, and sat down at the table. The stew had been good when I first made it, but like most soups and stews, reheated it was fantastic.

"So what buried treasure did you find?" I asked. "Any gold doubloons in Aunt Ida's attic?"

My parents, rather than answering, simply gave each other a look, their eyes dancing with something like glee.

"What?" I said, putting my spoon down. "You found something?"

"Maybe," my father said, grinning. "Come take a look."

I followed the 'rents back into the living room, where a

very old, very dusty wooden clock was propped on the trunk that was serving as coffee table. The clock stood about three feet high and was composed of two sections, the lower a dark wood cabinet with simple but elegantly curved legs and a scalloped edging at the top, the upper the actual clock case. This was made of the same wood as the cabinet and, except for two brass urn-shaped finials at the top front corners, was totally Yankee in its simplicity. The brass dial behind the glass clock face was perfectly round, with engraved Roman numerals marking the hours. I liked the clock. It had a certain austere charm. But it sure didn't look like it was going to go far toward my new furnace.

"You found a clock," I said, pointing out the obvious.

"Not just any clock," my mother said. "A Massachusetts case-on-case shelf clock"—*Whatever that means*—"made by Samuel Mulliken."

She pointed to the bottom of the clock face where, sure enough, "Sam'l Mulliken" was incised on a brass plate in graceful script.

"And who, as the British say, is Samuel Mulliken when he's at home?" I asked. I still wasn't taking this very seriously.

"You'd know if you watched *Antiques in the Attic* like every other normal person," my mother said.

"I watch it," I protested. "I'm just not *obsessed* with it."

My mother ignored my interruption. "The minute I saw this clock, I knew I'd seen it before," she said. "Come and take a look at this."

I followed her into the guest bedroom, where she'd set up her laptop on a small table by the window. She opened a tab and clicked on a video. The first thing I saw was our clock. Or something very like our clock. It wasn't dusty and it was missing the brass finials on the top, but as far as I could tell it was pretty darn close to Aunt Ida's clock. I watched as a slim blond man, who I was pretty sure I'd seen before on the show, excitedly explained the clock's history to its owner.

"Samuel Mulliken was a member of a very important family of Massachusetts clockmakers," he said. "This case-on-case clock was probably made around 1750. It's missing what would have been brass finials and the original glass has been replaced, but it's still a wonderful, and very rare, example of Mulliken's craft."

Then he asked the owner, as they always do, "Do you have any idea what it's worth?"

The clock's owner replied, as they always seem to, "Not really."

"Well, at auction this could go for as much as . . ."

There was a dramatic pause. And then the appraiser named a sum that would not only buy me a new furnace but even a new roof. And maybe a secondhand car.

There was another pause while the clock's owner digested the news of this windfall. Then he said, as they always seem to, "Wow. I had no idea."

FOURTEEN

~~~~~

TRUTH BE TOLD, I wasn't convinced that Aunt Ida's clock was going to turn out to be the twin of the *Antiques in the Attic* find, but in any case, I didn't have much time to think about it. Veronica Barnes's grasshopper brain was already onto something else, and I was on call as driver. Apparently, she'd gotten Julie Bruni to agree to meet with her to discuss the Mayo case. I wasn't averse to going along, as I had a few questions for Julie myself and I hadn't yet had a chance to ask Martin for his eggnog recipe. But I was surprised that my mother was following up on an angle that she'd dismissed earlier.

"I thought you were going to leave the Brunis to the authorities," I said.

"I have to write a follow-up on the case for today's online *Clarion*," my mother said. "I still need to cover the basics."

"I'm also surprised Julie Bruni agreed to talk to you," I said.

"We agreed that most of it would be on background and off the record," my mother said. "Mostly I want to hear her side of the story, get a sense of how seriously she and her brother took these rumors about Mayo coming after them. But she'll probably want to make a statement, get her side of the story out there."

I could just hear my mother in my head, convincing Julie Bruni how important it was that the Brunis, not the rumor mill, begin to control the story. It was true, of course, but it was also standard journalistic practice to encourage a source to talk.

We left my father carefully dusting the clock. "Do not, under any circumstances, try to clean or polish it," my mother commanded. "We want the original patina untouched." Whatever that meant.

"You sure you don't want to come with us into town?" I asked him.

My father got that cagey look on his face that I was getting used to.

"No thanks, sweetheart. I've got plans with . . . a friend."

Again with the plans. But I knew better than to ask. And my mother seemed unconcerned, which, for a woman so congenitally curious, meant she knew exactly what those plans were and she wasn't going to tell me either. *Fine. Be that way.*

WHEN MY MOTHER and I walked into the Ginger Jar, Julie was sitting at a small corner table sipping a cup of coffee and scrolling through her cell phone. She looked drawn and pale. Martin was wiping down the bar. He looked, well, like Martin always looked. Awesome. It was the midafternoon lull, when the lunch crowd has long gone and the evening shift hasn't yet begun, though I could hear banging and talking and laughing from the crew in the kitchen.

As we walked over toward Julie, she looked up and made an effort, it seemed to me, to pull herself together. She shook my mother's hand as she introduced herself and then turned and smiled at me.

"I want to thank you for that video piece you and Jenny Singleton did on the Ginger Jar for the *Clarion*," she said. "Honestly, I think it's the only thing that's working for us in this whole god-awful mess."

"I'm happy it's been helpful," I said in all honesty. I didn't have the nerve to ask her if she'd seen or heard about the "Santa is dead" video.

"Why don't you come along back to the office where we won't be interrupted," she suggested. She seemed to think that I was part of the package, so I followed the two of them past the bar. To tell the truth, there was no place I'd rather *not* revisit than the office where Caleb Mayo met his fate, but inquisitiveness won out over squeamishness.

As it turned out, the office held no traces of the recent past. The room was clean and neat, with a potted poinsettia on the desk. Julie sat behind the desk and my mother opposite her in the only other chair in the room. I stood next to the file cabinet, now all closed up and tidy, and tried to make myself inconspicuous. Or as inconspicuous as someone of my height can be. I needn't have worried. Julie was all business, and the only person she wanted to get down to business with was Veronica Barnes.

"The longer this investigation drags out," she said, "and from what I can tell it's not exactly moving along, the worse the impact of all the rumors on our business. You talked about us taking control of the story. What do you need from me to do that?"

"Well, first of all, let's get a statement from you about the tragedy for the record."

Julie nodded and looked briefly at some notes she'd made on a pad of paper lying on the desk. "We're devastated that someone could have used our premises for such a crime. And going forward we will, of course, make sure that the back entrance to the building is never left unlocked, even for a short time."

I saw my mother nod appreciatively to herself as she

scribbled down Julie's words in her reporter's notebook. In one fell swoop Julie had managed to place the blame for the crime on an outsider.

"Our thoughts and prayers are with Caleb Mayo's family, of course," Julie continued smoothly, "and we have every confidence that the police will soon find whoever did this terrible thing."

She sat back. "Will that do?" she asked bluntly.

"It'll do for the record," my mother said, equally bluntly. "But, off the record, we know you lied about that chemical tattoo on your brother's wrist. We know that it's the active ingredient of Ecstasy and that it's a common, let's say, advertisement for dealers. I'm not going to put that in the story, obviously. So was Martin a dealer? Did he have a police record? And did Mayo know about it?"

Julie shook her head firmly. "Absolutely not. Martin has no police record. They checked that when we applied for our liquor license."

My mother didn't look surprised. I knew she must have run a check herself. I also knew she was heading toward something.

"So he'd never had any run-ins with the law on that score?" she said.

Julie looked uncomfortable. "Well, every kid has runins with the law," she hedged. That was news to me, but whatever.

My mother pressed on. "And if, hypothetically, your brother had had a run-in with the law as a minor, that record would, of course, be sealed."

Julie nodded. "*And* expunged. *If* that had happened." She glared at my mother fiercely. "Which it *didn't*," she added for emphasis.

I could understand her protectiveness. There was something about Martin, a kind of unworldliness, that could inspire that kind of response.

"Understood," my mother said.

"Look," Julie said, "let me tell you a story. I have a friend"—*hoo boy*, the old *I have a friend* approach—"a really nice boy I'd known since we were kids. We were close, but he got in with the wrong crowd as a teenager, got into clubbing, you know?"

My mother made a little sympathetic noise, and Julie took a deep breath and continued. "A bunch of them thought it was cool to sell a little E on the side. My friend was way too scared to go that far, but he liked to look the part, you know, with tats and all?"

Julie looked closely at my mom, significantly. It was clear she was talking about the tattoo on Martin's wrist but didn't want to be completely explicit. My mother just nodded her understanding and Julie resumed her story about her "friend."

"Well, one night his buddies got caught offering a tab to an undercover cop. My friend was just hanging with them at the time, but he got pulled in as well. The good news was he had nothing on him except a little weed and clearly not enough for intention to distribute. This was before marijuana was legalized, so it was a misdemeanor, but the judge could tell my friend was basically a good kid, so, since he was underage and it was a first offense, he was just given six months of community service in a drug rehab clinic. It was the best thing that could have happened to him. That experience did exactly what it was supposed to do—scared him straight. He never touched recreational drugs again. And his record was expunged five years later."

"I see," my mother said. "So your friend"—I was impressed that she didn't put any stress on the word—"would have nothing to fear from an examination of his legal record?"

"Nothing at all," Julie said passionately. "He's a good man who's built a good life and he doesn't deserve to be hounded or subjected to vile rumors."

Her voice caught in her throat and her eyes flashed fire.

There was no pretense now as to who her "friend" was, though my mother affected not to notice.

"Well, he's lucky to have you in his corner," my mother said mildly, standing up to leave and holding out her hand.

Julie leaned across the desk and shook it firmly. "Thank you for understanding. And please let me know if you need anything else from us."

This was my opening. "Actually," I said, "there is just one thing. . . ."

Once outside the Ginger Jar, my mother turned to me, precious eggnog recipe clutched in my hand, and said, "I'll tell you what I understand. I understand that that woman would do anything to protect her brother."

U SUALLY WHEN JASON and I went out for dinner, I'd try someplace new that I'd heard about or that had been recommended by a friend. I called this "research." But that night, I wanted familiar faces and familiar food. Life had been a little too exciting recently. So I decided on the Crying Tiger, where I knew Madam Phi's hospitality and spicy Thai noodles would warm us.

Madam Phi herself, elegant in her long silk skirt and high-necked blouse, led us to a quiet corner table, followed by a server bearing two glasses of sparkling wine and a plate of delicate shrimp spring rolls in almost translucent wrappers.

"With our compliments," Madam Phi said, bowing slightly. "So many new customers have come to us since seeing your wonderful movie." She meant the Cape Cod Foodie video that Jenny had created of Madam Phi showing me her greenhouse. She always called it "the movie," like it was *Casablanca* or something.

"You were the one that made the movie wonderful," I said, "but thank you." I reached for a spring roll with my chopsticks. "These look delicious."

"But not as delicious as you do," Jason murmured uncharacteristically after Madam Phi left us and we clinked glasses. Maybe he was getting as fed up with this going-slow thing as I was. Or was he feeling guilty about something? I was almost tempted to ask him outright. But the problem with asking a question outright is that you may not like the answer. Intellectually, I recognized that open communication was the foundation of a good relationship, and I was fine with talking about the good stuff. But I really didn't like talking about the bad stuff. Words, to me, had enormous power. They made things very real, very permanent. If you don't talk about the bad stuff, maybe it's all in your head, maybe it will go away. Better just to change the subject.

"You're not going to believe this," I said, "but my mom thinks she may have found a very valuable antique clock up in Aunt Ida's attic."

Jason raised his eyebrows. "How valuable?"

I told him and the eyebrows went even higher. "So you're an heiress," he said, grinning. "Somehow that makes you even more attractive."

And once again I wondered why I'd ever doubted him.

"Don't get your hopes up, you gold digger," I said. "My mom tends to get overexcited about things like this. And I haven't heard anything more about it, so I suspect her research hasn't really come to anything. But if it is worth something, whatever I get is going right into the pockets of Stan the Heater Man."

"Dang," Jason said. "I never liked that Stan."

We laughed and dug into our pad kee mao, which I love as much for its name (it translates as "drunken noodles") as for its wide rice noodles cooked in a combination of Chinese broccoli, eggs, onion, meat, chilies, garlic, soy, and a little oyster sauce. It was saucy and sticky and indulgent and just what I needed.

By unspoken agreement, Jason and I declined to discuss

anything that might put us off our food, like a certain murder, and kept the chat during dinner to light topics, like my plans for the all-edible Christmas tree and the Feast of the Five Fishes.

"My dad's springing for one lobster for the fish pie," I said, laughing. "Bless his parsimonious New England heart."

"Don't knock your dad," Jason said with a smile. "He's a great guy. I really enjoy his company."

Which was an odd thing to say, I thought, since Jason hadn't actually spent much time in my father's company. But if Jason liked my dad, then who was I to second-guess him?

"And can I spring for something, too?" he asked hesitantly. "I was thinking maybe fresh oysters to start? You'll recall that I'm a demon oyster shucker."

I was suddenly hit with the memory of Jason when I'd first known him, working the oyster bar at the Logan Inn, his long black hair pulled back at the nape of his neck, the muscles of his forearms sliding smoothly under his tan skin as he deftly shucked bivalves and uncapped beer after beer.

"What?" Jason asked. "Why are you looking at me funny?"

I'm looking at you funny, I thought, *because you're still as hot now as you were then.*

What I said was, "I'm just, um, excited, um, about the oysters." *Calm yourself, Sam.* "Helene is bringing champagne for predinner drinks. What could be better than champagne and oysters?"

"I'll take that as a yes," Jason said, but he looked pleased at the reception his suggestion had gotten.

As we left the restaurant, I was as thrilled as a kid to see that snow, a rarity on the Cape, had begun to fall while we'd been eating. There was already almost an inch on the ground and more was falling fast, but Jason had the Harbor Patrol's four-wheel drive, so the roads wouldn't be a problem. We drove in companionable silence for a few minutes, and in spite of myself, my thoughts turned to murder. I really needed some more possible leads that would point my mother away from her crazy mob idea.

"You're not officially on the Mayo case, right?" I asked.

"Not officially," Jason said, his eyes on the road, "but Hammond is an old friend from when I worked in Bourne, so Vivvie Peters has been keeping me up to date."

Vivvie. Not Lieutenant Peters, not even Vivian Peters. *Vivvie. Is it Vivvie who's been keeping you so busy?* I wanted to ask. But of course I didn't.

Instead, I asked, "How much can you share?"

"How about you ask me what you want to know, and I'll share what I can?"

"Sounds good to me," I said. "Is Martin Bruni still in the frame? Because Tom Wylie told my mom that the rumor about the board doing due diligence on the Brunis again was a no-go. And Julie Bruni hinted to us that Martin's Ecstasy tattoo was just a youthful indiscretion."

I didn't feel I was betraying any confidences there. And it could only help the Brunis if Jason passed it along to Lieutenant Hammond. *Or Vivvie,* the voice in my head taunted me.

Jason nodded. "Well, obviously I can't talk about who's being investigated, but Hammond is no fool. You and your mom aren't asking any questions that he hasn't asked himself. I'll just say he's keeping an open mind."

"Are they any closer to finding the weapon?" I asked.

"Not really," Jason admitted as he slowed to make a careful turn onto Memorial Road. "All the lab can tell them is that it was spherical, maybe a little larger than a softball, and very hard and, presumably, heavy. How heavy depends on the strength of the guy wielding it."

"But not a rock?"

"Probably not. The indentation in the skull was too regular."

I winced and changed the subject from forensics. "And no sign of this weapon, whatever it was?"

Jason shook his head and switched the car's windshield wipers to fast to keep up with the increasing snowfall. "A search of the surroundings found nothing that meets the description. Which means the killer probably brought it with him. Which argues for premeditation."

But I wasn't so sure. Something was nagging at me, something about the back room of the Ginger Jar . . .

And then in a burst of inspiration, it came to me.

"I've got it!" I announced. "Santa was conked on the coconut with a coconut!"

FIFTEEN

I DON'T KNOW WHY I was being so flip about it. There's nothing funny about being conked on the head with a coconut. Well, maybe a little bit funny. But my theory, it seemed to me, made sense.

"There was a crate of coconuts in the restaurant's back room when Jenny and I came in there," I continued. "I tripped over it."

Jason never even took his eyes off the road. "And?"

"The average coconut is just a little larger than a softball and weighs about two pounds."

"How do you know how much a coconut weighs?" he asked.

"Chefs know these things," I said. "I also know that the best way to open a coconut is to tap it around its equator with the back of a chef's knife."

"Well, far be it from me to question the expert," Jason said dryly.

"Anyway, what if someone came in, picked up a coconut from the back room, and whacked Mayo on the head with it in the heat of the moment? A strong man could have made it work."

"True," he admitted, "but a coconut shell is covered with hairy fibers, which definitely would have shown up even in a superficial forensic examination. And there was nothing like that in the wound from what I understand."

Dang. So, whatever the weapon was, it looked like a coconut was out.

But there was another possibility. What was it Jenny had said? *"Those suckers are heavy even if they are small. They can do real damage."*

"What about a candlepin bowling ball?" I offered. "It's the right size and shape. Smooth and pretty heavy. A strong man could use it as a weapon."

"You may have something there," Jason said, slowing as we bumped off Memorial onto the sandy road leading into Bayberry Point. "It's the perfect weapon, but the man was definitely killed where he was found so that would mean somebody sneaked into the Lanes to grab a ball before following Mayo into the Ginger Jar."

"Not necessarily," I countered. "Wally Lipman was already at the Lanes and his Camaro parked outside by the time Mayo got there. Tom Wylie says Mayo didn't like the Lanes having a full bar. I saw that supposed kitchen of theirs and Mayo could have shut the bar down, at least briefly, for violations."

"Go on," Jason said as he navigated around a pothole the size of Colorado.

"Mayo recognizes Wally's Camaro—because who wouldn't—and decides it's a perfect opportunity to make Wally squirm. He jumps out of his car, goes into the Lanes through the open back door, and finds Wally, I don't know, taking inventory or something."

"Except Wally wasn't in the back room," Jason put in. "Remember? He was in the front of the house, stocking the bar."

"Okay," I said, reshuffling the deck mentally. "Maybe it makes more sense if none of this takes place in the Lanes. Let's say Wally has just arrived, just parked his car. Mayo sees Wally in it. He doesn't need to go into the bowling alley. His quarry is right there in the back lot, probably getting out of the car now. So Mayo trots over to Wally, says he's sorry but he has to do the right thing and inform his fellow select board members that the bowling alley is in violation."

Jason frowned doubtfully, and I could understand why.

"I know," I said. "I can see Wally snatching up a bowling ball, maybe from his car, and lashing out in the heat of the moment. But then what? Did he carry Mayo's body over to the Ginger Jar to divert suspicion from himself? That seems a little too clever for the likes of Wally Lipman."

"Nobody carried that body anywhere," Jason said, shaking his head. "The forensic evidence clearly showed that Mayo died where he was found."

"So, maybe he followed Mayo over to the Ginger Jar and took the opportunity to kill him there?"

Jason swung into Aunt Ida's driveway, parked, and turned to me. "So you think Wally followed Mayo into the Ginger Jar and hit him on the head with a bowling ball because of a possible threat of a brief shutdown of the Lanes's bar?"

"Yeah," I admitted. "Maybe it's a little weak. But could you mention it as a possibility to, um, Vivvie?"

"Sure," Jason said. "I think Lipman's worth following up, even if the motive is pretty weak. And the candlepin ball as a weapon is definitely something they should be investigating."

"And there could have been other people Mayo was bullying," I pointed out. "A lot of bowlers have their own balls that they might keep in their cars."

Like Mrs. Mayo, I suddenly thought, and was relieved when I realized that she wouldn't have had the strength required to do the deed.

"And what about time of death?" I asked. "How closely can they estimate that?"

"It looks like two to three hours before you found him."

I did some quick calculations in my head. "So basically from shortly after the cleaning lady propped the back door open to around the time the Brunis arrived."

"Right," Jason said.

"So really anybody could have come in the back way before the Brunis got there and while the cleaning lady was working in the kitchen?"

"It's possible, I suppose," Jason said doubtfully. "But if it happened then," he said, "you'd be looking for an unknown someone with an unknown motive who through sheer luck saw Mayo going into the back of the building. Remember, his wife said he only decided to go in on the spur of the moment. *And* this unknown assailant with his unknown motive also happened to have an unknown weapon on hand with which to do Mayo in." He smiled at me to take the sting out of his words.

I smiled back ruefully. "Okay, okay, I can see why it makes sense to look first at possible known assailants with possible known motives and opportunity."

I didn't have to add that I really didn't want Martin Bruni to be the primary suspect. I didn't think Jason did either. Martin seemed like a nice guy. A little naive but sweet. Plus, I really liked his sister. She was badass. But I, of all people, knew that liking or not liking a suspect is not evidence of either their guilt or their innocence.

"Don't let it bother you too much," Jason said. "There's not going to be much more headway made on the case until after Christmas anyway."

*C*hristmas. WHY DID the word fill me with such agita, as Nonna would say? Maybe because it was only *three days away* and I still had *so much to do*. Make and decorate the cookies for the tree. Trim the tree. Wrap my presents. Shop for the Feast of the Five Fishes. Prepare and cook the Feast of the Five Fishes.

And, oh lord, I suddenly remembered that my father would be expecting to make his usual roast beef dinner on Christmas day itself. I couldn't deny the poor guy that reprieve from his healthy diet. He was inordinately proud of the *one meal a year* he cooked, which was, in all honesty, pretty darn simple: roast beef with horseradish sauce (Dad's tip: Just mix a couple of tablespoons of jarred horseradish into a pint of sour cream. Actually pretty delish), cheesy broccoli casserole, and baked potatoes with lots of butter, sour cream (obviously Dad's secret ingredient), and chives. Clean up would be the province of my mother, who had long ago claimed this role after I had announced at age eleven that her meat loaf looked like cat food and from now on, I would do the cooking in our household.

But all of this feasting still required planning and shopping by yours truly.

So when Jason declined my invitation to come in for a "nightcap" on the grounds that, *surprise*, he had a busy day tomorrow, I didn't really object. So, it had become alarmingly clear, did I.

SIXTEEN

B USY, AS IT turned out, but super fun. The snow had
tapered off overnight, but when I let Diogi out the next
morning there was enough on the ground to make me feel
like I was living in a snow globe. The sky was a brilliant
blue, and the long branches of the low-growing pitch pines,
delicately frosted with snow, looked like something out of
a Japanese woodblock print. At first Diogi regarded this
changed world with great suspicion, standing in the doorway, sniffing the air, putting one paw hesitantly into the
white stuff, then drawing it back in alarm. Diogi, except for
when he thinks his human is being threatened, is a complete chicken.

It was beginning to look like he was never going to do
his business and I would simply freeze to death in the doorway, even with my flannel jammies and woolly bathrobe
on. At last, inspiration struck. Reaching down, I scooped
up a handful of snow, patted it into a snowball and threw it
out into the yard, calling, "Fetch!"

Diogi didn't even stop to think. Thinking has never been

his strong suit anyway. Barking joyfully, the silly dog charged out after the snowball, only to be completely flummoxed by the white ball's curious disappearance when it hit the ground. His look of confusion made me laugh out loud.

Taking pity on him, I threw another snowball, this time calling, "Catch!"

Diogi leaped up, snatched the snowball neatly out of the air, and did another doggy double take as the ball dissolved in his mouth. A ball that you *drank*? No matter. In Diogi terms, this was a great new game. I threw him a few more and then left him happily rolling in the white stuff while I closed the door and went back to run my frozen hands under warm water.

At nine sharp, as promised, Jillian rolled in in her Jeep. I let her in through the kitchen door and watched in awe as she unpacked two huge ziplock bags of cookie cutters in the shape of everything from Christmas trees to fat little Santas to angels and stars (including, I was delighted to see, a Star of David for Helene). Animal shapes abounded, from dogs and cats to—oddly—frogs.

"I love frogs," Jillian said, as if that explained everything.

I'd provided the ingredients for the cookies and their frosting, but Jillian, being the expert, had held firm on bringing the decorations—an assortment of little glass jars containing candy confetti, a rainbow of variously colored sprinkles, little silvered sugar pearls, tiny red and green stars, and miniature red hots. It was a sugar smorgasbord.

I introduced Jillian to my parents, though, as it turned out, my mother already knew her and her husband, Andre, through a series she'd written a few years back on Black-owned businesses on the Lower Cape. Andre was the proprietor of Camping & Co., a chain of very successful stores selling high-end hiking and camping equipment and the endless associated "gear" so beloved of outdoor enthusiasts. Of which I am not one, I freely admit. I like a nice sail or walk in the woods, but you are *never* going to catch me sleeping in a tent. Not unless it comes with its own bathroom.

There followed the usual "How are you liking Florida?" and "Oh, we love it" and "Bet the weather is better down there" and "We'd be wearing shorts if we were home" (*home*?) until I couldn't stand it anymore and suggested that the 'rents let Jillian and me get to work.

"Actually," my father said, "we've got a full morning ahead ourselves, don't we, Veronica?"

He had that *I've got a secret* look on his face again, but I figured it had something to do with Christmas, so I didn't take the bait. I like a holiday surprise as much as anybody.

"Yup," my mother said. "Tommy should be dropping off the rental any minute."

"Tommy of Tommy's Garage?" I asked. Tommy Byrne was the best mechanic in town and he sometimes rented out his loaner cars if they weren't needed by his clients. "You're renting one of Tommy's cars?"

So much for saving money on car rentals. Tommy was cheaper than the car rental chains, but not by much.

"We thought we'd take a drive," my father said, again with the hush-hush look. *Fine. Surprise me.*

ONCE ROBERT AND Veronica were safely off on their secret mission in Tommy's rental Toyota, I presented Jillian with one of Aunt Ida's wonderful old-fashioned flowered aprons, and a veritable blizzard of baking began.

"The first thing you have to realize about these cookies is that they are not your usual crumbly, delicate holiday cookies," Jillian warned me as she weighed out the flour. (Tip: Real bakers weigh flour rather than measure it. So they tell me. I am not a real baker.) "These bake up hard. They have to, to stand up to all the decorating and hanging on the tree and all. But kids love 'em. My kids used to eat them so fast the tree was empty in two days."

"I really don't care as long as I don't have a naked tree on Christmas Eve," I said.

Once the dough was made, Jillian popped it in the fridge to chill before we rolled it out. We used the wait time to make good old-fashioned stove-top popcorn (much more tender than the microwaved version) for popcorn and cranberry strings, which were going to be that night's assignment for the 'rents and Jenny's boys. Then we painstakingly unwrapped a couple dozen miniature candy canes from their individual plastic packets and put them into a bowl for tree-trimming time. And then, to my absolute delight, Jillian produced a bag of drugstore chocolate balls wrapped in gaily colored foil and a box of wire ornament hangers. She fished out one of the hangers, saying, "You see? You unbend this little hook at the bottom and just stick the end straight into the chocolate ball."

I took to this chore happily. This gave me the opportunity to pop a few chocolate balls into my mouth in my official role as taster. They were great. They were chocolate.

Once Jillian had rolled out the chilled dough, the good times really began to roll. Is there anything as much fun as using cookie cutters? There is just something magical about creating recognizable shapes—a frog! an angel! Diogi!— from what had been a big shapeless lump. For those of us with absolutely no artistic talent, it is as close to the creative process as we are likely to get. Jillian also made a friend for life by sneaking Diogi little bits of leftover cookie dough when they thought I wasn't looking.

Jillian then showed me how to use a straw to punch neat little holes about a half inch from the top of each cookie. "After they're baked and decorated, you can thread some red yarn or ribbon through the holes for hanging them," she explained.

While the cookies baked, Jillian and I broke for lunch. My folks rolled in as I was preparing tuna sandwiches made with Italian tuna packed in oil (which can be expensive, but is *so* worth it if you buy it on sale) drained and mixed with mayonnaise, lots of chopped celery and sweet onion, and served open-faced on toasted sourdough bread.

"Oh, good," my dad said as he hung his jacket on a hook by the kitchen door. "Tuna on sourdough, my favorite. I'm starved."

Thanks for letting me know you'd be back for lunch I didn't say. I just opened another can of tuna. Because that's what the adult in the household does when the kids come home hungry.

The four of us managed to demolish lunch in record time with Jillian and me jumping up occasionally to pull out one sheet pan of cookies and sliding the next one in. In about an hour, we had several dozen of what Jillian, quite accurately, called "the cutest cookies on God's green earth."

"Genius," I said. "You are an absolute genius. You have saved my life."

"No," said Jillian. "You've saved mine. You have no idea how much I've missed doing this since my kids flew the nest." I knew Jillian's son, an engineer living in Maryland, and daughter, a doctor in Boston, were both busy starting families of their own.

"You must miss them," my mother chimed in.

Yeah, I thought, *like you miss me.* Which was unfair, given that I was the one who had moved off Cape first and had only come back under duress. But still.

"Well, every stage of life has its new wonders," Jillian said with one of her wide, joyful smiles. "Andre and I are driving out early on Christmas day to see Deb and our daughter-in-law, Rayya. We did the same thing last year when we visited Shaun. We'll leave at the crack of dawn to be there in time to help them celebrate little Matthew's first

Christmas. We have an entire suitcase full of presents for him already packed."

"I'm so glad you could come on Christmas Eve," I said. "We'll be starting early because of Jenny's kids, so you should be home at a reasonable hour."

"We're looking forward to it," she said. "And to bringing the surprise dessert. I guarantee it will be in the theme."

Oh, yay, the surprise dessert. I could not even begin to imagine what a fish-themed dessert might be. Failing to find words to express thanks, I simply tried to look enthusiastic. And, I'm sure, failed miserably.

My parents took Diogi off for a walk while Jillian and I patiently iced four dozen cookies with a simple white frosting of confectioners' sugar and water.

"This needs to harden a little before we add the decorations," Jillian said. "When are you expecting Santa's little helpers?" By which she meant the Three Things, who, in an excess of Christmas spirit, I'd invited to help decorate the cookies.

"Jenny's bringing them over after they get out of school— so soon, I guess," I said.

At just that moment, an unholy din broke out in the driveway.

"That must be the little darlings now," I said.

A volley of joyful barks joined the chorus outside, by which I gathered that Diogi had brought my parents back from his walk.

Within minutes, the entire circus had invaded my kitchen.

"Auntie Sam! Auntie Sam!" Evan shouted. "There's snow! Outside! Piles and piles of it!"

I don't know when or how I became Auntie Sam to Evan. It made me feel about a hundred years old. But if my little friend wanted to call me his auntie, who was I to complain? If I was perfectly honest with myself (which I tend avoid at all costs), it made me feel, I don't know, loved?

"And look what we've got," Ethan announced, waving

some kind of lime-green plastic contraption under my nose. I leaned away and on further inspection could see that the contraption was a semi-flexible plastic stick with a kind of cup on the end. Each boy had one, each in a different Day-Glo color.

"You've got toilet plungers?"

This was greeted with gales of laughter.

"Noooo!" Eli responded with all the disdain of an eight-year-old for the adult's lack of technological knowledge. "It's a snowball thrower."

I looked at Jenny inquiringly.

"Early Christmas presents," she explained. "The snow won't last long. And, quite frankly, I'd give them a pony if it would give me an hour to myself."

"*I'd* like a pony," I said automatically. But I knew I would never get a pony, no matter who I asked.

"You can't believe how much farther you can throw with these things," Eli the Info Kid informed me solemnly. "It's science."

"I'm sure it is," I replied equally solemnly. "Now why don't you guys go out and show Diogi how they work."

As the boys trooped out, Diogi leading the pack, I said to Jenny, "There. My contribution to your sanity."

I introduced Jenny to Jillian, and we moved into the ell, where we sat on my squishy couch in front of the fire in the woodstove with cups of tea and chatted about nothing in particular. It was lovely. For the first time in days, I felt my little knot of anxiety about Jason begin to dissolve. A small voice in my head, a nice voice, not my usual hectoring one, whispered, *All will be well, and all will be well, and all manner of things will be well.* The words were familiar somehow. Had I read it? Had I heard it somewhere? No matter. It was, like tea with friends, a great comfort.

But the boys, with the unerring instinct that kids seem to have for detecting adults indulging in time for themselves, soon broke up our little party.

Eli came pounding into the ell, tears welling and clutching his right ear.

"Ethan hit me with a snowball!" he yelled, pointing back with his other hand at his older brother, who raced in behind him. Diogi and Evan followed close behind. It was up for grabs which of the two was more mesmerized by the drama.

"Did not," Ethan yelled, and then, when Eli removed his hand to reveal a very red and puffy ear, rapidly backpedaled. "Anyway, not on purpose. You ran right into it. It's not my fault the thrower throws so hard."

"It's the velocity, you dope!" Eli yelled back, still clutching his ear. "Don't you know anything, you dumb jock?"

"Enough," Jenny commanded over the din. Amazingly, both boys quieted immediately. I will never understand how she does it.

"Ethan, I made it very clear that the throwers were just for target practice. Your brother is not a target. Accident or not, you need to apologize."

"Sorry," Ethan muttered.

"And, Eli, you need to apologize for saying unkind and untrue words to Ethan."

"Sorry," Eli said reluctantly.

"Now come sit here next to me and let me look at that," Jenny said. Eli sat on the couch and leaned against his mother while she gently examined the injured ear.

"I can see that that must have hurt," she said, and he looked somewhat mollified.

Jenny turned to the perpetrator of the outrage. "Ethan, you go into the bathroom and run a washcloth under warm water. Then wring it out and bring it here."

Ethan did as he was told.

"Now you take care of your little brother," she said, standing up from the couch. "Hold that on his ear until he feels better."

Ethan sat down on the couch and, as if a switch had gone

off, held the warm compress to the side of his brother's head with amazing tenderness. Meanwhile, Evan climbed onto the couch on Eli's other side and patted his knee.

"Good," Jenny said. "Now the grown-ups are going to go into the kitchen. When Eli feels better, you three can join us there to decorate the cookies."

As one, the three boys whooped with glee. It appeared the crisis had been averted.

WELL, I CAN'T say the cookies were exactly beautiful, but they certainly were eye-catching. The boys' overall approach seemed to be "more is more." Red hots and silver balls elbowed each other for space on the same little angel. One frog appeared to be wearing solid gold lamé. Rainbow confetti encrusted Evan's Diogi cookie.

Jillian, Jenny, and I threaded red-and-white-striped twine through the holes in the top, and in about an hour we had four dozen sparkling decorations almost ready to go.

"Now we leave these flat to dry overnight," Jillian said, "so all their beautiful decorations don't fall off when we hang them on the tree."

The boys groaned, patience not being their strong suit.

"But we want to decorate the tree," Ethan complained.

"And you will," I assured him. "When you come over on Christmas Eve, we'll all decorate the tree together." More groans.

"Christmas Eve is, like, forever away," Evan countered.

Inspiration struck. *Play the guilt card.*

"It's just two days," I said. "And that way your dad can help with the tree. I'd hate him to miss the fun, wouldn't you?"

Deep down, I thought that Roland would probably quite happily miss all the fun but, bless their naive little hearts, the boys fell for it. All three nodded philosophically.

"And remember," Jenny put in, "we still have the popcorn and cranberry strings to make tonight."

All three boys again groaned in unison. I had the distinct impression that whatever popcorn and cranberry strings were forthcoming would be the product of Jenny's enthusiasm alone.

I T HAD BEEN a long, lovely day, and after a quick meal with my folks and even quicker good night call from Jason (*All will be well*, I had to remind myself), I fell into bed exhausted. And, of course, could not sleep. I hadn't thought about the Mayo murder for almost twenty-four hours, but now unanswered questions formed themselves into a loop in my brain that I could not seem to shut off.

Who had Mayo come to confront when he'd had his wife drop him off behind the Ginger Jar? The Brunis or Wally? Or had Mayo lied to his wife about talking to someone? Maybe that had just been an excuse once he saw the open back door of the Ginger Jar. Had he seen an opportunity to try to sneak in and see what dirt he could find on the Brunis? And when the Brunis arrived, had they found him rifling through their papers and struck him down on the spot?

But that seemed unlikely, too. Why kill the man if, as Julie seemed convinced, there was nothing he'd be able to find out about Martin's youthful indiscretion? Plus, though Julie definitely had the momma-bear-protecting-her-cub instinct, she certainly didn't have the physical strength for the job. Which left Martin. Was there a killer behind that sweet smile and shy demeanor?

But worse than all these unanswered and seemingly unanswerable questions was the one that I had been trying to avoid.

I couldn't stop thinking about Helene's animosity toward Caleb Mayo. What on earth had the man said to send a nice high school girl like Beth into such a tailspin and to turn the usually sensible and objective Helene into his sworn enemy? I understood that Helene felt she had to keep what she'd learned from Beth confidential, but this was a murder inquiry. And if she wouldn't go to the authorities, then it was up to me to find the answer to one simple question: *What was Helene keeping from me?*

SEVENTEEN

T HE NEXT MORNING I knew what I had to do. The
library was closing at noon for the long weekend, so
my best bet was try to catch Helene and, hopefully, Beth
before they locked up so that we could talk in peace. That
would give me the afternoon for my food shopping for the
Feast.

There was no sign of my parents as I wandered into the
kitchen, though I could hear my mother in the guest room
yakking away on her cell. I could only hope that she was
not irritating her little mob friend with an early morning
call. I really, really needed to find that woman some new
avenues of exploration. I gulped a quick cup of coffee,
while Diogi reacquainted himself with the white stuff, now
enticingly laced with bunny prints and bird tracks and, no
doubt, all sorts of intriguing attendant scent.

"Enough with the bloodhound impersonation," I called
to him as I pulled on my parka and stepped out through the
kitchen door into another clear, bright, and very cold day.
"We're going to the library."

Diogi has a very limited vocabulary, mostly along the
lines of "walk" and "dinner." But he definitely knows "li-

brary." That is because Helene sometimes takes him there for story time, where the preschoolers are bribed to sit quietly and listen with the promise of being allowed to pet the "big doggie" afterward. Diogi *wuvs* being petted. I barely had time to open Grumpy's passenger side door before he galumphed up onto the seat. Looking at him sitting there for all the world like a rock star impatient for his driver to *get a move on*, it occurred to me that my big puppy was turning into a big doggie indeed. He barely fit in a space designed for two human passengers.

"I'm gonna need a bigger boat," I said to myself, paraphrasing Roy Scheider in *Jaws*. This apparently annoyed Grumpy, who declined to start for a good ten minutes.

"A bigger boat and a *better* boat," I muttered to myself.

Nonetheless, we made it to the Fair Harbor Free Public Library, one of my all-time favorite places in the world. As a child, I'd spent many a winter Saturday devouring Nancy Drew mysteries in one of the old sprung wingback armchairs in the children's reading room. Nancy Drew turned out to be just a gateway drug. By my teens I was pulling the Agatha Christies and Dorothy L. Sayerses off the shelves as fast as I could read them. About a decade ago, the library had been the recipient of a sizable bequest from the matriarch of a family that had summered in their Fair Harbor big house for generations. As a result, the original modest brick Victorian building with its white gabled front porch was now dwarfed by an addition twice its size and as sleek and up-to-date as the original had been shabby and old-fashioned. And yet the two managed to coexist in a surprising harmony. Even the old sprung armchairs remained, though spiffed up with fresh slipcovers.

As I walked in, I saw Helene in the children's section overseeing a plump, dark-haired teenage girl in a monumental reshelving operation. It would be hard to miss Helene, resplendent in a yellow turtleneck sweater, a red-and-black-checked midi skirt, and brown leather ankle boots. I, in contrast, was wearing jeans and a Gap sweatshirt. As was the teenage girl. What does that tell you?

I waved and walked over.

"We had middle school book club this morning," Helene said by way of greeting. "I told them each to pick *one* book to read over the holiday and they literally pulled *every* YA title off the shelves in their search."

"That's your fault," I said. "That's what happens when you get kids excited about reading."

"Good point," Helene said. "Big mistake on my part."

Diogi in the meantime was greeting the girl with his usual enthusiasm, which meant attempting to lick her face.

"Diogi," I shouted. "Sit!"

Needless to say, Diogi did not sit.

"Diogi," Helene said quietly. "Sit."

Diogi sat.

The girl patted him on the head and smiled at me. "Hi," she said, "I'm Beth."

She had clear gray eyes, a straight nose, and a wide mouth. She wore no makeup and her dark hair was pulled back into a ponytail held by a red scrunchie. Her smile was like sunshine. I liked her immediately.

"Hi," I said. "Samantha Barnes. But just call me Sam. I'm your boss's neighbor. I'm guessing you already know Diogi."

"Oh, yeah," Beth said. "We're old friends." She gave Diogi one last rub between the ears and turned back to her work.

I cocked my head toward Helene's office. "Can you talk for a minute?" I asked.

"Sure," she said. "We're closing soon, but Beth can hold the fort out here until then."

We moved into the office, shutting the door behind us. It took far less persuasion than I'd expected to get Helene to agree to let me ask Beth about her encounter with Mayo.

"The man made some claims that unnerved the girl," Helene explained. "But I did some research and found out his assumptions were unfounded. I think she'll agree to talk to you now that we know there's no genuine threat."

"That's great," I said. "Thank you."

"Just let me go out and lock up," Helene said, "and I'll ask her if she minds talking to you."

There was a brief colloquy in the YA section before Helene came back into the office with Beth.

"I hear you want to talk to me about Mr. Mayo," the girl said, sitting down in the chair opposite mine, while Helene settled into her desk chair. "I'm not sure it's right to talk about him now. I mean, I don't want to bad-mouth the guy now that he's, like, dead, you know?"

"I just need to understand how the man operated, Beth," I assured her. "We can withhold any judgment calls. And even if Mr. Mayo wasn't the nicest guy in the world, he still didn't deserve to die like that. Someone snuck up behind him and deliberately killed him with a blow to the head. And no matter how you look at it, that is wrong."

I was a little surprised at my own vehemence until I realized that it was because I truly believed what I was saying. Murder, no matter what the motivation, no matter how great the provocation, is wrong. It's that simple.

Beth, who had paled at my description of Mayo's death, seemed convinced.

"Okay," she said, nodding. "I'll just tell you what happened and you can, like, make up your own mind about the guy."

"Perfect," I said, for all the world as if I didn't have any preconceived notions myself.

"Well, he came into the library last week sometime— actually I think it was two days before he, um, died?"

I nodded to show I was following, but didn't interrupt.

"He wanted to do some online research. He saw me in the computer lab and asked Ms. Greenberg if I could help him."

I nodded and asked my first question. "Mr. Mayo asked for you specifically?"

"Well, he saw me and I guess he recognized me. We both live in south Fair Harbor even though his house is, like, huge and ours is just, well, normal. But I've sold Mrs. Mayo Girl Scout cookies and wrapping paper to support the glee club since I was a kid. So I guess I was a familiar face."

"What did he want to research?"

"He said he wanted to check out some guy who was dating his niece. Said he'd heard he'd gotten arrested for dealing drugs or something in college and was worried about that. That seemed kind of reasonable to me, so I told him the trick is to google the name plus other keywords like the name of the college and something like 'arrest' or 'violation.' You'd also want to check out dot org websites. He looked kind of lost, so I wrote it out for him on a piece of paper, but he still wasn't getting it, you know? I don't think he even knew what a keyword was."

She shook her head at this amazing ignorance. I didn't dare tell her I wasn't entirely sure what a keyword was, either. I'm a foodie, not a techie.

"So I figured I had to start at the beginning. I told him I'd show him an example. I typed in my name plus Fair Harbor, Massachusetts, and sure enough my Instagram and Twitter account came up. Then, just for good measure, I added 'arrest.' I knew it wouldn't bring anything up, because I am, like, the world's biggest goody-goody. But I was wrong. Something did come up."

Beth stopped, looking stricken at the memory.

"What?" I asked gently. "What came up?"

"My aunt," she said quietly. "I'm named after her. What came up was an arrest record for my aunt."

THE ACCOUNT FLOWED more smoothly after that hurdle. Beth was a smart girl, a logical thinker, and she told her story straightforwardly and without self-pity.

When she was twelve, her parents had been killed in a car accident. She had been taken in by her father's sister, with whom she was very close, even though, as she said, "we are, like, total opposites." As far as Beth knew, her aunt had always lived on the Cape, had never been in any kind of trouble with the law. But that fateful Google search showed otherwise.

What had come up was a scanned, archived story from a Maine newspaper about her aunt from thirty years ago. Apparently, in her early twenties she'd left the Cape to work on a sport fishing boat out of Rockport, Maine.

"It's crappy work, crewing charter boats," Beth added. "The tips are good, so I get why she did it, but sometimes the passengers who go out can be, like, total jerks, you know?"

I knew. I'd known a few boys in high school who had worked the charters in the summer. They'd hated it. A bunch of middle-aged businessmen on a boat for four hours with two coolers full of beer can get pretty obnoxious.

Apparently that had been the case that day. According to the news story, one client had brought his ten-year-old son along and had become enraged when the boy, rather than being properly enthusiastic about killing fish, had started to cry. He'd smacked the boy on the head, and when Beth's aunt shouted at him to stop, had raised his hand again to the boy. At which point, the aunt had lashed out at him with the gaff she used to pull caught fish over the side of the boat. Its hook just missed the man's eye. The man had pressed charges for aggravated assault, but the judge had instead sentenced Beth's aunt to six months of anger management therapy.

"Wow," I said when Beth came to the end of her story. "I'm glad she got off with just the therapy, but it might have been better used for that boy's father."

"Yeah," Beth said, grinning a little. "I'm not sure it really took, anyway. She still has a tendency to fly off the handle when she thinks someone's acting like what she calls an asshat."

I had to smile. I hadn't heard that term in a while. It had been a favorite of my Grandpa Barnes. "So, I take it Mr. Mayo saw the story you pulled up?"

The grin faded. "Oh, yeah," she said. "He saw it. I was so shocked I didn't even realize he was reading it over my shoulder."

"And what did he say about it?" I prompted gently. *Now we're coming to it.*

"He told me . . ." She paused and gathered herself. "He told me that a person with a criminal history of physical violence can't be a foster parent."

I glanced at Helene questioningly and she nodded. "I did some preliminary research when Beth told me what he'd said. Technically, her aunt's record could have been enough to disqualify her for kinship guardianship."

"But what was worse," Beth rushed on, "was that Mr. Mayo said that even though he didn't want to, he was going to have to report her to the 'proper authorities.' He said it was the 'right thing to do.'" Beth's eyes filled with tears as she made air quotes around the phrase. "Can you believe that? I have no other relatives. I'm only sixteen. I'd be taken away and put into foster care. My aunt has never raised a finger to me. She *loves* me. How was telling the 'proper authorities' the *right thing to do*?"

At this, the tears spilled over and Helene moved out from behind her desk to put a calming hand on the girl's shoulder.

When the storm subsided, I asked gently, "And what did your aunt say about this when you told her?" *Your aunt with the anger management issues.*

Beth shook her head firmly. "Oh, I didn't tell her."

"You didn't tell her?"

"No, Ms. Greenberg said to wait. She wanted to do some

more research, maybe check with some legal experts before we did anything or said anything to anyone."

"That was good advice," I acknowledged. Trust Helene to know when and how to turn the temperature down.

"It was," Beth said and smiled up at Helene, still standing next to her. "Mostly on account of because of what she found out."

"And what, exactly, did you find out?" I asked Helene, not adding, even though I wanted to, *and when were you going to tell me?*

Helene was unfazed. "The man's threat was hollow. I finally managed to trace the judge on the case. He's long retired but he remembered it well. The plaintiff had been verbally abusing his young son for most of the trip. When he'd cried at the coshing of the fish, the father had threatened to 'give him something to cry about' and slapped him. The boat's captain was up on the bridge negotiating some unexpected chop and missed the scene. The young crew member who'd helped to pull in the fish was standing frozen with shock. Beth's aunt, in contrast, had shouted at the father to 'back off the kid' and when he'd raised his hand again to the boy, had hit out wildly at the man's arm with the gaff, shouting at him again. He'd turned toward her and the gaff hit him in the face."

"That explains the suspended sentence and the anger management slap on the wrist," I said. "But what about her fitness for guardianship?"

"The judge told me that the incident, with its mitigating factors, 'could not in any way be construed as making the aunt unfit for guardianship.'"

"Well, thank goodness for that," I said.

"Yeah," Beth said. "I actually told my aunt the whole story today. She was totally cool, like, not freaked out at all. Like she wasn't even surprised. Of course, I started out by saying there was nothing to worry about."

The relief I felt was tremendous. How truly awful if this

nice girl's aunt had been a suspect in Mayo's murder. But Beth's story had confirmed for me Helene's estimation of Mayo. Here was a man who had gloried in his petty power and had cloaked his bullying in rectitude. And, it seemed, here was a man who had learned the power of internet research. What else had he found out? And about whom? And, more to the point, had he told them of his discovery because *it was the right thing to do*?

I thanked Beth for her willingness to talk to me and she responded with a cheerful "No problem." The resiliency of youth is wonderful.

I turned to Helene. "You won't forget about picking up Jason's present tomorrow?"

"Not on your life," she said with a grin. "I know how busy you'll be."

And just like that, the freight train known as the holidays was once again barreling down the tracks at me.

EIGHTEEN

T HE HOLIDAYS, AS anyone will tell you, are not traditionally the time to go around tracking down bad
guys. The holidays are traditionally the time to freak out.
Especially if you have guests coming over for eggnog and
tree trimming followed by a five-course meal. In exactly
twenty-four hours. So I went with my traditional *oh god, oh
god, oh god*.

I spent the rest of the afternoon in a whirl of food shopping and prep. I'd placed an order well in advance at Snyder's, the local fish market, and the pickup was scheduled
for that afternoon. This would allow me to start prepping
that night and begin cooking first thing in the morning.

I'd hoped for some help from the 'rents but they had
unaccountably disappeared again by the time I got back
from the library. *Jeez, I'd asked them for one thing. Just
take the dog out for his walk while I do the shopping. And
did they listen? Did they do what I'd asked? No, they did
not.* Once again I reminded myself to *never have teenagers.*
Children, maybe. I was getting to like the Three Things.
Teenagers, no.

So I added some thermal long underwear under my

jeans and an extra down vest under my hooded parka before venturing back out to take Diogi for a quick walk
around Bayberry Point. And, in truth, the weather, though
unusually cold for the Cape, was actually quite nice. As my
Grandpa Barnes had been fond of saying, "There is no such
thing as bad weather, only inappropriate clothing." The sky
was a brilliant blue; the northern Canadian air crisp and
clear; and I reveled in brief, sparkling glimpses of Crystal
Bay through bare trees that would not leaf out for another
four months.

A FTERWARD, I LEFT Diogi snoozing in his patch of
sunlight in the kitchen and set off on my quest for
food. Sitting in Grumpy while he warmed up again, I read
through my menu one last time to make sure I hadn't forgotten anything on my grocery list. (And, yes, I do create
and print out menus for special meals. It makes them, well,
special):

THE FEAST OF THE FIVE FISHES
Tree Trimming Coconut Eggnog
Champagne and Wellfleet Oysters
Madam Phi's Shrimp Spring Rolls
Angel-Hair Pasta with Clams
Nonna's Fish Pie with Saffron and Leeks
Calamari, Pine Nut, and Baby Spinach Salad
Dessert à la Surprise

I would make both alcoholic and nonalcoholic eggnog
and Helen was providing champagne to go with Jason's
oysters. A bottle of sparkling cider would serve as bubbly
for the boys. I also thought it would be a good idea to put
out some clam dip and Cape Cod Potato Chips (*best ever*
potato chips) for the kids. The shrimp rolls were going to
be delivered by the Crying Tiger that afternoon. In addition

to the various fish involved, the fish pie would require frozen puff pastry. (Tip: Frozen puff pastry is awesome. When I publish my "Why Bother?" list, making your own puff pastry will top it.) I didn't actually have to buy saffron (which is optional but I love it as much for the flavor as for the rich color it imparts) since I'd brought my last precious pinch with me from my New York pantry and now seemed like the perfect time to use it. In honor of Nonna, I was going with the Italian approach of a light salad to end the meal.

I picked up the basics at Nelson's Market, including two coconuts, which I'd special ordered. I then made my way to Snyder's Fish Market with its heady, briny aroma of fresh fish. (Tip: Fresh fish smells like the sea, not like fish. If the fish smells fishy, don't buy it. At Snyder's it always smells like the sea.)

When it was my turn at the register, Mr. Snyder, with his neatly trimmed silver beard, spotless canvas apron, and broad Cape accent greeted me as he had been greeting me since I was five years old. "Well, look who's here (*heeyah*). Little Samantha Barnes (*Bahns*)."

It never seemed to occur to Mr. Snyder that the last time I'd been "little" was when I was actually five years old.

"Hi, Mr. Snyder," I said. "It's good to see you again."

"I hear you're back for good, now that you're on the internet and all."

Oh god. I never knew what people meant by that. Were they talking about Samantha Barnes, the Cape Cod Foodie, or Samantha Barnes, the world's most reluctant YouTube star?

"You ought to do a piece on the fish market (*mahket*)," Mr. Snyder added.

Whew. A faithful online reader of the *Clarion*.

"That's a great idea, Mr. Snyder," I said, meaning it. It would be the perfect opportunity to talk about sustainable fishery. "I'll talk to my editor about it."

"You do that," he said, and began to lay out my order for approval. "A half pound each of cod, haddock, and monk-fish; a quart of the chopped clams; a pint of clam broth; one and a half pounds fresh squid; five dozen littlenecks; and a one-and-a-half-pound lobster, parboiled four minutes, just like you ordered."

I looked at the mosaic of glistening seafood before me and nodded happily. "It's all beautiful, Mr. Snyder. Thanks so much for putting it together for me."

I handed over my credit card and waited for the damage. Which wasn't as bad as I thought it might be. Probably because my dad had paid for the lobster earlier that day. My plan was to mix the lobster meat in with the other fish, but make a fantastic stock from the shell, which I would use to infuse the creamy sauce with lobstery flavor. We ex-chefs have lots of sneaky penny-saving tricks like that.

I came back to a still-empty house, which was weird (*Where do they go? What are they doing?*) but not the worst thing in the world. I'm actually happiest working alone in my kitchen. I like to put on some Adele and wail away while I chop and slice and mix and stir and just generally have a fine old time. Diogi likes this, too. Diogi's favorite song in the world is "Rolling in the Deep." His floppy ears perk up and we both sing along on the chorus. It's really fun.

I put the groceries away, then turned to prepping the fish pie, cleaning as I went. (Tip: *Clean as you go.* Cannot be stressed enough. *Clean as you go.*)

When everything was ready, I poured the whole yummy mess into a buttered oval casserole. This went into the fridge to rest overnight. Tomorrow I would top it with the puff pastry and pop it in the oven to cook while we dug into the earlier courses.

With the main course essentially done, I prepped the squid for the calamari salad and put it into the fridge. I saved the tentacles in the freezer, as I'd noticed that kids (and some adults, namely Jenny) are squeamish about them.

Fine. More for me. One night I'd have some battered and flash fried for a midnight snack.

Finally, I put the frozen puff pastry into the fridge to defrost overnight, and scrubbed the littlenecks so they'd be ready to go for the pasta course. There, I'd done as much in advance as it was possible to do.

It was well past dinner time, so I finished up the last of the lentil stew and tidied the kitchen again, wondering as I did so where my parents had gotten to. You'd think they'd call or text or something. I was sweeping the floor (Nonna used to say the dishes aren't done until the floor is swept), when they finally bustled in.

"We're back!" my father shouted as they slammed through the kitchen door.

This startled Diogi, who had been happily snoring under the kitchen table. He leaped to his feet, smacking his head on the underside of the table, thus adding his wounded yips to the sudden chaos.

"No kidding," I responded with heavy sarcasm, which neither of my parents seemed to notice. Which was annoying. In addition, neither of them was carrying any shopping bags. Which was also annoying. So much for my surprise gift.

"Where've you been?" I asked as I busied myself tying up the garbage.

"Your dad had some stuff to do, so I dropped him off," my mother replied briskly as she hung up her coat. "I had an appointment in Boston."

Immediately, the little voice in my head was asking worriedly, *Does that mobster guy live in Boston? Is that who you had an appointment with?* But my mother's tone had been clear—don't ask.

Fine. Be that way.

"Are you hungry?" I asked instead, my tone studiously neutral. "You want some dinner?

"Oh, no thanks, sweetheart," my dad said, still oblivious

to my coolness. "We stopped and had a bite in Chatham."
And you couldn't have let me know?

"Okay, then," I said. "I'm just going to take the garbage out and hit the hay. Come on, Diogi, you, too."

"Night, night, sleep tight," my mother sang out, just as she'd done when I was a child.

I was suddenly undone. I put down the bag of garbage, came back, and kissed both my parents on the cheek. Let them have their secrets.

"Don't let the bedbugs bite," I sang back, just as I'd done when I was a child.

NINETEEN

~~~~~~~~~

DECEMBER 24 DAWNED bright and clear, although as I gazed sleepily out the window across from my cozy bed, I could see wisps of cirrus clouds being blown in from the northeast. Maybe snow again for Christmas? That would be lovely.

In truth, everything seemed lovely that morning. Jason had called the night before just as I was climbing into bed, and if there is anything nicer than your man telling you he's found the perfect Christmas gift for you, I don't know what it is. I'd chided myself for my unfounded worries and had nodded off with visions of silver earrings dancing in my head.

Also, today was the Feast! All my previous nerves had settled down in the knowledge that everything that could be done in advance had been done in advance. The rest of the day would be spent doing what I loved best—cooking for family and friends and, better yet, sitting down to a fabulous meal with them.

I piled my hair up on my head with a clip to keep it off my face while I worked and slid into jeans and a flannel shirt. I found myself humming "Good King Wenceslas" and wondering idly what the "feast of Stephen" actually was. And if the word "festive" came from the word "feast."

The 'rents, too, were in a jolly mood. By the time I got out to the kitchen, my father had already been into town for a fresh-baked loaf of banana bread from Belinda's Bake Shop (there are no shoppes in Fair Harbor, thank goodness).

"Your breakfast, madam," he said with a flourish as he set a few still-warm slices in front of me on one of Aunt Ida's blue willow plates. "No fuss, no muss. I figured you didn't need anyone messing up your kitchen this morning."

"You're a champ," I said, as I slathered the first slice (of many) with Irish butter.

"Where's Mom?" I asked through a mouthful of heaven.

"Oh, she's a little busy," my father responded cagily.

"Please tell me she's not still trying to talk to that mob guy," I said nervously.

"No, no," my father assured me, laughing. "Apparently, even organized crime shuts down for the holidays."

"But she's going to make the eggnog, right?" I asked, getting back to the business at hand. My mother is no cook, but she shakes a mean cocktail.

"Of course I am," my mother said, coming into the kitchen with two dusty glass pitchers in her hands.

"Where on earth did you find those?" I asked.

"In the cupboard next to the dining room fireplace."

Aunt Ida's dining room is a long, narrow room between the kitchen and living room, which, because I only ever ate in the kitchen, I tended to think of as a glorified hallway to the rest of the house. I could see that it had its charm, with its whitewashed walls and arched plaster ceiling. It also boasted a small fireplace at one end, and six small windows, three on each side. I'd scrubbed the floor and the windows when I'd moved in and even peered into the cupboard by the fireplace once or twice but had been discouraged from exploring its depths by the number of mouse droppings decorating the shelves.

"*Eeuuw*, mice," I said at the recollection. "Better you than me."

"Don't be such a wimp," my mother said as she filled the pitchers with hot soapy water. "Those droppings were ten years old if they were a day. Anyway, I've already emptied the cupboard out and scrubbed it. Now all we have to do is vacuum and dust and move the table in."

"Wait, *what*?" I exclaimed. "Move *what* table into *where*?"

"The *dining room* table into the *dining room*." Like it was obvious.

"I don't *have* a dining room table," I pointed out.

"Of course you do," my father said mildly. "It's in the attic. Seats twelve. It's in pieces right now, but Jason's coming over to help me put it up."

I was beginning to catch the drift.

"We're going to eat in the dining room?"

When had my parents taken over my party? I was beginning to think I'd liked it better when they'd been acting like teenagers.

"Well, of course we're eating in the dining room," my mother said, her dark eyes flashing, hands on hips, brooking no argument. She had never looked or sounded so much like Nonna. "It's the Feast of the Seven Fishes."

"Five fishes," I corrected her weakly.

"Whatever," my mother said, dismissing me. "Don't you worry about a thing. We'll take care of the setup. Just you get the food on the table."

The rest of the morning was a whirlwind of activity. I pulled the thawed puff pastry from the fridge and rolled two sheets out thinly. (Tip: Puff pastry is delicate. Flour your work surface and your rolling pin and try not to use too much force or you'll lose some of that flaky yummy puffiness.) I cut the first sheet into a large oval with a pizza cutter, and then draped it over my fish pie casserole. I used the second sheet to cut out a bunch of little fishes with one of Jillian's cookie cutters. These I placed on the top sheet creating a school of miniature fishes. I stood back and looked at my handiwork. *Adorbs.*

I was putting the fish pie back into the fridge when a pair of strong arms wrapped around me from behind and warm lips nibbled the nape of my neck.

"Yum," Jason's voice murmured. "Delicious."

I closed the refrigerator door and leaned back into his embrace. I had missed this.

"Oh, good, Jason's here! You're just in time. The table's ready to go."

At the sound of my father's voice, Jason and I sprang apart like guilty teenagers. Apparently I was going to keep on missing Jason until my beloved parents went back to Florida *where they belonged.* This unaccustomed thought was a measure of my frustration. Filial love only goes so far.

B Y THREE IN the afternoon, I was ready. There was a brief moment of excitement when Madam Phi's delivery guy, bearing two dozen freshly made shrimp rolls, knocked at the kitchen door. Diogi, who had once again been dozing, scrambled up and began barking madly, as apparently a dog is supposed to do when somebody knocks to announce that they are planning to break into your human's house. Helene had followed with two bottles of champagne, which she wedged into my very full fridge, and Jillian brought around an absolutely amazing chocolate caramel cake that had been baked in one of those curved, fish-shaped molds (*brilliant!*).

But most gratifying of all was the miracle my parents and Jason had wrought in the dining room. A long rose-wood table took pride of place, with twelve mismatched wooden chairs around it, somehow united by their simplicity. Aunt Ida's blue and white china glowed against the table's sheen, and low brass candlesticks holding beeswax tapers marched along the center of the table. The "kids' table"—actually Helene's card table made fancy with a starched white tablecloth—was a mini replica of the adults' but without the candles (because the 'rents aren't stupid). In lieu of curtains, pine boughs garlanded the room's sparkling windows, and more candles stood sentry on the white wooden mantelpiece. This brought a lump to my throat. Nonna had loved candlelight for special dinners.

"You were right," I said to my mother, blinking back tears. "We did need to have Nonna's Feast in the dining room."

"Your mother's always right," my father said briskly. For his Yankee temperament, my mother and I were veering dangerously close to outright emotion. "Now I'm going to go take a nap, and I suggest you do the same."

I haven't taken a nap since I was three, Dad, but whatever.

I did decide to take rest, though, lying comfortably on the couch in the ell with Diogi scrunched in next to me. When I'd been going through Aunt Ida's things, I'd found a treasure trove of dog-eared Golden Age mysteries on a bookshelf in the long-disused front parlor. For the past couple of nights I'd been rereading one of my all-time favorites, Dorothy L. Sayers's *Murder Must Advertise*.

After only a few pages, I was seeing a lot of parallels to my current situation. An amateur detective (okay, it's Lord Peter Wimsey, but still), a dead body, too many suspects . . . Okay, I'm not an amateur detective. More like an amateur snoop. But in spite of my best efforts (*it's the holidays, Sam; take a break*), I found my mind wandering to my own mystery.

I gave up and grabbed the pad of paper that I'd been using for my endless to-do list. Flipping to a clean page, I wrote at the top "Suspects—Pro and Con." I figured if I could get it all down on paper, I might be able to shut off the loop in my head, at least for the next twenty-four hours. I loved Christmas; I really wanted to be there for it.

About forty-five minutes later, I had what I thought was a reasonable list of suspects and the reasons for and against their possible role as the perpetrator, as a real detective (like *Vivvie*) might term it. I tried very hard to be objective, which made me feel hard-hearted in some cases and like a pushover in others. But at least it was a start.

The mob—Pro: Possible motive in Mayo's refusal to sell Cape Concrete; inclined to violence to achieve ends. Con: Killing on spur of the moment unlikely and unprofessional; other options to buy are open to them; probably not prone to carrying candlepin bowling balls with them, in which case, what was the murder weapon?

Martin Bruni—Pro: Possible motive in concern that Mayo might have evidence to shut them down; strong enough; only alibi is his sister. Con: Julie says record expunged, which would reduce motive; probably not a bowler, so hard to imagine him running across the parking lot, swiping a ball, and coming back to hit Mayo on the head with it; seems like a gentle person.

Julie Bruni—Pro: Same possible motive as above; only alibi is Martin; strongly protective of her brother. Con: Not strong enough to kill with one blow, no matter the weapon.

Wally Lipman—Pro: Possible motive if Mayo was looking to shut down the Lanes's bar for food violations; near premises; very strong; has own candlepin balls; not too smart, drinks too much, volatile temperament. Con: Possible motive is weak as violations easily fixed; alibi? (Jason checking with Hammond/Peters).

I looked over my list and sighed. Every suspect seemed to have at least one circumstance that made them in some way unlikely. Either I hadn't found the right one or I wasn't any good at this murder stuff. Probably both.

TWENTY

I PUT THE LIST back on the coffee table. *Leave it to the professionals, Sam. Not your circus, not your monkey. You have a holiday dinner to host!*

And just like that, my mood lifted. I jumped in the shower, toweled off, blow-dried my hair upside down to give it a little lift like Jenny had advised me (*which worked!*), wiped on some mascara and some red lipstick (just to be seasonal), slid into a floaty red silk dress that I'd bought back in the days when I made steady money, and added a dangly pair of earrings in the shape of Christmas trees.

I was ready to celebrate.

So, it appeared, was Jason. I wasn't surprised when he knocked on the door of the ell at precisely five o'clock. This time I was ready for him.

"Oh lordy, would you look at what Santa brought *me*," he said as I opened to door to him and pulled him inside. *What on earth had I been worried about?*

The man was looking pretty yummy himself. He was wearing a soft gray-and-white tweed blazer over a black button-down shirt open at the collar and new black jeans that fit him only too well. His thick, wavy hair had recently seen the ministrations of a barber, but one lock was still insisting on falling enchantingly over his brow. And then I stopped staring at him and closed my eyes.

Because Jason Captiva was kissing me.

The moment was shattered by the sound of the Three Things outside whooping and hollering and just generally ruining everything with their holiday cheer.

"Auntie Sam!" Evan yelled as he banged on the door to the ell. "Eli says that in ezzackly six hours and forty-three minutes it will be CHRISTMAS!"

"Bah humbug," I muttered as I pulled away from the sexiest man on Cape Cod.

But Jason just laughed and walked over to open the door.

The boys were dancing with excitement and burst through like a human explosion.

"Hey, what's wrong with your face?" Ethan said, stopping dead in his tracks. "You look like the Joker or something."

Mortified, I turned to check myself in the mirror over the bureau. Sure enough, the snogging had smeared my red lipstick pretty much all over my face. I wiped it off quickly with the back of my hand while trying to think how to explain my disheveled appearance but the boys had already lost interest in me.

"We have a present for Diogi!" Evan said, proudly brandishing a package that looked like he'd wrapped it with his eyes shut. "It's dog biscuits but don't tell him. It's a surprise."

"I won't tell him," I promised soberly. "He's in the kitchen. Why don't you guys go find him?"

Whooping again, the three crashed through the connecting door from the ell to the kitchen, shouting for Diogi. I don't know how mothers do it. I really don't. Three minutes with the little hellions and I was ready for a nap.

I was reapplying my lipstick when Jenny and Roland stuck their heads through the door. "All clear?" Roland asked. Roland can be unexpectedly funny. Even when he doesn't mean to be. Especially when he doesn't mean to be.

I laughed, the open lipstick still in my hand. "I sent them into the kitchen to torture the dog."

"Good plan," he said, carefully wiping his feet on the doormat and walking in. "Merry Christmas!"

He held out two lovely bottles of crisp Sicilian white. (Tip: When people ask what they can bring, do not say *Whatever you'd like to drink*. Say, *Two lovely bottles of crisp Sicilian white* if that's what you want. They *asked*, for Pete's sake.)

"Thank you!" I said, taking the wine from him and handing it to Jason. "And Merry Christmas to you!"

I leaned back toward the mirror to give my mouth a final touch-up.

"You know you're going to need to blot that, right?" Jenny said as she walked in, closing the door behind her. "Otherwise it's going to smear all over your face."

"Now you tell me," I muttered, and reached for a tissue. I am woefully lacking in the girly-girl tricks of the trade.

"Where are the others?" Jason asked Jenny. "I thought you were bringing Miles and Sebastian and Krista." Jenny, who has never been much of a drinker, had offered to be the night's designated driver, much to everyone's delight, particularly Roland's, who seldom lets himself go, but when he does, he *really* does.

"Your parents called them in through the front door," Jenny said. "Jillian and her husband had just arrived."

"But Jenny thought we ought to check on the boys first," Roland said.

"*And* I wanted to give you this," Jenny said, holding out a box wrapped in silver paper and curly gold ribbon.

"Ooh, a present!" I squealed, reaching eagerly for the box. "I *love* presents. Is it a pony?"

"Ha ha," she said, grinning at me. "Open it now. It's for tonight."

She didn't have to tell me twice. I pulled off the wrappings like a greedy three-year-old and then gazed adoringly at what lay inside.

"Oh, Jenny," I said, "it's a star for the top of the tree. And it's beautiful."

This was true. The star was actually in the shape of an intricate snowflake, encrusted with delicate gold and silver beads.

"I've never seen anything like it before," I said as I gently lifted it out of its bed of tissue paper.

Tears came to my eyes. *What was going on with all this emotion stuff? Happy tears twice in one day?*

"Thank you," I said as I tried to blink away the evidence. "It means a lot to me."

Jenny looked uncomfortable. "Well," she said briskly, "if we don't get a move on, there won't be any eggnog left for Rolly."

And with that, the four of us went to join the festivities.

WELL, YOU WIN the Great Eggnog Debate," my mother said with absolutely no rancor (and my mother *hates* to lose). "Best recipe *ever.*"

She took another sip of the foamy concoction and rolled her eyes with pleasure. "Of course, it helps that the drinks master herself made it." *There's the Veronica Barnes we all know and love.*

Veronica Barnes did not look like a woman who had spent the day vacuuming and making coconut cream. Seated on the couch sipping her drink, her dark hair pinned up and a crisp white blouse tucked into a floor-length black velvet skirt, she looked absolutely regal.

"I wish I'd made enough for two glasses each," she said smacking her lips in a decidedly un-regal fashion.

"No way," I admonished her. "First of all, I'm not killing everyone's appetites with what is essentially dessert in a glass, and second of all, two rum cocktails and we'd never get this tree trimmed."

"Nonsense," Helene put in from her seat on the sofa next to my mother. "Drink up. The menfolk are doing all the work."

Which was true. Miles and Sebastian (dressed in competing Ugly Christmas Sweaters) had done their bit by painstakingly draping the tree with precisely looped popcorn and cranberry strings. And to my great surprise, Jason and the rest of my guests, including the Three Things and my parents, had very sneakily gotten together and agreed that each of them would give me one actual ornament for the tree. "And we'll keep doing it every year until you don't seem so pathetic," Krista said, only half kidding.

Soon I had a collection of fourteen glittery ornaments that Jillian's husband, Andre, had hung with great deliberation as each was unwrapped. Andre's hobby was watercolor landscapes, and he wasn't, as he put it, "going to leave the decorating in the hands of amateurs."

"You *are* an amateur," his wife remarked dryly. And then they shared a smile that made every other person in the room think "Yes, *that* is how it is supposed to be."

I N ADDITION TO their enviable relationship, Jillian and Andre were well matched sartorially. Jillian was wearing a sleeveless black sheath dress with a kente cloth stole patterned in vibrant shades of orange, and Andre had donned a camel hair sport jacket over a cream turtleneck sweater and dark brown slacks.

Once the ornaments were placed, Andre consented to letting the Three Things do their worst, and they threw themselves with their usual abandon into finding just the right spot for each cookie and foil-wrapped chocolate ball. It was true that I'd promised them a second glass of the nonalcoholic eggnog as a bribe, but I think they'd have been just as enthusiastic without it. These kids were nothing if not wholehearted in their endeavors.

The rest of us lazy bones then seated ourselves around the living room fireplace, sipping our eggnog and nibbling on salted Spanish almonds from a little Dedham pottery bowl that my mother had rescued from the dining room cupboard. I was unreasonably pleased that, like my mother and Jillian, the other ladies had acknowledged the occasion by dressing up. Jenny was fifties-style perfection in an emerald green slubbed silk shirtwaist. Helene was resplendent in a floor-length caftan in a silvery fabric that highlighted her silver curls. And Krista, never one to be outdone, was sporting red velvet jeans topped by a gold lamé camisole top.

We were all enjoying the warm blaze that Roland—playing to type with a Christmas tie featuring the Grinch who stole Christmas—had laid and coaxed into being.

"This is why we marry them, you know," Jenny said to me with a sigh of pleasure as she stretched her hands out to the blaze. "Because they know how to make fires."

"And because they kill spiders," my mother chimed in.

"And that," Jenny agreed solemnly.

I glanced over at Jason and asked, with the foolhardy courage of a woman who has downed a rum cocktail, "Do *you* know how to make a fire?"

"I am a master at making a fire," he said significantly (having also downed a rum cocktail), and laughed as I began to blush. It doesn't take much for the man to get me flustery. "But I don't kill spiders."

"Wimp," Jenny said.

"I *catch* spiders and put them outside," he continued.

Jenny looked suitably impressed. I gave her my "How great is this guy?" look, and she nodded her understanding. *Strong but gentle.*

Roland took the beaded snowflake topper from its box and walked over to the tree, saying, "You also marry us because you need someone tall enough to put the star on the top of the tree."

Actually, I don't, Roland, I almost said but didn't. Roland may be an awkward guy, but his heart is very much in the right place.

The tree was finally trimmed and suitably admired by all except Diogi, who, though he didn't bark, had returned to his initial marked suspicion of the interloper now that it was so outlandishly dressed.

"I don't think we have to worry about him eating the decorations," Sebastian said, but he still sounded worried. Sebastian's default mode, I was coming to understand, was worry.

"Chocolate, as I'm sure you know, is very bad for doggies, so we put the chocolate balls up high just in case," Eli reassured him in his best little professor imitation. Except that professors don't, as a rule, say "doggies."

If I can help it, I am not the kind of host that disappears into the kitchen for last-minute prep while everyone else is sitting around having a good time. I am a big believer that, if your kitchen is big enough, get your friends in there with you and put them to work. It's much more for fun for everybody.

So when the time came, I herded my guests back to the kitchen, pulling Helene aside to ask her quietly about my present for Jason.

"Nothing to worry about," she reassured me. "I picked it up this afternoon and I'll bring it by tomorrow. When are you opening your presents?"

"Around nine, I guess," I said. "We have to be at the

children's carol service at All Saints at eleven. Ethan has a solo. Is nine too early for you?"

"Not a bit," Helene said. "I have to admit, though, that the present is going to be kind of hard to wrap." We both laughed and followed the crowd into the kitchen.

I brought out Helene's champagne and some sparkling cider for the boys and the Munsells, who, because of their early wake-up call the next morning, had decided not to indulge further after the obligatory eggnog. Helene's two bottles would provide one full glass of bubbly each, which was about right. (Tip: First rule of a multicourse meal—do not ply your guests with too much to drink unless you *like* people passing out in your chocolate caramel cake.)

While Miles popped the champagne corks, almost giving Diogi a heart attack, Jason stood at the kitchen sink opening the Wellfleet oysters with a skillful twist of his shucking knife and setting them on a platter of crushed ice. I popped the fish pie in the oven and artfully arranged two shrimp spring rolls per person on small salad plates, ready to go out to the dining room. (Tip: Second rule of a multicourse meal—serve *small* helpings of each course. There is *nothing* worse than stuffing your guests. Unless it is getting them looped. See above.)

Miles poured the champagne and cider into the waiting glasses. And then I really don't know why I did what I did next. Maybe it was because we as humans have some deep need to say thank you for all the wonder of our lives. And suddenly I was filled with wonder and thanks.

"To Aunt Ida," I said, lifting my glass.

"Aunt Ida," my guests echoed, raising their glasses in turn. And we drank to Aunt Ida.

DINNER WAS A huge success, if I do say so myself. Helene was touched by my inclusion of a Thai version of Chinese takeout, and Rolly's wine was perfect with the spring rolls and the pasta. The fish pie, its pastry top all puffy and golden from the oven, was maybe the best I'd ever made—all silken saffron sauce wrapped around chunks of fish and lobster. Jenny was initially wary of the calamari and arugula salad but ended up having a second helping. And the Three Things were completely over the moon for Jillian's chocolate caramel fish-shaped cake.

Also, thanks to Jillian, I even got a new restaurant review assignment out of it. My mother had been telling her that she wanted to add more fish to her and my father's diet, but had run out of ideas.

"Then you've got to try that new seafood restaurant in Wellfleet, the Fish House," Jillian said. "It will inspire you."

Jenny, sitting on Jillian's other side, snorted. Jenny is a confirmed meat-and-potatoes girl. "Wellfleet. They're a bunch of hippies in Wellfleet."

Jillian laughed. "Well, they do tend to be freethinkers," she said, "and thank goodness. The food was great!"

My ears pricked up. "Great how?" I asked.

"They've taken typical Cape Cod fare to the next level," Jillian said. "Great as in super-fresh fish, all local produce, and a twist on everything from mussels to codfish cakes. Their lobster roll, for instance, is warm lobster salad wrapped in a savory crepe."

"Well, that sounds confusing," Krista put in.

"It kind of was," Jillian admitted. "But good. Really good."

"Also sounds like good copy," Krista said, looking at me significantly. "You want to give it a try?"

"Let's make it a girls' night out," I said. "You want to come with?"

Krista gave a little moue of distaste. "I'll wait until I read your review."

So that was that. More money in my pocket!

* * *

B Y THE END of the evening, I was tired but happy. I handed each guest their gift of homemade fudge as they were preparing to leave and thanked them again for coming.

"Actually, there were seven fishes if you count the three in the fish pie," Eli pointed out, shrugging on his Avengers puffy jacket.

"Nobody likes a know-it-all, Eli," I said, and he grinned delightedly at me. At eight he was beginning to get my humor, which was kind of fun. These kids weren't all bad.

Of course, I was full of the milk of human kindness at that point in the evening. And some very nice eggnog, champagne, and white wine. Not too much. Just enough. Plus, my father and Jason had insisted that they'd do the cleanup once everyone was gone, which, in a house without a dishwasher was probably the best present they could have given me. Barring an actual dishwasher, of course. Or a pony.

I was in the ell, curled up on the couch, watching the flames in the woodstove burn down into glowing embers and reliving my lovely evening in my head, when a soft knock came on the connecting door and Jason poked his head in.

"Oh good," he said. "I was afraid you might be asleep."

I smiled at him. "Come in," I said, patting the seat next to me. "Come sit by the fire for a minute before you go."

He settled himself in, wrapping one warm, tweedy arm around my shoulders. As always, I was amazed by how well we literally fit together. I snuggled a bit closer.

"Mmmm," I murmured.

He turned his face slightly toward mine. "You are the best thing that has ever happened to me," he murmured.

So why do you always pull away, Jason? a little voice in my head asked. *What is so important that you always leave?*

But then the little voice fell silent.

Because Jason Captiva was kissing me.

TWENTY-ONE

A ND THEN HE left, of course. But I kept remembering his voice in my head. *"You are the best thing that has ever happened to me."* The feel of his lips on mine. If Jason needed to take it slow, then I would take it slow. Because he was the best thing that had ever happened to me, too.

Which is why, when I unwrapped Jason's present the next morning, I was hardly disappointed at all. I mean, what girl wouldn't be thrilled to receive her very own life jacket personalized with her very own initials? A man who kisses like Jason Captiva can be forgiven for not understanding about *jewelry*.

I put the life jacket, in all its yellow and orange glory, on over my jammies, saying proudly to my parents, "No more stinky old rental boat life jackets for me!"

Jason, who'd arrived at precisely eight that morning, as ordered, looked absurdly pleased by my enthusiasm, and I wanted to hug him to pieces.

My parents, bless their big hearts, presented me with a tiny box (good things, small packages, etc.) containing an even tinier glass bottle with a quarter ounce of beautiful red Spanish saffron threads.

"You shouldn't have!" I gasped. The best Spanish saffron is very pricey. Saffron adds a distinctive bright yellow color and a subtle flavor and aroma to heavenly dishes like Italian risotto Milanese, French bouillabaisse, Spanish paella, and Indian biryanis. It is the dried orange-red stigmas of a particular kind of crocus, each gently harvested by hand. It takes almost seventy thousand crocus flowers to produce one pound of dried saffron. Hence the price tag. The good news is you only need a few threads to season and color an entire dish, and this bottle held enough to last me at least a year.

"It was totally selfish," my father said. "We wanted to replenish your supply so you'd have no excuse not to make us a paella this summer." My summer paella, that classic Spanish seafood and saffron rice dish cooked outside over a wood fire in an enormous paella pan that I'd found at a yard sale when I was fourteen, was legendary.

"But I don't have my paella pan anymore," I said ruefully.

"Oh, yes you do!" my mother said, dragging an enormous, awkwardly wrapped present about the size and shape of a satellite dish out from behind the couch.

"I don't believe it," I said as I uncovered my old friend, blackened by years of great cooking. "You kept this when you moved?"

"We kept a lot of stuff," my mother said. "We rent a storage unit in Hyannis."

Well, *that* was interesting. Is that where they'd been on Friday for the entire afternoon? They'd been looking for my old paella pan? That seemed unlikely. But still, it was interesting that my parents had hedged their bets when they moved to Florida.

Handing them their presents from under the tree, I said, "Well, this isn't quite as exciting as a paella pan."

My mother opened her volume of Mary Oliver verse almost prayerfully, and immediately lost herself in the pages.

My father unwrapped Thoreau's *Cape Cod*, but just stared at it, saying nothing.

"Don't you like it?" I asked.

He looked up at me. "I love it," he said with uncharacteristic emotion. "I love Cape Cod." I wasn't sure if he was talking about the place or the book. Maybe both. "And it will help me with my research."

"What research?" I asked.

My father's face lit up with a kind of shy pride. "Research on my book."

"Your *book*?" I said. "You're writing a book? Like a *real* book, with chapters and everything?"

He smiled. "Yup. Chapters and everything. I have a contract with a university press for a book on famous Cape Cod sea captains."

"You're kidding me!" I exclaimed. "Why didn't you tell me?"

He smiled again, this time broadly. "We only just signed the contract. That's where I was yesterday. I didn't want to jinx anything by talking about it in advance."

I went over and hugged him, which is a measure of how pleased I was for him and how proud. I am not given to a lot of hugging. Of course, I didn't tell him I was pleased and proud. I figured the hug did that.

But even my father's exciting news couldn't compete with my gift for Jason.

Precisely at nine, Helene materialized at the door into the living room with what appeared to be a tiger-striped ball of fluff in her hands. She marched over to Jason and plopped it into his lap.

"Merry Christmas from Sam," she said, stepping back. "Ho, ho, ho."

For a moment Jason sat very still, staring down at his little surprise, which had unwound itself into a tabby kitten with four tiny legs, a merrily twitching tail, and a triangular face overfilled with enormous green eyes. The kitten looked up at him with a steady curiosity. Jason gently picked her up in both hands and brought her up to his face.

"Hello, little one," he said softly.

Well, that did me in.

I knew Jason loved cats. There wasn't an animal that Jason *didn't* love. But he'd often talked about his childhood cat, Mrs. Miniver, named for his mother's favorite movie.

"Mrs. Miniver waited for me every day at the bus stop," he'd told me. "She sat on my lap while I did my homework, slept on my bed at night. That cat got me through a lot."

I knew Jason's mother had battled several bouts of breast cancer before finally succumbing about ten years ago. I could only imagine what a comfort Mrs. Miniver had been to that sensitive boy. And as I'd pondered what to give to a man who literally had no interest in *stuff*, who *wanted* nothing, I began to think about what he might *need*. And what I thought he might need was some quiet companionship, a pet that, unlike a dog, would be fine with his unpredictable absences for work but be equally happy to see him when he finally walked in the door. What my introvert needed was another introvert. In other words, a cat.

A cat who was now softly batting him on the nose with one small paw.

And just like that our hearts were won. Every single person in the room said, "Aww!"

"Do you like her?" I asked unnecessarily.

"She's great," he said, returning the kitten to his lap, where she gazed around complacently at her new fan club. "What's her name?"

"I thought I'd leave that up to you," I said.

"Well, then, that's easy," he said with a grin. "She's Ciati." He pronounced it "see-AY-tee." "To match Diogi."

I smiled delightedly. How like Jason to remember me telling him that when Helene had first introduced Diogi to me, I had asked if there was a cat named C-A-T.

I went over and rubbed the kitten gently under one ear. "Hello, Ciati," I said. "Welcome to the madhouse."

Ciati's response was a contented purr.

In all of the excitement, none of us had been paying any attention at all to Diogi, who had finally had enough. Lumbering up from his spot in front of the fire, he pushed his way past me and nudged the kitten with his nose.

Anticipating disaster, I tried to pull him back, but Helene put a hand on my arm. "Nothing to worry about," she said. "Diogi and Ciati are old friends. I've been socializing them for two days. Most dogs are very gentle with kittens anyway."

It was true. Ciati was hailing Diogi with a delighted mewing and the same tap-tapping on his nose with which she'd greeted Jason.

And so Ciati joined the family.

BEFORE SHE LEFT, Helene pulled me aside.

"Do you have any free time this afternoon?"

"I'll be free in the late afternoon. We should be done with Dad's roast beef dinner by, say, four. Would that be okay? What's up?"

"There's something Beth and I wanted to share with you at the library. It's closed, of course, so we'll have the place to ourselves."

I didn't know whether to be excited or worried.

"I'll be there," I said.

THE CHILDREN'S CAROL service was equal parts hilariously funny (Evan as a wise man in a homemade crown that was almost as tall as he was) and incredibly touching (Ethan singing "O Holy Night" in his pure boy's soprano). My father's roast beef dinner was exactly as it always was. Delicious. Meat, potatoes, broccoli swimming in cheese. What's not to like? Jason looked like he'd died and gone to heaven. I did the cleanup and then headed off to the library to find out just what exactly Helene and Beth had in store for me.

By the time Grumpy and I were rolling into the library parking lot, I was consumed by curiosity. What was so important that Beth would give up her free time to spend Christmas Day at the library?

I knocked on the locked door. Helene let me in and led me to the computer lab, where Beth was sitting at a PC in the far corner. She looked up with a smile as I entered. She was wearing a cheerful red turtleneck sweater and track pants, and she'd pulled her shiny brown hair into a loose bun at the back of her neck. Which caused me to ask myself, not for the first time, why I'd never been able to master the loose bun. My attempts always made me look like Miss Almira Gulch riding her bicycle in *The Wizard of Oz*.

"Hi, Beth," I said. "I like the sweater."

"Thanks," she said, her smile growing broader. "It was my Christmas present from my aunt."

Something told me that Beth didn't get a lot of new clothes and my heart ached a bit for the girl.

"So what's going on?" I asked, gesturing to the computer in front of her.

Beth pulled the chair at the next carrel over next to hers.

"Have a seat," she said. "I have something to show you."

I draped my coat over the back of the chair and sat down.

"I got to thinking after we talked the other day," Beth said. "Mr. Mayo got me wicked upset with what he said about my aunt, so I walked away, you know, to kind of pull myself together?"

I nodded to show I was following.

"But he didn't leave when I did. He kept looking at the notes on how to do an advanced search and pretty soon he was typing and I guess searching for stuff on his own. He worked for about twenty minutes more and then left. I stayed away. I didn't want anything more to do with him or whatever it was he was looking for."

"Not surprising," I said.

Beth gave me a wan smile. "But after you and I talked, I started to think. What if Mr. Mayo found some dirt on somebody else? I don't believe that story of his about being worried about his niece's new boyfriend. And I'd heard he didn't like Martin Bruni, the super-cute owner of that new restaurant in town, you know?"

I nodded again. This was taking a long time, but I knew Beth had to tell her story in her own way.

"Yeah," I said. "I heard that, too."

"Everybody heard that," Beth said with a mischievous grin. "Mrs. Brennan in the town clerk's office is, like, the town telegraph."

I had to laugh. "So you figured Mr. Mayo was looking for something on Martin Bruni?"

Which made a lot of sense, particularly if Mayo was considering invoking the sound character clause

Beth nodded. "I did. So I went back to this computer, the one he'd used. We keep a record of who uses each PC, and nobody else has used it since him. So, easy-peasy, I checked his search history. First he searched the University of Massachusetts arrest records plus 'Bruni,' came up with nothing."

Good, I thought, in spite of all my efforts at objectivity.

"Then he tried the same U Mass arrest record but this time put in 'Lipman.'"

"As in Wally Lipman?" I exclaimed. "From the bowling alley? Martin and Wally both went to U Mass? That's kind of coincidental, isn't it?"

"Uh, duh, everybody who grows up near Boston goes to U Mass," Beth said, rolling her eyes.

She was right, of course. In my high school graduating class, the vast majority had gone on to U Mass, which not only had a great reputation but was a mere two hours' drive off Cape.

"So what did Mayo find?" I asked.

"Here," Beth said, looking rather pleased with herself and punching a few keys, "I'll show you."

She turned the monitor so that I could see it. The page that she'd pulled up was headed University of Massachusetts Arrest Log, December 2009, and there in stark black and white were the words:

(1) POSSESSION OF SCHEDULE III CONTROLLED SUBSTANCE
SUSPECT (1) LIPMAN, WALTER D.

"Well, well," I said. "I wonder exactly what controlled substance Walter D. Lipman was in possession of?"

"Oh, that one's easy," Beth said. "I found it in the archives of the college paper. It was anabolic steroids, you know, what some athletes and bodybuilder types take to bulk up?"

I didn't bother nodding. I'd finally realized that just because Beth finished most sentences with a Valley Girl upswing, she wasn't actually asking me a question.

"The question was whether he had possession with intent to distribute," she continued. "I guess he had quite a reputation on campus, but the police couldn't prove anything. If they had, he could have gone to jail for five years. As it was, he only got a year's suspended sentence and a thousand-dollar fine."

I considered what I'd just learned. This was a whole lot more damning than a couple of microwaved burgers. Had it indeed been Wally whom Mayo had gone to talk to the day he died? Did Mayo threaten to ensure the bowling alley would lose its liquor license not for minor food violations but because of Wally's drug-dealing history?

Helene interrupted my considerations. "Whoa, Sam," she said warningly.

"Whoa?"

"I don't like that look in your eye."

"What do you mean?" I asked innocently, knowing full well what she meant.

"You know full well what I mean," she said sternly. I swear the woman is a mind reader. Or a witch. "Just promise me one thing."

This time I was the mind reader. I already knew what she was going to say. We'd had this conversation before.

"Don't worry, Helene," I said. "I'll be very, very careful."

TWENTY-TWO

"ARE YOU SURE she's not part dog?"

I grinned up at Jason from where I was sitting on the floor of his apartment playing with Ciati. I'd come by first thing in the morning to see how the kitten was settling in, stopping first at the pet supply store out on Route 6 for some cat toys. Helene had handed over a litter box and some cat food to Jason before he'd left yesterday, but I thought it was very important that Ciati have her very own cat toys. There is nothing as hysterically funny as a kitten pouncing on a knitted mouse with purple tail feathers.

I'd been tossing the mouse across the room for about a half hour and had finally stopped because I'd gotten tired of going over to pick it up and throw it back the other way. Once I refused to play, it took Ciati about two minutes to figure out that if she brought the mouse back to me and dropped it in my lap herself, the game would go on indefinitely.

"She's the first cat I've ever known that plays fetch."

"She's exceptionally intelligent," Jason said with all the pride of a new parent. He was lying on his back on his ancient, ugly plaid couch, arms folded behind his head, as perfectly content as I'd ever seen him. Ciati suddenly lost interest in her mouse and leaped up and snuggled onto his chest. Jason reached one hand down lazily and scratched her gently under her chin for about ten seconds, by which time she was fast asleep.

"I'm hungry," Jason said, suddenly and expectantly. I love the way men do that, as if just by saying "I'm hungry," food will suddenly appear. *Not happenin' here*, I thought. Jason's apartment over the Harbor Patrol offices at Town Cove could be charitably described as minimalist. The living room furnishings consisted of the aforesaid ugly couch and an equally unattractive faux leather recliner facing a large screen TV that was only used during baseball season and then only when the Red Sox were playing. The Boston Red Sox were gods in Jason's book.

The kitchen was similarly spartan, furnished with an over-varnished pine table and four over-varnished pine chairs circa 1972 and equipped with very little in the way of utensils aside from a pasta pot and a battered aluminum frying pan (or, as I called it, burning pan). I knew from experience that the fridge would contain a few bottles of Sam Adams beer for Jason, some drinkable pinot grigio for me, and maybe a rind of cheese and some mustard. Jason got most of his food from whatever takeout place was handiest.

"There's nothing to eat here," I pointed out.

"Let's go to Nellie's," he suggested.

"Oh, yay!" I said, hopping up from the floor. Nellie's Kitchen is one of my favorite eateries in Fair Harbor. It only serves breakfast and lunch and nobody thinks it's odd to order banana pancakes at two in the afternoon. Because Nellie makes the best banana pancakes ever. Everybody knows that. (Tip: What everybody doesn't know is Nellie's secret ingredient, discovered by yours truly—a touch of brown sugar in the batter, which gives them that little crispy, caramelized edge.)

Jason sat up and gently placed Ciati, still snoring, in a corner of the sofa.

"Back soon," he whispered. *Smitten by a kitten*, I thought, smiling to myself.

Nellie's was doing a booming business in parents too exhausted by their children's winter break to cook *even one more meal*, but Jason and I managed to snag a two-top in a relatively quiet corner. I ordered my pancakes with a side of bacon, Jason had two eggs sunny-side up and a side of Nellie's fantastic sweet potato hash browns. I chowed down, alternately sipping coffee and making "this is really yummy" noises, until I could think straight about what I'd learned about Wally from Beth.

"I need to run something by you," I said, putting the thick white coffee mug down on the table. "It might be nothing, but it might also be something Lieutenant Hammond and Detective Peters ought to know about if they don't already."

"I thought you had something on your mind," Jason said, dipping a corner of his buttered toast in the melty yolk of his egg. "Tell me about it."

I told him about Mayo asking Beth how to research a person's background and then looking for whatever dirt he could find on Martin Bruni. I omitted the newspaper article about Beth's aunt and Mayo's baseless allegations, as Beth had told me that in confidence and it was no longer relevant. When I got to Beth's subsequent examination of Mayo's search history and what the selectman had discovered about Wally Lipman, I paused.

"Do you remember hearing anything about Wally's arrest when it happened?" I asked. "I was living in New York then, but my parents never said anything about it."

Jason shook his head. "He probably had a Boston-based lawyer, and his mother must have kept it very quiet, as any parent would."

"But with a drug arrest on his record, it would be against the law for him to be a bartender, right?" I asked. Anything to do with drugs, Jason would know. It was a big part of his job.

"Not necessarily," Jason said. "There's no state license for bartenders, and the Lanes is a local, family-run business. Nobody would question Wally working as the bartender there."

"But what if he's a part owner?" I asked. "As a part owner Wally's conviction as an adult would be enough for the board of selectmen to close the Lanes's bar down, wouldn't it? So Mayo was really onto something this time."

"*If* Wally's a part owner," Jason admitted. "We don't know that that's actually the case." His eyes slid away from mine and he pretended to be absorbed in wiping the last of the egg yolk off his plate with the final corner of his toast.

But I wasn't having any of that. "You could find out," I said. "You have access to those kinds of databases."

He looked back up at me. "I do," he said. "And so do you. It's all public information online."

"I've tried," I admitted. It was true. I'd spent about an hour at it the night before until I wanted to throw my laptop out the window in frustration. "But it's a maze. You know how to navigate it."

"Okay," he said, giving in. "I'll check it out when I get back to the office."

I leaned across the table and kissed that man right on his yolky mouth.

B ACK AT THE Patrol headquarters, Jason went upstairs to collect Ciati and then brought her down to the office where she sat bolt upright on his lap, her green eyes intent on the PC's cursor as it jumped around the screen. It took Jason about three minutes to pull up the information that, indeed, Walter D. Lipman had been named a part owner of the Lucky Strike Lanes when his mother had bought the place.

"Here's how I see it," I began.

But Jason was busy talking baby talk to the kitten and wasn't listening.

"Put that cat down and pay attention," I commanded. They both ignored me.

I continued anyway. At least I could get it straight in my own head.

"As a selectman, Mayo could easily find out if Wally was a part owner."

Jason looked up from Ciati long enough to nod in agreement.

"So," I continued, "when Mayo sees Wally in the deliveries lot, he's all excited to tell him about his little research project and that the chances are good the bar will be closed down. How much do you think that would eat into the Lanes's profits?"

"Significantly," Jason acknowledged. "I can't imagine there's a fortune to be made from the pure sport of candlepin bowling."

"I agree," I said. "Certainly for the Ladies League, the sport seemed to be how many glasses of white wine you could pack in before hubby comes to pick you up."

"Okay," Jason said. "So now Wally has a real motive. But on another issue, why did Mayo even go to the Ginger Jar? As far as he knew from his internet search, there was nothing concrete on Martin Bruni."

"Maybe he was on a high from lording it over Wally and just decided he'd keep his lucky streak going by sneaking in and taking a peek at the Brunis' files in the hopes he could find something. Remember, aside from Wally and Mrs. Lipman's cars, the only other vehicle in the lot is Liz the Cleaning Lady's truck. So clearly the only person in the Ginger Jar is the cleaning lady. And she won't hear him sneaking around because she's in the kitchen with country music blasting."

"And he knows that how?"

Suddenly I was excited. "Remember, she said she'd opened the kitchen window a crack for ventilation. So maybe Mayo hears the music through the window, peeks in, and sees her mopping the floor. Maybe he thinks as long as he's on a roll, he'll just go in, snoop around a little, see what he can find in the office."

Jason looked skeptical. "That's a lot of maybes."

"I grant you that, but let's just follow this scenario for a while, okay?"

Jason nodded, and I continued. "So Wally's pretty upset, sees Mayo going into the back of the Ginger Jar, and decides to shut Mayo up before he can tell the select board what he'd discovered."

Jason looked skeptical. "But first he runs into the Lanes to grab a bowling ball and then runs across the deliveries lot with the ball in his hand? Risking being seen by his mother or a passerby or even the cleaning lady?"

"Maybe," I said (for about the hundredth time). "Or maybe he's got his personal bowling balls already in his carrier case. I know he's got one—I've seen it. Maybe he keeps it in his car. So there's nothing suspicious about him with a ball carrier."

"Okay, I'll give you that one," Jason said. "And what happens next?"

"Like Mayo, he knows the only person there is the cleaning lady. The radio is blasting from the kitchen window, so he figures she can't hear anything. Anyway, he grabs his carrier out of his car, goes into the Ginger Jar's back room, then into the back hallway, where he sees Mayo going into the office and shutting the door behind him. Wally pulls a ball out of the case, sneaks over, opens the door quietly, sees Mayo rummaging through the file cabinet, and whacks Mayo on the head with it."

"What about blood on the ball and on him?" Jason asked. "And before you get all snippy"—he took the sting out of his words by leaning forward and kissing me lightly—"I'm just playing devil's advocate here, okay? I do actually think you may be onto something."

"Well, thanks for that, anyway," I said as I gathered my

momentarily distracted thoughts. "There wasn't that much blood—you saw that." I tried very hard not to flash back to the image of Caleb Mayo dead on the linoleum floor of the office.

"True," Jason said. "He died from internal brain hemorrhage, not from the wound to the head and skull itself."

"And Wally wasn't wearing any jacket when I saw him later in the back lot. Maybe he'd had one on when he did the deed, and it took whatever mess there was. It might be a good idea to look around for that jacket if there was one."

"If there was one, it's probably wrapped around an anchor at the bottom of Crystal Bay," Jason said.

"So Wally probably wouldn't have had much to worry about," I continued, "except for a little blood on the ball itself. All he had to do was drop it back into his case, shut the office door behind him, and get out of there. He probably went right back into the Lanes and machine polished the heck out of that ball."

"Well, as a scenario, it works," Jason said. "And once the holiday break is over, forensics will be able confirm if a candlepin ball could have been used as a weapon. But I'm just not sure about your star player. Any number of people might have seen Mayo going in the back door of the Ginger Jar. And, you know, I bet a lot of the league players have their own bowling balls and carriers."

"Pretty much all the league players," I agreed, adding, "including Mrs. Mayo."

Jason raised his eyebrows. "You suspect *Mrs. Mayo*?"

"Not really," I said. "And anyway, you said yourself, a woman wouldn't have had the strength to crush his skull like that."

Jason nodded. "Maybe with a full-size bowling ball, which is larger and heavier and would have the advantage of centrifugal force, since you can really swing it using the finger holes. But not with a candlepin ball that you just hold in your hand."

"Centripetal," I said.

"What?"

"Centripetal," I said. "Centrifugal force is what you feel when you're in a car going around a curve and you lean away from the curve. But the real force, the force of the object itself, is centripetal, the force leaning *into* the curve."

"Good lord," Jason said. "The things you know."

"Didn't you take Mrs. Lipman's physics class in high school?" I asked.

"I took environmental studies that year," Jason said.

"Too bad. She was famous for her David and Goliath re-creation. She did it every year. I guarantee you that anyone who took that class understands centripetal force."

"But *I* know why the horseshoe crab is an essential part of our ecosystem," Jason pointed out.

"Well, I'm glad someone is on their side," I said. I find the essential-to-our-ecosystem horseshoe crab, which looks like a miniature prehistoric tank with is spiked shell and spear-like tail, pretty darn creepy.

"Anyway," I said, getting back to business, "given that it's likely a man we're looking for, all we need to do is figure out which of Fair Harbor's dozens of candlepin bowlers in the men's league had a murderous grudge against Caleb Mayo." I laughed in spite of myself. "I gotta admit, I'm glad I'm not officially investigating this case."

Jason snorted. "That's never stopped you before."

I grinned at him. "And it ain't gonna stop me now."

And then it came back to me. No, I wasn't officially investigating the case, *but my mother was*.

W ITH ALL THE excitement of the holidays, I'd kind of pushed my mother's obsession with the Rhode Island mob to the back burner. But now my worry was back in force. Not that I thought organized crime had had anything to do with Mayo's killing, but I didn't want any bad dudes annoyed with my mother for poking around in their business. And if she really had been to Boston the other day talking to her "source" about Hanson Construction, I was afraid there was a good possibility it might get back to the wrong people.

I could understand and even applaud my mother's journalistic conviction that she had to follow up this lead if she had some solid evidence, but as far as I knew, she had nothing. And I was increasingly convinced that the Mayo murder was personally motivated, not professionally (so to speak). It was time for me to double down on that approach and find something concrete to convince my mother. A tiny, insistent memory tried to make its way forward, but try as I might, all I could come up with was that it had something to do with the Three Things. Which was unlikely.

Maybe a walk would help. It would also be a welcome diversion from worrying about Jason, who had sent me packing because of some unspecified work that needed to be attended to.

Fine. Be that way.

Back home, Diogi greeted me as he always did—as if, despite all historical evidence, I had left that morning never to return. *At least my dog loves me.* We took a nice long walk around Bayberry Point. I was beginning to know some of my neighbors, including the O'Gormans, who had moved into the house across the way with their four exuberant kids in July. But even if the occasional car that crawled past us at the posted speed of fifteen miles per hour wasn't driven by someone I knew, I still gave the obligatory little half wave that Fair Harbor etiquette required. The drivers, of course, responded with the same little wave. It was nice. When I lived in New York, I never waved to anybody except my building's super.

It was a still, clear, crisp day that would have been very cold if there'd been any wind at all. But as it was, the brisk pace that Diogi set for our walks kept me comfortably warm. In the winter sun a thin frosting of snow still sparkled on the green branches of the pines, and the blue waters of Crystal Bay peeked tantalizingly through the leafless oaks. It's amazing how one sunny winter's day on the Cape can make you forget all about the endless gray ones. Once again, the magic of this great curve of sand and sea charmed me. And once again, I marveled that what had seemed at the time to be an unmitigated disaster had been in fact a road leading me back home. The Cape was exactly where I needed to be, when I needed to be there. And it still was. For me, the Cape held all the answers.

Which was why I wasn't surprised when, as Diogi and I headed back home along Snow Lane, the memory I'd been trying to catch hold of finally presented itself. *The Three Things with their snowball throwers.*

And suddenly, a flurry of other words and images slotted into place. And I had it. Almost.

TWENTY-THREE

I T WAS ELI the Info Kid who'd made the first connection for me when his brother had turned a snow toy into a missile launcher. "It's the velocity, you dope!"

And then there was what I'd said to Jason about centripetal force: "The real force, the force of the object itself, is centripetal, the force leaning *into* the curve."

The centripetal force that the biblical David, employing a whirling sling, had used to increase the velocity of a stone to the point where it could fell the giant Goliath. Ironically, it had been Wally's mother, Mrs. Lipman, who'd made the physics of that story real to legions of students.

Every year, Mrs. Lipman would take the sophomores in her physics class out onto the baseball field where she'd set up a huge straw-stuffed dummy, complete with an aluminum pasta pot helmet, in front of the backstop. Then she'd have them, one by one, play David by dropping a fist-sized rock into a knee-sock, whirling it around their head and letting it loose, sock and all, at the giant. My year, we didn't all hit the target (okay, *I* didn't hit the target), but by the time we'd each had a chance, the pasta pot was flying off Goliath's head more often than not.

So now it seemed to me that using a makeshift sling, anyone could have snuck up behind Mayo as he was absorbed in his search of the filing cabinet, whirled the sling once or twice to create that deadly force, and, because they were close enough to Mayo to hold on to the sling itself, be very sure that they would hit their target.

Anyone. Even a woman. Which opened up the potential suspect list dramatically.

Julie Bruni was the obvious choice. But not the only one. I came back to Mrs. Mayo. She was clearly delighted to be out from under her husband's thumb, and I, for one, could imagine her feeling pretty darn murderous after forty-some years of living with that man. As she'd said herself, "It adds up."

Had the tipping point been her husband's refusal to sell his business and join their son and his family off Cape? By her own account, she and Mayo had been arguing in the car that day about just that when he'd told her to let him out. She could have parked the car and followed her husband into the premises, could have found him rummaging around in the Brunis' private files. Had that been it? Not only was her husband ruining her life, he was actively trying, once again, to ruin someone else's. As she'd looked at her husband rifling through the file cabinet, had she thought to herself, *I'd like to bash that man's brains in*, knowing full well she had neither the strength nor the weapon to hand?

But her son had gone to Fair Harbor High. Had Tim Mayo taken physics? Had he come home one day and told his mom about David and Goliath and the rock in the sock? Had that lodged somewhere in Mrs. Mayo's memory? When she'd found her husband rooting around in somebody else's private life, had the David and Goliath story floated up into her consciousness as it had in mine? Was that when she'd quietly gone back out to the car and taken one of her bowling balls out of its league case? Now she had her rock. But what to use as the sling? Not the carrier case. Its square, quilted sides would obviously cushion the blow. What else would she have had to hand?

And that was where my theory hit a wall. Maybe, I thought, I was coming at this from the wrong direction. I tried again. Maybe the *sling* came first, the bowling ball second. Maybe it was the *sock*, not the rock that unleashed that memory.

I tried again to visualize what might have happened. Mrs. Mayo parking her car and following her husband through the back door of the Ginger Jar. I imagined her walking into the dim back room cluttered with groceries and supplies, the ghostly shape of Liz the Cleaning Lady's smocks pinned to the makeshift clothesline. Then coming out into the hallway, standing in shock at the doorway to the office, seeing her husband at that filing cabinet. Frightened at her own rage, eager only to get away, had she stumbled into the back room and been startled to stillness by a damp touch on her cheek? Had she reached out, only to find it was one of the cleaning lady's compression knee-highs hanging from the clothesline? Was that when the story of the rock in the sock had floated into her consciousness?

And with that I had it. Completely.

B Y THE TIME Diogi and I got back to Aunt Ida's house, I was actually relieved that, even though it was almost five and night had fallen, my parents were once again missing in action. All the better. It gave me some time.

Time for my great experiment.

I sent Jason a text, asking him to meet me at the Ginger Jar around seven for a quick dinner. By then I would have completed my experiment, and after I explained my theory to him, we might be able to convince the Brunis to let us take another look at the Ginger Jar's storeroom. I was grat-ified that he texted back right away, although his brief okay was slightly less enthusiastic than one might want. I really had to teach that man how to use emoticons.

I fed Diogi, assured him I'd be "right back" (for all the good it did), and convinced Grumpy to take me to town. I stopped first at Jenny's and explained what I needed from her. She went up and rummaged through her attic, then the basement, and finally what she called the junk room, where she at last dug up a sparkly pink carrier case from under a pile of skateboards. She took a candlepin ball out and handed it to me.

"I don't even want to know why you need this," she said.

"I'm going to prove that the Bible is true," I said, taking the ball and dropping it into my shoulder bag.

"That was my first guess," she said.

A quick stop at CVS and the grocery store, and I had everything I needed for the great experiment. But by this point it was almost seven. There wouldn't be time to get home, try out my theory, and still get back in time to meet Jason. Any sensible person would have put the experiment off until the next day. But I am not a sensible person. Hence my starring role in several infamous YouTube clips. When I have decided on a course of action, it is virtually impos-sible for me to wait on it. Besides, I was almost positive that even a limited trial run of my idea would prove the theory I'd come up with on my walk. The pieces fit too neatly.

So no waiting. I had to give it a try. I parked in the deliv-eries lot behind the Ginger Jar, which was only dimly lit by a weak bulb over the back door of the Lucky Strike Lanes. Which was fine. I really didn't want anyone to see me whirl-ing a homemade sling around my head like some kind of lunatic.

Still sitting in Grumpy's driver's seat, I unwrapped the very attractive pair of thickly opaque compression knee-highs I'd bought at CVS. Then I slipped Jenny's candlepin bowling ball into the top of one of the socks. The ball slid down to the toe, where it bulged like a mouse that had been swallowed by a snake.

I had to try it. Just once.

I stepped out of the truck. I looked around and, seeing no one, grabbed the top of the knee-high, and took an experimental whirl. It worked like a charm. It certainly felt lethal. I couldn't wait to get home and test it on what I was calling in my mind "the victim," the out-of-season and thus very expensive watermelon that I'd picked up earlier at Nelson's. But the hottest man on Cape Cod was probably already waiting for me inside the Ginger Jar, so that would have to wait.

I turned to open the truck door and toss my "weapon" back inside, but was halted by the sight of a squat, burly figure coming out of the back door of the bowling lanes. Wally. With something dangling from his hand. I shrank back against the truck, willing Wally not to see me. The last thing I needed was another little encounter with my unlovely Lothario.

Luck was with me. Wally walked over to his Camaro, beeping to unlock it, opened the passenger side door, and tossed in what the interior light revealed to be his ball carrier, replete with his initials stamped in gold. Very tasteful. He slammed the door shut and walked around to the driver's side door. But before he could get into the car, the back door of the Lanes opened again, a woman's tall figure silhouetted against the light behind her.

"Walter, before you go, could you help me with these boxes that just came in?" his mother called out to him.

"Can't it wait until I get back?" he asked sulkily.

"They're blocking lane seven. It will just take a few minutes."

"Okay, okay," Wally ceded ungraciously, and headed back toward the Lanes.

Without relocking his car.

What else could I do? I really didn't want Caleb Mayo's killer to be Mrs. Mayo. I *liked* Mrs. Mayo. If it had to be anybody, I would prefer it to be Wally. You'd think by this time, I'd know better than to let my personal likes and dislikes guide my detecting, but some people never learn.

I scurried over to the Camaro. This would be my only opportunity to check out Wally's carrier case. I wasn't thinking about rocks and socks anymore. Walter wouldn't need anything but his own strength to whack Mayo on the head with a bowling ball. Not that I expected to find anything on any of the balls themselves. I knew he used the Lanes's machines to clean them. But what about the carrier?

I opened the Camaro's passenger door, dropped the sling on the seat, and leaned in to grab the carrier case on the floor. I unzipped the case and carefully took each ball out and set it on the seat. The interior light would be enough, I thought, for me to check the inside of the case for bloodstains. When it was empty, I leaned in farther to hold the case up to the light.

"Hey, hot stuff, you trying to tempt me with that booty?"

My first confused impression was of a vise on my bottom. Not a vise. Wally's hand. *Eeuuw.* Grabbing me. Hard.

Startled, I grabbed the sling and stepped back out of the car, whirling around to face my attacker. There was a sickening crack, and in the glow from the Camaro's interior lights I watched in confusion as Wally's leer turned in an instant into a grimace of pain.

"Shit, girl!" Wally screamed, grabbing his left arm with his right hand. "What'd you do that for?"

I looked blankly down at the sling in my hand. Apparently, when I whirled around, it had whirled around as well. And connected with Wally's arm.

"What, are you crazy? You broke my arm!"

Actually, it kind of looked like I had. So if nothing else, I now knew the sling worked.

"What on earth is going on here? Walter, what's happened to your arm?"

Mrs. Lipman was coming around the front of the car, her face a combination of concern and outrage. Before Wally could respond, she turned to me.

"Samantha, what happened here?"

I responded with the usual eloquence I am known for in times of stress.

"Um, it was an accident. He, um, startled me by, um, touching me"—grabbing my butt, actually, but I wasn't going to say that to Mrs. Lipman—"and I kind of, um, turned around too fast and sort of hit him, by accident"—I trailed off and held out the knee-high with its sagging weight—"with this."

Mrs. Lipman stared at the sling in shock. Clearly, she knew exactly what it was. Well, she should. She invented it, after all.

She turned back to her son, who was leaning against the car, still clutching his arm and moaning softly.

"Let me see," she said, her tone softening, and reached toward the arm.

Wally flinched. "It really hurts," he whined.

"I'm sure it does," his mother said crisply as she examined the arm in the light from the open car door. "Just hold it close to your chest until I can get a sling on it and get you to the hospital."

But Wally wasn't going to go anywhere without getting back at me first. "Ask her why she was in my car. Why she was stealing my bowling balls."

Well, that burned me up. "I wasn't *stealing* your bowling balls," I exclaimed and then wished I hadn't. What I'd said begged the question *So what were you doing with them?*

Sure enough, Mrs. Lipman turned her gimlet eye on me. "Explain yourself, Samantha."

Feeling like a kid who was *definitely* going to get detention, I knew I had to think fast. Whereas telling the truth and nothing but the truth makes me stammer, I am fairly fluent when I am, shall we say, *embroidering* the truth.

"I had some kids at my house recently and they were using one of those snowball throwers, which made me think about the David and Goliath sling experiment. I wanted to show it to them." *Like I would ever.* "I made one out of a knee-high and a bowling ball and was carrying it with me"—*please don't ask why*—"when your son snuck up behind me in the dark, grabbed my rear end, and said something pretty disgusting. It startled me and I swung around and the sling hit him on the arm. I didn't do it on purpose, but now I kind of wish I had." I was definitely getting my dander up.

Mrs. Lipman looked at her son is dismay. "Walter, did you really do that?"

Wally was unabashed. "I was just trying to be friendly. She's a tease. Always has been."

Okay, this was war. But before I could get my next volley in, Wally added, in what I thought was an obvious attempt to distract his mother from his own rotten behavior, "Why don't you ask her what she was doing with my bowling balls. Why'd she snoop around in my car? Why'd she take the balls out of their carrier?"

Damn.

"I'd like to know that, too, Samantha," Mrs. Lipman said. Not unreasonably.

That's when Wally went over the line. "We should call the police on her," he said triumphantly.

"That's what you want, Wally?" I responded hotly. "You want the police? In that case, maybe you'd like to tell them about your visit from Caleb Mayo the day he was killed."

Wally looked at me blankly. His mouth opened and closed like a goldfish. *"Wha'?"*

Mrs. Lipman, on the other hand, was perfectly composed. In fact, she gave me The Look, and I almost lost my nerve. Almost, but not quite.

"You remember, Wally," I added with heavy sarcasm. "When he told you that he'd found out about your little secret and that he was going to use it to shut down the Lanes's bar?"

Wally finally found his voice. "That's a lie. I never saw Mayo that day."

The thing was, I actually believed him. The guy sounded totally confused.

"Anyway," he added, not particularly intelligently, "nobody knows about—"

"Walter," his mother said sharply, "that's enough."

She turned once again to me. "What were you looking for, Samantha?"

The woman wasn't stupid. She'd worked it out. She knew what I was looking for.

"Evidence," I said, avoiding specifics. "Not on any of the balls, they're easy to clean, but in his carrier case. He couldn't get rid of it, it's personalized. The police would want to know what happened to it."

"Assuming the police had any reason to suspect my son of being involved," Mrs. Lipman said. "Which they don't. Which he isn't."

"How do you know?" I shot back.

"He's not that smart," Mrs. Lipman said, her eyes filled with something like resignation. I was tempted to point out that it doesn't take a lot of smarts to hit somebody on the head with a candlepin bowling ball, but was almost immediately ashamed of my snarky attitude. I'd always respected Mrs. Lipman. Intelligent, principled, dedicated to science and the truth. How very sad that she should be mother to this not very bright, not very principled, not very truthful son.

And then, to my amazement, she reached into the car, picked up the carrier case, and handed it to me.

"Here," she said. "Give it to the police, have them check it. They won't find anything. I've got to take Walter to the hospital."

TWENTY-FOUR

WHAT ON EARTH is that?" Jason asked as I plunked down Wally's carrier case on the table in front of his half-finished Sam Adams.

"Walter Lipman's candlepin ball carrier case," I said dully. I was coming down from the not very pleasant adrenaline rush of my encounter with the Lipmans and felt like I'd run a marathon. "Could you order me something very sweet and very alcoholic before I explain?"

Jason, who, when he drank at all tended to stick to beer or wine and on whom the Ginger Jar's concoctions were wasted, grimaced at the description but went obediently over to the bar. There he engaged Martin in a brief discussion and came back with something tall and crimson and foamy in his hand.

"Martin's version of a Cape Codder," he said, placing the drink in front of me. "Made with fresh cranberries, some kind of honey with a fancy name I can't remember, fresh lime juice out of some weird machine . . ."

"A centrifuge," I said.

"Of course," Jason said dryly, "a centrifuge, what else? Plus lots of vodka."

I took a gulp and almost choked. Lots of vodka indeed.

"Whew," I said. "That'll put hair on your chest."

"Good lord, I hope not," Jason said. "Maybe you just want to sip it."

I tried that with much better results.

"It's actually delicious," I said, wiping a little of the foam off my upper lip. "I need to know what kind of honey that is."

"But first *I* need to know why you're carrying Lipman's bowling balls," Jason said. "Are you going steady now?"

"Very funny," I said. "And it's not his bowling balls," I corrected him. "Just the carrier case."

"Oh, okay, now I understand," Jason said with unnecessary sarcasm.

So I told him the whole story, starting with my biblical brainstorm and ending with Mrs. Lipman's present of the carrier case. Jason listened carefully, nodding occasionally to indicate he was following, except when I got to the part about Wally groping me. At that point he got very, very still, and I thought it was a good thing that Wally was safely in the emergency room of Hyannis Hospital.

When I got to the end of my recital, there was a long pause as Jason absorbed what he'd heard.

"So let me get this straight," he said finally. *Uh-oh.* "You got to thinking about David's sling and centripetal force . . ."

"And increased velocity," I added.

"And increased velocity," he amended patiently. "And somehow you thought maybe a knee-high stocking and a bowling ball would make a good sling."

"Not somehow," I protested. "I did some very logical deduction there."

"You did," he acknowledged. "That was very impressive." I gave a little self-satisfied smirk, which didn't last long.

"I'm just questioning the wisdom of your decision to try your little experiment at night in the deserted back lot of a restaurant where somebody had been killed the week before by, we suspect, somebody who also uses that back lot."

I was encouraged by the "we suspect" part. Not so much, though, by his point about me hanging around in dark corners with suspected murderers.

"You know what I'm like," I said hotly. "When I have an idea, I have to go with it. I can't just sit around. And anyway, as it turned out, I had a pretty effective weapon in hand."

Jason laughed ruefully, and I was relieved that the tension was lifting.

"You're right," he said. "You've proved more than once that you can take care of yourself. I should know that by now. I know I shouldn't try to change you or tell you what to do. It's just the caveman in me trying to keep you safe, even in retrospect."

I reached across the table and put my hand on his. "You are the most highly evolved caveman I know," I said. "And besides, even cavemen have their uses."

"Glad to hear it," he said, grinning at me. *Whew, disaster averted.*

"So, will you give the carrier to Lieutenant Hammond?"

"I think he's already left for Bourne," Jason said. "We were both at the station, where I was catching him up on what you'd found out about Lipman's record. But Vivvie should still be there." *Vivvie again?* "I'll just run this over to her. It'll only take me a few minutes. Are you okay waiting for me here?"

"Sure," I said. "I'll order us some food in the meantime, okay?" In times of emotional stress, food is my cure-all.

"That'd be great," he said, standing up and leaning over to kiss me gently on the mouth. That's another thing I love about Jason. There is no such thing as a perfunctory kiss. Every kiss is deliberate. And meltingly effective. *Vivvie* was effectively erased from my mind.

I ordered myself another of Martin's Cape Codders, but nonalcoholic this time. I felt it would be unbecoming to be asleep at the table when Jason got back. After a lengthy perusal of the menu (next to Golden Age mysteries, menus are my favorite reading material), I ordered a tasting of hand-crafted Vermont cheeses, a small bowl of ale-steamed mussels fragrant with garlic and Dijon mustard, and a trio of sliders—a beef burger topped with fresh guacamole, a lamb burger topped with eggplant tapenade, and a salmon burger garnished with mango salsa. *There, that should hold me . . . I mean us.*

I asked my server, a fresh-faced boy who hardly looked older than Evan, to bring the cheese plate while I waited for Jason to get back from talking to *Vivvie. So his kiss hasn't totally reassured you, Sam?*

I was consoling myself with alternating bites of Unusually Sharp Cheddar, I Can't Believe It's Not Butter Triple Crème, and We're Not Kidding Hot Pepper Colby, when I heard a familiar voice hailing me. I looked up to see Beth Voorhees coming out of the hallway next to the bar wearing her red Christmas sweater and a big smile on her face.

"Beth!" I said. "It's good to see you. Are you here for dinner?"

"No," Beth said. "I'm just waiting for my aunt. Her truck is in the shop, so I'm driving her. She's in the back room getting her stuff."

At first, I couldn't quite process what I was hearing. Why would Beth Voorhees's aunt be in the Ginger Jar's back room?

It wasn't until I saw Liz the Cleaning Lady stomping out of the hallway with an armful of cleaning smocks and knee-highs over one arm that I managed to put it together. *Liz the Cleaning Lady was Beth's aunt.*

Actually, it made sense. I hadn't really thought about it, but I realized now that I knew that the cleaning lady's last name was Voorhees. She'd told me when I'd written the check for her help with my basement.

But hadn't Beth said that she and her aunt had the same

name? That was how she'd accidentally googled her aunt's run-in with the law when she'd meant to be searching for herself. How do you search "Beth Voorhees" and come up with "Liz Voorhees"?

And then the penny dropped. She hadn't searched "Beth Voorhees." She'd searched her full name—"Elizabeth Voorhees." "Liz" and "Beth" were both short for "Elizabeth."

"Liz the Cleaning Lady is your *aunt*?" I asked, just to make sure. "*That* Liz, who works here?" I pointed over to Liz, now in indignant conversation with Martin, who was shaking his head and shrugging.

"Yeah," Beth said. "She actually quit the Ginger Jar today. I'm not sure why. The pay was pretty good and she liked the hours. But it's okay. She's got another gig at Shawme Manor starting tomorrow."

By this time Liz had plowed her way over to her niece. From the look on her face, she was clearly in no mood for chitchat.

"Come on, let's get out of here," she said brusquely, nodding briefly at me. "This place makes my tired ache."

Beth rolled her eyes at me, gave me a little wave, and followed her aunt out the back way, while I sat stunned, trying to process what I'd learned.

Liz the Cleaning Lady was Beth's aunt. Liz the Cleaning Lady, who'd been alone in the Ginger Jar for more than an hour during the time when Mayo was killed. Liz the Cleaning Lady, who'd made no secret of her feelings about Mayo. Had Beth lied to Helene and me about not telling her aunt about Mayo's threat? I couldn't really believe that.

But what if Mayo *himself* had told Liz? What if he'd seen her truck in the deliveries lot and decided this was a golden opportunity to taunt her with what he'd found out about her history? Had he come in to tell the cleaner what he'd learned and what he planned to do about it? Had she "flown off the handle" when she'd realized that she risked losing her beloved niece if Mayo reported her?

This was not good. I really didn't want it to be Beth's Aunt Liz. And not just for Beth's sake, although that was paramount. I just simply couldn't believe that Liz, for all her gruffness, was a killer. I *liked* the woman. *Again with the personal likes and dislikes, Sam?*

Okay. Let's put personal feelings aside. Had Beth taken Mrs. Lipman's physics course before the teacher retired last year? Had she, in fact, told her aunt about the sling experiment? Liz certainly had access to compression stockings. *Oh lord, had Liz Voorhees just walked out of the Ginger Jar with part of the murder weapon?*

TWENTY-FIVE

I STRUGGLED WITH WHAT to tell Jason when he got back to the Ginger Jar a few minutes later. On the one hand, he needed to know what I'd learned. On the other hand, I knew I was in big trouble. I decided to go with the truth, mostly because I'm a terrible liar and because *this is a murder investigation, Sam.* But first things first. I gestured to the server to bring us the steamed mussels. Jason loved steamed mussels. The last thing I wanted was a hangry Jason when I told him my news.

The mussels were great. Small, but not so small that you didn't get a good mouthful of seafood deliciousness out of every open, glistening shell. As we were sopping up the broth with some lovely, chewy bread, I thought it was safe to broach the subject of Liz the Cleaning Lady. I was wrong.

When I finished my recitation, Jason put his bread down uneaten and got very, very still. "So you're telling me Liz Voorhees had a motive for Mayo's murder."

"Only if she knew what Mayo had found out," I said. "And Beth says she didn't tell her."

"Which is why you didn't see fit to tell anyone, least of all me, about this before now."

"I didn't know who Beth's aunt *was*," I protested. "I certainly didn't know that she was someone *on the scene*."

"You knew the authorities were looking for anyone with a motive," Jason reminded me.

"Any *man* with a motive," I reminded him. "I hadn't come up with the sling idea then."

"*Anybody* with a motive," Jason pointed out. "You should have shared that information with the police."

He was right, and I knew it.

"I'm sorry that I didn't tell you Beth's story," I said. "I was sure and I still am sure that Beth was telling the truth when she said she never told her aunt about Mayo's threat. She trusted that Helene would find a solution. And Helene did find a solution. So, in my mind, it wasn't relevant. It wasn't until I realized that *Mayo* could have told her aunt that I put it together. And just for the record, I'm telling the authorities, i.e., *you*, now. And I sincerely doubt that they would have ever put this together without me."

Jason laughed, a bit ruefully. "I know," he said. "Once again Miss Marple comes to the rescue."

Miss Marple, as Jason well knows, is my very favorite Agatha Christie sleuth. You can have Hercule Poirot with his little gray cells. I like the nosy old lady with her deep knowledge of human frailties.

"Well, if you put it like that," I said with false modesty.

"No, I mean it," Jason said seriously. "You have a knack for putting things together and for listening, *really* listening, to what people are saying. And you do share your information—once you see fit. I just wish you would see fit a little earlier."

"It's only that I promised Beth that I'd keep what she told me confidential," I said. "I have to say I feel really bad about breaking that confidence even now."

"It's a murder investigation, Sam," Jason reminded me

gently. "There's no such thing as confidential in a murder investigation. And remember, this is just information, not a measure of anyone's guilt or innocence. Although I have to admit, it doesn't look so good that Liz Voorhees is clearing out of the Ginger Jar so fast. It looks like she's trying to stay under the radar. Hammond is around here a lot."

"Or maybe she just doesn't like working at a place where people get killed," I pointed out.

"Come on, Sam. Does Liz the Cleaning Lady strike you as the squeamish type?" Well, he had me there. "And in your sling theory, the compression hose actually belonged to her."

Now was the time to tell Jason that Liz had just walked out the door with her knee-highs in her hand. But I wasn't ready to go there yet. Maybe first I could demolish my own suspicions.

"But anyone who went into the back room could have grabbed a knee-high from the clothesline."

"*If* they'd even noticed they were there," Jason pointed out. "Liz Voorhees *knew* they were there. The back room is where she kept her stuff."

A little bell pinged in the back of my memory, something I thought I remembered Liz saying the day Mayo died. But I couldn't be sure. I wasn't exactly thinking straight at the time.

"Okay," I said, coming back to the topic in hand. I really didn't like where this was going. "Let's think about this. Liz is mopping the kitchen when Mayo comes in, talks to her for we don't know how long, and then leaves the kitchen. He then goes into the office. Unbeknownst to him, Liz has followed him and sees him go into the office. She then runs over to the bowling alley, sneaks in, takes a bowling ball, comes back, drops the ball in the knee-high, and goes in and kills Mayo with it. And then goes back to mopping the kitchen. Does that make any real sense?"

Jason looked at me quizzically. "Make sense how?"

"Look," I said, "running over to the Lanes to take a ball was both risky in terms of witnesses seeing her go in and then come out with the murder weapon in her hand."

"Maybe she was too angry to care," Jason said. "Even her niece admits that she has a temper. And her record doesn't do her any favors there."

This was getting very serious. "Jason," I reminded him, "we have *absolutely no proof* that Liz Voorhees knew about Mayo's threat to Beth. Until we do, there's no provable motive."

"True," Jason said, "but there's a probable one."

"And how likely is it that she came up with the sling idea just like that?" I added.

"Beth Voorhees might have taken that physics course," Jason pointed out. "Maybe she talked to her aunt about it at the time. In any event, I'll talk to Hammond about all this. He's in Bourne tomorrow but back in Fair Harbor after that. If he thinks it's worth following up—and I think he will— he's going to need to hear this directly from you. And then Beth and her aunt."

I really didn't like where this was going. I should have just let my mother tangle with the mob.

"Listen," I said, leaning forward across the table, "could I check out one thing before you take this to him?"

"Whoa," Jason said, holding up one hand, which was still holding the piece of bread he'd failed to eat. "You are *not* going to talk to Liz Voorhees. You are not going to talk to a possible suspect in a murder investigation. Not your job, Sam. Plus, it's dangerous."

"I know, I know," I said. "Not Liz. Jillian. She and Andre are driving back from Boston tonight. When I saw Liz earlier this evening, she was clearly annoyed by something. Maybe when she applied for the Shawme Manor job, she told Jillian what it was that was bothering her."

"And how would that have anything to do with Mayo's death?"

"Well," I said, "there was something Liz said that day in the Ginger Jar after Mayo was killed. I'd like to find out what she meant by it. Because if it was about what I think it was about, I think it would make it unlikely that Liz is the killer we're looking for."

Jason rolled his eyes and sighed. "Could we stop with the mystery and you just tell me what she said and what you think it means?"

"Only if you promise not to roll your eyes again."

"Promise."

And so I told him. And he did not roll his eyes.

"Okay," he said. "But I want you there the day after tomorrow when I talk to Hammond, no matter what you find out."

"I promise," I said.

I pulled out my phone and texted Jillian. u back from boston?

Her response was yes followed by a sad-face emoji.

ok to come by tomorrow am at manor for quick chat?

This time I got a thumbs-up emoji.

"We're on," I told Jason. "She's usually in her office by nine. I'll go see her first thing and get right back to you."

"I don't know why I let you get away with this stuff," Jason said, shaking his head ruefully.

"Don't worry," I said. "I'm not going to do anything foolish."

And yet, for some reason, Jason didn't look like he believed me.

I gestured to the server for our sliders, which he, not being as inexperienced as I'd assumed, had clearly asked the kitchen to hold back until his customers looked like they were friends again. Once we'd finished them off, we left in our separate vehicles. This was beginning to feel like a pattern.

The rental car was in the driveway when I pulled in, but Aunt Ida's house was dark, for which I was grateful. I love my parents, but there are times when all a girl wants is a warm bed and a good book. Jason's reference to Miss Marple had left me longing for Christie's safe, if murderous, little world of St. Mary Mead, so I tiptoed into the front parlor and pulled *A Murder Is Announced* from the bookshelf.

I AWOKE THE NEXT morning from a very confusing dream in which I, wearing sensible walking shoes, a brown tweed suit, and a felt cloche on my head, was chasing a piglet with a Santa hat in her mouth through crooked streets lined with thatched-roofed houses and shops. Pigs, I knew in my dream, were very smart and I was convinced if I could catch this one, she would lead me to the killer I was searching for. But every time I got close enough to grab her, she slid through my hands. "She's a very slippery little piglet," I said aloud, waking myself in the process.

I opened my eyes to see Diogi eyeing me balefully from what he considered his side of the bed.

I looked at the clock. Six thirty.

"Sorry," I said. "I didn't mean to wake you. Go back to sleep."

Diogi immediately closed his eyes and began to snore gently. It's amazing what that dog will choose to understand.

I, on the other hand, found myself unable to go back to the land of Nod. Resigned to my fate, I stumbled into the bathroom. As I stepped into the claw-foot bathtub, I blessed Aunt Ida once again for rigging it with a shower. Nothing like a shower for washing away a frustrating dream.

But not completely. It kept coming back.

"She's a very slippery little piglet."

That was an odd thing to say. And why was I so sure the piglet was female? A very slippery female. I was hoping she could lead me to the killer, but every time I tried to hold on to her, she slid through my hands. She evaded me.

And now that I thought about it, someone else had evaded me recently. Or at least evaded my questions. Wilma Mayo. It seemed to me now that when I'd asked her specifically who her husband was planning to talk to when she'd dropped him off, she'd avoided a straight answer.

Okay, so I'd told Jason I was just going to talk to one person, but it wouldn't hurt to pay a little call on Mrs. Mayo, too. I could probably fit it all in before I met Jillian at the Manor at nine. Then I'd go back to Jason with what I'd learned.

That's what I told myself anyway.

WILMA MAYO REGARDED me doubtfully through her partially opened front door. This was not the jolly lady of our first two encounters. I wasn't surprised. First of all, it was too early for wine, and second of all, I was pretty sure she regretted our conversation in the bowling alley. Something she'd said had sounded like an evasion to me then, and I suspected that she knew what I'd come for.

"Hi, Mrs. Mayo," I said. "Could I come in? I'd just like to talk to you for a minute. It's about a friend of mine."

Her look of suspicion faded a bit, and when she saw Diogi, who had refused to be left behind, still sitting in the truck she said, "Of course. And bring your dog in, too, if you'd like."

Ah, dogs. The great icebreakers.

"Thanks," I said. "If you're sure you don't mind . . ."

"No," she said, finally smiling. "I love dogs. But Caleb would never have one. Too much trouble, he said." *Well, he was right about that at least.*

I went back to gather the beast, though I put him on his leash just in case. Diogi's greetings tend to be exuberant.

But my fears were groundless. Diogi, like so many large dogs, has a natural gentleness around older people and little ones. He greeted Mrs. Mayo like a gentleman and was welcomed with a bowl of water in the kitchen.

While Diogi slurped the water happily, Wilma and I settled ourselves at her kitchen table with freshly brewed coffee served in real coffee cups with matching saucers.

"How pretty," I said, admiring the delicate, rosebud-strewn china.

"Thank you," she said, coloring a bit with pleasure. "I love using my nice things, but Caleb thought they should stay in the china cabinet just for display. I broke one once and he didn't trust me with them after that. I'm terribly clumsy I'm afraid."

Was there nothing this man couldn't find fault with?

"No more than any of us, I'm sure," I said.

Wilma smiled at me then. "It's very kind of you to say so, dear."

I decided to jump in while I was ahead. "Mrs. Mayo, there's something I want to ask you."

And suddenly the smile faded. "About Caleb's . . . passing?" she asked guardedly.

"Well, in a way. About something you said the other night at the bowling alley."

Wilma's gentle face took on a stubborn cast, but I pressed on.

"You said that your husband didn't tell you who he wanted to talk to or what he wanted to talk to them about."

"That's right," she said, sounding rather relieved. "He never said who he was going to see."

"And you also said you never saw him again after you dropped him off."

Here Wilma looked a bit more cautious. "Well, I didn't," she said. "I never *saw* him again."

"But you *heard* him, didn't you?" I said.

Mrs. Mayo went pale, and I knew I'd hit my mark.

"How do you know that?" she whispered.

"Your husband wasn't wearing his Santa hat in the Ginger Jar. But the police found one outside the Ginger Jar's kitchen window. I think it was your husband's hat. And I think you dropped it there."

Wilma said nothing, just looked at me. But her hand shook as she placed her cup back into its saucer.

"I think that after you dropped your husband off, you drove to the elementary school parking lot behind Town Square. That's when you realized that he had left his Santa hat in the car. You had some time before the tree lighting, so you thought you'd walk back up Main Street and give it to him. It would only take a few minutes. And it wouldn't be right for Santa to arrive for the festivities without his hat. But you didn't see him on Main Street, did you?"

Wilma shook her head in a silent no.

"So you went around to the deliveries lot to look for him. You saw the open back door to the Ginger Jar. And as you walked over to it, you *heard* him talking to somebody inside, didn't you? What you told Detective Peters was true. I think you always try to tell the truth. You never *saw* your husband after you dropped him off, but you *heard* him."

At this she nodded and finally spoke. "In the kitchen. The window was open a crack and I could hear music coming out. Country music. You know, that cute song about Grandma getting run over by a reindeer?" The question was rhetorical. Everybody knows "Grandma Got Run Over by a Reindeer." It is one of those Christmas novelty songs that gets trapped in your head and *will not stop.* I just nodded and Mrs. Mayo marched grimly on.

"Well, I could hear someone singing along, a woman, I wasn't sure who. But then all of a sudden the music stopped. And I heard her say, 'Hey, I was listening to that' all cranky-like, and I recognized her voice. It was Liz the Cleaning Lady."

"Who was she talking to, Wilma?"

Faced with a direct question, Wilma did what she had been conditioned to do her whole life. She told the truth.

"It was Caleb. He said he had to talk to her, that it was his 'duty.' He started talking at her, the way he does, all high-and-mighty, all this stuff about her hitting somebody once and a bunch of legal rigmarole. But I finally figured out what he was talking about." And for the first time, I saw tears in Wilma Mayo's eyes. "He was telling her that he was going to make sure she would lose her niece, that lovely girl, Beth. I know Beth. She used to sell me Girl Scout cookies."

"And what did Liz say to that?" I asked gently.

"She said she'd see him in hell first," Wilma said, almost in a whisper.

There it was. Proof that Mayo had told Liz Voorhees about what he'd found out. And that he'd threatened her with losing Beth. That Liz's response had been an angry one.

I tried to hide my dismay. "And what did you do then?"

"I left." Mrs. Mayo sobbed, the tears spilling over and down her cheeks. "At that moment, I hated Caleb. I threw his stupid hat on the ground outside that window and I left. As I was going, I heard the radio come back on, even louder this time, and I thought, Good for you, Liz. Drown him out. I don't even remember walking back to Town Square. I remember being surprised that Caleb never showed up, but I was glad. I never wanted to see him again."

"But you didn't tell Detective Peters what you'd heard?"

"No," Wilma said. "I told her the truth, that Caleb didn't tell me who he was going to talk to and that I never saw him again. But I didn't tell her about *hearing* Caleb and Liz the Cleaning Lady talking. I felt like if that poor woman killed him, I could understand it, I really could. I know now that's wrong, but I was still just so *angry* with him. And later I figured out that just because Caleb was threatening the cleaning lady, that doesn't mean she killed him, right? I mean, Caleb made *a lot* of enemies. And by then everybody was saying a woman couldn't have done it anyway. So I thought to myself, Why should I give Liz and Beth Voorhees any more troubles than they already have? Can you understand that?"

I nodded and reached across the table to touch her still-shaking hand. "Of course I can," I said. "Absolutely."

Which was true. I understood a lot of things now. I just wished to heaven I didn't.

Mrs. Mayo nodded her head firmly, as if she'd come to a decision.

"I'm glad I finally told someone," she said. "I think I'd better go talk to that nice lady detective again, don't you agree?"

What could I say? Ask Mrs. Mayo to continue in her deception? But Mrs. Mayo didn't know what I knew, that a woman could indeed have killed her husband. But you don't withhold evidence in a murder inquiry, no matter how good your intentions. I had learned that lesson all too well last spring.

"You do think I should tell the police, don't you?" Mrs. Mayo asked again, unnerved by my silence.

"Of course I do," I said again helplessly. "Absolutely."

B ACK IN THE truck, I texted Helene while waiting for Grumpy to warm up, which was never a rapid process. I pulled off my gloves and typed is beth working today

Helene had proudly mastered the art of texting this past summer but had never subscribed to the notion that grammar and punctuation have no place in those messages.

No. She's home today. Do you need her address?

yes thanks

Helene duly sent me the required information. I didn't even want to think how Jason would react if he knew, after what I'd just had confirmed, that I was going to Liz Voorhees's house, even though I was fairly sure she wouldn't be there. Today was supposed to be her first day of work at Shawme Manor.

Beth and her aunt lived on a much more modest street in south Fair Harbor than the Mayos. As I pulled up in front of the tidy half Cape on its quarter acre of neatly raked sand and scrub pine, I was relieved not to see Liz's truck in the driveway. Things would be simpler all around if I could just get the information I needed from Beth. And to be honest, I didn't want to face Liz.

I took a deep, calming breath. Which didn't work.

"You stay," I said to Diogi, who knew exactly what I meant. Stay is *not* his favorite command; it took Helene weeks and a whole bag of jerky sticks to get it into his thick head. He sighed noisily and plopped himself down dejectedly in the seat. I hardened my heart against him. I didn't have time for some doggy reunion with Beth. This was not a social call.

Beth greeted me cheerfully at the front door and led me into a tiny, spotless kitchen with a wallpaper frieze of yellow ducks and blue-and-white-checked café curtains at the windows.

"Can I get you a cup of coffee?" she asked. "Aunt Liz always makes a whole pot and takes the extra in a thermos, but I guess she forgot this morning, what with her new job and all. She says you have to take out a mortgage for a cup of coffee to go at the Coffee Café and people who do that are numbskulls." Well, then, count me a proud numbskull. The Coffee Café's cappuccino is worth its weight in gold.

"No coffee me for me, thanks. I can't stay long," I said, having decided to head over to the Coffee Café as soon as I possibly could. "I just have one quick question for you."

I wasn't sure how to continue. I was hoping against hope that Beth's answer would work in Liz's favor. But what if it didn't?

Beth just looked at me politely. There was no evidence that I could see of anxiety or fear.

"What do you need to know?" she asked.

I plunged in. "Did you take physics last year?"

"You bet I did," Beth said, cheerfully. "Aced it, too."

Helene was right. Beth was a smart girl.

But as I walked out the door, my heart was a stone in my chest.

D IOGI AND I arrived at Shawme Manor at nine on the dot, just as Jillian was opening the front door. She was wearing a very chic, very simple camel hair dress and a pair of gold hoop earrings that set off the glow of her deep brown skin. I was wearing faded sweatpants with a fleece sweater of indeterminate color and no earrings to set off my winter-gray skin. *Once again Samantha Barnes sets a world record for not even trying.*

"Have you had breakfast?" Jillian asked as Diogi and I made ourselves comfortable in her office. "I made cornbread this morning."

"I did," I admitted. I'd had a huge bowl of homemade granola with Greek yogurt and a hefty drizzle of local honey. "But I'm a big believer in second breakfasts."

Jillian grinned and carefully levered a deep golden square out of the baking tin on her desk, put it on a paper napkin, and offered it to me. It was still warm from the oven, and I almost swooned. Diogi sprang to attention, and Jillian offered him a square as well.

"Do you make cornbread every morning?" I asked through a mouthful of savory, crumbly goodness.

Jillian snorted. "If I did, I'd weigh two hundred pounds in about a week. No, this was a special treat to make up for missing my girl and her family already."

"The holiday was that good?"

"The holiday was great," Jillian said, her eyes misty. "Matthew is a total cuddle bunny and Deb and Rayya's house is so pretty and comfortable. And Boston is such a great town. Maybe Andre and I shouldn't wait for when we retire to move to the city."

"Jillian," I said firmly, "you are exactly *where* you should be, *when* you should be."

Okay, so I stole that line from Helene, but at one time it had helped me through a very difficult period in my life. And still did.

"You think?" she said, pursing her lips doubtfully. "Anyway, time to stop feeling sorry for myself." She sat up straighter in her desk chair and assumed her professional "let's get down to business" mode. "What's so urgent that you had to drag the hound out of bed at the crack of dawn?"

Damn. Time for the tough stuff. I took a deep, calming breath. Which didn't work. It never does.

"I hear that Liz the Cleaning Lady is working for you," I said in a rush.

Jillian nodded. "Yes, she started this morning. She's doing the public rooms like the dining room, the TV room, and the sunroom."

She didn't ask me why I was asking. She just waited for me to continue in my own way. It occurred to me that years of counseling distraught relatives had probably taught her the virtue of simply listening quietly.

"Do you have any idea why she left her job at the Ginger Jar?" I asked.

"Well, she told me it was her idea, but of course I checked with the Brunis for a reference," Jillian said. "You can always tell if someone's been fired or let go, even if the previous employer doesn't say that explicitly. But in this case, Julie Bruni seemed sincerely sorry to lose her."

I nodded. "Yeah, I think so, too. I saw Liz last night and she gave the distinct impression that *she* had fired *them*. She was super pissed off about something. I was just wondering if she told you what it was that prompted her to leave."

And here I held my breath. So much depended on Jillian's answer.

And the answer, when it came, was exactly what I'd expected. Not wanted. But expected.

I stood up slowly, saying, "Thanks, Jillian. I appreciate your help."

Jillian raised her eyebrows and said, "Well, if that's what you look like when you appreciate someone's help, god knows what you look like when you don't."

"I'm sorry," I said. "It's just one of those situations when there's no good answer."

Just heartbreak.

TWENTY-SIX

D IOGI AND I walked back to Grumpy in mutual despair. I because of what I now strongly suspected had happened in the Ginger Jar the day Caleb Mayo met his end. Diogi because nobody had offered him another piece of cornbread. As I was waiting for Grumpy to clear his throat before starting, Jason texted me.

forensics says Lipman's carrier case clean

also witnesses saw him through window stocking bar during time frame

So not Wally. Which meant things really did not look good for Liz Voorhees. There was only one person who could help. Unfortunately, this person was not a member of my fan club. My next step was inevitable. For me, anyway. Maybe not for anybody with reasonable impulse control. I went looking for this person. I went looking for Mrs. Lipman.

As I had no idea where she lived, my only hope was that she'd be at the bowling lanes. It was a measure of my desperation that I was willing to run the risk of another encounter with the vile Wally in order to talk to my old teacher.

When I pulled into a parking space in front of the Lucky Strike Lanes and shut off the ignition, Diogi gave me a "don't tell me" look.

"Sorry, bud," I said. "You're staying in the truck this time." Diogi gave me a look of complete disdain and turned his back to look out his window. I was dismissed.

The noise that greeted me as I walked through the glass double doors was hellacious. There appeared to be some kind of birthday party going on with at least two thousand ten-year-old boys screaming and carrying on and, unaccountably, actually hitting the candlepins, which only contributed to the din.

I looked hesitantly at the bar, but it appeared to be manned only by some teenage girl filling one ice-filled plastic cup after another with Coke and Dr Pepper. Just what these kids needed, more sugar and caffeine.

I vaguely remembered seeing a door marked "Office" down past the restrooms, so decided to try there first. Sure enough, once I had pushed past a stream of little boys crowding into the men's room, no doubt to create even more havoc, I found the office. The door was firmly shut, and taking another deep, calming breath that didn't work, I knocked on it.

"Come in," a familiar voice said.

Phew. Mrs. Lipman not Wally. I turned the handle and pushed the door open. Oops. Spoke too soon. Mrs. Lipman *and* Wally. They were seated on opposite sides of a worn metal desk covered with neat piles of paper. Wally's left arm was in a cast. When Mrs. Lipman saw me standing in the doorway, she stood and put out one hand as if to stop me in my tracks. She was, as always, neatly and conservatively dressed in black slacks, low shoes, and a navy wool sweater. Her long face was haggard, as if she hadn't slept in days, and it seemed to me that she had shrunk into herself even more in the twenty-four hours since I'd last seen her. Which was odd, since she surely knew by now that her son had been alibied.

Wally, for his part, was looking at me as if he expected me to attack him again, which was almost comical considering that he outweighed me by at least seventy-five pounds.

"I'm, um, sorry to, um, bother you, Mrs. Lipman," I said inadequately. "I know you, um, probably don't want to ever see me again, but I, um, need your help."

She couldn't have looked more surprised if I'd asked her for a million dollars.

"My help," she said. "*You* want *my* help."

"Well, not for me exactly," I said, taking a step into the tiny room but not closing the door behind me. "For someone else. You're the only one who can help her."

"What the hell is this?" Wally demanded, half rising from his chair.

I flinched in spite of myself, and Mrs. Lipman said, "Walter, that's enough."

Wally sat back down, still scowling at me but momentarily under control. This was a guy who could really use some obedience training from Helene.

"Is there somewhere, um, more private we could talk?" I asked Mrs. Lipman. *As in, away from your son?*

Mrs. Lipman looked like she had made some kind of decision in her own mind. She stood up from the desk.

"We'll leave Walter to finish up the paperwork." I wondered at the wisdom of leaving Walter with anything to do with reading and writing but held my tongue. "I sometimes take a walk in the mornings around Trout's Point. You can walk with me there if you feel you must talk to me."

As an invitation it wasn't exactly gracious, but I would take it. I had to take it. Whether I wanted to or not.

"Sure," I said. "I'll follow you in my truck."

As I pulled out onto 6A behind Mrs. Lipman's tan

Honda, I said to Diogi, who was still conspicuously sulking, "Good news. We're going for a walk."

Next to "treat," "walk" is Diogi's favorite word in the English language. He leaned over and gave me a nice sloppy kiss on the cheek to show that we were friends again.

"Ugh," I said, wiping his slobber off with my arm, leaving a nice snail trail on the sleeve of my parka. Diogi just wagged his butt happily in his seat. We were *going for a walk*.

I didn't bother explaining to him that we were going for a walk with a woman who by all rights should hate me, who had no reason to go along with what I was going to ask her to do. No reason except that, at least once upon a time, she had been a good person with real integrity. A person who would do the right thing in the very best sense of the term. I was hoping against hope that she was still that person.

As GRUMPY BUMPED down Bathsheba's Lane toward the Trout's Point Conservation Area, I wrestled us around the dirt road's deep potholes that the residents purposefully did not fill, knowing that it was a surefire way to keep any cars that ventured down it going at or below the fifteen-mile-per-hour limit posted for all of Fair Harbor's private roads. It didn't bother me. I knew the lane as well as I knew Trout's Point itself.

Trout's Point is a pristine thumb of land carved millennia ago by two saltwater rivers leading out from Crystal Bay. One empties into my own Bower's Pond, the other into Bathsheba's Cove, home to Nauset Sailing Club, my home away from home as a kid. The point itself was named for the Trout family, who had lived on the thirty-five-acre property in solitary splendor for generations, their dignified yellow clapboard house at the very tip of the promontory commanding an extraordinary view south down Little Crystal Bay.

By the late 1980s, only one Trout remained in the yellow house, the redoubtable Miss Alexandra. Off-Cape developers, recognizing (they thought) easy pickings, flocked to her with offers to buy the property. Imagine, they said, how much easier her "golden years" could be with all the money they were willing to pay her. She'd be a millionaire. She could move into a nice modern house closer to town with a full-time housekeeper, a nice car instead of her old Jeep, and even a driver.

But Miss Trout, sitting straight-backed in her rattan peacock chair, her hands resting on her Malacca cane with its brass knob in the shape of a duck's head, was having none of their nonsense. She *liked* the old inconvenient house where she'd lived happily for almost eighty years. She *liked* living alone. She *liked* cooking her own food and sweeping her own floor. She *liked* driving her old Jeep into town to shop for her groceries. But the house was expensive to keep up in the manner to which it had become accustomed, and this Miss Trout *didn't* like.

So, Alexandra Trout came to the town of Fair Harbor with an offer they couldn't refuse. In exchange for life tenancy, she would sell the property to the town as a nature preserve for a sum considerably less than what the developers had offered, but still considerable.

"I'm sure you'd like me to just hand my property over for free," she said waspishly to the board of selectmen. "Well, I may be old but I'm not crazy. I like money as much as the next person."

So the town handed over its check, and Miss Trout carried on with her life exactly as it always had been for the next twenty years. When she died at one hundred, she left her remaining dollars (still considerable) to the Fair Harbor Historical Society, on the condition that they move the yellow house to an appropriate site in town and use it as the society's headquarters. They were delighted to comply.

As we turned into the conservation parking area, Diogi, with that walk radar that all dogs seem to have, began to whine as if he just couldn't wait one more second to get out of the truck.

"Calm down, my canine companion," I said as I put Grumpy into park next to Mrs. Lipman's Honda. "You're not going anywhere until I get a leash on you. This is a nature preserve, not a dog park."

After Diogi introduced himself politely to Mrs. Lipman, we waited while she grabbed a walking stick out of the back seat of her car.

"All hickory," she said, hefting the heavy stick in her hand. "Helpful with uneven terrain and unfriendly canines."

"Do you have a dog?" I asked in a weak attempt to jump-start a conversation as we walked over to the entrance to the main trail through the park.

Mrs. Lipman smiled wanly. "I did. A golden retriever named Bear. He died last year."

Great first move, Sam. Remind her of her dead dog.

"I'm sorry," I said, meaning it. I couldn't imagine losing Diogi. I *wouldn't* imagine losing Diogi. Time to change the subject.

The main trail through Trout's Point winds in a circle around the property with various side trails leading over to Bathsheba's Cove and its river on one side and Bower's Pond and its river on the other. I pointed to where you could just glimpse the entrance to the river leading to Bower's Pond on our right.

"I used to come here all the time with my friend Jenny after sailing club," I said. "We'd slide down the hill there to a sandbank along the river. There's was a little freshwater spring bubbling up just at the edge of the water and a vein of real clay that you could actually make into little cups and saucers."

But Mrs. Lipman was not particularly interested in memories of my golden childhood. She looked pointedly at me and took a swipe with her stick at an unsuspecting pine cone on the path in front of us, sending it flying.

"What is it exactly you wanted my help with, Samantha?"

"There's a bench on the waterfront a little farther on," I said. "Maybe we could sit there and talk."

Mrs. Lipman just nodded and we walked in silence along the sandy path through the pines and pin oaks toward the clearing where the Trout house had once commanded its expansive view down Little Crystal. Even Diogi seemed to sense that this was not an occasion for joy, and for once stuck close to me instead of tugging at his leash. After about five minutes, the ground sloped down to a small, sandy beach. The entire expanse of Little Crystal Bay was spread out in front of us, a deep blue in its bowl of green hillsides, the sky a paler robin's-egg blue above. In spite of the circumstances, both Mrs. Lipman and I seemed to be compelled to stop and take it in.

"Crystal Bay is the largest contiguous bay along the Cape Cod National Seashore," Mrs. Lipman said, almost as if she'd been transported by our surroundings back into teacher mode. "The indigenous Nausets referred to it as Monomoyik, which translates to 'Great Bay' in English. It's an enormously important and delicate ecosystem."

"I'd forgotten that you taught environmental science, too," I said.

"For a few years," Mrs. Lipman acknowledged, "until I could finally convince the school board that the subject was important enough to spring for a full-time teacher in that specialization."

I was encouraged that we were at least talking, even if it was about ecosystems.

"There's the bench," I said, pointing down to the beach.

"It's pretty sheltered, so we'll be a little warmer while we talk."

"While *you* talk," Mrs. Lipman corrected me pointedly. But she started down the slope of the path toward the bench, using her stick, so I assumed I was to follow her.

But as she made her way to the bench, I took Diogi down to the tide line and let him sniff out all the wonderful seashore smells. With any luck, he would find a yucky dead fish and could roll on it. *Fine. Whatever.* I just needed to be able to think about what I would say to Mrs. Lipman. I couldn't afford to mess this up. It seemed to me that this no-nonsense woman would appreciate a straightforward approach. Once I'd gathered my thoughts, we made our way to the weathered wooden bench, where I sat down.

"I have a theory about who killed Caleb Mayo," I began.

"Yes, I know," Mrs. Lipman said dryly. "You think my son did it."

I wasn't going to insult her intelligence by denying her claim.

"Well, I know better now, but, yes, I did think it was a possibility," I said, "given what Mayo knew about him. . . ."

"What you *assumed* Caleb Mayo knew about him," Mrs. Lipman corrected me.

I continued as if she hadn't spoken. "And what I'd learned about Mayo himself."

"Such as his overweening sense of white male privilege wrapped in the banner of moral superiority?"

"Well, I was going to say his delight in seeing people squirm," I said. "But that, too. You see, I knew from my, um, source in law enforcement that the blow was struck with something round and about the size of a softball but obviously heavier. It seemed to me that a candlepin bowling ball would fit the bill. But it would take someone quite strong to use it to strike a killing blow to the skull. Which is why, when I found out that Mayo had pulled up your son's record online, I thought it more than possible that he

could have confronted Wally and Wally could have . . ." I
trailed off.

Mrs. Lipman stood up from the bench and looked down
at me.

"Killed him," she supplied. "You thought Walter could
have killed him."

"No, I thought he was a possible suspect," I said, wish-
ing she would sit down or at least put down that stick of
hers. "If Mayo threatened to shut down the Lanes's bar
based on Wally's record, then he had motive, he had opportunity, he had access to the possible weapon, and he is
very strong."

"What made you change your mind?" she asked.

"A couple of things," I said. "But most of all, I believed
your son when he denied that Mayo had confronted him. He
seemed genuinely, um"—"clueless" was the word I almost
said but caught myself—"confused when I brought it up."

"He *was* confused," Mrs. Lipman said, sitting back
down on the bench as if suddenly weary. "He had no idea
what you were talking about."

I could have said something here, but I decided to hold
that thought, to see how things progressed. "Also," I continued, "I could imagine him striking out in the heat of the
moment, but following Mayo over to the Ginger Jar, maybe
to throw suspicion onto someone there? That sounds like
premeditation and planning and he isn't that"—I almost
said "smart"—"that kind of a guy," I finished lamely.

"No," his mother said, almost apologetically, "he's not."

"And, of course," I added, "there's no forensic evidence
pointing to him *and* it seems he has witnesses who saw him
stocking the bar at the relevant time."

Mrs. Mayo allowed herself a thin smile at what I had to
admit was a justified moment of vindication.

"So I'm assuming you've decided to wrongly accuse the
Brunis?" she asked.

This, I thought, was just mean. On the other hand, I was

encouraged that she was prepared to defend those who were wrongfully accused.

"I'm not in a position to accuse anyone," I said as neutrally as possible. "That's for the police to do. But, no, I don't think it's either of the Brunis. Martin and Julie are both alibied by their cleaner. Nor do they have any real motive, since they knew that Mayo's threats to shut down the Ginger Jar were just a bunch of hot air."

"And, as I'm sure you know, any number of people heartily disliked Caleb Mayo," Mrs. Lipman pointed out. "I strongly suspect that the police will never find this public benefactor, and I for one hope they never do. So, once again, I fail to see why we are here and what exactly it is you think I can do for you."

She stood again, and I feared she was ending our conversation. Nonetheless I took a minute to collect myself before I answered.

"I'm afraid that, based on some new information that I and others have a responsibility to share with the police, they will arrest someone else for the crime." I stressed the word "crime." I wasn't going to go along with her "public benefactor" approach to justice. "The case against this person is very strong."

Mrs. Lipman blanched. "And who, exactly, is this someone else?" she asked through lips that barely moved. I could see the knuckles of the hand that held the walking stick go white as she clenched her fist around it.

"Elizabeth Voorhees," I said quickly.

For a moment I saw relief in Mrs. Lipman's eyes before her face went from apprehensive to blank in a nanosecond. No, more than blank. She looked completely bewildered. "And *who* is Elizabeth Voorhees?"

"Liz the Cleaning Lady," I said.

"Liz the Cleaning Lady," she repeated, incredulous.

"You know her?" I asked.

"Of course I know her. Everybody knows her." I couldn't

tell from her voice whether this was a good thing or a bad thing. "And you think Liz the Cleaning Lady killed Caleb Mayo?"

"It looks pretty bad for her," I said.

"This time, Samantha Barnes," Mrs. Lipman said coldly, "you really have gone too far."

TWENTY-SEVEN

W HAT REASONS DO you have for making this assertion?"

I was almost surprised she didn't add, *and what proof do you have to support your hypothesis?*

I took a deep, calming breath (which never works). "Well, maybe the easiest way to start is with the facts," I said.

Mrs. Lipman nodded. Now I was speaking her language.

"Forensics puts the time for Caleb Mayo's death between a little after ten, when Liz arrived at the Ginger Jar to start cleaning, and eleven fifteen, when the Brunis arrived. Meaning that Liz Voorhees was alone at the Ginger Jar for an hour. Mrs. Mayo dropped her husband off at the back lot shortly after ten, because, she says, he'd recognized someone's car. The only cars in the lot at that time were yours and Wally's."

I paused, and Mrs. Lipman said, "I hear a 'but' in there."

I nodded. "But the police aren't stupid. They are going to ask themselves what if it was Liz the Cleaning Lady's *truck* that Mayo recognized? What if it was Liz Voorhees whom Mayo was going to talk to?"

I waited for my companion to ask why Mayo would want to talk to Liz and about what, but she stayed obstinately, and in my view significantly, silent. She no longer seemed surprised, though she did seem to be struggling with how to respond.

"You see," I continued, "Mayo found out something about Liz, something that he thought made her legally unfit to be her niece's guardian. Her niece is Beth Voorhees. She took your physics class last year."

"Yes, I remember Beth Voorhees," Mrs. Lipman said. "She's a very intelligent girl."

"I agree," I said. "And a very nice one, too. She loves her aunt with all her heart, and when Mayo told her that he'd have to report her aunt to the authorities, she was terrified."

Finally, Mrs. Lipman showed some surprise. Perhaps even outrage. "He told the *girl*?"

I nodded. "He said it was the right thing to do."

"Of course he did," Mrs. Lipman said flatly.

"But Beth, wisely, decided not to tell her aunt until she had more information on the accuracy of his threat. Quite frankly, she was afraid her aunt might 'fly off the handle,' as she had a history of a short and sometimes violent temper."

Mrs. Lipman stood and began pacing in front of the bench as she thought this through. "But the girl did not tell her aunt, so her aunt would have had no motive to kill Caleb Mayo."

"Unless *Mayo* told Liz what he'd found out and what he planned to do about it," I said.

Mrs. Lipman snorted. "And she broke his skull with a well-aimed blow of, what, her mop? She'd hardly have had the strength."

Sarcasm aside, I was pleased that Mrs. Lipman was defending Liz Voorhees. I needed her on Liz's side.

"No, not a mop," I said. "A sling."

Mrs. Lipman had the good grace not to pretend she didn't know what I was talking about. She stopped her pacing and sent another stray pine cone flying with her stick.

"A sling," she repeated. "Like the one you broke Walter's arm with."

So I hadn't been wrong then when I'd suspected that Mrs. Lipman had immediately recognized what I'd used to break her son's arm.

"I think so. I won't go into all the details, but something reminded me recently of your David and Goliath sling experiment."

"I'm glad I could help," Mrs. Lipman interrupted dryly, staring away from me out into the bay.

"Yes, well, it made me think about centripetal force and how maybe a candlepin bowling ball in something like a knee-high could be used as a weapon by anyone, even a woman. That's when I remembered Liz the Cleaning Lady's knee-high support hose in the back room. One of those, I thought, would make the perfect sling. That's what you found me trying out last night."

"On my son's arm," she said grimly, swiping at another innocent pine cone.

"That was an accident," I protested, made nervous by her aggression. "But you have to admit, it proved my hypothesis."

And for the briefest of moments, I thought I saw a slight smile on that grim face.

"So this is what could have happened," I continued, relieved. "Some of it I know did happen. Some of it I'm hoping you can help me prove didn't happen. But here's the scenario the police will inevitably put together: Caleb Mayo sees Liz Voorhees's truck and takes his chance to lord it over the cleaning lady.

"He hears the radio in the kitchen, goes in, turns it off, and tells Liz what he knows and what he plans to do about it. She is furious and tells him where he can shove his threats. Maybe he's a little nervous now, realizing that with Liz he's bit off more than he can chew, and he clears out of the kitchen. But when he hears the radio come back on and realizes she's not coming after him, he can't resist the opportunity to check the Brunis' office for something, anything, incriminating on them.

"Liz, who has been fuming in the kitchen, comes out into the hall, only to see Mayo disappear into the office, closing the door behind him. She opens the door, fully prepared to tell him exactly what she thinks of him, and sees him rummaging around in the Brunis' files. This is the last straw. This is a man who lives to ruin other people's lives. Someone should bash this guy's head in and put the world out of its misery. She'd do it herself if she could. She'd just go over to the Lanes and get herself a bowling ball and smack him right on his lousy head. But she's about five feet tall and ninety-five pounds. And Mayo is a big guy. It would be like David and Goliath. And maybe that's when she remembers what her niece told her about your physics class, about your rock-in-a-sock sling, about that poor scarecrow. She has just the sock she needs right there on the clothesline in the back room."

Mrs. Lipman turned back to me, her face resolute, as if she'd made a decision. "So you think this poor woman went across to the Lanes and took one of our balls to use in this compression sock sling of hers?" I couldn't tell if she liked this idea or thought it was ridiculous. I was hoping desperately that it was the latter.

"It seemed like a possibility."

She shook her head. "I was in my office that morning doing paperwork. I often leave the back door unlocked for convenience while I'm there, so I don't have to turn off the alarm every time we get a delivery. But I do have a little motion detector on the door just in case someone comes in unannounced, shall we say. If anyone opens the back door, a buzzer sounds in my office. Nobody came into that back room. Nobody took a bowling ball from our premises. It's a preposterous idea."

It was as if I'd suggested the earth was flat. Not that I was complaining. This was exactly what I'd been hoping for.

"Actually, I agree," I said. "It seems too premeditated, not to mention risky and time-consuming. Before I came up with this sling theory, I'd wondered if the weapon could have been a coconut from the box in the back room of the Ginger Jar itself. But forensics found no coconut fibers in the wound, so I shelved that at the time. But covered by thick compression hose, the fibers *wouldn't* get into the wound."

By this point, Mrs. Lipman was looking at me like I was some kind of out-of-control avenging demon. I felt terrible, but I kept going.

"Unfortunately, I mentioned this coconut idea once to, um, law enforcement. As well as my sling idea. And my compression sock idea."

"Haven't you been a busy girl." Mrs. Lipman sat back down on the bench next to me, stick in hand.

I tried to steady myself, to keep things neutral. "Someone is going to put it all together. Liz slides a coconut into a knee-high, gives it a whirl. She walks into the hallway, gently opens the office door, peers in, and sees Mayo excavating the Brunis' files. She sneaks up behind him, begins to whirl the sling, at which point he realizes that something is happening and turns just slightly toward her. The sling with its coconut missile slams into his head."

I sat back, trembling, almost sick with the images I'd conjured up. Then I waited.

So much depended on what Mrs. Lipman said next.

"I fail to see why you are favoring me with this, this, this *fantasy* of yours," she said coldly.

"It's not a fantasy," I said. "At least not the part about Mayo telling Liz what he'd found out and what he intended to do about it. Mrs. Mayo heard them talking from outside the kitchen window."

Mrs. Lipman went a little pale. "So you're counting on me to somehow give Liz Voorhees an alibi for the time of the actual murder? To lie to the police?"

"No," I said. "I think the last thing you would do is lie outright. Avoid the truth, yes, not tell the whole truth, yes. But not out-and-out lie."

"You've lost me again."

But I hadn't. She knew it and I knew it.

"I'm counting on you to save Liz Voorhees from going to jail for a crime she didn't commit, despite all the evidence against her. I'm counting on you to keep Beth Voorhees out of foster care and at home with the aunt she loves and who loves her. I'm counting on the woman I remember from my high school days. The woman, the scientist, for whom truth is sacred. Even if it means great personal sacrifice."

I paused, and finally added, "I'm counting on you to tell the police that you killed Caleb Mayo."

And then Mrs. Lipman really scared me. Mrs. Lipman began to laugh.

TWENTY-EIGHT

ONCE SHE'D GAINED control of a laughter that was somehow completely mirthless, Mrs. Lipman looked at me and said, "Obviously, you're more intelligent than I gave you credit for in high school, Samantha." *Well, thank you. I think.* "Why don't you tell me how you reached this conclusion."

I supposed I should have been frightened. After all, I was sitting in the middle of nowhere with a woman carrying a rather threatening hickory walking stick who could well be a murderer. But I wasn't frightened. Even if Mrs. Lipman had killed Caleb Mayo, I never thought for a moment that she would harm me. And if she wanted to know my reasoning, I was willing to tell her.

"Mostly it was how you acted and what you said when you found Wally and me in the back lot after my little sling experiment. If Wally was clueless about Mayo's discovery, and he sure seemed to be, you were not. You stepped forward as if you were about to say something, then stopped and simply glared at me. I think you realized at that moment that Wally's confusion was a point in his favor, so you said nothing and just gave me one of your looks."

"My looks?"

"Actually," I said, "The Look. The one you used to give us in high school when we stepped out of line."

Mrs. Lipman almost smiled. "Oh," she said, nodding. "That look."

"And," I continued, "you were so sure that your son had nothing to fear that you actually gave me his carrier case to have it checked by forensics. How could you be so sure unless you knew who the killer really was? But, in hindsight, what really pointed to you was what you said in Wally's defense. 'He's not that smart.'"

Mrs. Lipman nodded. "It just slipped out."

"At the time I thought that was kind of an odd thing to say. I hadn't mentioned a sling as a possible weapon in Mayo's murder. I'd just said that Wally might have used a candlepin ball as a weapon. You don't have to be very smart to hit someone on the head with a bowling ball. Even Wally was capable of that. But eventually it came to me. When you said your son wasn't that smart, *you were staring at the sling in my hand.* You knew exactly what it was and why I had it. It didn't surprise you at all. Because you had made it yourself. To kill Caleb Mayo. Who had threatened to expose your son's troubled past and deal a crippling blow to your business."

I stopped and turned to Mrs. Lipman, who was staring out across the expanse of Crystal Bay all the way to the horizon where sea met sky, the stick lying forgotten across her lap.

"I'm sorry, Mrs. Lipman," I said. "I'm truly sorry."

"Don't be sorry," she said. "Never be sorry for searching for the truth. It is the foundation of all scientific advancement. All truth is good."

Well, maybe so, but it certainly didn't feel good at that moment.

"You know, Samantha, as much as I was able, I told the truth about what happened that morning. It was true that when I arrived, I saw no one in the deliveries lot. However, I failed to mention that, a little later, I went back out to my car to get some files I'd forgotten and saw a gentleman in a Santa costume walking toward me. It was not until he got closer that I realized it was Caleb Mayo, primarily because of that unfortunate nose of his. What did surprise me was that he was clearly coming to talk to me. Caleb Mayo and I have had a long and unhappy professional relationship for years, starting when I applied to Fair Harbor High School as a science teacher more than thirty years ago, when the man had just been elected to the school board. Perhaps I should explain that as background, Samantha?"

"Of course, Mrs. Lipman," I said politely

"Mrs. Lipman," she repeated quietly, almost to herself. "It all started there. With Mrs. Lipman." She turned slightly toward me. "You see, Samantha, I wasn't *Mrs.* Lipman. I was *Miss* Lipman."

I didn't see, but I had a feeling I would soon.

"I'd come from a school system in a suburb of Milwaukee. When I first interviewed here, I mentioned that I was a single mother. No one batted an eye or asked about the circumstances. That is, until I sat down with Caleb Mayo, who began with, 'And where, may I ask, is *Mr.* Lipman?'"

I felt my hackles rise at the nerve of the man, but said nothing. I didn't want to stop the flow of Mrs. Lipman's recollection.

"I wanted this job. I needed this job. But I immediately knew the kind of man I was dealing with here—self-righteous and trigger-happy with it. I knew he would not approve of 'divorced mother.' And the actual 'unmarried mother' would be completely reprehensible. And so I did what I'd sworn I'd never do. I lied. 'I'm a widow,' I said. Now, a widow, *that* was respectable. So a widow I became and a widow I stayed. Nobody checked, nobody asked questions. And, in truth, saying I was a widow made everything so much easier, particularly with Walter, who was just a baby at the time. I made his imaginary father as dull as I could, so as not to encourage questions. 'Your father was an accountant. He died in a car accident.' This was infinitely preferable to the truth about his real father—a married man who wanted nothing to do with me or his child when I became pregnant."

I didn't say anything. There was nothing to say.

"Things went along fairly smoothly after that. I was eventually made head of the science department, and when the post of principal became vacant, it was a natural progression to apply. I was in my midfifties with almost thirty years of teaching and administrative experience. But Caleb Mayo was against my application from the first. He had another candidate in mind, Kevin Inglesby, a person with far less experience but two overwhelming advantages, in Mr. Mayo's eyes."

"Which were?" I asked.

"One, he was a man. And, two, that he didn't push new-fangled ideas like an environmental studies curriculum."

"And was the school board convinced by these arguments?"

"Apparently not. But that didn't stop Caleb Mayo. He took it upon himself to call the principal from my old school, now long retired. He asked him if he saw any reason why I shouldn't be promoted to principal. Absolutely not, my former boss said. He'd been terribly sorry to lose me, but, of course, completely understood why I'd needed to make a new start. People, he said, were not so understanding in those days and in that part of the country about women who weren't married getting pregnant and choosing to raise the child on their own—particularly when they were teachers. He thought I'd done the right thing by moving to a part of the country where people had a more liberal attitude. Good soul that he was, he assumed that I'd been open about my circumstances. It never occurred to him that

I would have lied about them. But now the truth was out, and Caleb Mayo had all the ammunition he needed to claim I was unfit for the principal's job."

"But all this happened thirty years ago," I protested. "Surely your record and reputation as a teacher outweighed the circumstances that brought you to Fair Harbor. People really aren't bothered by the concept of single motherhood. If anything, they think it's a brave choice."

"Perhaps. I would like to hope so. But that's not the cudgel that Caleb Mayo decided to use. The day after his phone call, he told me what he'd learned. He was, he said, not concerned that I was an 'unwed mother.'"

"He actually used that term?"

"Oh, yes, and with great relish," Mrs. Lipman said with a grim smile. "But, he said, what he could not overlook was that some thirty years ago I had lied on my application forms. He was right. When I was initially interviewed by the board, all they had in front of them was my résumé. Once I'd passed that review, I'd filled in the formal application forms, in which I stated that I was a widow. The form included a sworn statement that all the information I'd provided was correct and truthful. To include false or misleading information was then and still is grounds for dismissal."

Now it was my turn to express my frustration. I kicked out at a pine cone at my feet, missing it entirely but sending a spray of damp sand all over Diogi. He promptly shook himself all over, spraying the two of us in return.

"So," Mrs. Lipman continued, as if nothing had happened, "Caleb Mayo said, given the 'gravity of my actions,' as he put it, he would have to take what he'd learned to the school board. Not that he wanted to, he said, but it was 'the right thing to do.' We both knew that even if the board met in closed session, the word would get out. Caleb Mayo would make sure of that. But, he assured me, he didn't want to 'ruin my reputation.' As if I or anyone cared about my circumstances thirty years ago or even if I'd lied about them on a job application."

"But he knew what you *did* care about," I said.

She nodded. "Yes, he knew. What I did care about was that if he went to the board, Walter was certain to find out that I had been lying to him all his life. So Mr. Mayo proposed a solution: I would simply withdraw my application for the principal's post, and he would drop the whole thing."

"And you agreed," I said.

"I agreed. Even though I was sure he was looking forward to years of holding what he knew over me."

"But you didn't give him that satisfaction," I said. "Not only did you withdraw your application for the post, a year later you retired altogether."

"Well, I hope that was a disappointment to him," she said with another wry smile, "even though he insisted that his only concern was that a person of 'absolute probity' become principal of Fair Harbor High School. I have to admit it was amusing to me that he thought Kevin Inglesby was an example of absolute probity. There's a secret drinker if I ever saw one."

I remembered the victory dance at the bowling alley. Not goofy? Drunk?

"When I learned that Irwin Smith was selling the Lanes, I thought that might be a solution. At least for Walter, who'd been having trouble finding his feet." *Well, that's one way of putting it.*

"But you gave up a job you loved," I protested. "You gave up your ambitions, your identity as an educator, Mrs. Lipman."

Her face twisted then. "I didn't give it up. Caleb Mayo took it from me. I went from training generations of young people how to think critically to taking inventory of Lucky Strike Lanes T-shirts." The bitterness in her voice was palpable. "The only thing that made it bearable was that I'd never have to see or deal with Caleb Mayo again."

"Until last week."

She nodded. "Until last week. You see, it wasn't Walter whom Caleb Mayo wanted to confront. It was me. I think you will find that what Caleb Mayo really likes, *liked*, to do is pick on women. Particularly women in a position of weakness, women who can't or won't fight back. My Walter is a strong young man. Caleb Mayo wasn't going to go face-to-face with him. But he knew what losing our liquor license could mean to the Lanes. To me. He cornered me in the back lot and began to talk at me. He took his time, enjoying the unfolding of his tale. It seemed to take forever, hours and hours, but it probably was no more than ten minutes. He told me what he'd learned about Walter's . . . mistakes. That he intended to report Walter, who is a co-owner with me of the Lanes, to the town's select board. He said it was the right thing to do."

"And you decided you had to stop him."

"No. Not at all. Not then. I admit that for a moment I felt a brief rage, like a lick of fire through my veins. But I was too stunned, too shocked to argue, to think. I just turned and walked away. And then something stopped me. I glanced back and saw him going into the open back door of the Ginger Jar."

I really don't want to hear this, I thought. *Why do you always get involved, Sam? Why can't you learn?*

"And then I thought, no. I am not helpless. I am not weak. I will stand up to Caleb Mayo. I will ask him what kind of a man takes away a woman's livelihood, not once but twice? What kind of man will not give a young man who made one mistake a second chance? It wouldn't do any good, but at least I would have the satisfaction of holding a mirror up to him, forcing him to see himself."

I thought of Helene's words when I asked why Mayo had

chosen to play Santa: "*to hide from himself what kind of man he really was.*"

"It couldn't have been two minutes since he'd left me. I crossed the delivery area, vaguely aware of some kind of country music coming from the kitchen window, which was open a crack. I walked into the back room, tripping over a crate of coconuts placed inconveniently near the door, knocking a few to the floor, and almost pulling down a clothesline full of wet compression hose and a few smocks that I assumed belonged to the cleaner in the kitchen."

At least I'm not the only clumsy one, I thought irrelevantly.

"As I made my way into the hallway, I was aware that the music had stopped and I heard voices coming from the kitchen. That seemed very odd to me. Caleb Mayo was not the kind of man to stop in for a friendly chat with a cleaning lady. So I went over and peered through the little window in the one of the kitchen doors, where I saw Mayo in conversation, if you could call it that, with the cleaner. It did not look like a friendly chat. She looked as if all the blood had been drained from her body, as if the mop she held in her hands was all that was holding her up. I pushed the swinging door open a crack. I heard Caleb Mayo threatening legal action to take away her adopted niece. At this, the fire in my veins rose again. What worse fate could there be than to have a beloved child taken away from you?"

All this, I realized, explained why Mrs. Lipman hadn't been surprised when I'd said Mayo had confronted Liz, but had been appalled when I'd told her he'd threatened Beth as well.

"Shocked to my core, I turned and left the building. I thought I would wait in the lot until Mayo came out, but when he didn't, I went back in, curious as to what was happening. Ever the scientist. I peered into the hall from the back room just in time to see Caleb Mayo slipping into the Brunis' office. I tiptoed across, opened the door a crack, and peeked inside. His back was to me. He was going through the Brunis' file cabinet."

Don't tell me, Mrs. Lipman. I really don't want to know. But it was too late for that.

"And that's where you got it very right, Samantha. That's when I thought, *enough is enough.* This man will not ruin this woman's and this girl's lives like he's ruined mine. I will stop him. And if I go to jail for it, so be it. But how? What could I do? Hit the man on the head? With what? The obvious choice was a ball from the Lanes. But that would certainly point to me, or worse, Walter. Not to mention that, though a candlepin ball would be enough in the hands of a strong man, it would be ineffectual in mine. What could I use instead and how could I increase the weapon's velocity and force? It took about a nanosecond for me to resolve both questions. There was a box of coconuts right to hand. And there were those compression socks on the clothesline. No one knew better than I how effective a sling I could make with those two things. Particularly if I timed and aimed the blow exactly right. At this, the fire in my veins was replaced with ice. I had a workable hypothesis based on science. Now I only had to prove it correct."

Mrs. Lipman paused. I really, really didn't want to hear the details of what happened next. But I was committed now, and I would have to see this thing through to the end.

"Tell me," I said. "Tell me what you did next."

Mrs. Lipman nodded and took a breath. "I closed the door gently, went back into the storage room, pulled one of the stockings off the line, and dropped the largest of the coconuts into it. Then I walked back to the office, the sling in my hand. When I opened the door, Caleb Mayo was so intent on his dirty work that he never noticed. My thought was I would take two steps forward until I was about three feet behind him, calculating that this would be the best parabola for the swing, creating the most centripetal force. Centripetal force is when—"

"I know what centripetal force is, Mrs. Lipman," I said quietly. "I learned about it from you."

"Oh, of course you did. Well, I'm glad something stuck." *You shouldn't be*, I thought. *It was your undoing.*

"My plan was this. I would give just a little cough, just enough for him to hear it. My calculations were that he would only half turn, as his hands were deep in the files, presenting me with the most vulnerable portion of his skull, the pterion, which you probably know as the temple. I knew that just beneath this thin bit of skull is the middle meningeal artery. If you get hit with due force on this spot, this artery can rupture, causing unconsciousness and eventually death from pressure on the brain. When you hear about someone dying from a single blow in a bar fight, that's probably what happened."

"How do you even *know* this?" I asked.

"Ironically, Kevin Inglesby told me. He'd brought his biology class out to watch the sling experiment. Afterward, in the teachers' lounge, he man-splained to me how a single blow to the temple could have taken Goliath down. So I was fairly confident that I could make it work."

She stopped, almost as if she'd come to the end of the story.

"And then . . ." I prompted her.

"And then, nothing," she said. "I did nothing. I couldn't go through with it."

My heart leaped.

"You couldn't go through with it," I repeated.

"I couldn't," she said. "There was a chair in the hall next to the office door. I put the sling down on it, and I turned around and left. You may not believe me, but that's what I did. Nothing."

Here's the thing. I *did* believe her. Mrs. Lipman as a killer had never made sense to me. But all the evidence had pointed either to Liz Voorhees or to her. I did not believe it was Liz. And I no longer believed it was Mrs. Lipman.

"I believe you," I said firmly. "I believe you walked away. I believe you didn't kill Caleb Mayo."

Mrs. Lipman looked at me steadily, letting my words sink in.

"Thank you, Samantha," she said. "But you must realize that means I cannot alibi Liz Voorhees, much as I would like to. Indeed, my story, if it is even believed, would point the finger at her as Caleb Mayo's killer. In effect, I gave her the weapon."

"I do realize that," I said. "But I still don't think she was the killer."

"You continue to surprise me, Samantha Barnes," Mrs. Lipman said dryly.

I told Mrs. Lipman about finally remembering what had been niggling at me about Liz ever since I first found Mayo's body.

"When I asked her if she'd touched anything in the office, she said, 'I'm not the one taking other people's stuff.' And when she quit her job at the Ginger Jar, she was clearly annoyed by something that Martin didn't seem to take very seriously. I began to wonder: Had someone taken something of hers? Possibly one of her compression hose? They aren't cheap, and for a woman with her income, she would feel the loss even if Martin didn't think it was such a big deal."

Mrs. Lipman nodded her understanding.

"So I went to Jillian Munsell, who runs Shawme Manor," I continued. "Liz had applied there once she decided to leave the Ginger Jar. Jillian told me that Liz had said somebody at the restaurant had 'light fingers,' that they'd taken one of her 'special socks.'"

"Well, then, that's a point in Liz Voorhees's favor," Mrs. Lipman said. "If she'd made the sling out of one of her support hose, why draw attention to its disappearance?"

"That's exactly what I thought," I said. "Why, if she had used it as part of a weapon, would she even mention it? The only answer was that she *hadn't* used it. She hadn't killed Mayo."

"So that led you to me."

"Yes, I'm sorry. It did."

"No need to apologize. You were only going where the evidence led you. I take it you haven't told anyone your theory about me as the killer yet?"

If this were a TV show, here is where you would shout at the screen, "Don't let her know that, you dope! Now she'll knock you on the head with that stick of hers!"

But this wasn't a TV show. And despite the fact that Helene would no doubt later chide me for not being very, very careful, I told Mrs. Lipman the truth.

"No," I said. "I haven't shared that with anyone yet."

Nothing happened. Mrs. Lipman did not hit me on the head with that stick of hers. All she did was ask, "Why did you come to me first?"

"Truthfully," I said, "I didn't think anyone would believe me. All you would have to do is deny seeing Mayo that day. So no motive and certainly no proof. But Mrs. Mayo is going to the police to tell them that she also heard her husband threaten Liz and that Liz said she'd see him in hell first."

"Oh," Mrs. Lipman interrupted, "that is not good."

"No, not good," I agreed. "So I decided that my only hope was the possibility that you would confess to save her from being convicted of a crime that you'd committed."

"You thought I was a murderer, but you also thought I'd sacrifice myself for someone else?"

"Yes," I said. "I don't know how to explain it, but I thought the Mrs. Lipman I knew would do that."

"I still can, you know," Mrs. Lipman said. "I can and will go to the authorities with my part in this terrible story. Quite frankly, it would be a relief to finally tell the truth. I am deeply uncomfortable with lies. But part of that truth is, I am not sorry that Caleb Mayo is dead. Had he died in his sleep, I would have rejoiced. But I am deeply ashamed that Caleb Mayo died because in a moment of rage, I left behind a weapon for some other poor soul to use to kill him and thus ruin their own life. But I'm afraid, my dear, that it won't absolve Liz Voorhees. Indeed, the authorities may feel that I made it easier for her to have done the deed."

"Yes, I know," I acknowledged. "But it also means that anyone nearby could have seen Mayo go into the Ginger Jar followed by you. And then, when they saw you come out, gone in themselves, seen the sling, and used it to kill Caleb Mayo. It opens the door to possibilities other than Liz."

"I would hope so," Mrs. Lipman said. "But I'm afraid it's far more likely that the authorities will decide that I am the killer. They will surely realize that there are very few people who would see an old support hose with a lump in it on a chair and say to themselves, aha, I can use this as a weapon. No, I'm afraid they will recognize that the killer has to be someone who, one, knew about the sling experiment and would recognize the sling for what it was; two, had a good reason for wanting to kill Caleb Mayo; and three, was either very lucky or, more likely, knew precisely where to aim the sling to do the maximum damage. And I'm afraid the only person who fits all those criteria is me. Nonetheless, I'm fully prepared to go to the authorities with my story."

"You were always planning to do that, weren't you?" I asked. "There was no need for you to tell me the whole story unless you planned to take it to the police."

"Not always," she admitted. "My sincere hope was that the case would remain unsolved. When Walter was cleared, I thought all was well. But given the weight of circumstantial evidence against Liz Voorhees that you outlined, I cannot remain silent. I can't stand by and let an innocent person be accused of a crime that I very much doubt she committed. I have to come forward."

And then she gave me The Look. "As you knew very well I would, Samantha."

"Well, I *hoped* you would," I acknowledged. "I wouldn't say I *knew* you would. And let's not forget that I actually believed you'd killed Caleb Mayo."

"But only as a result of rational thought," Mrs. Lipman said, as if somehow that absolved me. "And you were very close to the truth. I came very close to that truth. I'm sorry I underestimated you in high school, Samantha. I should have recognized your potential."

There was the old Mrs. Lipman I knew and loved, dedicated to her profession, to her students, to radical honesty. I was relieved to have her back.

"I didn't give you much to work with," I said with a smile. "As I recall, I spent most of my time in your class cracking wise with my friends."

"Oh, yes," she said with some of her old brisk manner. "That Miles Tanner and Jennifer Snow. You were quite a troublesome trio. Not that I blamed you. I knew what it felt like to be a bit of a misfit. And I must admit, I liked you all. You were really quite amusing."

"We liked you, too, Mrs. Lipman," I said sincerely. "And we loved your class."

"Thank you, Samantha," she replied with some of her old dignity. "And now, let's go talk to the authorities and let them clap me into handcuffs if they wish."

But to tell the truth, I wasn't really listening. My brain had started doing that thing where snippets of information—things people had said to me, things I'd seen, things I'd forgotten—began to line up like soldiers coming into formation.

"No, Mrs. Lipman," I said, vaguely, "they're not going to clap handcuffs on you."

"If not me, Samantha, then who?"

"Give me a minute," I said.

To give her credit, Mrs. Lipman simply sat and waited.

It wasn't a just minute. Maybe five. Maybe ten. I honestly couldn't tell you how long I sat there, putting it all together. Finally I looked up at my companion.

"The person they'll be clapping into handcuffs," I said, "will be Kevin Inglesby."

TWENTY-NINE

_{~~~~~~~~}

T O GIVE HER credit, Mrs. Lipman did not give me one of her usual "would you care to explain your evidence for this preposterous hypothesis" looks. Instead, she simply waited for me to do so.

When I'd finished, she stood up from the bench, carefully brushing a few stray pine needles off her slacks, and said, "Given what you've told me, Samantha, I think it behooves us to speak to Mr. Inglesby before I incriminate myself or Liz Voorhees with the police."

Then she paused and gave me what I swear was a mischievous smile. "It's the right thing to do."

As it turns out, by "we" Mrs. Lipman meant me. But that was fine. We planned my little conversation with Kevin Inglesby carefully. Both of us were hoping that the man would fold like a two-dollar umbrella when confronted with the case against him. Because there was absolutely no evidence to support my contention.

"The only problem is finding him," I pointed out. "We don't even know where he lives."

"Ah, but we do know where he plays," Mrs. Lipman said.

I looked at her blankly.

"At the Lanes," she said with a little sigh at my obtuseness. "He plays at the Lanes. On league night. And tonight is league night."

Which is how I found myself back at the Lucky Strike Lanes, once again surrounded by a cacophony of bowling balls rumbling down the lanes, downed bowling pins clattering, shouts of laughter and banter. I found Kevin Inglesby exactly where Mrs. Lipman had said he would be, with the Oddballs in their usual lane seven.

This was not the Kevin Inglesby I remembered from before. Yes, he was clearly under the influence of the five beer bottles I counted on the table in front of him and the one currently in his hand. But this was not the Kevin Inglesby of the victory dance. He wasn't even bowling, just sitting on one of the lane's molded plastic seats, sucking down a beer. He'd clearly decided to sit the game out in favor of getting himself quietly loaded. And he looked like hell. If he'd shaved in the past week, you'd never have known it. His eyes were red rimmed and his mouth was curiously twisted, as if he'd eaten something bad and couldn't get rid of the taste. It was a curious combination of despair and bad temper, and it made me very certain that I was right about Kevin Inglesby.

It also should have made me very, very careful.

Instead, I walked over to him, my bag slung over my shoulder and a reporter's notepad in my hand.

"Principal Inglesby?" I said, tapping him on the shoulder gently to get his attention.

The man pulled himself together with an obvious effort. As I had pointed out, he was the principal of Fair Harbor High, after all.

"Yes?" he responded cautiously, and I could almost hear him asking himself what fresh hell this could be.

"My name is Samantha Barnes and I'm looking into the death of Caleb Mayo for the Cape Cod *Clarion*," I lied. But it was okay because I had my fingers crossed.

The man blanched and took a long pull from his beer, noticed that it was now empty, and took up another one, still capped, but said nothing.

"I have a theory about Mr. Mayo's death," I continued, officiously flipping the notepad open as if to check my notes. "And I thought that before we published the piece you might want to comment on this theory."

"Why would I want to do that?" he asked with a kind of false bravado.

"Because it involves you, *Principal* Inglesby," I said. He stiffened again as I laid the stress on his job title. "And I thought you might want to make a statement, get your side of the story out there." *You see, Mom, you taught me well.*

And with that, all the bravado was gone. He didn't even pretend not to know what I was talking about. He stood up, swaying just a bit. So not totally out of it. Yet.

"Let's get out of here," he said.

Yesss.

"Okay," I said. "We can talk in the office." Where, I did not add, Mrs. Lipman will be hiding in the supply closet, taping our conversation.

"No," he said truculently. "Outside." He pointed with the unopened beer toward the hallway that led to the Lanes's back room and through it to the deliveries lot.

Oh god, oh god, oh god.

I made my decision in an instant. We had only one shot at this, and I was going to take it.

"Okay," I said.

I went through the hallway, Inglesby following me. We went out through the back door, which swung open easily, almost silently, and then clanged closed behind us. My eyes probed the dark lot beyond the light cast by the wire-encased bulb over the door. No cars except for the Lipmans' and the Brunis' Tesla. No people. It was a chilly night. And Fair Harbor is a town where the sidewalks roll up pretty early anyway. Nobody was out who didn't have to be out. Inglesby and I were alone.

Well, I was determined to make the best of it. Surely Mrs. Lipman would begin to wonder where I was if I didn't turn up in her office soon. Hadn't she said something about a buzzer that sounded when the back door was opened? But could she hear that from the supply closet? I decided to believe she could. I turned to face Inglesby.

"Over there," he said, gesturing to the shadows outside our dim pool of light. "Nobody needs to know our business." As he stood there, beer in hand, he looked a lot less like a high school principal than a barroom thug.

I told myself to stop being fanciful. This was my chance. I moved over a bit into the murk, telling myself a few feet wasn't going to make any difference. And I was fairly sure that, given his alcohol level, Inglesby would admit what he'd done. If I stated the case against him forcefully enough.

"Okay," I said firmly, "here's my theory, Principal Inglesby. You killed Caleb Mayo."

Inglesby looked at me, unsurprised, swaying slightly. I could almost see him trying to put on his "I am the principal" face, the mantle of authority.

"Why would I kill Caleb Mayo?" he asked. "He's my champion. He got me my job."

"He *was* your champion," I corrected him. "But that changed recently. When your drinking problem became a lot more noticeable. Even to Caleb Mayo. His wife told me she'd tattled about your victory dance at the Lanes to her husband and 'he did not like it one bit.'"

Inglesby glared at me. He knew exactly where I was going.

"When I first started reporting on this story"—fingers still crossed—"Tom Wylie at the Windward told me that Mayo 'had a real bee in his bonnet' about drinking, was always asking him who he had to shut off, who had gotten his car keys taken away. I wonder if Tom Wylie ever had to take your car keys away. And if he told Mayo that."

At this point, Inglesby tried to take a swallow from the beer in his hand, only to find the bottle still capped. He stared at it uncomprehendingly. I brought his attention back to me. "Also, Wilma once said something about you riding your bike down Main Street at the Santa Selebration," I continued. "Which makes me wonder why you weren't driving, considering how cold it was."

Inglesby tried again to gather his dignity. "It's a conscious choice, given the rate of global warming. When I can, I use the bicycle."

I shook my head. "Or maybe you weren't *allowed* to drive. Maybe, I thought, you'd had your license suspended? Maybe for drunk driving? And, if so, I wondered if Caleb Mayo knew about it."

"I don't have any DUI," Inglesby protested. "You can check on that. Believe me, if I had a DUI, everybody in this damn town would know about it."

The man had exchanged aggrieved dignity for a kind of aggressive self-pity, and it made me uncomfortable, but I pressed on.

"That occurred to me, too," I said. "And then I remembered something that Chief McCauley said to the detective in charge of the murder investigation, something about being 'tight' with Mayo. What if you had been pulled over, given a Breathalyzer and then—what with you being the high school principal and a pillar of the community and all—had just been given a warning? Wouldn't it make sense, in that case, for McCauley to go to his friend and school board member Caleb Mayo and put a friendly word in his ear? Tell him to make sure the high school principal cleaned up his act so he didn't look like a fool for putting you in the job?"

Inglesby said nothing. My eyes had adjusted to the darkness by now and I could see him looking at me like a cornered rat. It was kind of scary. But I pressed on.

"And here's the worst part. When you were stopped, you told the patrolman you were speeding because you were late for picking up some kids on the debate team to take them to a competition in Hyannis. That, of course, was before you were Breathalyzed."

This, actually, was total conjecture on my part. Well, on the part of Mrs. Lipman. But it made sense. As we'd been marshaling our arguments, she'd recalled a friend of hers who was still teaching at the high school complaining about what she called the principal's "la-di-da" attitude.

"She's the advisor to the debate club," Mrs. Lipman had explained. "Apparently, Inglesby was supposed to help ferry some students to a debate in Hyannis but never showed. He claimed car trouble, which my friend did not believe for one minute." She had paused and then added, "And now that I think about it, that was about the time he became the great global citizen and stopped driving altogether."

It didn't take long for us to put two and two together.

"You were *fully intending to drive in that condition with kids in the car*," I accused Inglesby. I had fully intended to be neutral, to keep the temperature down, but I have to admit, I wasn't succeeding. "And once Mayo found *that* out, you were not his golden boy anymore."

"You stupid, nosy girl," the cornered rat snarled. "You can't prove any of this."

Where are you, Mrs. Lipman? one side of my brain was shouting. But the other side was saying, *Keep it up, Sam—you're getting close.*

"I can prove it," I lied. "It's just a matter of McCauley confirming it." *Easier said than done*, but Inglesby didn't know that. Was McCauley really going to admit that, knowing what he knew, he hadn't taken Inglesby's license away?

"And anyway," Inglesby said, leaning into me, his breath sour in my face, "I didn't need Caleb Mayo to be my best friend anymore."

He all but said *not once he'd gotten me the principal's job*. But I noticed he hadn't bothered to deny that Mayo knew about his little encounter with the law. *Score one for Sam.*

"Yeah, you did need Mayo," I shot back. "Your contract is up for renewal this year. And if Mayo could make you principal, Mayo could make you unemployed. And that," I announced triumphantly in my best Miss Marple imitation, "was exactly what he told you he was going to do when he saw you at the Selebration in front of the Ginger Jar. Wilma saw you and Mayo saw you. He told her to stop the car so he could talk to someone. And that someone was *you*. Caleb Mayo told you he wasn't going to support renewing your contract."

Again, Inglesby didn't bother denying any of this.

"And I did what?" he asked. "Hit the guy on the head with my trusty bicycle lock?"

"No," I said. "You hit the guy on the head with the sling you found in the Ginger Jar when you went in to beg Mayo to reconsider."

There was a shocked silence, and I knew I had it right. But Inglesby wasn't giving up without a fight.

"You're talking crap," he growled.

"I don't think so," I said. "I think Mayo took you into the back lot where you could talk in private and told you his plan. You knew you'd never get another job in education if all this came out. You pleaded with him to give you another chance, but Mayo wasn't having any of it. Instead, he came all Mr. Rectitude on you, made you feel even smaller than you already did. I can only imagine how infuriating that must have been."

If I thought the sympathy vote might get Inglesby to confess, I had another think coming.

"You need to shut up right about now," he said quietly, and his fingers clenched the beer bottle in his hand. *Okay, fine, anger also loosens the tongue.*

"And then he left you there and headed into the Ginger Jar. I think you decided to wait for him to come out, to try to convince him once more to reconsider. But instead of Mayo coming out of the restaurant, Mrs. Lipman went in. So you decided to wait some more. Then she came out again. But no Mayo. You must have been beside yourself by that point. You needed to *talk* to the man. So you went looking for him."

"This is all bull," Inglesby said, slurring his words just a little. "You can't prove any of this."

He was right of course. Which is why I had to get him worked up enough to admit something, anything. I continued as if he hadn't interrupted.

"You went into the back room of the Ginger Jar and then began walking down the hall. There was some kind of loud music coming from somewhere but nobody was in sight. That's when you noticed what looked like one of the slings from the David and Goliath experiment on a chair outside a door marked 'Office.' Curious, you picked it up. It was still in your hand when you looked into the office and saw Caleb Mayo with his back to you, searching through the file cabinet."

By this point Inglesby was looking at me as if I were some kind of demon. I could almost see his brain, fogged by alcohol as it was, trying to make sense of how I could know all this.

"And then, it came to you," I continued inexorably. "It came to you that you could literally solve all your problems with one blow. You stepped into the room, and when Mayo turned to see who had come in, you whirled the sling, hitting him at the exact point on his temple that you knew would do the most damage."

Inglesby made a kind of weird, scary noise, almost like a growl at that, but I didn't stop.

"I don't blame you"—fingers still crossed—"for what you did. He was a malicious man, happy to ruin your life. He'd never give you another chance. You knew that. You just did what had to be done."

And that's when things got *really* scary for yours truly. I realized too late that I'd been very foolish to expect my reconstruction and false sympathy would make Inglesby think I was on his side.

He stepped toward me and said, very slowly and very quietly, no longer slurring his words, "And you're not going to give me that chance either, are you?"

Before I could respond or even make a sound, the hand with the beer bottle was swinging back. I knew in a split second what was coming. That bottle was going to hit me on the forward swing at the exact point on my temple where Kevin Inglesby knew it would do the most damage.

"Not so fast, dude."

I couldn't even process it. It looked as if Kevin Inglesby's arm had literally disappeared.

And then he screamed with pain, and I realized it hadn't disappeared. It had just been twisted behind his back.

By Wally Lipman.

THIRTY

"HOW DID YOU know?"

I took a break from scarfing down the best oyster stew *ever* and looked at Jenny, my eyebrows raised.

"How did I know that we could actually find something you would eat at an all seafood restaurant? It's my *job* to know that."

"No, you big dope," Jenny said, popping another tiny fried codfish cake into her mouth and wiping a dribble of dipping sauce off her chin. "How did you know that Kevin Inglesby killed Caleb Mayo?"

"Oh, that," I said uneasily.

It had only been three days since Wally Lipman had stepped out from the Lanes's back door and subdued my attacker with one swift move. And, even more impressive, with one hand, seeing as I'd broken his other arm. *For which I am deeply sorry.*

As it turned out, the buzzer on the Lanes's back door had alerted Mrs. Lipman, and she'd gone into the back room to see what was going on. She'd heard me and Inglesby talking outside and opened the door a crack. This had not been part of our plan, but she would adapt to the change, still be my secret witness. But first she went back into the Lanes to get her son. Just in case things got out of hand. She'd told him earlier about my scheme to try and crack Inglesby and save her from being a suspect in Mayo's murder. And apparently, you don't mess with Wally when he's defending the woman who's defending his mom. Even with only one good arm, Wally had incapacitated Inglesby within a matter of seconds once it was clear what he intended. Wally Lipman saved my life. Wally Lipman is my friend forever.

But so far I hadn't been able to bring myself to talk about what had happened, or almost happened, with anyone. There is no joy in finding a murderer. There is only justice. I hadn't even spoken about it to Jason, who seemed instinctively to understand my reluctance.

"Of course he understands," Helene had said. "When introverts are distressed, they retreat inside themselves. It would seem completely natural to him if you didn't want to talk about it."

"Well, it doesn't seem natural to me," I said. "I like a lot of yammer, yammer, yammer when I'm distressed. Is introversion catching or something?"

Helene had laughed. "Not as far as I know. I wouldn't worry, though. The time will come when you'll be ready to talk about it. Or somebody else will decide you're ready to talk about it. Just not Jason."

Apparently, Jenny had decided the time had come.

"C'mon, Hercule Poirot, spill it," she commanded. "Tell us how you used your little gray cells to solve the Mystery of the Dead Santa."

I looked around the table. The girls' night out at Wellfleet's Fish House had done a lot to restore my usual faith in humanity. My mother had approached the dinner with her usual reporter's zeal, peppering our poor server with questions until he was forced to bring out the chef to answer them all. Jillian had guided us to her favorite items on the menu, including a wonderful Portuguese kale and linguica soup (a Provincetown staple) in which the kale had been julienned into lovely slivers and the linguica carefully removed from its casing. A day boat fish sandwich that might have just been very, very good was transformed into fantastic with the addition of a tartar sauce made with Old Bay seasoning. And Jenny's crispy little codfish cakes proved that she will eat pretty much anything if you deep-fry it. I did my usual discreet tasting of everyone's dishes, making mental notes for the enthusiastic review I fully intended to write.

But now, it appeared, I was going to have to explain myself.

"First of all, I didn't *know* it was Kevin Inglesby," I said. "I'm no Hercule Poirot. How could I be? He works with the police and gets to listen to evidence and testimony. I'm more of a Miss Marple, an amateur who has to rely on gossip or just a friendly talk over a cup of tea. Or coffee in my case. I have never been so over-caffeinated in my life than this past week."

"Also, like Miss Marple, you have a friend in the force who helps you out a bit," Helene said with a grin.

I gave her a look of mock outrage. "My *friend in the force* will tell you that, more often than not, it works the other way round."

"*And* Sam has a knack for knowing the right questions to ask," my mother chimed in.

I wasn't sure if this was professional or maternal pride. Probably professional. My mother doesn't do maternal pride. Not on the outside anyway. I blew her a kiss across the table.

"It's just that when something niggles at me, I can't let it go," I explained. "It's like trying a put a name to that elusive spice you're tasting in a new dish at your favorite restaurant. I can't rest until I figure it out, because in my head I want to know the whole recipe."

Jenny did one of those circles with her hand that means "c'mon, c'mon."

"Okay, okay," I said. "Anyway, like I said, I didn't *know* it was Inglesby. I went through a lot of other suspects first."

"And there was always the possibility that the death was a mob hit in retaliation for Mayo refusing to sell his company to them," my mother broke in.

"Seriously, Mother?" I said. "I can't believe you're still banging that drum."

"Nah," she said dismissively. "I gave up on that a long time ago." *Really? Then what were you doing on all those mysterious day trips before Christmas?*

"*Whatever*," I said with a sigh. "As I was saying, there were a lot of other local candidates for Mayo's killer."

I went through the whole roll call—Martin Bruni, Wally Lipman, Wilma Mayo, Liz Voorhees. They loved my accidental candlepin-ball-in-the-compression-hose experiment on Wally.

"Oh, jeez," Jenny said with relish, "I wish I'd been there to see that. Except for when Mrs. Lipman got mad at you."

"Yeah, that was uncomfortable," I admitted.

And then I explained why I'd suspected Mrs. Lipman, at which point Helene interrupted. "And then," she said, her voice cold, "You decided that the intelligent next step was to go for a nice long walk on a deserted property with a woman you thought was a murderer and tell her all about your suspicions?"

Helene seems to feel it is her role to scold me for what she feels is risky behavior. Goodness knows, somebody had to do it. My mother sure wasn't going to. She saw that kind of behavior as completely normal.

"I wasn't afraid of Mrs. Lipman," I said. "Even if she had killed Mayo, I knew she'd never hurt me. I just knew that."

Jenny nodded. "Of course Mrs. Lipman would never hurt you," she said as if it was obvious. Which it was, to us.

"But I also knew, or hoped I knew, that if I told her how strong the case was against Liz Voorhees, she would turn herself in to prevent that miscarriage of justice."

"But if I'm following this correctly," my mother said, "she didn't do it."

I nodded. "She couldn't go through with it."

"Of course she couldn't do it," said Mrs. Lipman's number one fan.

"So why did this woman tell you what she had planned to do?" Jillian asked. "She certainly didn't have to do that."

"You're right, Jillian," I said. "No one had seen or heard Mayo talking to Dorothy Lipman. But she knew it was Liz's only chance, even if it was a slim one."

"Yes," Jenny said, "that sounds like Mrs. Lipman."

I nodded. "There was every chance the police wouldn't believe her 'I did nothing' defense. But I believed her."

"So the next obvious question," my mother said, "was if she didn't kill him, who did? And somehow you came up with the principal of Fair Harbor High School."

I nodded. "It was something Mrs. Lipman said—that the police should be looking for someone who, first of all, knew about the David and Goliath experiment; who, second, knew how to aim the sling to do the most damage; and who, third, had good reason for wanting him dead. And there was only one person I could think of who satisfied at least two of those criteria. Kevin Inglesby. He'd seen the experiment and he was the one who told Mrs. Lipman about the skull's vulnerability at the temple. And once we figured out his motive, he was the obvious choice."

"Well done, Miss Marple," Helene said, leaning across the table and patting me on the arm. "Very well done, indeed." And she winked at me. So I guess I was forgiven for not being very, very careful.

"Once he was in custody and learned that Mrs. Lipman had taped our little encounter," I concluded, "Inglesby admitted the whole thing."

This I'd learned from Detective Vivian Peters, who seemed to feel that I deserved to know it, seeing as the man almost cracked my head open with a beer bottle.

"As I'd guessed, while he was waiting for Mayo, he'd worked himself up into a frenzy. And when he had that sling in his hand and saw Mayo with his back to him, well, he said he 'just went crazy for a minute.' He attacked Mayo with the sling, stuffed it in his pocket, and ran away."

"Leaving the man to die," Helene said.

I nodded. "Leaving the man to die."

I looked at the somber faces of my dining companions. I had totally ruined girls' night out.

And then my mother saved the situation. She gestured imperiously to our server. "Garçon, more wine, please."

THIRTY-ONE

~~~

I HAVE NEVER BEEN a big fan of New Year's Eve parties. First of all, nobody is particularly interested in food, so the nibbles, if there are any, tend to be pretty meh. And then there's the hangover. Who decided the first day of a new year should be spent with a killer headache? This year, I decided, would be different. As my Aunt Ida would advise, I would begin as I meant to continue.

Also, as I may have mentioned earlier, my birthday happens to fall on January 1. Not that it's important or anything.

But this year I would save my celebrating for my birthday. I would spend a quiet New Year's Eve with Jason and a few glasses of bubbly and wake up relaxed and refreshed. On New Year's day, I would go southern and cook the traditional meal of black-eyed peas with sausage, a mess of sautéed greens, and lots of buttery cornbread, setting the stage for a year of prosperity and good luck. Then I would cut myself a huge slice of an unbelievably yummy birthday carrot cake. (Tip: Use walnut flour instead of wheat flour. So, so, so good. And your gluten-free friends will love you forever.) Then I would blow out the candles and make my wish. I already knew what the wish would be.

Jason, not being a fan of parties in general, was more than happy to fall into line with my plans. Some old Fair Harbor friends had invited the 'rents over to welcome the New Year with them. Jenny and Roland would be home, trying to keep the Three Things under some kind of control as the evening spiraled further and further past their usual bedtime. Sebastian was on call (as always), so he and Miles had plans to curl up on his sofa in front of the TV and quietly sob their way through *An Affair to Remember*. Helene was spending the evening with Liz and Beth Voorhees, who wanted to thank her for all her efforts on their behalf. Jillian and Andre, being the good folks they were, apparently always spent New Year's Eve at Shawme Manor, lifting a glass of champagne with any of the residents who actually made it to the midnight hour. And Krista had announced her intention to (and I quote), "smack my bottom down on a bar stool at the Ginger Jar and give that hunk of man a Krista kiss at midnight." This made me all flustery, so I didn't ask what that actually meant.

So Jason and I would be alone at last. Maybe there would be some, ahem, *fireworks* at midnight. Maybe we would even talk. I was ready for that, and I hoped he was, too.

I'd regained my usual optimism over the days following Kevin Inglesby's confession. Things were beginning, I thought, to work out. Mrs. Lipman had put the Lanes up for sale. She'd told me that after she'd come so close to spending the rest of her days in jail, she'd gone to the Barnstable County Correctional Facility with a proposal to teach environmental studies as part of the prison's educational program for women inmates and they'd jumped at the chance to have her.

Wally seemed to have grown up overnight and finally found the nerve to tell his mother that he wanted to set himself up as a personal trainer. For men only, thank goodness. I honestly thought he might make a success of it.

One night Jason and I saw Mrs. Mayo at the Ginger Jar. I almost didn't recognize her. She was wearing a pink track suit and her hair had miraculously turned from browny gray to gold. She was seated at a table with a very good-looking older gentleman. When she saw us, she came over with one of Martin's piña coladas in her hand and greeted me like an old buddy. Her gentleman friend, she said, was someone she met on an online dating app for what she called "Silvers." It was nothing serious, she said. Just for fun. She told me that Hanson Construction had asked if she would reconsider her husband's earlier decision about selling Cape Concrete to them. She, however, politely declined their offer, and said they were "perfect gentlemen" about it. Instead, she said, she was selling the business to a consortium of the plant's employees, which she thought was the "right thing to do." Her plan was to move to Florida to be closer to her son and his family. Then she gave me a kiss on the cheek and trotted back to her date and her new life.

I T HAD ALL been going so well. Jason and I had agreed to start our New Year's "stay-bration" with a late supper, to avoid that endless wait for midnight. I, of course, had spent more time planning the meal than my New Year's outfit, which resulted in a frantic, last-minute throw-everything-from-the-closet-onto-the-bed frenzy of discarded outfits. I finally landed on a rather slinky black number that I'd bought online years ago in a moment of weakness and had never had the nerve to actually wear. *Well, tonight things are gonna be different, Sam.*

Jason arrived at ten, very sexy in his black jeans and black button-down shirt (*definitely* gonna be different), bearing a bottle of champagne in one hand and Ciati in the other. I don't know whose greetings were more heartfelt, mine and Jason's or Diogi's and the kitten's.

Jason lit a fire in the woodstove and popped the cham-

pagne (giving Diogi another minor heart attack), while I
found Etta James on my playlist and set out a small platter
of Italian antipasti on the coffee table. As I put it down, I gave
Diogi The Look, which I'd been practicing and which he
clearly understood to mean "don't touch if you value your
life." The animals, of course, immediately claimed the
warmest spot right in front of the fire, leaving Jason and me
with the whole couch for ourselves. We clinked glasses and
looked deep into each other's eyes as we drank. Yup. *Very*
different.

"You look beautiful," Jason said. "I mean, you always
look beautiful, but tonight you look especially beautiful."

The evening continued like that, though not with a great
deal of talking (I mean, after a comment like that, what
else needs to be said?), just a kind of quiet electricity passing between us. After we finished off the antipasti, we
moved ourselves and the champagne bottle to the ell's little
cherrywood table, which I'd set with Aunt Ida's china and
a few tea lights.

Jason lit the candles while I went into the kitchen to
fetch our individual ramekins of coquilles Saint Jacques,
which I'd made that afternoon and had put back in a low
oven to warm just before my man arrived. We ate our scal-
lops in the glow of nothing more than candles and firelight,
and I thought the evening couldn't be improved. Actually,
my dessert of key lime pie topped with two sparklers that
I'd lit before bringing it out proved me wrong there. Everything, even the most wonderful evening, can be improved
by key lime pie. And sparklers. Now I *knew* the evening
couldn't get better.

I was wrong. As I stood to clear our dessert plates, Jason
stood, too. He took the plates out of my hands, set them back
on the table and pulled me into his arms. The immortal Etta
was singing "At Last," and Jason and I began to dance.
Slowly, barely moving, our bodies fitting together in perfect
harmony. I lost track of time, until Jason finally pulled away.

"It's almost midnight," he said softly. "Shall we send the kids to bed and celebrate in private?"

"I thought you'd never ask," I said with a little wicked grin. *And you have no idea how much I mean that*, I didn't add.

But before we could entice Diogi and Ciati out of the ell and into the kitchen with promises of treats, the New Year arrived. With a bang. Literally. Actually, lots of bangs. As in fireworks. Really, really loud fireworks. From the O'Gormans' house across the street. Which might have been kind of fun and festive (even metaphorical, if you know what I mean) except for Diogi's reaction.

Which was sheer terror.

In some kind of deep primordial part of his doggy brain, he knew that he was under attack. And he knew just what to do. Take cover. In the bathtub.

Where he got the idea that the bathtub was a place of safety, I cannot imagine. Maybe that same deep primordial part of his doggy brain. Whatever it was, it took him about two seconds to push through the bathroom door and throw himself into the tub, where he trembled like the puppy he still was for all his great size. So I did the only thing I could do under the circumstances.

I crawled into the tub, too.

As I held the trembling dog in my arms, I looked at Jason beseechingly. "What do we do?" I asked. "I can't ask the O'Gorman kids not to celebrate New Year's."

"No, probably not," Jason said. He'd followed Diogi and me into the bathroom and was sitting on the rim of the tub with Ciati mewing discontentedly in his lap. She wanted to get in the tub, too.

"It'll probably be over soon," Jason said, as the bangs continued unabated and he dropped the kitten into our little group hug. "It just sounds like firecrackers, maybe Black Cats, and some roman candles." *Black Cats? How is it that men know this stuff?* "Until then, unless you can think of something else to do to soothe Diogi, we just have to wait it out."

"Put on Adele," I said.

"What?"

"Put on Adele," I repeated. "Put on 'Rolling in the Deep.' Loud."

Jason looked at me like I had finally lost it, but did as I had requested. Okay, ordered.

And that's how my parents found us when they got home. In the bathroom, Diogi, Ciati and I in the tub, Jason perched on the rim, all of us singing along to Adele at the top of our voices.

THIRTY-TWO

I AWOKE ON MY birthday, otherwise known as New Year's Day, alone in my bed. Except for my dog. Who appeared to have fully recovered from his nervous collapse the night before if his enthusiastic morning slobber kiss was any indication.

"That was not exactly the birthday smooch I was hoping for," I muttered as I pushed Diogi away and rolled myself out of bed.

But I wasn't as disgruntled as I sounded. Sure, the evening hadn't ended as I'd hoped. Or, it was clear, as Jason had also hoped. So at least we were on the same page there. And the sheer, deep pleasure we'd taken in each other's company still thrummed through me. Jason and I were going to be all right. We'd still struggle, we'd still have questions to answer and challenges to face, but we'd do that together.

Starting this morning apparently.

Before we'd said goodbye the night before, my parents' hysterical laughter still ringing in our ears, he'd promised to come around first thing in the morning to give me my birthday present.

"First thing in the morning" for Jason is a very small

window of time between sunrise and, maybe, if you're lucky, just after you've had your first cup of coffee. So I was up and at 'em. I wasn't taking any chances. I *wuv* presents.

I wandered blearily into the kitchen. My mother was sitting at the table perusing some legal-looking piece of paper, and my father, bless his heart, was making coffee.

"Happy birthday, kiddo!" he said as he handed me a mug of legal stimulant. "You're up early."

"Happy birthday!" my mother chimed in, looking up from whatever it was she was reading so closely. "Listen, your dad and I have to leave in a couple of hours if we want to get to Boston in time to catch our plane, so he's eager to get breakfast on the table." *Yeah, because it will be the last time that man sees a pile of pancakes for months.* "But first we have a little surprise for you, Sam."

"Okay," I said, all flush with happiness and excited about getting another present. "Lead me to it."

My mother and father led us out to the living room, where my mother with a grand flourish pointed at the case clock she'd found two weeks ago.

"Do you remember what I told you this might be worth?"

"Yeah," I said. "Something like a gazillion dollars." I didn't have to add that I hadn't thought much about it since, what with finding a murderer and all.

"Yeah, about that," she said. "In fact, probably more than the one I showed you online, according to the nice man I met with at the auction house in Boston." *So not a meeting with the mob.*

And then it hit me. *More than the one we'd seen online?!*

"That's amazing, Mom," I said, as I sat down weakly on the couch. "I can't quite take it in."

With a grin, my father chimed in. "You see, Sam, Santa Claus *isn't* dead."

I glared at him in (almost) mock outrage.

"But that's not the best part," she said proudly. She held out the legal-looking paper. *Uh-oh.*

"What's that?" I asked faintly.

"This is an application for your appearance on *Antiques in the Attic*!"

Oh god, oh god, oh god. Once I got over my shock, my dad handed me a second cup of coffee.

"Thanks," I said as I took the mug gratefully. "Apparently Jason's coming by to give me my birthday present."

I carried the mug over to the kitchen window, took a large gulp, and looked at the empty driveway. "Good," I said. "He's not here yet."

"Actually, he is," my father said, smiling broadly. "He's down at the dock."

None of this was making any sense to my bleary brain. I took another gulp of the coffee, hoping it might help, and went over to the picture window that looked out to Bower's Pond. Though I could see some of the pond from that vantage point, the dock itself was hidden by a small grove of pitch pines.

I turned back to my dad. "He came by boat?"

"In a manner of speaking," he said cryptically. *Okay. Whatever. Be that way.*

"Tell him I'm in the shower when he comes up, okay?" I asked.

"Sure thing," my father said, reaching over with the coffeepot and topping my mug up.

I felt bad about my grumpiness. I leaned over and kissed him on the cheek.

"Thanks, Dad," I said. "You're the best." I almost said "I love you" but the poor man looked uncomfortable enough.

When I came back out into the kitchen twenty minutes later, clean and fully caffeinated, I felt better. And I felt a whole lot better when I saw Jason at the table in some kind of confab with my parents. He stood up and gave me a chaste kiss on the cheek, but his eyes were the eyes of the man who'd danced with me the night before.

"Happy birthday, Sam," he said quietly.

Suddenly, I felt very shy. "Thank you," I replied, almost in a whisper.

My mother, being impervious to sentiment, broke the spell, singing out, "Happy birthday, Sammy baby!" She knows I hate it when she calls me Sammy baby. It amuses her no end.

I held my empty mug out to my father. "More coffee needed, please."

"Jason has a present for you," my mother said, an enigmatic smile on her face.

I looked at him over the edge of my mug. "Is it a pony?" I asked.

"I'm afraid not," he said.

"It never is," I said, doing my best imitation of a disappointed three-year-old.

Jason grinned and then suddenly got all serious.

"Let me explain," he said. "I know I've been, um, kind of AWOL recently." *That's one way of putting it.* "But I found this present, so I bought it, and it needed a lot of work, and I really wanted to get it done in time for your birthday." *Found a present? That needed a lot of work?* "And, honestly, I don't think I could have done it without your dad's help." *All those mysterious disappearances had been to help Jason with a birthday present for me?*

"Jason," I said, "you're a lovely man and I really appreciate you trying to explain, but I'm just more confused than ever."

"Argh," he said. "Sometimes I'm really bad with words. Just come down to the dock with me, okay?"

"Okay," I said.

We pulled on our jackets and made our way down the hillside path to the pond, Diogi leading the way. At the bottom I saw the Harbor Patrol Boston Whaler tied up to Aunt Ida's old rickety dock.

"I still don't get it," I said, turning to Jason. "It's just the Whaler at Aunt Ida's dock."

"Not the Whaler," he said. "That."

He pointed about fifty feet out onto the pond, where a lovely Baybird sailboat, its white mainsail neatly furled and its deep navy topsides freshly painted, lay bobbing at a mooring. I knew the boat immediately, even if it was almost unrecognizable in its meticulously restored condition. It was my family's old Baybird, the sailboat of my deeply happy childhood, sold when my parents had moved to Florida.

"Oh, Jason," I breathed. "You found it and brought it back to life. It's the *Nellie Bly*."

"Not anymore," Jason said. "Look again."

And at that moment, a puff of wind turned the boat's stern toward the shore. Painted on the transom in gold letters was its new name: *Miss Marple*.

I turned to the man who had done this for me. This man who in his every spare minute had worked on a gift that honored not only my childhood, my family, and my love of the sea but also my determination to see justice done.

"Oh, Jason," I cried as I threw my arms around him. "It's even better than a pony!"

ACKNOWLEDGMENTS

After writing two Cape Cod Foodie mysteries, I've learned a lot about the book biz, but mostly this: It takes a village to publish a book. It takes a wonderful agent (thank you, thank you, thank you, Sandy Harding!), it takes super-talented editors (and I have two of the best, Jenn Snyder and Michelle Vega!), and it takes a meticulous copy editor (thank you, Martha Schwartz, for being my safety net!). And then to get that book into readers' hands, it takes a whole crew of publishing pros (like brilliant cover artist Julia Green, mellifluous voice narrator Patti Murin, dedicated publicist Stephanie Felty, and marketing maven Elisha Katz!). Villagers, I thank you, Sam thanks you, and of course, Diogi thanks you.

And, even more wonderful, I've learned this: It takes other writers. I simply cannot say enough about the friendship and support offered to this newbie by so many brilliant and talented authors. What would I have done without the wise counsel of Roberta Isleib (aka Lucy Burdette); my new pal (and Facebook guru!) Krista Davis; the incredibly generous Elizabeth Gilbert; the lovely Edith Maxwell (aka Maddie Day), who has been kindness itself; and (be still my heart!) the uber-talented Deborah Crombie. I cannot thank you enough for your encouragement and generosity of spirit. I promise I will pay it forward.

RECIPES

A Warm and Cozy Dinner for Christmas (or any Winter's) Eve

You can relax—I'm not going to encourage you to make Sam's Feast of the Five Fishes! We are not all ex-professional chefs (least of all me). Instead, I'd encourage you to make this much simpler but incredibly delicious dinner, perfect for a special night with family or friends when the weather outside is frightful and the fire is so delightful . . .

BRAISED LEEKS WITH PARMESAN

These meltingly tender leeks make a terrific appetizer. If you can find real Italian Parmigiano-Reggiano at your grocery store go for it, but domestic parmesan is absolutely fine if not. And do grate it yourself—the difference in taste and texture is amazing. You can make this ahead of time and simply reheat it in the oven or on the stovetop for about 10 minutes before serving.

(SERVES 4)

4 large or 8 small leeks
3 tablespoons butter
Salt to taste
½ cup freshly grated parmesan

Trim the bulbous root ends and the dark green parts of the leeks, leaving only the white and light green parts.

Cut each leek in half lengthwise and then cut each half again crosswise, making 16 total pieces, each 3 or 4 inches long.

Wash the pieces under cold running water, fanning them open gently to get rid of any hidden grit but keeping the pieces whole.

Lay them in a sauté pan large enough to accommodate them in one layer. (It's fine if they are a bit crowded and overlap a little.)

Add the butter, a little salt, and enough water to just cover the leeks.

Cover the pan and cook on medium-low for 15 to 25 minutes, or until the thickest part of the leek at the base is fork-tender.

Uncover the pan and turn the heat up to high. Move the leeks around gently with a spatula until all the liquid is cooked off and the leeks are lightly browned.

Add the grated parmesan and serve.

BUTTERMILK-BRINED
ROAST CHICKEN

~~~~~~

*The only difficult part of this recipe for a supremely tender
and flavorful roast chicken is remembering to start brining
the bird a day before you plan to cook it. Other than that, it
couldn't be simpler! I like to cook it in a cast-iron pan, but
a small roasting pan is fine, too.*

(SERVES 4 TO 6)

2 tablespoons of kosher salt or 4 teaspoons fine salt
2 cups buttermilk
1 (3- to 4-pound) roasting chicken

Twenty-four hours before you plan to cook the chicken, mix
the salt into the buttermilk. Put the chicken in a gallon-size
resealable plastic bag and pour the buttermilk over it.

Seal the bag and turn it over a few times to cover the
chicken with the buttermilk. Put it on a rimmed plate and
refrigerate. (Turn it over the next morning and once or
twice during the day.)

Take the chicken out of the fridge an hour before you
plan to cook it to bring it to room temperature. Preheat the
oven to 425°F, with a rack set in the center position.

Take the chicken out of the bag and lightly wipe off the
buttermilk. Tie the legs of the chicken together with butch-
er's twine and put it in a cast-iron skillet or shallow roasting pan.

Put the pan in the oven with the legs facing the rear.
After about 20 minutes, when the chicken starts to brown,
reduce the heat to 400°F.

Continue cooking for another 40 minutes or so, until the
chicken is brown all over and the juices run clear when you

insert a knife down to the bone between the leg and the thigh. (Check occasionally to make sure the skin isn't over-browning, and if it is, loosely tent the bird with some aluminum foil.)

When the chicken is done, remove it to a platter and let it rest for 10 minutes before carving and serving.

OVEN-ROASTED BUTTERNUT SQUASH WITH ROSEMARY AND GARLIC

You can slide this into the oven when you put the chicken in. If the squash is done before the bird, just take it out and slide it back in to warm up while the chicken is resting.

(SERVES 4)

4 tablespoons olive oil (or a neutral oil like canola, if you prefer), divided
1 large butternut squash, peeled and cut into 1-inch cubes
3 or 4 sprigs fresh rosemary or 1 tablespoon dried
1 large clove garlic, minced or thinly sliced and tossed with a little oil

Preheat the oven to 425°F.

Pour 1 tablespoon of the oil onto a full-size sheet pan and spread it around with your fingers or a basting brush.

Place the squash in a bowl with the remaining oil and toss to coat evenly.

Pour the squash onto the sheet pan and spread the pieces out into a single layer, putting the rosemary on top.

Slide the pan into the oven and cook for 20 minutes, then take the pan out of the oven, toss the squash pieces with a spatula, and sprinkle the garlic on top.

Roast for another 20 to 25 minutes until the squash is very tender and the pieces are nicely browned on at least one side.

BLENDER CHOCOLATE MOUSSE

Yum. Just yum. And easy?! The hot sugar syrup melts the chocolate and cooks the eggs. If you can find dark chocolate chips, you don't even have to chop the chocolate. And if your grocery store carries cold-brew coffee concentrate, you don't have to brew the coffee. Do take those eggs out of the fridge at least an hour before making this, though, to bring them to room temperature.

(SERVES 4 TO 6)

¾ cup heavy cream (plus more if you want whipped cream on top)

2 large eggs, at room temperature

6 ounces dark chocolate, roughly chopped (or dark chocolate chips)

¼ cup granulated sugar

¼ cup water

¼ cup strong (brewed) espresso (or very strongly brewed coffee or cold-brew coffee concentrate)

½ teaspoon vanilla extract

¼ teaspoon kosher salt

In a large bowl, whip the cream to medium glossy peaks, about 3 minutes. Set aside in the fridge.

Once the eggs have reached room temperature, crack them into a blender and add the chocolate. Cover and blend on medium-high speed for a minute or so. Turn the blender off.

In a small saucepan over low heat, combine the sugar and water and stir until dissolved. As soon as the syrup begins to boil, turn off the heat.

Turn the blender back on and slowly pour the hot sugar syrup into the chocolate mixture. (If your blender top has a removable filler cap, take it out and pour the sugar syrup through that, which will keep any splattering to a minimum.) The hot sugar syrup will melt the chocolate and cook the eggs. Keep the blender running and add the coffee, vanilla, and salt. Blend for another minute or so until the mixture is very smooth and has cooled to room temperature.

Fold ½ cup of the chocolate mixture into the chilled whipped cream until smooth, then add the rest of the chocolate mixture to the cream mixture and fold until there are no streaks.

Pour into individual bowls or glasses and let the mousse set in the fridge until firm, at least 2 hours or up to 24 hours. Serve chilled with extra whipped cream, if desired.